# WICKED ANGEL

JAINE DIAMOND

*Wicked Angel*
Jaine Diamond

Copyright © 2023 Jaine Diamond

All rights reserved.

No part of this book may be reproduced, scanned, uploaded or distributed in any manner whatsoever without written permission from the publisher, except in the case of brief quotation embodied in book reviews.

This book is a work of fiction. Names, characters, places and incidents are the product of the author's imagination or are used fictitiously. Any resemblance to actual events, locales, organizations or persons is coincidental.

Published by DreamWarp Publishing Ltd.
www.jainediamond.com

Cover Design: DreamWarp Publishing Ltd.
Cover Photo: Michelle Lancaster @lanefotograf
Cover Model: Chad Hurst
Back cover image: Downtown Vancouver

# Wicked Angel

*For my man.*
*Thank you for teaching me that my tears are never wrong.*

**villain**

*noun*

An immoral or antagonistic person; an antihero.

# Prologue

**Angeline**

We all make mistakes.

We all fuck up royally from time to time.

We all harbor painful regrets, sorrows, and even secret shames.

Things we wish we never did.

And other things we only wish we never did because we know they're wrong, even if they felt right. Things we're so deeply confused about that the torment wedges deep inside, twisting like a knife between our ribs with every breath, until we fear that our boyfriend is about to find out.

Or, wait. Maybe that last part is just me?

Point is, we all make mistakes.

Some we hope to be forgiven for.

Some we don't deserve to be forgiven for because… if we could do it all again…

We'd still fuck up.

The night I fucked up, all I wanted was a quiet place to make a phone call in the middle of a loud house party. So I stepped outside and walked across the grass, away from the house into the dark, alone, for just a moment. But all it really takes is a moment for the world to crash into oncoming space junk.

"Hey, Angel."

I jumped a little at his voice floating out of the dark, a tidal wave of goosebumps running down my body. My heart lurched. My nipples pricked. My fingernails dug into my palm as I took a slow, deep breath and turned to find him sitting in the shadows.

"Hello," I said softly. I sounded like a young girl. A girl so much younger than I was. A girl who was deeply uncertain, suddenly, of the place where her feet met the earth. I was only twenty steps or so from my boyfriend. And from my older sister. Ten steps from a house full of friends. Any one of them would've saved me in that moment, if they could.

But the door was closed. No one could see me. Or him.

No one could see *us*.

Instead, it was all left up to me, and I fucked up.

Crimson and gold flared in the night as he clicked his lighter and fire-light danced across his gorgeous face. His name was Johnny. He was the older brother of one of my best friends.

He was a mistake, long before anything ever happened between us.

Nothing had ever happened between us. But I'd crushed on him so hard and for so long, just the sight of his face, flickering in and out of the dark as that lighter sparked the joint in his hand, turned my stomach to a mass of snakes. Because I knew. I knew something very, very bad was about to happen.

And I was going to let it.

"Angeline Delacroix." He said my name slowly, like he was tasting it. Like he was really hearing it for the first time since we'd met, years ago. Every syllable so soft and sensuous on his lips in the dark.

Then he got to his feet, standing up to his full height, looming over me. I got a better look at his face in the moonlight. His eyes were wet with some emotion I couldn't identify. He looked high or drunk, or both.

He looked tormented.

It took my breath away.

His hands slid up around my bare neck, so suddenly I didn't even pull away. By the time his fingers had slid under my ponytail to cradle my skull, I'd gone almost limp. I dangled there in his hands as his watery eyes tripped into mine.

He was gone. Somewhere far away and somewhere deep inside me, all at once, as he looked into my eyes.

My heart fluttered like a trapped butterfly. My hands went to his waist, grabbing onto him, and his eyes flared. I didn't pull him to me or push him away. I just held on. I didn't even know what was happening except that in the utter chaos of this miraculous, fragile event called life, his orbit and mine had suddenly collided and locked together. And I couldn't move.

"Wh-why did you call me Angel?" My voice shook. My fingers dug deeper into his waist. I could feel his heat through his T-shirt.

Despite my name, no one had ever called me Angel.

His watery, dark-aquamarine eyes dropped to my lips. "First time I ever saw you…" he said, his voice rough and dark as sin, "you were wearing a shirt with a kitten on it. With wings. A fucking sequined kitten. You remember that?"

"No."

*Yes.*

But… he remembered what I was wearing the first time we met?

"And some short little shorts…" His eyes wandered down. "With bare legs. And high-heeled boots. And you know what I thought?"

I swallowed.

He leaned in, until his lips were so close to mine I could smell him—all his rough and ready maleness and his sweet-smoky aftershave and the alcohol on his breath. I could smell the joint burning down between his fingers, so close to my face. I could taste him in the air between us like an instantly addictive drug. "I thought, I bet she's even prettier when she begs."

I sucked in a breath. I knew he was about to kiss me.

I didn't move.

My core lit on sweet, heavenly fire as his lips met mine.

And yes, I kissed him back.

Because you know what? Life isn't easy.

We don't always get what we want.

We don't always want what we get.

Inside, we are nothing like what others think we are when they look at us.

We are deeply misunderstood.

And we are complicated. We are so many things; more things than we are not.

I *felt* so many things in that moment as Johnny O'Reilly kissed me in the dark, with only the moon and stars as witness to our seeking tongues, our pounding hearts.

He broke the kiss, abruptly, and I held my breath, reeling. My hands dropped away from him.

What the hell did I just do?

He turned my head in his hands and kissed my neck. "I'll take my time…" he rasped in my ear. "I'll make you purr." His tongue drifted up the curve of my ear and I shuddered.

"Don't," I whispered. I pressed my shaking hands to his chest and stepped back an inch.

"Don't… what?" He looked amused, maybe. And for a split second in the shifting moonlight through the trees, as his eyes met mine again, he looked broken.

I didn't feel amused. Or broken. I felt confused. I was reeling with emotions. So many feelings at once, I couldn't lock onto a single one of them.

But I knew I didn't owe him any explanation. I didn't owe him anything. I had no idea if he knew I had a boyfriend, but in the end, none of that was his responsibility.

I wrapped my arms around myself as his eyes dragged over me, slow.

Then his hands released me, gently. He brought the joint to my lips. I took a small, hesitant drag, breathing in the musky smoke. He took a drag, too, his eyes never leaving mine.

"You should go back in the house," he said softly, exhaling smoke into the air.

I should've. But for some reason, I lingered.

"I leave you out here all alone, in the dark…" He gestured into the darkness, his joint leaving a wisp of smoke and sparks in the air. "What kind of man would that make me?"

I wanted to tell him that I knew exactly what kind of man he was. But the words got choked up in my throat.

*You kissed him.*

It was sinking in, like teeth ripping into my heart. I cleared my throat and turned, forcing myself to walk back to the house as my body flushed with heat. And with hunger.

Guilt.

Shame.

"Good night, Angel," he breathed behind me, and a shiver ran down my back. I could hear the whisper of gratification beneath his words, and something strangely sad.

And for some reason, I felt bad about leaving him standing there all alone, in the dark. But I didn't turn back as my insides churned, my emotions still reeling in a chaotic tumult as the world spun around me, upside down and inside out.

*You kissed him and you loved it.*

In one sudden, unexpected moment, the entire trajectory of my life had subtly changed. Though I wouldn't know it until later.

I wouldn't say that it was that single, broken kiss that ended my relationship with my boyfriend, Flynn.

But I would say it was the spark that lit the fire, that in the end, burned our whole house down.

# Chapter One

**Angeline**

*Three years later…*

"It's not me, Angeline," Flynn said evenly as I poured him an orange juice. "It's you." His flinty gray-blue eyes met mine across the small table in our apartment kitchen, daring me to argue.

But how could I say a thing, when all the breath had left my lungs?

It was the meanest and probably the truest thing he'd ever said to me.

Flynn was not a mean guy. He could be stoic, even rigid. He was hard on the outside but soft on the inside, if you could burrow down deep enough to find it.

I'd tried.

And he'd tried—to be everything I'd ever wanted in a man. I would've told him I was sorry that he'd failed at that, but I'd told him I was sorry a thousand times, for a thousand things, and all it did was put bandages on top of bandages.

We were broken beyond repair, and I was afraid in my heart of hearts that he was right.

It was me.

I got up to plate his breakfast while biting my lip, hard. The eggs were about to burn. I laid the plate of sunny-side-up, back bacon and mixed fruit, his favorite, in front of him, like I did pretty much every morning. Then I kissed him on the temple, knowing it was the last time I'd ever kiss him. I breathed in his scent.

He tensed, but said nothing else.

What was there to say?

We'd both said more than enough last night. The ghosts of that argument, just one of so many and yet *the one*, the final, insurmountable one, clung in the air around us. The shadows under his eyes matched my own. There was no sleep in our home last night. Who could sleep when the end was so near? When the still, silent darkness was so empty and yet so loud with his hurt, and with mine.

We both knew this was coming. We both knew it had to end.

At least he was brave enough to end it.

I never would've let go of him if he didn't cut me loose first. Flynn knew as much.

I knew it, with a crisp, torturous certainty as I left the apartment and headed downstairs. As I stepped out into the morning light, shoving on my sunglasses as the tears started to flow.

---

Once the tears started flowing, they didn't stop.

I spent the rest of the morning at a table in the back of a café, hiding out behind a fake plant, on and off the phone with my mom, my sister and my three best girlfriends while I sipped latte after latte. Until I couldn't dam the flood any longer and locked myself in the washroom to let it all pour out.

Then I ordered up a panini for lunch on the café's app. I was starting to feel sick from all the lattes, and realized I never actually ate breakfast this morning.

*Because Flynn broke up with you.*

I went up to the counter before the panini was ready and paced, collecting pitying looks from the staff. I suddenly noticed how much the place had cleared out since I first set up camp. I stuffed some money in the tip jar and checked my phone, and was embarrassed to discover that it was almost noon.

I texted one of my besties, Shayla.

**Me:** I'm getting pity from the staff. Do I look that sad?

I took a selfie, doing my best to smile, and sent it to her.

**Shayla:** Beautiful. I'd swipe right.

I laughed under my breath.

**Shayla:** You will get through this, babe.

**Shayla:** And for the record… I can't believe he did this to you after everything you've been through together. I hate him.

**Me:** Don't hate him. Please. He's one of the good ones.

My fingers shook as I sent the text. I stared at my own words, struggling not to burst out crying again as the screen swam; I really had to stop doing that. My eyes would swell closed. At this rate, I'd be in terrible shape for the meeting with my boss this afternoon.

When my lunch was ready, I forced myself to eat while I skimmed entertainment news and didn't read an actual word of it. When I was finished, I locked myself into the washroom again, this time to try to fix my makeup.

*There is no need to cry. Crying won't change anything.*

*It's the middle of the day.*

*You are a professional and you have an important business meeting.*

This was what I told myself as I shuddered with the effort to hold back the wracking pain and sadness that threatened to split me open whenever I looked into my own eyes.

Then I headed out to meet my boss, to discuss my new role at her company.

*Don't worry*, I tried to soothe myself, *you got through the worst of it.*

Because this day could only get better from here. Right?

---

"Unfortunately, we just don't have a role for you at this company."

I sat across from Danielle Duke, legendary publicist, so-called "queen-maker" of the local entertainment scene and my absolute professional role model, and tried not to let my chin wobble. I'd been crying so much today, it was a definite possibility that I might melt down into waterworks right here in her polished, glass-walled office.

Danielle saw it. "Oh, darling." She got to her feet, strode to the bar and poured something. She thrust a cut crystal tumbler at me. "Have a scotch."

I took the heavy glass, my fingers shaking. I felt like I was falling through the floor. Nothing fit together right anymore. My feet on the ground, my ability to breathe in my own body, the walls holding up the ceiling.

*It's not me.*

*It's you.*

"I don't understand," I managed.

Danielle sat behind her desk and reclined in her leather chair. She regarded me across the wide slab of slick marble. There was nothing on the cold surface but her phone, a sleek laptop and an agate paperweight with no actual papers beneath it. She didn't seem to do much work here. No; this was where she met with colleagues and clients to display how successful she was. Ones she wanted to impress or intimidate.

I'd never even stepped into the building before. I did all my work for her remotely.

Maybe this should've been my very first clue that this wasn't going to be a happy meeting.

After a moment, she broke the silence. "What don't you understand, Angeline?"

I took a breath. Then I took a sip of scotch. The instant it hit my throat, I coughed violently. God, that burned. I'd never drank scotch before.

She thought this would help me right now?

I set the glass carefully on the desk and looked up into her eyes. Danielle regarded me dispassionately. She wore a bright pantsuit, crimson red, with a luxurious, silky blouse, her hair in a sleek inverted bob. I was pretty sure I recognized the lipstick she'd paired with the suit: *Soul-crushing Red.*

There were tubes of it on the glass display along the wall beside me, along with other makeup from my sister's celebrity makeup line, *Kiss & Tell.* And a framed album. And magazine covers with my sister on them. It was like a holy shrine.

"Well… all I ever heard from you," I said carefully, "was that I would have a role at this company, after the internship."

"Not would, darling. Could."

"So, then… why can't I?" I sniffled back the tears and snot that threatened to gush forth in an unholy flood, knowing I sounded like a sad little girl who'd been denied a play date with the cool girl at school.

Danielle's phone lit up on her desk for about the dozenth time since I'd sat down and she'd crushed my soul. It made no sound, but her eyes flicked to the glowing screen. Like whatever was on it was more important than my fledgling career evaporating around me.

"Look, Angeline." She finally looked me in the eye again, almost impatiently. "You have a way about you. It's very… sweet. I know you mean well. But it's just not going to work."

"I thought we worked well together."

"We did. You did everything I asked, and I've appreciated your enthusiasm. Your work ethic was never in question. It was your… how shall I put this delicately…" She tapped a black-tipped acrylic nail on the marble desktop.

"Please. You can be indelicate. Just…" I swallowed against the sick feeling in my gut. Rejection. *Failure.* Sitting here beneath the framed poster of my sister's solo album cover from a few years back—her name in gold letters, *ELLE*, and the album title below, *BOLD*, her pretty face gazing down on me—it felt worse, somehow. "I want to know."

Danielle studied me for a long moment. Then she said bluntly, "You get too personally involved with clients."

I blinked at her, confused. "What?"

"Too *emotionally* involved."

I blinked again, trying to force back the tears that were threatening. Again. God, I was fragile today. "Emotionally involved? How? I mean, I care about—"

"You're very emotional, sweetie," she observed, with no emotion whatsoever. "Passionate. There's nothing wrong with that. It just has no place in our clients' lives."

"But—"

"I can't be any plainer than that."

"I… I try to treat them like family. You told me, when you hired me, that we—"

"You were never hired, Angeline. This was an internship. And it's done now. I would've liked to offer you a position, for Elle's sake, of course. But I can't."

*For Elle's sake.*

Not for my sake.

Because Elle was the entire reason she'd given me the internship in the first place. Because my big sister, the rock star, one of Danielle's most high-profile clients, had asked her to take me on. I knew that. And yet hearing those words, right now? *For Elle's sake…*

After all I'd done for Danielle, how hard I'd worked to prove that I wasn't just some spoiled little sister of a star client looking for handouts and favors… it killed the last glimmer of desperate hope that I might change her mind.

How was this happening?

When I woke up this morning, it felt just like any other day. At least, for that split second before I remembered the fight I'd had with Flynn last night, and that I was waking up alone, on the couch.

I swallowed the bile that was creeping up, making my throat burn in the wake of that throat-punch of scotch. "Because… I'm too emotional," I reiterated quietly, forcing the words out.

"Correct." Danielle's black-tipped nails played with her phone case, like she was halfway somewhere else. Like she was itching to *be* somewhere else.

*This conversation means nothing to her.*

*I have no actual value to her.*

The saddest part of it, the most pathetic part, was that I had no idea until right now.

I cleared my throat. "Could you give me an example, please?" She frowned, and I really tried not to beg. "I don't want to make the same mistake in the future."

"Angeline… How can you not know what I'm talking about?" She poked at her phone impatiently as it lit up again, then shoved it aside. "Look. Next to your sister, Brianna MacMillan is one of my biggest clients."

"I know." Brianna was a model I'd met last week at a party. Danielle herself had introduced me as her "lovely assistant."

"And you bought a drink for her date last night."

I stared at Danielle, struggling to comprehend.

*That* was what she meant by "too emotional"? She thought I was trying to hit on our client's date?

My head spun, replaying the events of last night; seeing Brianna at the fundraiser I'd attended with my sister. I didn't even know she had a date. She wasn't with a man when I saw her. Last I heard, she was dating JC Bissette, the lead singer from Johnny O'Reilly's band, but as far as I knew, he wasn't there.

"What date?" I asked.

Danielle leveled me with a look. "Johnny O'Reilly."

"But…" *How?*

Yes, I'd seen Johnny at the event. And yes, I'd gotten him a drink. But if he was there with Brianna, I had no idea. My mind twisted itself into knots, seeking answers I didn't have. Johnny was dating Brianna MacMillan? Since when?

"He said… he said he was thirsty!" I spluttered. "He said he'd get pawed if he waded through the crowd to the bar and the waitress was taking forever. So I got him a drink."

"He was flirting with you."

"No, he wasn't." I took a breath. Going on the defensive wouldn't help. I just wanted to understand where I'd screwed up so badly. "You told me, on the first day we met for coffee to discuss the internship, that we do whatever it takes to make our clients and their loved ones comfortable." Johnny O'Reilly was not our client. But still… wouldn't we treat a prospective client with the same courtesies?

"I meant winning their trust," Danielle said. "Assuring them that our clients are in capable hands. That we protect their interests in the public eye."

"I thought… I thought I was going above and beyond by wading through the crowd so he didn't have to."

"Well, Brianna did not see it that way."

My mouth drifted open again, then snapped shut. "Did she complain about me?"

Danielle just looked at me, and I could practically hear the vault door shutting in my face. As "our" clients became hers once again, and I landed firmly on the outside of the inner circle.

Instead of answering me directly, she said, "You know who *will* complain, as soon as I pick up their calls?" She tapped her phone. "Brianna's other representatives. Her agent has been in my ear all morning."

My stomach twisted. I wasn't even sure why. I didn't do anything wrong.

Did I?

"What can I do to fix this?"

"It's no longer yours to fix, Angeline. You didn't tell me you met with Johnny O'Reilly last night." And there it was, in her tone; an accusation. She thought I'd betrayed her somehow?

"Yes, I did."

"This morning," she clarified. "You didn't tell me when it happened. I had to find out from Twitter first."

"I told you I talked to him at the fundraiser." I'd gone with Flynn and my sister, and a bunch of my sister's friends, while Danielle attended another event. She knew that. "If someone Tweeted about it—"

"You talked to him," she echoed. "Presumably, while representing me and my company."

"Of course. Isn't that what I'm supposed to do?"

"What did he say to you?"

"He said we should talk about his new album coming out. He's a prospective client. So, I listened."

"And you sat at his table for most of the night."

"He kept talking," I said softly, realizing how bad it sounded in retrospect, in the context of this conversation. "There were a bunch of people at the table…"

Danielle sighed quietly, like I was a very dumb little girl. "Did it not occur to you that he might be trying to make his date jealous?"

My stomach sank. "I thought he was there alone."

"Did you not see the Tweets?"

"What Tweets?" *Shit.* What was she talking about? "I didn't see anything."

*Did Flynn?*

"Your name wasn't on the photos," she informed me. "Yet. You're officially the 'mystery sweetheart' who dined with Johnny O'Reilly last night. But as far as the wide world knows, the photos say it all."

"But… we weren't 'dining' together! It was a music industry fundraiser. People came and went from the table all night."

"And yet, you sat."

"At a table with a prospective client who invited me to sit with him."

"At a table with a rock star who was there with another woman." Danielle very briefly rolled her eyes. "A woman who, incidentally, is dating the lead singer of his band."

I had no idea what to say to that.

Brianna was dating them both??

How was this my problem?

As the brother of one of my best friends, I'd known Johnny O'Reilly for many years. Like my sister, he was a rock star, and I often ran into him at events and parties. I didn't always talk to him. The last three years, I didn't talk to him at all if I could avoid it.

But the fundraiser was a work thing, and I was there representing Danielle. I'd sensed an opening when Johnny casually asked about my job at Danielle's company. He'd never done that before. He never really talked to me about work, or about anything at all.

Ever since that mindfuck of a night when he'd kissed me out of nowhere, we weren't exactly best buds. Last night, I'd even put aside my general loathing of the man to get him a drink and listen to him talk about himself, because I wasn't just me at that fundraiser; I was work me.

But I had no idea he was there with a date.

"I thought Johnny was single," I said, in my defense. Not that it mattered, really. Because I was not "emotionally involved" with him.

"Is that what he told you?"

"No. I just… know." Or I thought I did.

I tried not to bring any personal stuff into this job. And I'd never even thought of suggesting to Danielle that we try to land Johnny O'Reilly as a client, just because I knew him through his sister. But last night, the opportunity presented.

Danielle shook her head, like she was deeply disappointed in me for not getting it. "He was toying with you, Angeline. Giving you attention to upset Brianna."

"So… I'm to blame for other people's bad behavior?" I tried to rein my emotions in. "I thought that was exactly the kind of thing you wanted me doing at parties. You know, making connections for you."

Danielle's eyes burned into me, making me feel small, when I was not small. I did not deserve to be talked down to, and yet… "Let me ask you, Angeline. Do you know how to make a connection with a man without flirting with him?"

"I wasn't trying to flirt with him," I protested, but my voice faltered. I really wasn't.

But her words hit deep.

They were so very similar to words Flynn had leveled me with whenever he felt I'd overstepped a line at some party. Being too friendly—too warm, too kind, too sweet—to any other man who wasn't him.

It was a reoccurring fight, one neither of us ever seemed to win.

Including last night.

I'd told him that he was being overly jealous about the attention I'd paid Johnny at the fundraiser. We weren't even on a date; we were both working last night. Flynn as Elle's bodyguard. Me as Danielle Duke's intern, a publicist-in-training.

But now I asked myself… was he actually right?

"I know where the professional line is, Danielle." The tears were drying up now, my hurt replaced with a need to stand up for myself. "I may be 'passionate' and, I don't know… overly patient… but I listen to people and I try to treat everyone with kindness and respect."

"Here's the thing, darling," Danielle said impassively. She leaned forward, bracing her elbows on the table and entwining her fingers. "Clients, and their families, and their partners, and their friends, and even prospective clients, will all behave badly at times. Some of them behave badly most of the time. It's not our job to get manipulated by it. It's our job to sugarcoat whatever they put out into the world. I've said it before and I'll say it again. They take a shit, we sprinkle it with sugar before it floats downstream."

I wrinkled my nose. Honestly. She'd given me that same metaphor the first day I started interning with her.

I never knew that she meant it quite so seriously.

But the look on her face was dead serious when she told me, "We don't let them convince us that the shit they just took is actually ice cream."

"You think I'm naïve," I concluded.

"Not naïve. *Sweet.* So sweet, you think everyone's serving up ice cream even when they're not. And that would be a detriment to this company, if I were to hire you."

I tried to swallow the lump that had formed; my throat was still burning, but I picked up the scotch. As I slugged it back—the whole damn thing—Danielle looked almost amused.

I winced and set the glass on her desk before standing up and looking her in the eye. My mentor. My would-be boss. All at once, standing here with my stomach burning and my heart in my throat, I was glad she didn't hire me. Deeply glad.

Maybe I hadn't found my place here at her company, under her expert wing, like I thought I had. This was my very first job, internship or not, ever. And I'd never wanted anything like I thought I wanted this job.

When she let me go, my entire self-worth could've been ripped out from under me. Especially considering the morning I'd had.

But instead, this conversation only made me realize what I did not want.

I did not want to end up like the woman in front of me.

"Well, I'd rather see the world as one giant ice cream parlor than a toilet." I picked up my purse. "And for what it's worth, I was not flirting with Johnny O'Reilly, and I'm terribly sorry if I offended his date. Thank you, sincerely, for everything you've so graciously taught me. And for giving me a chance. I'm really sorry it didn't work out. "

I scurried to the door before my eyes could start leaking again; I could feel the dam stretching, about to burst.

"You're welcome," Danielle said behind me. "Keep that chin up, sweetheart."

And that did it.

Something about the way she called me *sweetheart*—like I was some cute little kitten she could just brush aside?—made me stop in my tracks. Hadn't people spoken to me like that my entire life? My sister's friends? My sister's boyfriends?

Even people I met professionally through Danielle's company.

What the hell was it about me that brought that on?

I turned slowly on my heel and looked at her, sitting there on her leather throne. My sister's publicist. *The queenmaker*. In her designer suit with all the trimmings. Her age so hard to peg because of all the fillers in her face. The measure of her soul even harder to get a lock on through the imperious shit-and-sugar metaphors. She was already on her phone, typing.

"Danielle?"

"Hmmm?" she hummed, without looking up.

"I will prove you wrong."

The silence in the air was so taut, it hurt when I sucked in a deep breath, trying to calm my heart. I'd never told anyone off in my life. I didn't even know how to do it.

As much as I wanted to right now.

Her eyes finally lifted to mine. "I hope you do," she said, her intent neither here nor there. She either meant it or she didn't believe me at all. Who could say? Danielle Duke wasn't exactly the most forthcoming, warm or sympathetic person.

She was nothing at all like me.

"One day," I told her, my voice wobbling a little as I clung to my shredded pride, "I'll be the queenmaker in this town."

Then I dashed out the door before she could refute it.

# Chapter Two

**Johnny**

The windshield wipers beat back the weather, a slow, monotonous thud, as the rain on the glass turned to blood. There was an old rock song playing on the car radio.

And a stranger in the front seat.

I jerked awake.

For a long, dark moment, it felt like someone was in the room with me.

"*Shit.*" I released the breath I'd been holding in a burst. I sat up in bed, my chest tight, my heart thudding like a wild, spooked animal trapped in a cage.

I swiped my hand over my face as the world took shape around me. Empty.

*Safe.*

Four walls and a bed, last night's clothes tossed across a chair in the corner. I was alone, my ragged breathing the only sound.

Dull light crept in at the edges of the floor-to-ceiling windows, the blinds shut tight. I picked up my phone and checked the time. It was just after one in the afternoon.

Squinting into the light of the screen, I thumbed over to the app that controlled the blinds. They slid all the way open across the expansive wall in front of me as I adjusted the slider and blinked into the glaring sunlight.

Then I dropped the phone on the bed and fell back onto the pillow. It felt damp and cold. I'd been sweating in my sleep. I rubbed my face, struggling to wake up fully and get my bearings. I was at home, in my own bedroom, but everything felt off, like it always did when the nightmare invaded my dreams.

I always had the nightmare when something was wrong. When something was bothering me, even if I didn't know what it was yet.

Maybe it was all the vodka last night. It had been a long fucking time since I'd slept in this late. But then again, I didn't get home until the sun was coming up. Because—

Brianna.

*Fuck.*

I ran my hand absently down my body. Naked. Felt like I needed a shower. Did I even take one, when I got home this morning?

I couldn't remember. Everything was kinda hazy.

I dragged myself out of bed. I hated sleeping late. Felt groggy and off all fucking day. I liked my morning wellness routine. But I also liked an endless night, a lot of booze, and an enthusiastic woman. These things butted up against my diet, my workouts and my music regimen at sharp fucking angles.

I picked up my phone again and turned on some music; my *Wake Up* playlist started rocking through the speakers all over the house. I mercilessly cranked the volume to ear bleeding levels, then staggered into the bathroom and got the shower running, as I tried to remember what day it was. My phone said it was Friday and according to several messages from my manager, Yash, I had a meeting with my record company in just over an hour.

I thumbed through the messages, swiping away the ones from Brianna without reading them, instead opening the ones from Yash. *Where are you? Can you make it or not?*

I texted him back. *I'll be there.*

Then I got in the shower and soaped off last night. Dripping wet, I shut off the water and stalked over to the patio doors, opening them to the fresh air. It felt cool on my hot skin. It was June, warm but not yet hot outside.

Naked and steaming, I stepped out onto the upper patio that ran the length of my bedroom and bathroom. Could've headed downstairs through the house, but I liked going this way better.

I glanced down into the backyard, then next door, but no one seemed to be around. The whole lot, including the adjacent one next door that I'd bought a few years back and integrated with mine, was surrounded by tall, old trees, blocking out the view of neighboring houses. Maximum privacy.

I walked down the stairs to the deck that surrounded the pool, then under the stairs, past the giant party hot tub. And into the "gym" at the back of the house, which was really more of a state of the art fitness center equipped with every tech innovation I could get my hands on, from an AI adaptive bike to a Red Light Therapy bed. I didn't have time for any of those right now, or for the sauna, unfortunately.

I went straight to the in-ground cold plunge pool. The water inside was just several degrees above freezing.

I hated this part, but the shock to my lymphatic system was the quickest way to jumpstart my day, improving stress management, boosting performance of my immune system and a myriad of other health benefits. Polar opposite of last night: this would suck during and feel amazing afterwards.

I cupped my balls and jumped. Just before I crashed into the water, I shut my eyes.

And I saw his face.

The man in the front seat.

Then the cold hit my system, whiting out everything else. Like an ice-cold shot of electricity through my core.

Shock.

Alertness.

*Focus.*

My dad's words to me, like they sometimes did, smashed into me. Something from the Bible. Something he'd misinterpreted. *Immersion in the lake of fire.* He thought it would make me feel better. That it was a purifying, a cleansing by God.

That we all were worthy of this cleansing and must seek it out.

Even me.

I didn't believe him or his holy words. Even then, as a kid, I knew that the lake of fire wasn't a cleansing. It was a punishment.

The eternal burning of the wicked.

My feet hit the bottom and I shot to the surface. Inhaled, like a baby sucking back its first breath, about to scream.

Reborn.

Everything wiped clean, reset, for just a moment.

For just a moment, there was no car. No blood-rain on the windows.

No man in the front seat.

There was only this.

*Pain.*

Which meant only one thing: I was alive.

*You were wrong, Dad. We don't need to seek it out.*

*If we're meant to burn, it's already happening.*

———

When we arrived downtown, my hulking, live-in bodyguard, Lamar, escorted me up the elevator of BHR Tower, home of my record label, Brick House Records.

Lamar then waited for me out in the Brick House reception area while I went in to talk to Trey Jones, owner of Brick House and a guy I'd known for years. I was texting my buddy Dane as I followed Trey's assistant into his office; the west coast offices of Dane's company, Valhalla Media Group, were also in the building, and I wanted to know if he was in the office today and wanted to meet up for a late lunch or something.

When I looked up from my phone, I was greeted by two dour-ass faces. Yash and Trey got to their feet as Trey's assistant shut the door behind me. Trey, looking toned and slick in a designer button-down with the sleeves rolled up, standing behind his desk, and Yash, my manager and longtime friend, comparatively doughy in an orange Polo shirt and jeans, hovering in the foreground, looking sweaty.

"What's with the long fucking faces?" I greeted them casually as I went to hug Yash, then shook Trey's hand across the desk.

"Johnny," Trey greeted me neutrally.

"Sit down, bro." Yash scratched at his beard, a wild and wiry thicket that crept up his cheeks and down his neck. Yash was basically the opposite of Trey Jones in the way he conducted business. He wasn't exactly sloppy, but he didn't give a fuck about grooming or fashion. Told me once, long ago, that he was never going to be "that guy" so why bother. He knew his place in a room with a guy like Trey.

And with me.

Yash brought brains and logic to the equation, and a generous dose of anxiety.

Trey brought polish, a high bar and a capacity for over-achievement.

I brought chaos and talent.

Yash's words, not mine.

"How many coffees have you had today, buddy?" I asked as we all sat down; Yash looked twitchier than usual.

He laughed uncomfortably. "Not enough for this conversation."

I glanced at Trey, who sat back in his chair looking relaxed but not happy. Trey Jones would be the first guy in the room to try to charm you, find common ground, influence your mood with a compliment. Usually it was, *Looking good, Johnny. That a new tattoo?* Or, *When are we going for drinks?*

Not today.

"Look, Johnny. JC walked out."

I heard Yash's words, but they didn't sink in. He stared at me in silence, waiting on a reaction.

"Walked out," I repeated slowly. "Out of where?"

"He walked out on *us*," Yash clarified. "He's left the band." He twitched, rattling his wood-bead bracelets. It was a nervous tick, and it drove me crazy. I should've stolen all his bracelets one night on tour while he was sleeping and burned them.

*Walked out.*

By the time I'd processed, I was already rejecting this information outright. My lead singer was not leaving the band. "No. He's not going anywhere."

"Johnny." Yash tried to hold my gaze, but kept looking away. Another nervous tick. "He's gone for good this time. I spoke with him this morning. He's not coming back."

"Of course he is." I leaned forward in my seat. "And why am I just hearing about this now?" I looked from him to Trey.

Trey returned my look with a cool detachment. *This is your problem, not mine.*

No. I could not lose my lead singer. I *would not* lose my band.

I would not lose this record deal.

Not when I was positioned to get everything I'd ever wanted, professionally.

We'd been through way too much as a band to get where we were now: standing on the fucking precipice of breakout, top-of-the-charts success.

The kind of success we'd never quite achieved. Yet.

We had a strong lineup, after so many changes in the band in the early days. Our sound had matured. We'd dialed in our live performance. We'd been working with some great lyricists. We even had the right management, most days; Yash believed in us, had stood by me since fucking high school. Even if he wasn't the barracuda I would've sometimes liked him to be, he was fucking loyal and that had massive currency with me.

And now we had Cary Clarke coming on to produce our new album.

I truly believed this was the missing ingredient—one of the hottest producers in the business to collaborate with, to take what we could do in the studio from great to outstanding on our next album. We had Cary's studio, Little Black Hole, to record at. And we had the right record label; Brick House Records had recently launched the Players, the first rock band on their largely hip-hop focused label, into the rock 'n' roll stratosphere.

My band, Breakneck, was about to follow suit.

Finally. Fucking finally, after all these years, we were going big.

"It's Breakneck's turn to shine," I reminded them both. How many times had Trey said those words to me, almost ad nauseam, since we'd inked this deal earlier this year? Even he didn't know how close the band had been to breaking up—yet again—just before the deal was signed. That ink was the glue that had held us together. "We've got everything lined up and the band isn't going anywhere. We have a contract."

Neither of them spoke.

"Why are you both looking at me? JC is contractually bound to make this album."

Yash scratched his hairy neck. "Yeah. Not if he sues, though, Johnny."

*What the fuck?*

"Why would he sue? He's not gonna sue. JC wants this album as much as any of us. Noah, Miles. We all want this."

"You sure about that?" Trey said mildly, assessing me with his dark eyes.

"What does that mean?" I countered.

"You're the only one here, Johnny," he pointed out.

"Because JC is home, in New York, I assume. And Miles is home in Toronto. And Noah's in L.A. for a few days off. So what?"

"He meant," Yash said, "you're the only one we called in here today."

I looked at Yash… as his words shifted the entire meaning of this meeting, tipping everything into focus, an uncomfortable clarity settling over me.

Reading the emotions of others wasn't exactly a strong suit of mine, but I could see the tension on Yash's face, the sweat gleaming on his forehead.

When the hottest rock band in town, and now one of the biggest bands in the world, Dirty, signed their first record deal, they had their friend, Brody Mason, as their manager. Working with Brody had worked for Dirty their entire careers. I was only in high school when Dirty's first album hit the charts, but I figured if that worked for them, it could work for me. So I'd recruited my buddy Yash, who was a violinist and nerd who'd started helping me manage the meagre earnings from my first few paid gigs in high school, to be my manager.

The only issue with that over the years? Yash had never had Brody Mason's balls.

Which was why he was blindsiding me with this shit.

"So, what is this?" I asked him, then looked at Trey. "An intervention?"

They didn't deny it.

"Maybe you should think about intervening on JC's attitude," I suggested. "Or Miles' crippling need for reassurance every time he plays a note." I got up and headed for the door. What was the point of this conversation?

"You're always up and running, Johnny," Yash said, sounding weary. "Just stop for a fucking second, okay?"

"Running?" I stopped inside the office door and turned back to him.

"Running," he repeated. "Faster. Harder. Until you can't fucking run anymore, you get me?" He clawed a hand through his tangle of hair. "You can't ignore this. You've gotta deal with this head on."

"How am I not dealing with this?"

He sighed quietly, but this time his eyes held mine. "You fucked up, my friend," he said.

And I realized…

He fucking knew. Maybe they both knew.

About last night. The fundraiser.

Fucking Brianna.

"It's all over the internet," he added grimly.

"Like I care," I said evenly.

I didn't, really. It still surprised the hell out of me, the kind of trivial junk the media and the world at large were so interested in. Like, who the fuck cared? Which was why I generally stayed away from it.

It was just noise, and I had enough noise of my own to deal with on the best of days.

Yash knew I didn't keep social media apps on my phone, or the fucking internet. No one but my closest friends and whatever women I was seeing had my phone number. And none of them had said anything to me. So whatever was "all over the internet" couldn't be that bad.

*Bad enough to have Yash sweating.*

"Why don't you come sit down," Trey said cooly.

I sat back down and sighed. "You're gonna tell me this problem with JC is entirely my fault?"

"That's not what anyone's saying," Yash assured me.

"Except JC," I challenged.

"We all need to take responsibility for our shit," Yash said diplomatically. "We all know the band has had some struggles. But we were feeling really tight when we signed this record deal."

"Yeah. We were."

"So what happened?"

"Nothing happened."

Yash cleared his throat. "Well, last night, something happened that was… unacceptable… to JC. So, now we need damage control, or we've got a serious problem."

I knew he was right.

I could feel Trey's eyes on me.

What happened last night… what I *let* happen… If JC was seriously this pissed about it… It could threaten everything, from our current recording contract to our ongoing career as a band. I didn't exactly think about that when my lead singer's girlfriend had my cock in her mouth, though.

I mean, if you could call her his girlfriend. What kind of girlfriend does that shit?

"This is our fifth fucking album," I reminded them both, "and we're not going anywhere."

"There's a window, Johnny," Trey reminded me right back. "Cary just finished up with the Players' album. It's now or never. The Players are going on tour with Dirty in September. They've got rehearsals, video shoots. They're scheduled—"

"Yeah. I know. You don't have to explain to me how busy they are—"

*Video shoots.*

It hit me, suddenly. The Players were holding auditions for one of their music videos in town, and my sister was auditioning as a dancer. And I fucking forgot. That was today, right?

I pulled out my phone, checked the time, and sent a text to Shayla. *You auditioning?*

When I looked up again, Trey and Yash were exchanging a look at my expense.

"What? I'm listening. I was texting my sister."

"I need to impress upon you, Johnny," Trey said, "how important it is that we hit those dates in the studio. We lose Cary and the studio mid-August. That means we need the album—"

"You'll have your album. I'm fucking here. You know who isn't here? JC. He wants to walk out on the band, fine. Let him throw his tantrum." I looked to Yash for agreement, but he just looked sweaty. "We've all seen this before."

"I don't think this is like before," he said.

"He'll come around."

"Wish we all knew that for sure, brother," Trey said evenly. "Four guys in the band. You all need to be onboard to make this work."

"We go into the studio as planned. We can start without him. He'll come around," I repeated.

Trey and Yash exchanged another look.

"We need JC, Johnny," Yash told me. "We need lead vocals."

"I fucking realize that." I got to my feet again. "We'll have lead vocals." I looked Trey in the eye and he held my gaze. He nodded slightly, like, *Let's make sure we do, then.*

I headed for the door and I heard them getting up behind me, to see me out. Yash would probably follow me out and repeat himself like fifty times, as if I didn't get the fucking message already.

*Fuck, JC.*

This was definitely about last night. Obviously, I'd fucked up. Read the situation with Brianna wrong? Not the part where she tore off my pants, that part was pretty fucking clear. But the rest of it.

Her and JC…

How he felt about her?

But no matter what I'd done, this was ugly. Unfair. We were a band. We'd made a commitment.

And it wasn't like JC was pure as the driven snow. The fact that Yash and Trey were looking at me like I was the only one who'd ever fucked up in this band, or fucked around?

Fuck that. I knew the truth.

JC knew the truth.

There were no angels in this band.

I just needed to go talk to him, set this thing straight.

"I'll take care of it," I told Trey, as I shook his hand before leaving his office.

And the thing was, I totally believed that I would.

I once heard that if you put a frog in water and turned up the heat slowly enough, the frog would boil alive. It would die. It wouldn't jump out of the pot before it got too hot.

And I wondered if the same thing would happen to me.

Maybe when you got used to the heat, you failed to read the cues. Maybe, in truth, you just didn't want to read them.

To recognize that just one more degree could be the one to end you.

# Chapter Three

**Angeline**

"How beyond fucking cool would it be if I landed a role in a Players video?" Shayla linked her arm with mine as we wandered up the sidewalk. It was just past nine and downtown Vancouver was starting to light up around us as the sun went down. She smoothed her long, straight strawberry-blond hair, exaggerating the roll of her hips in her short skirt as she eyed a passing convertible with the top down and a bunch of guys in it.

After I'd watched her dance audition this afternoon, where she'd wowed absolutely everyone including the members of the Players, their management team and everyone else in the dance studio—by pole dancing in a pig costume, of all things, then stripping out of it—the two of us had met up with our girls Courteney and Larissa for dinner in the West End. We'd laughed until we cried as I played Court and Larissa a video I made of Shayla doing her pig routine to a Toadies song, "I Want Your Love."

It was seriously one of the best things I'd ever seen in my life.

Shayla performed with such confidence and wit, *in a pig costume*, and still somehow managed to bring it home with a super hot ending, stripping down to a sparkly bikini. She was an amazing dancer. Plus, the whole routine was choreographed by her, right down to the costume and song choice, she'd totally nailed it, made it unique and memorable, and I'd be shocked if she didn't get a role in the video.

Dinner had turned into drinks, and now the four of us had walked all the way across downtown amid Friday night traffic, heading over to Champagne nightclub.

"Beyond fucking cool," I agreed. Shayla was still flying high off the adrenaline from her audition. The Players were one of the largest bands to break out of Vancouver in recent years; second only to my sister's band, Dirty. I knew how important this day was to Shay, and I didn't have it in me to put a damper on it by telling her that her brother's behavior at the fundraiser last night—where I thought Johnny and I were talking business, but apparently he was just being a fucking asshole—had cost me my job.

I mean, he wasn't the whole reason Danielle dismissed me. But he was a giant part.

"Maybe I can get a role, too," Larissa mused. Her curvy bod was swathed in a cute purple velour track suit, her dark, curly hair wound in braids on top of her head; she'd been rocking this "stylish student" look since going back to school. "Maybe they could film me cramming for an exam?"

Shayla laughed.

"Yeah, maybe if I hang around on set," I put in, "they can cast me as 'girl standing around doing nothing' in a scene." I tried to smile and not feel too sorry for myself, but it fell flat as the lingering pain of the day's events overshadowed it. I noticed no one laughed, but I did catch my friends passing an uneasy look between them.

It just reminded me of all the crap I was trying not to think about. Getting dumped. Getting fired. Unfortunately, it was all I could think about. Shayla's audition had been a welcome distraction, but it was only temporary relief.

Courteney wrapped an arm around me and gave me a little side-hug.

When we arrived at the door to Champagne, Ronan Sterling, the Players' head of security, was standing right inside the nightclub's entrance with some other men. My sister was part owner of the new club, as was Ronan's wife, Summer Sorensen; Summer was the Players' keyboardist and my sister's best friend. As we walked in, Shayla made no small work of checking out the guys—they looked like bouncers, possibly in training for opening night—as I said hi to Ronan and gave him a hug.

"Hey, sweetheart," Ronan greeted me. "Elle's inside." He also hugged Courteney, whose husband and brother were both members of the Players. Then he drew open the massive, tufted suede interior door for us and we wandered inside to soak in the vibe. I hadn't been inside since the renovations were finished.

The walls were the first things that drew my eye. Painted flat black, they displayed a number of massive paintings that had been commissioned for the space. Katie Mayes, wife of my sister's bandmate Jesse Mayes, had painted them; semi-abstract paintings of people playing musical instruments, in bold color patterns. The paintings were interspersed with large, black-and-white portraits of Vancouver-based rock stars, photographed by Amber Cope; Amber was married to another of my sister's bandmates, Dylan Cope.

The art really gave the place an eclectic yet elevated feel.

"Wow, VIP lounge, but take it to the next level," Larissa remarked. "Trey is going to love this." Her older brother, Trey, was a record company exec, owner of Brick House Records, the Players' record label. And a man of serious taste.

"I think you're right," I agreed.

"Forget your brother," Shayla said. "Mine is gonna *live* here."

"Yeah, pretty sure I can see Johnny O parked right… over… there." Courteney pointed out a deeply curved booth. "You know, holding court over his salivating fangirls…" Inside the large booth was a table and several large velvet ottomans that left plenty of room for babes to flock around a VIP. And possibly blow him without anyone knowing.

"Yup. Say goodbye to the Ruby," Larissa marveled. The Ruby was a local nightclub that had been a favorite hangout of many music industry VIPs, historically.

No surprise, my sister and her team had really outdone themselves. This place was backstage VIP room meets luxury penthouse with a side of back door gambling club. There was something sexy and illicit about the dark, curving walls and the sumptuous furnishings, the gleaming, mirrored decor, and the deep corners lined with hidden booths. They'd kept those booths from the existing design, but everything else had undergone a serious facelift.

The lighting was on point, glowy and subdued interspersed with sparkling chandeliers. The large dance floor at the back of the massive space was bedazzled in lights that bounced off a series of mirrored disco balls. There were a couple of guys in the raised DJ booth, maybe testing out the sound system, and staff working away, unpacking supplies and stocking the glass-shelved walls behind the two long bars, which had been completely rebuilt.

Where it used to say *Artemis* in neon along the entry wall, it now said *Champagne* in mirrored script.

The Artemis Club had been a fixture in the Vancouver party scene for several years, but like so many bars and clubs, it had changed ownership many times. Most recently, Summer—who, before she became a member of the Players and a rock star herself, was known as DJ Summer and had gotten her start at the Artemis—had heard that the current owners wanted to sell. She'd appealed to my sister, and together they'd convinced Dylan Cope that he should sell his portion of the nightclub he co-owned down in L.A., bring his money back up to Vancouver, and the three of them should buy the Artemis.

They did.

An extensive reno followed, and they were now putting all the finishing touches on it for the grand opening party next weekend. It was sure to be the hottest club in town—and yet another win in my sister's ongoing success story.

"This all is just… *wow.*" Larissa stood, open-mouthed and staring at one of the larger-than-life black-and-whites on the wall—a portrait of rock star/music producer Cary Clarke, wearing jeans and nothing else, and doing nothing at all but leaning against a wall with a guitar leaning next to him. His ankles were crossed, his hands dangling at his sides and his blondish hair falling over his face as he looked down at the ground, smiling. You couldn't even see his eyes, but the effect was…. breathtaking.

"Dayyyyum, that Amber Cope is one incredible photographer," Shayla observed.

“It doesn’t hurt when your subject is scrumdiddly-fucking-umptious,” I pointed out, mostly to tease Courteney.

“Ugh. Quit ogling my brother.” Courteney glanced at the image; she was fourteen years younger than Cary and loved him to death, but with her thick blonde hair and hazel eyes she looked more like him than she cared to admit. She headed over to another image; Dylan Cope backstage, dressed in his typical performing attire—kilt, boots and no shirt—twirling a set of drumsticks. He was standing at the side of the stage, looking out into the crowd—a blur of faces and glowing cell phones—while the stage lights shone through his jaw-length, wavy hair.

I stood with her, staring at the image for a long moment. Marveling over how only a guy like Dylan Cope—so easygoing, charming, likable—could have a hot picture of himself up on the wall of his own bar and not come across as a self-important douche. Guaranteed, Dylan wasn’t the one who put that image on the wall, though. His wife, as the photographer, and Summer, as a woman who knew how to give the public what it wanted, were for sure at work here.

“These are amazing,” I gushed. From where I stood, turning in a slow circle, I could see equally stunning portraits of the Players’ lead singer, Ashley Player, and another local singer, Dean Slater, along with a portrait of my sister, and many others. It was such a beautiful tribute to the city’s most accomplished musicians, and many of my sister’s friends.

And those were just the ones I could see; there were many hidden nooks and crannies where the curving walls disappeared out of view.

Then I saw the portrait of Johnny O’Reilly and stopped in my tracks.

In the giant photo, he was onstage with his guitar, all sweaty and sensual and looking every inch his ridiculously beautiful self. Toned, tattooed. Thick blonde hair that was naturally dark at the roots. His sex appeal oozed through that image, almost choking me where I stood.

I cleared my throat as my sister suddenly appeared, manifesting out of God-knew-where, as VIPs tended to do. A concerned look marred her face as she beelined for me across the empty club, and I realized belatedly that the concerned look was for *me*. “Angie.” She reached for me, crushing me into a hug.

“Elle.” I hugged her and released. Jeez, I wasn’t broken. Felt like she was trying to hold me together or something, like she was worried I'd shatter if she let go too fast. "Uh, hi. Nice club."

"Oh. Thank you." Elle looked around distractedly like she'd just remembered where we were. Then she looked me over with that concerned face, her steely gray eyes skimming over my sheath dress, a pale blue-gray knit that matched my eyes, which I'd worn for my meeting with Danielle today. I'd made it my own by adding a brooch, a glittering faux-diamond bunny. Just 'cause.

Elle, as always, looked beautiful, her platinum blonde hair in a high, sleek ponytail, her slim figure poured into jet black skinny jeans and an offensively overpriced designer hoodie. Even lowkey, my big sister looked like a rock star, with her glittery manicure, many silver earrings and the lavishly studded wedge sneakers that added inches to her height. I was five-five, she wasn't much taller, but right now she towered over me in my ballet flats. I didn't like it.

"Everything ready for the big night?" I tried to keep it light, because the last thing I needed was to dissolve into waterworks in front of her, right here. She could probably tell just looking at me that I'd already cried a river today.

"Getting there." She studied my face, like she was searching for the tracks of my tears. "I tried calling you. You didn't pick up."

"I was at Shayla's audition."

"How did it go?"

"Much better than my meeting with Danielle Duke."

She gently squeezed my arms. "Oh, babe."

"Did you know?"

"No. I didn't know. Of course not. Angie, I would've told you. She called me right after you left her office to tell me."

I glanced at my friends, who were still ogling the rock stars on the walls. "I'm gonna get a drink with the girls, if that's okay. Is the bar open?" Elle had invited me to come down for some free drinks tonight if I wanted to; I had no idea I'd want to take her up on that so badly until today happened.

"Of course." She turned to a dark-haired woman behind the bar.

"Whatever the girls want," she called over, indicating me and my friends. "It's on the house. But put their taste buds to work."

The female bartender had turned and I recognized Merritt. Dark hair with blunt bangs, visible tattoos and a black band T-shirt; she had a memorable look. Merritt worked at Cary Clarke's recording studio, Little Black Hole, where the Players had recorded both their albums.

I waved at her. "Hey, Merritt. How the hell did they rope you into this?"

She laughed. "Night job. I was bartending at a club up the street, and Summer recruited me. I'll just roll out a bunch of stuff for you ladies to taste test? We're trying out a bunch of drinks for the cocktail menu tonight."

"Yes, please," I gushed, a little too enthusiastically.

Merritt winked at me. "Have a seat. I'll bring out a round."

I waved my girls over to a high top table in the middle of the room, from where we had a great view of, well, everything. When I told the girls we were taste testing cocktails for the rest of the night, they cheered—and started waving tip money in Merritt's direction. She laughed again.

Elle gave a big-sisterly sigh, and reconvened with her posse, a group of people I loosely recognized; her assistant, a couple of members of Dirty's management team and some others, who were gathering around a table near the back of the club.

At least her bodyguard was nowhere to be seen. Last thing I needed was to run into Flynn right now.

I was way too sober for that.

---

I spent a good half hour or so relaying the scene in Danielle Duke's office, in detail, to my girlfriends, who'd demanded it. Though I left out Johnny's whole part in it, for Shayla's sake. They cringed in sympathy and rallied to comfort me as we sipped purple concoctions in fancy cocktail glasses, kindly provided by Merritt and my sister.

And then, of course, came the scene that started off this day from hell:

the breakfast table breakup. I was less detailed about that one and way less keen to talk about it, and got it over with as quickly as possible.

"I'm telling you," Shayla announced when I'd finished, "the good ones don't break your heart like that."

"I don't believe that's strictly true," I choked out. "But I really don't want to talk about him right now."

"How bad was it?" Larissa asked gently. "Not talking about him, I promise."

I groaned. "He was… very civil. You know Flynn." Actually, he was extremely unemotional about the whole thing, but I didn't want to talk about that, either. I'd put the man through enough emotional turmoil over the last three-and-a-half years, he deserved some peace. In other words, me out of his life.

*Tears threatening…*

I made a gross snuffly sound, choking back my misery with a cocktail napkin to my nose. "I'm okay, really," I pronounced, as my friends eyed me with concern.

"You're not," Courteney observed. "But that's okay."

"How many times have you listened to Harry today?" Larissa asked knowingly.

And I admitted, "Too many to count." Harry Styles' epic ballad "Sign of the Times" was my crying song, and all my besties knew it; if I had that song on repeat, the situation was dire.

God, Flynn probably hated that song. He'd probably developed PTSD from hearing it play after every fight we had, and would be triggered every time he heard it for the rest of his life. But for me, that song was a healing balm.

"Oh, babe," Shayla commiserated. "The LBS is here for you."

I tried to smile.

The LBS was the "Lil Brat Society," the tongue-in-cheek support group the four of us had formed together, many years back. When we all met, Shayla, Courteney, Larissa and I had quickly bonded over our similar lots in life: we all were little sisters to public figures in the music industry. I wasn't the only one who lived in the shadow of my glamorous older sibling.

Thank God.

No one except these three girls knew exactly what that particular aspect of my life was like, and no other humans on the planet had ever been more unfailingly supportive of me.

"I know you don't want to talk about him," Courteney said. "But… I thought you two were working on it?"

"We have been. For a while. It's… not working."

"Angie, I'm so sorry," Larissa said. "I know you love him."

"Yeah, well. The feeling is not mutual anymore."

"Sweetie." Courteney got up and came around the table to hug me.

I bit back the swell of emotion and the tears that threatened, again. I'd cried enough today, for fuck's sake. "Thank you."

"Tell us what you need."

"Nothing, I promise. I'll be okay."

Courteney eased back into her seat, looking doubtful. Actually, they all looked pretty doubtful. "What are you gonna do?" she asked sympathetically. "Like, where are you gonna go? Back to your parents' place?"

"No. Uh-uh. That's just too sad. I'm way too old for that."

"Hey, no one's too old to run back to their parents for love and recovery when they've been wounded," Shayla said. "It's human. It's what we do."

"Just be glad you have parents to run back to," Courteney said, and I knew what she meant. My parents were awesome. I'd just feel like such a loser crawling back to them. I was twenty-seven, almost twenty-eight. Way closer to thirty than twenty. Wasn't I supposed to be self-sufficient by now?

"If not your mom and dad, then who?" Larissa pried gently. Because sadly, we all knew I didn't exactly have enough savings to pay first and last months' rent on an apartment by myself, plus utilities and all the rest.

"Well…" I sniffled. "Flynn said I can keep living in the apartment for now."

Silence.

Music played in the background, Post Malone brooding away about running in circles, and my girls just looked at me. Then their eyes slid around the table, from face to face, as they decided telepathically who was nominated to kick my ass.

Shayla, of course.

She'd just taken a swig from her sparkly pink travel mug—she'd been dumping her cocktails into it—and slammed it on the table. It said, rather fittingly, *Big Dick Energy*. "What, in his bed? He thinks he can break your heart, then keep helping himself to the all-he-can-eat lady buffet? Hell no!" For such a wisp of a human, she was damn loud.

"Not in his bed," I hissed quietly. "Of course not. And say it a little louder. I don't think the DJ quite heard you." I glanced at my sister's table, way across the club, but they weren't looking at us. "He, uh, cleaned out the second bedroom. You know, his gym-slash-office-slash-man-cave."

"Already?" Larissa said.

"Yup. He's sleeping in there. You know, neither of us wants to…" *Sleep in the bed we shared while the other one is still in the apartment.* I couldn't even bring myself to say it, knowing the dam would probably burst again if I did. "And he made me a little nest on the couch last night. After our fight."

The girls all looked at each other again. It was getting mildly annoying.

"I guess… that's nice," Courteney offered. But the look on her face said *Like fucking hell I'd be sleeping on a couch nest if Xander broke up with me.*

They were right to hate the idea, probably. But what choice did I have?

I slumped over my drink. The purple ones had been replaced by blue ones, a while ago. Maybe there were green ones too, in between. "Guys, I know. As nice as he's trying to be about it, it blows."

"Well, thank Christ we don't have to break it to you," Shayla said. "But let me be clear. You cannot, and I repeat, *cannot*, live with your ex."

"It's only for now. You know, until I land on my feet."

"Land on your feet?" Larissa said carefully. "He ripped the rug out from under you, Angie. It may take a while to, you know, land on your feet again."

"You're staying at my place," Shayla announced.

"I am not."

"Babe. This is not the time to get stubborn and independent."

I laughed. We all knew I was the last thing from independent.

I didn't even realize how entirely dependent on my boyfriend I was until this afternoon, when Danielle told me I had no job. Flynn paid for the apartment, all the taxes and utilities and whatever. He paid my credit card bill. I didn't even know what he paid for.

I didn't even have an income.

Somehow, with Flynn, I never felt like I needed anything. Including a job. I was free to enjoy our life together. He took care of me financially. I took care of him in other ways; cooking, massages, doing his laundry, looking after the apartment. Making things nice for him. He never complained about that part. It worked for us.

But now I was a woman with no job, no work history, and virtually no money. Worse, I was a woman with no purpose and no idea what she was doing with her life when she woke up tomorrow.

"I mean, he told me I can stay as long as I need to." My tone was growing uncertain. "Although that was when we both thought I was getting a job offer today. In reality, 'As long as you need to' probably meant 'Until your first paycheck comes in.' You know, the paycheck I'm not gonna have anytime soon."

"Shayla's right," Courteney said slowly. "You should move in with her. She has the space. I'd welcome you into my home anytime, you know that. But Xander and I have such a small condo. You'd be on a couch nest, for sure. You're welcome to, of course, but that's all I can offer."

"I know," I assured her. "It's fine."

"And you know Jason and I don't have the space, either," Larissa said. "I'm so sorry we can't help." I knew that, too. Larissa and her boyfriend had moved back in with his parents while they both finished their advanced degrees.

"It's okay you guys, really. I don't need a bed. I've got the couch for now. All my things are there. I'll move out as soon as I can. I'm not even worried about that part." I wasn't. Mainly because I was just trying not to think about it. "It's just… I've never been on my own before."

"Pfft, it's not half bad," Shayla said. "I'm telling you. You'll be just fucking fine."

"Shay, I have no job."

"Who needs a job?"

"Says the woman who has no job," Courteney poked, "and yet her bills somehow get paid."

"By her wealthy parents and her older brother." Larissa sipped innocently on her blue drink.

"Hey!" Shay jabbed a gleaming fingernail in each of our faces. "Every one of you has accepted handouts, swag and goodies from your parents and/or successful older sibling at some point. Not to mention a BMW." She aimed her fingernail at Courteney.

"Sure." Larissa set her drink down, unfazed. "But you're the only one who accepted a whole house."

"Who wouldn't accept a house??"

"Uh… us?" Courteney smirked as she sipped, enjoying the opportunity to tease Shayla. Shay teased the rest of us—Courteney especially—so relentlessly.

Shayla huffed indignantly. "Um, hello. You lived in your brother's poolhouse just so you could lie around the pool in your bikini and try to seduce his best friend." She conveniently left out the part where the whole seduce-him-in-your-bikini thing was basically her idea.

"Hey, that man I seduced is now my husband," Courteney reminded her.

"Come to think of it," Larissa teased Shay, "why aren't you putting your brother's pool to more use?"

"Yeah, Shay," Courteney put in. "How many of your brother's friends have you seduced now?" She already knew the answer to that. We all did.

"Only one," Shayla sniffed. "And we're currently on a break."

"And why is that?" Larissa pressed, loving this.

Shayla waved her hand dismissively in the air. "Because Johnny got all aggro about it."

"And threatened to stop paying your bills," Larissa teased.

"Since when do you care what your brother says about your love life anyway?" Courteney inquired, stirring the pot.

"Since he threatened to stop paying for Netflix if she didn't stop making out with his lead singer," Larissa supplied.

"I was halfway through *The Walking Dead*! That's like, a billion seasons! You can't just stop in the middle!"

"And her manicures," Courteney elaborated, "and her credit cards, and everything else—"

"Anyway," Shayla interjected, "who cares who pays the bills? Money is just money. I'm my own woman." An obnoxious *DING!* so loud we all heard it over the music shook her phone on the table and she grinned, beaming self-confidence. "And hey, maybe I have a job. As the hot dancer in the Players' new music video!"

My phone lit up next to hers.

"Ooh!" she exclaimed. "Maybe that's Flynn, begging to get you ba… ack…" Her smile fell at the look on my face.

"It's not like that, Shay. And it's never going to be. It's over."

"Sorry. You know I think all men should grovel. It's my go-to." She added solemnly, "I'll never bring it up again."

"Thank you."

"Can I check my phone?"

"Of course."

We both picked up. I read the texts I'd just received from Summer.

**Summer:** Tell Shayla her audition was among the most ridiculous things I've ever seen. And I've seen some things.

**Summer:** Also, you can tell her she's hired.

"I got the gig!" Shayla squealed. "My agent says I got the Players video!"

"Yes, you did." I smiled and showed her Summer's messages.

Courteney semi-screamed and jumped off her chair to strangle Shayla in an exuberant hug. "You're gonna be in a video with my husband!"

They screamed together, jumping up and down.

I laughed. They did this often. Like whenever someone they knew had some huge success; usually Courteney's husband, Xander, or her brother, Cary. Or occasionally, even Shayla's brother, Johnny.

This time, Shayla was a part of the success, and it *was* exciting. I'd never known Shayla to have career aspirations, per se—she'd dragged her feet about entering the work force about as much as I did, though she was a few years younger than me, so she had time—but she'd never committed herself to anything like she did to dancing.

When Courteney was done mauling her, Larissa got up and hugged her, then grabbed her face and looked her in the eye. "I am so proud of you."

"Stop it!" Shayla started crying. "You're the worst." She hugged Larissa for a long time.

Then it was my turn. I hugged Shayla long and hard. "You did it," I told her. "You worked so hard, all those years of dance, and you did it. You've earned your turn in the spotlight." When we finally pulled apart, she was crying and I was mopping tears from my face trying not to cry.

She really did it. All on her own.

No matter who her brother was, or what doors his last name might open for her, I'd seen her dance today. She'd earned this gig, one hundred percent.

The fact was, no matter how confident or skilled Shayla was, she'd lived most of her life in the inevitable shadow of her older brother. Johnny O'Reilly was gorgeous, a talented musician, and he'd become pretty famous. I understood that shadow Shayla lived in all too well. This moment meant more to her than she'd ever admit, even to us.

As we settled back into our seats, I realized how much all my girls had grown since I'd met them years ago. They'd all accomplished something, become someone, and were on their way to accomplishing so much more.

Shayla as a dancer.

Larissa, who'd been working so long and hard at her education, and would one day have a prestigious career and no doubt make beautiful babies with Jason.

And Courteney, who'd worked for years on a biography about her brother's former bandmate and best friend, Gabe, who'd died while on tour, years ago, had finally had her dream come true. Earlier this year, *The Life and Death of Gabe Romanko* had been published by a major publisher. It hit the New York Times bestseller list. Since then, she'd been busy with a promotional tour, giving interviews and doing the thing she'd dreamed of: telling Gabe's story.

As for me…

As I looked around at my friends, it hit me—how hard I'd stalled out. This was the worst day I'd ever experienced, in a pretty charmed life. But it wasn't just today that my life halted in its tracks.

It never really got going in the first place.

For all of my twenties, I'd spun my wheels, because I wasn't really sure where I was going.

And so, I'd gone nowhere.

"Hey," Courteney said, and everyone looked at me. I realized I'd checked out of the conversation and was probably sitting here looking sullen and sad.

"Hey." I tried to smile.

"How're you doing?"

"I'm okay," I reassured them all.

Shayla frowned. "Are you sure you won't stay with me? You could come home with me tonight."

"I'm okay, really. I'll figure it out. I'll get a job. Who knows," I added dryly, "maybe my rock star sister can get me another gig." I waved a hand in the air to indicate the club. "Maybe they'll even hire me here—" Unfortunately, just then, Merritt was walking up to our table, and I hit her drink tray with my flailing arm—knocking the entire thing, drinks included, crashing to the floor.

"Oh my God." My hands went to my mouth.

"It's okay," she said quickly. "Totally my fault."

It wasn't her fault. At all.

"I can't believe I did that." Tears flooded my eyes again. *Holy shit.* I was not fit for public consumption today.

I should've just stayed in bed.

Maybe if I'd done that, this whole terrible day would've just passed me by. I'd wake up tomorrow and none of it would've happened.

But I knew, no matter what I did tonight, when I woke up tomorrow morning, Flynn would not be mine.

He'd never be mine again.

"I'm so sorry," I gushed, as Courteney and Larissa mobilized to help Merritt pick up the mess and Shayla wrapped an arm around me. Our eyes met.

"You will be okay," she asserted.

"I know." I didn't, but I forced the words out.

"We'll get another round," she said solemnly.

I laughed.

When Merritt came back with another tray full of drinks, I was careful not to knock it out of her hands. Clearly, I didn't have much of a future slinging cocktails. At least that was settled. I could tackle the rest of my unemployment dilemma tomorrow.

Until then… I drank the night away with my girls.

I told myself that maybe if I went home late enough and drunk enough, I wouldn't have to run into Flynn or think about him at all. I'd just see the closed door of his man cave and know he was where he wanted to be —alone.

And I could just cry myself quietly to sleep in my couch nest.

But as it turned out, that plan, like the rest of my life today, went to shit.

# Chapter Four

**Johnny**

The sky was a deep blue-black as I drove south from my house in Kitsilano toward Noah's house in Dunbar-Southlands. My drummer and one of my best friends, Noah Vaughan was currently in L.A. but I'd spoken with him on the phone this afternoon. Over FaceTime, he'd straight-up told me *I'm staying with Breakneck. If JC wants to leave, that's his choice.*

Unfortunately, not everyone was so clear on where they stood.

My bassist, Miles, who was at home in Toronto, told me over the phone that he was waiting on updates "from everyone" to "see how things pan out." Because he was a pussy like that.

After the little intervention or whatever the fuck that was in Trey's office, I'd stopped into Dane's office to use one of his boardrooms to make some calls. To my bandmates. To my lawyer. To my dad, who was the only one I went to, besides Yash, for business advice.

*Talk to him,* my dad advised me. *You're business partners and friends. There's nothing between you that you can't work out.* It was a nice vote of confidence, even if my dad didn't know half the shit that had gone down between JC and me over the years.

After making those calls, I had a late lunch downtown with Lamar and my friend, Shane; Dane was too busy with work to join us. Then Lamar and I headed home, where I paced the fuck around while I tried to reach JC. He was the only one of my band members who didn't answer my calls all day. But when I was leaving Trey's office building—and I told Yash never to fucking blindside me like that again—Yash basically told me that if I could stop JC from walking out, this was fixable.

*We can salvage this,* Yash said. What he meant was: *You can salvage this.*

Because sometimes, Yash was a fucking pussy, too.

He also told me that Trey Jones was more concerned than he was letting on. *Without JC,* he said, *we lose the voice of Breakneck. We lose that trademark sound.*

*Are those Trey's words,* I asked him, point blank, *or are they yours?*

*Both,* he told me. *We all know the songs don't sound the same without him. Look at every established band who's ever tried to replace their lead singer. How many have stayed successful? And how many have endured criticism for the rest of their careers because 'he doesn't sing like that other guy.'*

And fuck him, but he was right.

But I could hardly convince JC to change his mind if I couldn't find him. No one seemed to know where he'd disappeared to, and it took me most of the day to find out. When he finally resurfaced, he was here, in Vancouver. He'd flown out and called Noah when he landed, told him he was crashing at his place.

When I pulled into Noah's driveway, the exterior lights and some interior lights were on. I knew JC was here. I revved the Hellcat's roaring engine before I shut the car off, so he'd hear me coming.

He couldn't hide forever.

"You want me to come with?" Lamar asked me from the passenger seat.

*Yes.* There was a small part of me that wanted Lamar, the human tank, to punch JC in the face so I didn't have to bruise my hand doing it myself.

*You're not punching him,* I told myself. *No matter how much you want to.*

"No. We're just talking."

Lamar gave me a look that said he'd be watching, just in case.

I'd barely gotten out of the car when my phone buzzed. My sister's name, *Shayla*, flashed onscreen, and I stopped on my way up to the house.

Bad fucking timing. But in case it was important, I picked up. "Hey. How'd the audition go?" She'd texted me back this afternoon to confirm that her dance audition was today, but that was it.

"Johnny!" She squealed so loud in my ear, I had to move the phone away. "I got it! I got the gig!"

It took me a moment to process her words. It sounded like she was at a bar or a party or something. I heard the throb of music and her voice kept cutting in and out. "You got the video?"

"Yes!! Yes yes yes! I'm gonna dance in the Players' videoooo!!"

"Shay, that's—"

"I didn't even get to hear the song, it's like, top secret," she gushed, "but I danced my ass off, I wore this pig costume, I did this strip thing, AND I KILLED IT! It was epic! They picked meeee!" She shrieked again, and I could definitely hear her friends in the background, talking and laughing over the music.

I smiled a bit, despite my own situation. "That's great, Shay."

"What?! I can't hear you!"

"Where are you?"

"What?"

"Where. Are. You."

"Champagne!"

"It's open already?"

"No, it's closed! They're just setting up for the big opening party next weekend!"

"Shayla."

"Yes?"

"My ear is bleeding."

She laughed.

"I'm proud of you," I half-shouted, to make sure she heard me.

"I'm so excited!"

"Shayla?"

"Yes!"

"Never show me the 'strip thing.'"

"There's a video of it! I promise, it's more funny than sexy!"

"Uh-huh." I glanced up at Noah's house, where the door was still shut. "I'm sorry, I've gotta go."

"Okay! We'll talk later!" I heard some fumbling noises and she hung up before I could say goodbye, and I wondered if she was drunk.

Probably.

I put my phone away and any trace of a smile faded.

*Fuck.*

This time next year, my band was supposed to be as big as the Players. That was the plan. With this new album, and Cary Clarke producing, and Brick House Records…

But Yash called it. Without JC, we were in trouble. Who knew what Trey would say if we couldn't get him back?

If *I* couldn't get him back.

I didn't even want to think about that potential conversation. Not yet. Trey was playing nice today, being a gentleman—his specialty. But I'd seen the guy's gloves come off. There'd be no winning him back if we lost him now, over something like this. The man had an image to maintain, and he didn't like drama. Not among his artists, and not in his own relationships, business or pleasure. I'd known him long enough to know that.

I could not let this bullshit personal gripe between JC and me derail our band.

So I did my best to eat my pride as I walked up to the house, stood in the glow of the front porch lights and hardened myself for whatever I was about to face. Let JC throw his little tantrum, get it all out of his system. Then he'd be over it.

Like he always got over it.

Another week, at most, and he would've realized Brianna wasn't worth the trouble anyway.

I rang the doorbell, stood back and waited, which was bullshit. He probably heard my car. He took a long-ass minute to answer the bell, too.

When he opened the door he said nothing, just glared at me. The lead singer of my band, for better or worse, for the last almost-eight years, JC stood in front of me in a ripped T-shirt, jeans and bare feet, scripted ink wrapped around his throat just like the one I had across my chest. *Breakneck.* And he looked at me like we were already enemies.

Over the years, JC had changed. Become a better singer, but a worse friend. Started losing his hair, which was why he now shaved it off. Gained more tats and gradually lost his sense of humor. He'd become embittered by envy, by jealousy, by a never ending rivalry with me over every fucking thing. And the more he lost that battle, the more he hated me.

He'd just never admit to it out loud.

"What's this I hear about you leaving the band," I said flatly, when he said nothing.

"What's this I hear about you and Brianna?" He wasn't yelling, which surprised me.

And for the first time, I wondered who told him. Someone did. So what if his girlfriend was spotted with me at a party? We both happened to show up at the same event. It was what happened after the event, in private, that was the problem.

Did Brianna tell him herself?

He looked guarded, his eyelids lowered as he stared me down in silence. Which was not JC's style. The guy was way more likely to yell at me and throw shit around, ream me out, then freeze me out, before finally coming around. Being in a band with John Colton Bissette was like being in a relationship with a hormonal woman who was always peak cycle.

"You flew out here pretty suddenly," I observed.

He gave a short, bitter laugh. "Not for you."

Right. So he raced out here to see Brianna in person.

How humiliating for him.

Shit, had he even met the girl? Had a conversation with her?

Did he actually think she was in love with him or something?

She could not possibly be that good of a con artist.

I mean, she was gorgeous. And totally plastic. Exactly the type JC fell for, historically. But wasn't he past the days of falling for girls like that and thinking there was any substance to them?

Really, how stupid was he?

I took a step closer. He didn't move aside or invite me in, just stood right in the doorway. I wondered if he was alone. If Brianna was in the house. Or if his bodyguard was here with him. I didn't see or hear anyone else in the hallway behind him.

"Well, thank you for deigning to open the door for me," I said. "Seems like we should talk."

"About what? Pretty sure waiting on an 'I'm sorry' from you is a lost cause."

I considered how to put it, then went with, "There's a possibility that I misread your… involvement with her."

He made a disgusted sound. "And that's the closest to an apology I'm gonna get, I know."

"What do I owe you an apology for?"

"Only you would ask that question, Johnny."

"I don't think she's the kind of girl you think she is."

"What," he said bitterly, "like the kind of girl I was considering giving a ring?"

*Jesus.*

He wasn't, really.

Was he?

"I'd probably be rethinking that if I were you," I told him.

"The day I ask for your opinion on the matter, hell will have frozen over. So I'm afraid you'll be out a fiery chasm to slither back to after your next diabolical conquest."

Cute. And poetic.

If only the song lyrics he wrote were half as good.

"How about let's not make this about her," I suggested. "Last I looked, she wasn't in our band."

"Well, neither were you, half the fucking time," he fired back, his voice rising. *And here we go with the tantrum.* "You know how many times I heard you were out there, talking to some other band about leaving us and joining them? *Too fucking many*," he hissed at me, answering his own question. "You think I don't know you talked to Dirty behind my back? Trying to leave us for something better, every other fucking minute?" He shook his head, like that disgusted him even more than the

Brianna thing. "You want fame, you want money, and you want pussy, and you'd stab me in the fucking back to get any of it."

"That Dirty thing was years ago. And it was just a conversation. You're free to have those with other bands yourself, if you think you can find something better."

"Of course it was just a conversation. You think Jesse Mayes and Zane Traynor didn't see you coming a mile off? They were never gonna play backup to your fucking ego."

"So, you're my backup band, is that it?" As if I hadn't already listened to him moan and complain about living in my shadow, for Goddamn forever. Like every single time I co-wrote a fucking song, as if I had no right to assert my ideas. As if I had no voice.

And every single time I sang backup on a song and he didn't like it that people *liked* my voice. That our crew and our friends and our fans said I should sing more.

JC was the lead singer, and how dare I threaten his supremacy?

As if I ever wanted his fucking job. Yeah, I liked money, but you couldn't pay me enough to be the lead singer, in any band.

"You've had one foot out the door from day one," he accused. "You never wanted this band as much as you wanted a vehicle to become Johnny O, superstar, and you didn't give a fuck who you rolled over along the way. Well, I'm evacuating the fucking train wreck *before* you crash and burn."

So, maybe I couldn't change his mind.

I could hear his conviction on this. I could see it.

I'd never seen him like this before.

*Over fucking Brianna, of all things. Christ.*

"I'm not gonna crash and burn," I told him cooly. "Just because you're giving up, don't put that on me."

"Giving up?" He laughed bitterly. "If I gave up, it would've been years ago."

"Then what do you call this? Because it isn't fucking commitment."

"Commitment? Are you fucking kidding me?" He took a step out into the night, his eyes glittering as he lit up a cigarette. One of the man's many crutches; he always chain smoked when he was worked up about shit. "Do you want me to say it?" He blew smoke into the night air. "You actually want to hear me say the words."

"What words?"

"The *truth*. The fucking truth, Johnny. You're disloyal. You're untrustworthy. You're selfish as fuck. And whatever the fuck is eating at you—"

"Eating at me? Nothing's eating at me."

"I'm talking about whatever the fuck is in your head"—he made a jabbing motion toward my skull with his cigarette—"and wakes you up choking in the middle of the night—"

I turned on my heel and started back to my car. Fuck if I was standing there, listening to this shit.

"You think I don't see it? We all see it." He followed me down the driveway. "Something is *wrong* with you, man. Why do you think you have all those nightmares? Guilt, shame, regret, I don't know what the fuck it is, but you can't even trust *yourself* when you close your eyes. How do you expect anyone else to?"

I reached for the car door as my heart thudded, a sledgehammer in my chest. On the other side of the car, Lamar's door opened and he stepped out, eying JC.

"A guy turns his back," JC hissed behind me, "and you're right up his ass with a knife."

I turned to face him. "You always were melodramatic as shit, JC. Half the reason we had to pay a fucking lyricist on the last album, to fix all the sappy bullshit you wrote."

"Right. You're the rock star and I'm the fuck-up."

"You think that's what I did?" I asked him, half-curious. "I pulled a knife on her? That's how I got her naked?" Then I added, just to dig the knife in a little deeper, "That's how I made her moan my name?"

JC's eyes went flat and dead. I'd lost him. Whatever chance we had to negotiate this situation amicably, no matter the outcome, that was done for him.

Well, good. Good fucking riddance.

It was done for me the second he threw my nightmares in my face. Fucking disturbed me, that he knew that much. That he'd seen… whatever he saw.

So what the fuck more was there to say?

He just stood there, looking at me with those cold, dead-to-me eyes. But neither of us backed down.

What, was he waiting for me to describe it? How *she* instigated it? How she dropped to her knees and sucked me off, first chance she got?

*Don't fucking tempt me.*

Finally, he broke the standoff. "You sure it was your name she was moaning? 'Cause that's another thing I gave up for you. My fucking name. Couldn't have more than one Johnny in the band, so Johnny O it is, and Johnny Colton can go fuck himself. And now it's JC for the rest of my career, just to placate your fucking ego."

"So that's what it comes down to. Nicknames, and some girl you want to marry who gave it up to me the second your back was turned?"

His jaw twitched and he took a moment before answering. "You're right. It has nothing to do with her. It's about us. I don't care if she's Mother Fucking Teresa or the Whore of Babylon. You saw her with me. That should've been enough." He took a step toward me. "You gonna go fuck Dane Davenport's wife now? Or Lex's?" His eyes narrowed into slits. "Or did you already do that?"

I said nothing. Why was he even bothering? Throwing my married friends in my face, like I'd ever touch their wives? As if he'd ever been a friend to me like Lex or Dane were. Or like Noah or Shane, or any of my other actual friends. I tended to keep friends I trusted, and that went both ways.

The fact was there'd been a disturbing lack of trust, and respect, in my relationship with my lead singer for years, in both directions.

"We're supposed to be brothers," he pressed.

"We were never brothers, *Johnny*."

The truth of that pressed down on us, prickling with honesty. The kind of honesty we'd always skirted around with each other.

Well, no point in that now.

"It's probably best if we both walk away from this conversation now," I added flatly. "You really want out of the band? Don't let me to stop you. You want our relationship dead? Consider it buried."

"Believe me, it's buried."

"Don't make yourself too comfortable in Noah's house," I told him, opening my car door. "And don't think you can poison him against me."

"I don't need to poison anything. Your actions speak for themselves. Anyone wants to stand by you, stay onboard that crazy train, good luck to them."

"Maybe we'll see each other one day, on the charts. Breakneck versus whatever you put together."

"You think you're taking Breakneck?" He laughed under his breath. "The band isn't yours, Johnny."

"We'll see." I got into the car, and Lamar got back in on his side. "Good luck with your songwriting. I know a few lyricists who can help if you get stuck." I shut the door, but JC just kept going through the open window.

"Fuck you, man. Why don't you go play 'Long Train Runnin'' a few hundred times and get blackout drunk, then wake up next to someone else's woman?" The Hellcat roared to life and he shouted over it. "That's the pattern, isn't it?"

"I'll tell Noah and Miles you said hi," I replied.

"No need to tell Miles anything on my account," I heard him say as I started backing out. "But I will tell him you said goodbye…"

His voice faded out as I backed into the street, then floored it out of there.

I headed straight downtown, to a bar, where I asked Lex and Dane to meet us for a drink.

One drink turned into many.

I didn't even tell my friends what was going on with my band. Lamar didn't say anything. He was friendly with my friends, but the man was a vault. For all they knew I just wanted to get pissed. It was Friday night, after all.

Sometime in the night, I learned that my pussy of a bassist had walked out in solidarity with JC. Half my band was gone. I'd talked to Miles again, but that conversation went nowhere. Apparently he, too, had a laundry list of grudges against me that he'd been saving up for a day such as this. And apparently there was nothing I could say to stop my bandmates from leaving.

I really didn't know what to do about it.

Always thought one day I'd be walking away, leaving them.

Maybe that was why I'd always had one foot out the door. JC was fucking right about that. Abandonment was not an option; I was supposed to leave them, not the other way around.

But even though I couldn't stop them from leaving, I could salvage what I had left. I spoke to Noah again, and he reassured me that he wasn't leaving the band—what was left of it.

And all that was left of Breakneck by the end of the night, other than Noah Vaughan, was me.

———

By one a.m., Dane had gone home to his wife. Lex stayed a bit longer. His wife, Talia, had joined us, but the two of them had finally gone home.

I was drunk, but not blackout drunk.

And I didn't take anyone else's woman home with me.

When Lamar drove me home in my car, we turned into the front gate to find Angeline Delacroix in my driveway.

I surveyed the scene as Lamar rolled us to a stop.

What the fuck was this now?

The gate was already open when we pulled up, and there was an unfamiliar Mercedes-Benz parked in my driveway, still running. Hip-hop blazed out into the night, along with the voices of what sounded like three or four guys in the car.

And there was my sister's best friend, Angeline, wearing nothing but a giant, almost knee-length T-shirt and fuzzy pink slippers, trying to climb out of the Benz. While detangling herself from the seatbelt that had somehow followed her halfway out—and the grabby hands of some guy in the front seat.

I saw red. Literally.

It was like the rain on the windshield in my nightmare, everything in my vision suddenly turning to blood.

I got out of my car. Angeline was saying something about *Thanks for the ride!* and *Have a nice night!* in a fake-cheerful, slurry voice. And I heard the guys in the Benz—more than one of them—trying to convince her of something.

Adrenaline and an all-consuming anger lashed through my veins. I was moving forward, booze and rage and a terrible, sick dread squeezing like a fist in my gut as fight or flight kicked in.

*Fight.*

I didn't care that I was outnumbered. I didn't care that I didn't have a weapon. My reaction was automatic and total. It surged up from a dark, deeply buried place inside me as I laid my hand on Angeline's shoulder.

"Touch her again," I growled at the assholes in the car, in a voice that hardly sounded like my own. "I dare you."

# Chapter Five

**Johnny**

I watched the security gate shut after the assholes in the Mercedes took off, my heart still thudding but gradually slowing to a more normal pace. I shut the front door, clenching my jaw with anger.

As I turned to Angeline, she wobbled. I swooped in and grabbed her around the waist before she could fall on her ass. The way she'd wrapped herself around me while I walked her up to the house, I thought it was a show for the guys in the retreating car. But nope. The girl was falling down drunk. Literally.

Way drunker than I was, that was for fucking sure. The whole bullshit mess in the driveway had shocked me sober, maybe.

Maybe I should've let Lamar come inside and help me with this. After he'd caught my fist, though, stopping me from breaking that grabby asshole's face—something I'd be thankful for tomorrow—I'd been pretty pissed. As soon as I got Angeline into the house, I told him to go home. After making sure the gate was secure and those guys were long gone, he'd disappear into his suite around the far side of the house.

*Fuck.* I should've thanked him for doing what he was paid to do, which was make sure no one, most of all me, got hurt. But I just couldn't see past the rage pumping through my veins.

I realized I was still breathing hard as I held onto Angeline. I hadn't felt anything like that… hadn't felt much at all… in a long damn time.

Actually… I couldn't remember the last time I'd felt anything even close to that. It was disorienting.

I tried to tell myself it was the alcohol that was fucking with my head or something. Fucking with my emotions.

But that was wrong. Nothing fucked with my emotions.

Because I didn't really have any.

I looked down at Angeline. She'd sagged in my arms, clinging to me, but she seemed to gather her wits when our eyes met and pushed away. "You cost me my job, asshole," she slurred.

"What?"

"My job. Gone. Because of *you*." She jabbed me in the chest with her finger.

"What job?" Last I heard, she'd never had one. "That internship thing?"

"*That internship thing*," she parroted, mocking me with a voice that sounded nothing like mine but did sound like a snarky dick, "was a big deal to me! And you. Ruined. It." More chest jabs.

I wrapped my hand around her finger, disabling her weapon of choice. "I didn't ruin anything." What the hell was she talking about?

She burst out laughing, wavering on her feet again. My arm went around her again, pure instinct, and she ripped her finger from my hand. But she didn't push away this time. "You flirted! At the fundraiser! To ruin me!"

I scowled. "Explain."

"You invited me to sit at your table!"

"Uh, because you're my sister's friend? And you wandered by."

"And then you lured me in, blabbing on and on about your stupid band for like an hour, as if you even wanted to talk shop with me. To make your date jealous!"

I laughed.

She pushed at me and I let her go. "It's true!" she spluttered, indignant.

"It's bullshit, is what it is. If we talked about my band it's because you were asking me questions. Snooping for Danielle Duke."

Her jaw dropped. "I was working!"

"So was I."

"You played me! That's what everyone's saying. Stupid, sugary-sweet Angeline, falling for the lies of Johnny O like a dumbass ice cream lover while the whole world watches—"

"What the fuck are you even talking about?"

"—the latest bimbo to fall prey to his duplicitous charms!"

"That's quite a story. Who wrote it?"

"Danielle Duke. My *boss*. And like, everyone on Twitter." She slid her hands down her giant T-shirt, like she was expecting to find a pocket containing her phone, so she could offer up evidence of said Tweets. When she came up empty, she looked down, confused.

*Jesus.* The girl was a disaster right now. Her purse was on the floor next to her, though she seemed to have no idea. And where were her fucking pants?

"People see what they want to see," I informed her. "We had a conversation. At a public event. You're my sister's best friend. You're interning with Danielle Duke. We work in the same industry. And since you haven't clued in yet, your boss hates me."

"I wonder why?" she said dramatically. "And thanks to you, she's not my boss." She felt around her backside for her personal effects, still looking for that missing pocket. This time when she wavered, I resisted the urge to steady her.

Let her fall on her ass if she didn't want my help.

"Angeline."

She looked up, blearily, at the sound of her name. Almost like she'd forgotten I was here.

"Where's your purse?"

She blinked at me.

"It's on the floor, sweetheart," I filled her in.

The expression on her face changed as she held my eyes. Softened. "You saved me from those guys…" Suddenly, she was looking at me a lot like she did that night, three years ago. When I kissed her. At least, that was how I remembered her looking at me.

Awestruck.

And totally fucking confused.

I couldn't blame her for being confused that night. Or for walking away from that kiss. Because why the fuck was I kissing her in the first place?

Several reasons.

One, she was there. Two, she was beautiful. Three, I was pretty sure she'd been hot for me for a while. And four, I was completely fucked up that night over shit that had nothing to do with her.

Oh, and five, I had a long history of poor decision making when it came to women.

I fucking knew, even when I kissed her, that I shouldn't have. That I was the bad guy in that situation. I was often the bad guy. I knew she had a boyfriend. In that moment, I just didn't care.

But ever since that moment, she'd hated me. I knew that.

Couldn't say I was too fond of her, either. Boyfriend or no, she'd walked away from that kiss, never circled back around.

And now here she was, fucking looking at me like *that* for the first time in three years. While fucking wasted and wearing a T-shirt with her boyfriend's face on it.

I needed to dump her off on Shayla. Stat.

"Shayla!" I hollered.

We both stared at each other when there was no sound from inside the house. I already knew there was a slim to none chance my sister was home.

"I don't think she's home," drunk Angeline concluded, still staring at me.

"Where's your boyfriend, the bodyguard?"

She frowned.

I glanced down. There he was, smiling at me from the picture on her ugly-ass men's size XL T-shirt. It was a photo of her and him, on vacation or something, smiling at the camera. I'd seen him around often at parties, usually skulking around in the shadows on security duty; he worked on Dirty's security team, as personal bodyguard to Angeline's sister, Elle. But I couldn't remember ever seeing the man smile in person. He was ex-military, super stiff, and how he'd ended up with a candy-coated wet dream like Angeline Delacroix, I'd never fucking know.

"I wouldn't think Security Joe would be down with you getting a ride home with those assholes," I prompted when she didn't answer me.

"And why would you say that?"

"Because they don't seem like your type," I said sarcastically.

"And what's my 'type'?" she inquired, making sloppy air quotes on the word.

"You tell me. Judging by your actions, I'd say the over-protective, emotionally constipated type."

She recoiled, making a revolted face. "If you're talking about *yourself*, there was no *action*. I'm not here to pick you up, Johnny O'Reilly. *And his name is not Security Joe.*"

"I'm not talking about myself." Was that how she saw me? Over-protective and emotionally constipated? "I'm talking about Joe." I pointed at her shirt.

Her face screwed up. "His name is not Joe," she repeated. But I noticed she didn't say his name at all.

Next thing I knew, she was tearing the shirt off over her head in a fit of disgust or defiance or insanity. It got caught on her earring or something, because she struggled with getting it off, her face covered with it for way too long while the rest of her wriggled in front of me half-naked. She wore a see-through lace bra, light blue, with little matching panties. Her soft breasts looked sweeter than candy and her little pussy looked like the gateway to heaven and I didn't even try not to stare. She couldn't see me anyway.

By the time she'd gotten the shirt off over her head, I'd peeled off my T-shirt. She tossed hers down the hall with an aggrieved huff and I shoved mine at her.

She looked at it like I'd offered her the carcass of a dead, putrefying animal. "What is that?"

"It's a fucking shirt. You wear it over your body when you're standing in front of your best friend's brother, otherwise naked."

"I'm not naked," she said, pretty fucking indignantly for a woman whose nipples were clearly visible. But she glanced down and seemed to jolt into sudden awareness that I could see her nipples and her tiny swath of pubic hair, and her cheeks flushed pink so fast it was charming. I wasn't feeling real charmed, though, just residually angry.

She took the shirt and again, took way too long figuring out how to work it. This time, I looked away. Mostly out of pity.

She finally pulled on my shirt and covered herself. The yellow T-shirt reached the top of her thighs so all that was naked now were her pretty legs and the visions of lace-covered temptation in my head. She just stood there tugging down the hem, like that could make me forget what I'd just seen.

"Now what?" she said blearily.

Christ. Could I even leave the girl alone like this?

"Bedtime," I said bluntly. "Get your ass upstairs."

She balked and looked around, like I'd purposefully dragged her here to defile her or something. Did she forget where the fuck we were?

"You're in Shayla's house," I told her, trying to sound soothing and non-threatening. "You're going to go sleep upstairs. Alone."

She looked at me, eyes wide. "Okay." Then she turned to head for the staircase at the back of the foyer. She wobbled so hard her shoulder bumped the wall before I could catch her. I grabbed her shoulders to gently direct her toward the staircase. She headed there, wobbling every few steps as I held her shoulders to keep her aimed in the right direction. When we reached the bottom of the stairs, she shook my hands off. "I'm okay. I've got it."

She put one foot on the first stair, started to lift herself up, and keeled to the side.

I grabbed her, stopping her fall.

"Whooooa." She giggled, struggling up a few steps and then leaning a shoulder on the wall. She pushed herself up along the wall as I spotted her. Then she crumpled onto the stairs, giggling.

We'd made it up five steps. At this rate, we'd be here all night.

I smeared a hand over my face. I was too drunk for this. Seriously. I was half-tempted to call Lamar back in here to deal with this.

But then her hand suddenly grabbed my inner thigh in her blind attempt to steady herself, even though she was already sitting down, and that idea went out the window. I trusted Lamar with my life, not to mention my sister's. No way was I letting any dude carry Angeline up to bed in this state, though.

"Let's try that again." I offered my hand, and she took it. I pulled her to her feet—and caught her around the waist again when she fell right into me. Her breasts in that thin, no-padding bra flattened against me.

My dick stirred, because I wasn't dead, even though I tried to tell myself this was in no way enjoyable… even as I felt her soft tits drag against me through very thin fabric.

Nope. Definitely not asking Lamar for help with this.

She giggled in my arms.

Every time I tried to let her stand on her own she fell into me again, her body rubbing against mine, and my cock, based on previous conditioning, assumed this was foreplay, inconveniently growing hard. Her hands grabbed at my bare back, my waist, even my abs—as if that would steady her—almost like they had a mind of their own.

She blinked up at me as I gripped her waist and she finally managed to stand upright without pitching forward. She was one stair above me, which brought her close enough to kiss. I could taste the alcohol on her breath. She gave me a dopey smile.

"You're helpful." She hiccuped.

"Alright. Let's try this again." I turned her carefully. "Hold the handrail. And… up." She took two more stairs before she pitched to the side again. "What the fuck did you drink? Muscle relaxant?"

For some reason that made her laugh, which didn't help the muscular control situation. She sat right down on the stair, busting a gut.

"Stop laughing."

She kept laughing.

I waited for her to fucking finish, then told her, "Here's what's happening. I'm picking you up. I'm carrying you upstairs. You're going to let it happen. Otherwise, you're sleeping right here tonight."

She looked up at me with wide eyes again. "Okay." She blinked. "I like a decisive man."

I stared at her. "You are fucking drunk."

"I'm okay."

She was definitely not okay if she was saying shit like that to me.

I leaned down, slid my arms under her back and her knees, and told her, "Arm around my shoulders. Hold on tight." She followed orders and clung to me while I lifted her up and carried her up the stairs.

I was heading for one of the guest rooms when she suddenly said, "I feel sick."

I pivoted, fast, and went straight into the closest room—Shayla's bedroom—and through to the adjoining bathroom. I didn't even have time to get the light on. When I lowered Angeline to her feet in front of the toilet, she crumpled to her knees and hurled into the bowl. The sound was anguished.

What the fuck happened to this girl tonight?

I turned on the light and gathered her hair back carefully, holding it out of her face and out of the toilet while she threw up again, then again. Then she slumped against the toilet and groaned. "I hate this," she mumbled.

"What, being sick?"

"Being me."

I sighed. I was fucking tired, and self-loathing did not suit this girl. At all. "Angeline, you're a lovely person."

"You hate me."

"That doesn't mean you should hate yourself." I was trying to make a joke, but clearly, now was not the time. It went straight over her head. I could tell when she just blinked at me.

Then her eyes widened. "I have to pee. Right now. Get out, get out!" she shouted, scrambling up.

I got the fuck out, shutting the door behind myself. I waited in Shayla's room, turning on a light. After a minute, I heard the toilet flush and water ran for a while.

When it was silent again, I knocked on the door. "You okay?"

The door opened. Angeline stood there looking like a sweet disaster, her usually silky light-brown hair disheveled, her skin pale and her makeup smeared down her pretty face. She was playing with the hem of my shirt and her eyes looked blurry when they met mine. "I'm sorry I shouted at you." Then she started to cry.

"It's okay." I ushered her gently out of the bathroom. "You didn't shout."

"You helped me," she sobbed, falling into my chest. When she clung to me, I wrapped my arms around her carefully as she cried. "You're my hero."

Okay, we needed to nip this in the bud. She was not gonna love this, whatever she remembered of it, in the morning. As far as I could ever tell, Angeline couldn't stand me. Maybe she'd wanted to fuck me, once upon a time, but that was neither here nor there. As for actually admiring anything about me, there was no way. And calling me her hero? She'd hate that, for sure.

"You're like… my sexy guardian angel…"

Holy fuck.

"Let's just get you to bed." I tried to steer her around Shayla's bed so I could get her to a guest room, but she sagged right onto the bed as soon as she saw it. There was no getting her back up unless I picked her up again. And since she was somewhat in my arms and had almost pulled me down onto the bed with her—on purpose or by accident, I wasn't sure—and was now gushing, "You're sooooo gorgeous… You have amazing eyes… I like the way you scowl at me…" I was thinking that was a bad idea.

I held on just long enough to drag her into place and arrange her head on a pillow before detangling myself from her arms. But she held onto my neck, her eyes meeting mine when she confessed, "I had a crush on you. For four years."

My dick, which was now inconveniently hard again, throbbed at that look in her eyes. She'd never looked right into my eyes like that before, with that hungry look on her face.

She only ever gave me that look when she thought I wasn't looking, and even that was years ago. Now, when I met her eyes, she always looked away. Or looked annoyed.

She was gripping the back of my neck with surprising strength, holding me to her, and I didn't want to break away. I was not gonna kiss her or touch her or do anything. But something in me did not want to kill this moment, even though I knew I should. She was still looking into my eyes and this heated, raw-nerve feeling traveled down my spine and into my gut.

The vision of her pussy in her little lace panties flashed in my head, and I could easily imagine shoving myself into her. I could imagine kissing her. Again. Like I did that night. But this time, she'd be naked beneath me, her legs spread wide to take me…

"I'm gonna let go now," I said, my voice rough and raspy. She was the one holding on to me, though. "And let you sleep. Okay?"

"Okay," she breathed. But she was still holding on.

"You're safe here."

"Okay."

She didn't let go.

Her gaze dropped to my lips and that raw, hot feeling in my gut surged. Then she suddenly pressed her soft lips to mine. My breath caught in my throat as a sheet of lightning streaked through me, from my lips to my balls. My cock flexed.

So different from that other kiss…

That night, it was a warm, creeping shiver that swept through me, the thrill of kissing her and the dread of knowing it wouldn't change a thing.

This kiss was… hotter. Maybe because she instigated it. Even though she was drunk, it felt like a promise.

But I wouldn't hold her to it.

I wrenched away, breaking her hold. She flopped back on the pillow, gazing up at me. I could see the conflict in her eyes… like she couldn't quite decide if she should be upset, or try that again, or if any of this was even real.

There were still tears on her cheeks. At least she'd stopped crying.

I brushed them from her soft skin with my thumbs. "Good night, lovely."

"Good night Johnny," she breathed.

As I got up, I grabbed one side of the bedspread and folded it over her. I turned off the light and the bathroom light and heard her soft, ragged sigh.

Then I settled into a corner of the room in the dark, sitting on the floor with my back to the wall. I stayed right there while she slept. I was tired and it was the middle of the night, but it didn't matter anyway; even if I was at home, I probably wouldn't be sleeping.

At least Angeline crashing into my night had distracted me from my own problems for a while.

When I heard my sister come home, I went and hid in the bathroom up the hall. This night was already shitty enough. When Shayla had come upstairs and gone into her bedroom, I slipped down the stairs and out the back door, to my house next door.

I didn't have the energy to explain to her what I was doing in there with Angeline. Maybe tomorrow, I'd deal with that drama.

# Chapter Six

**Angeline**

I knew, as I cracked my eyes open, that I, Angeline Delacroix, was an unequivocal fucking disaster.

I felt mildly sick. Everything ached. My skull hurt and my mouth felt like I'd been sucking on croutons all night. Dry, bitter, and desperately in need of water. My face was flat on a hard, cool plank of greige engineered wood floor.

I was on the fucking *floor*.

I lifted my head, painfully, groaning. And caught a glimpse of some poor disheveled hussy, her hair mangled around her face, last night's makeup smeared, and her eyes bloodshot.

Oh, God. I was looking in a mirror.

The hussy was me.

I was regrettably, brutally hungover. I blinked at myself and slowly, stiffly pushed myself up on all fours. I couldn't have sugarcoated the situation to make myself feel better if I tried. Even me, sweet little thinks-everyone's-serving-up-ice-cream-when-they're-really-slinging-shit Angie. Because this shit was fucking messy. For one, I was wearing bedraggled slippers because I forgot to put shoes on before I stormed out of my—Flynn's—apartment last night. And a T-shirt with two giant, smiling faces on it, mine and Flynn's. A cheesy photo from our trip to Hawaii two years ago.

I blinked at myself in the mirror. Wait. I was not wearing that T-shirt anymore. This T-shirt was yellow.

I glanced down at it. "Oh—*fuck*." I leapt to my feet—too fast—staggered, and fell on the bed. "Ouch. *Shit.*" My head hurt so fucking bad.

I grabbed at the yellow shirt and stretched it out in front of me, blinking as I struggled to read it upside down. There were a bunch of words stacked on top of one another. COWGIRL... DOGGY... FACE... SIXTY-NINE... SCISSORS... THE CRAB... and at the bottom *Six popular sex positions as reported by AskMen.* I frowned. Why was I wearing a Thirty Seconds to Mars album T-shirt? A shirt that belonged to—

I looked up in abject horror as I heard a knock on the door, then Johnny O'Reilly strolled into the room like he owned the place—and a memory from last night crashed into me. His fist. His fist had almost smashed into the face of a guy in that car, out in his driveway, before we... came in here?

Together?

I could remember now, tearing off the Flynn-and-me shirt in a fit of upset, and Johnny taking his shirt off. This shirt. I could remember him shoving it at me. Arguing with me? But after that... it was pretty murky.

"Oh, shit," I stammered, "*no*." I gaped up at Johnny, wide-eyed.

He frowned. "You're alive. Good." I watched as he set a bottle of water on the bedside table. Next to a sparkly pink travel mug that said *Big Dick Energy*.

I looked around, blinking my surroundings into sharper focus as my brain struggled to do its thing. I recognized this room. And all the girlie decor and clothes...

Another door swung open and Shayla stepped out of the bathroom, and I shuddered with relief. "*Shayla.*" I'd never been so happy to see her. "Oh thank God."

She stopped in her tracks, wrapped in a bath robe, her hair wet from her shower, and looked from me to Johnny. "Huh?"

Johnny crossed his arms over his chest, and together they both watched me crawl weakly across the bed to the water bottle, struggle to open it, and suck back half of it. The only sound besides my gross chugging was the music playing faintly in the bathroom.

"This is your bedroom," I gasped at her when I came up for air, "thankgodthankgodthankgod." Then I fell over on the bed.

"Whose bedroom did you think it was?" She looked at her brother again, realization dawning. "Ew." Then she went to dig some fresh undies out of a drawer. "What are you doing here?" she asked him. "You just gave my girl a heart attack, thinking she woke up after the most disappointing one-nighter of her life, with *you*."

"The horror," Johnny drawled, unamused.

I cringed. Actually, the whole idea that he and I might have… was pretty laughable. And I highly doubted he'd be the disappointment in that scenario.

Unlike myself, he looked ridiculously put together right now.

Every blond hair was in place, the stubble on his jaw a perfect, sexy shadow, his sculpted bod needing nothing more to show it off than the sleeveless black T and soft sweats he was wearing. The artful, colorful tattoos up his arms and one side of his neck—the really expensive kind—only enhanced what nature gave him, which was a generous helping from the beauty pool. Gleaming jewelry, just the right amount to look glam and not trashy, white teeth, the works. He looked ready for a photo shoot. I looked ready for my "before" pics in a makeover column.

His deep, aquamarine eyes scanned over both his sister and me. "Just checking to make sure you were both still breathing. Did you drink the bar completely dry last night?"

"Depends which bar you mean." Shayla smiled at him, hip-checking her drawer shut.

"Any of them."

"Wellllll, let's just say that we do what we want and we don't need to ask your permission. Down with the patriarchy and all that." She smiled at her brother again and fluttered her panties toward the door like, *You scoot on along now*.

"Maybe you should ask my permission. You need someone to bounce your terrible ideas off of."

"I take offense, sir!" she lied. "Most of my ideas are *amaze*."

"Yeah? Leaving your friend to the horny wolves after giving her borderline alcohol poisoning? Brilliant."

"Hey, I didn't leave her anywhere," Shayla retorted, dropping the humor. "I dropped her off at her apartment, safe and sound. Leave no woman behind. You know that's my motto when I go out with the girls."

"Her apartment?" Johnny's eyes met mine. I grabbed one of Shayla's pillows and stuffed it over my face.

"Yes, *her home*," Shay said. "Whatever happened after that, I was unaware."

"Unaware?" Johnny echoed incredulously. When Shayla and her brother locked horns, they could go on like this for a while. I wasn't sure my headache could take it. "Are you *aware* that someone could've taken advantage of her, easily, in that state? She was trashed."

"Guys…" I uttered weakly.

"And where were you last night?" Shay fired back at him accusingly. "How did she get in here, drunk as a newly single skunk? And now she's wearing *your* shirt, hmmmmm? All by herself? Or did she have a little help?"

"Of course she had help," he shot back. "I found her in the driveway getting groped by a bunch of entitled douche-twats."

I peeked out from under the pillow to see Shayla's jaw drop. "Angie!" She whirled toward me. "Are you okay?"

"I'm fine," I croaked.

"No thanks to you," Johnny told his sister. "When I got here, she was alone with four guys. She came to *you* for help when she couldn't shake some clingy frat boys. Where were you?"

Shayla spun back to him and gaped for a second, then recovered. "Well, I thank you for helping her. Now get your hypocritical ass out of my house. You smell of last night's vodka binge, and I have to get dressed for dance practice." With that, she placed her hand flat on her brother's chest, backed him out of the room and shut the door in his face.

"We'll talk about this later," he growled through the door.

"No, we will not!" she sang back. Then she rushed over to me. "Angeline!" She tossed herself on the bed next to me, her bra and panties flying, and peered at my face. "Four guys?"

I plucked the bra off my neck where it landed. "Uh, there were only three guys. I think. You can get dressed if you want. Don't you have dance practice?"

"Fuck that." She snatched her bra back. "How much did you have to drink after I left you??"

I groaned. "Don't worry. I'm never drinking again."

"What happened?"

"Nothing." I sniffed, as more memories of last night flooded in. Then I moaned like a wounded animal. "Shayla… Flynn got home after I did and… he smelled like perfume, and…" I started crying, spluttering nonsensically as I tried to force out the words. "Gl-glitter…"

Shayla frowned, struggling to follow my weepy, broken sentence. "He smelled like glitter?"

"He was covered… in some girl's… body glitter!" I sobbed.

"Oh, for fuck's sake. Let's circle back to that later, but—"

"Let's not," I sniffled.

"But first, what's with these three guys groping you?!"

"Johnny's exaggerating. Only one of them groped me."

Shayla scowled. "Who were these guys? What were you doing with them?"

"Slippers," I hiccuped, and we both looked down as I stuck a foot in the air, where one of my now-dirty, ratty, virtually destroyed slippers dangled. I took a big breath and let it out. "Me and Flynn… we had a huge drunk argument and I ran out in my stupid slippers and our special T-shirt, and I forgot my shoes and I didn't even notice and then some guys pulled up in a Benz and we went drinking and then Johnny found me in your driveway."

Shayla sucked a breath through her teeth. She didn't like that little story, obviously. I couldn't blame her. "Angie… you got in a car with three guys you don't know?"

I sobbed again and took a breath. "They drove me home. Here, I mean. Eventually."

"But they could've—"

"Been much worse. I know." Lucky for me, they were obnoxiously confident that they might get something out of me, but they weren't aggressive about it. Though I was having a little trouble getting them to fuck off when Johnny showed up. "Your brother kinda saved me."

"Shit," she muttered. "He's a white knight once in his damn life, and now he's never gonna let me hear the end of it."

"Yeah… Sorry?" I sniffled again.

"Oh God, don't apologize. Babe, I should've been here. I went to Courteney's after we dropped you at home."

"It's okay."

She eyed me carefully. "I can't believe he tucked you into bed, though. Did he carry you up here or what?"

"Uh… What?"

"When I got home you were asleep on my bed. I tried to spoon you but when I woke up in the morning you were on the floor."

"Oh. I must've been really out of it." I frowned, trying to remember. I had a vague memory of trying to get up the stairs and bumping into the wall. And Johnny's hands… Being pressed against his body. And holding on tight, clinging to him. *Ugh.* I shivered now, embarrassed. I just hoped I didn't say anything stupid. "I think… maybe he did carry me up here…"

Also, the more I thought about it… I was pretty sure I blathered all over him. About Flynn?

I couldn't remember. There were tears, for sure.

"Well. At least you ended up in my bed instead of his…" Shayla gave me side eye as she picked at the pillow, and I knew what she was thinking. It was pretty much Shayla's idea of hell to have any of her friends, especially her best friends, mess around with her brother. Because she knew there was an approximately zero percent chance that situation would end with a happily-ever-after.

She did not want to have to deal with the messy fallout after one of her besties became just another notch on her brother's rock star bed post.

Who could blame her?

"Nothing happened," I insisted.

She narrowed her eyes a little. "How can you be sure? I know you, babe."

I blinked at her. "What does that mean?"

"It means, how can you be sure you didn't cop a feel when he carried you up here and put you to bed?"

"I didn't!" My face flushed hot, instantly. Because it did sound like something I would do, if I was drunk enough. I mean, it was Johnny.

I didn't like him. But I had been hormonally obsessed with him for a while.

Okay, for a few years.

My long-standing crush on him had frosted over, sure. But now it was almost worse. It was a hate crush. A terrible curse that had tortured me for way too long.

And Shayla wasn't blind. She knew how hot her brother was—to women who weren't related to him.

"I hope not. The thought of you touching my brother's dick makes me want to vomit."

"I did not touch your brother," I promised her. "I hate men right now, trust me."

"Me, too," she said supportively, even though it wasn't true.

"And don't worry. I hate your brother the most," I assured her, even though saying it felt kinda wrong. I knew I was supposed to be mad at Johnny, for the job thing, and I still was. I still hated him. But while I was drunk and vulnerable last night, he'd saved me. Who the hell knew what would've happened if him and Lamar didn't show up and run those guys off? But I said it for her. "He's a giant dick, okay?"

That made her smile. "I knew, all these years, you had a little bit of Mean Angie in you somewhere," she said proudly. "You need to let her out more often."

Hmm. Mean Me. "I'm not very good at that," I said tentatively.

"But sometimes, maybe you should be. Not everyone deserves your kindness, babe. Those gropey A-holes last night sure didn't."

"True."

*Flynn did.*

I felt a little ache in my chest. It still made me so fucking sad that I'd failed him.

She was right. I was way too nice to the wrong people. It was a gross pattern of mine. If a guy was a gorgeous mess, I'd be smitten in seconds. Add emotionally stunted, self-obsessed, unfaithful and wildly unstable to the mix and I was a goner—so long as he had a granite ass and a wicked smile. Flynn was the only truly decent, stable guy I'd ever dated, and it was the only long-term, serious relationship I'd ever had.

And I couldn't make it work.

I needed to seriously change my approach when it came to men or something. Because what I'd been doing? It sure as hell wasn't working.

"Okay… let me practice the mean thing," I said, trying Mean Me on for size. "Your brother Johnny is an arrogant, self-centered jerk."

She smiled again. "That's better. And damn accurate."

"Although… I'm glad he saved my ass last night," I said seriously. "Unfortunately… it was kind of heroic." In truth, I really wasn't sure how to reconcile the heroic thing with my hatred of him.

Shayla frowned. "Let's move past that part."

"Yeah. Let's." I smiled a little, for the first time today. "How about this. Even dicks can be nice sometimes. And sometimes we're all fucking jerks." My smile faded fast. "Flynn's never been one. But last night… last night was not good, Shay."

"Nope," she agreed.

"I was a jerk, too," Mean Me admitted.

"Hmm," she muttered. "He probably deserved it."

"I just wish I wasn't so drunk when I went back to the apartment," I lamented quietly. My head was still throbbing. "And Flynn, too. I've rarely seen him so drunk. And I've definitely never seen him smeared in some other girl's lipstick and glitter. The really sad part is I don't think he did it on purpose, to hurt me or anything. He was so drunk, I don't think he knew I could see her on him. I could smell her." My voice faded. "I'm so dumb, Shay. I stayed up waiting for him to come home because I wanted to talk to him."

"About what?" she asked gently.

"I don't even know. Anything. Nothing. When he came in and I got all mad about the glitter and perfume, I started telling him I was taking all his favorite things with me when I moved out, just to try to hurt him. I put on our shirt, the one with our stupid faces on it. He wears it around the house sometimes. And I told him he couldn't have it. It was the stupidest fight in the world." I sighed raggedly. "I know it's over. I know we're done and we're not going to be together anymore and we both have to pick ourselves up and move on. I just still love him, you know?" My voice broke a little. "I just… I didn't know he'd move on so fucking fast."

"It's because he loves you," she said gently. "He wants to get over you and he doesn't know how. He probably threw himself at the first skank he came across."

"Yeah. Probably." She was right, maybe. But I really didn't want to talk about it anymore. "Ugh."

"Men are the absolute worst," she commiserated solemnly.

"He's not," I admitted. "But we're a disaster right now. We can't be friends yet. Maybe not ever?"

Shayla gave me a sad look. "You don't know that."

"Either way, I can't stay with him in the apartment anymore. You were so, so right. What was I thinking?"

"You were thinking what you always do." Shay smoothed a chunk of my disastrous hair behind my ear and gave me a crooked, fond smile. "That everything would end up okay."

I fell into her arms then, and sobbed on her shoulder for a bit. I'd never cried so much in my life. But then again, I'd never had my heart broken like this before. I thought I knew what heartbreak was, all the times I was crushing on someone who didn't like me back.

That was child's play.

I'd just had a real, several year relationship with a man who loved me, and couldn't make it go the distance. Worse, I'd hurt him, time and again. I'd hurt us both, without ever meaning to.

Nothing I'd ever felt in my life had ripped my heart apart like this.

"You know what," Shayla said softly. "Some things do end up okay, though. Better than okay. You know why?"

I sat up and looked at her. "Why?"

"Because you're going to live right here. With me."

I laughed through my tears a little. I was such a freaking mess. "I wish," I sniffled. "And I love you for saying that. But I can't afford this place."

She made a *tsssht* sound, like that fact meant nothing. "Who *can* afford this place."

"Well… your brother."

Johnny had bought this property, next door to his, and had this house custom built on it. Shayla couldn't afford it either, but Johnny had paid for it. She said his plan was to eventually sell it, but we all knew he'd let Shayla live here forever if she wanted to.

As far as I could tell, the only warm spot Johnny O'Reilly had was for his sister.

She rolled her eyes. "This is my house. You're staying."

I wanted to raise some kind of protest, but I really didn't have any left in me. Where else would I go?

I was so fucking tired right now. Already. And the day had barely started. I wasn't even doing anything with my life yet.

I watched her gather up the underwear she'd dropped on the bed and head into her walk-in closet, then come back out with clothes slung over her arm.

"Shayla… thank you. I mean, if it's really okay with you…"

She met my eyes seriously. "I insist."

"I'll repay you, somehow."

"I'm not worried about that. You just take care of you, and the rest will work out."

She headed into the bathroom to finish getting ready for her day, and I fell back on the bed.

I knew Shayla believed what she said. But I also knew that she really didn't understand what I was going through. Her family had always taken care of her, but she'd never ask them not to. It didn't make her uncomfortable, at all, letting her brother and her parents pay her way until she could do it herself. If that day ever came—or not—seemed immaterial to her.

I really envied her. Shayla O'Reilly's self-worth was so unshakable, she didn't ever feel the need to apologize for taking up space.

"I'm sorry I'm such a mess right now," I told her after she reemerged from the bathroom, dressed in her dancing clothes, leggings and a tank top. I watched her brush out her strawberry-blonde hair in front of the wall mirror. "I won't always be this needy. I promise."

"It's okay to need things, Angeline." She turned to look at me sympathetically. "And it's okay to need people, too. You just have to learn when it's time to let go of the ones you don't need anymore," she added gently.

Flynn. I knew she was talking about Flynn.

And I knew, in my heart, that she was right.

But it was hard to let go of something you never really thought you'd lose. It was traumatic. And I didn't really know what my life would look like when I let go.

Would I go into free fall?

Would I crash and burn?

I had no idea. But I knew, no matter how scary it was, I had to take the leap.

I thought of Johnny last night, catching me over and over when I fell. The memories were coming back, even if I didn't want them to. Even if I didn't want to remember the feeling of him catching me in his arms, holding me up. Protecting me.

He didn't let me go until I was safe.

His strength just reminded me of Flynn's. Because Flynn could've held on, too. He was strong enough. He was way stronger than me, in so many ways. He could've held on and not let go.

But as hard as it was, Flynn had let me go, whether I felt ready for it or not.

Now I had to let him go, too.

# Chapter Seven

**Angeline**

After Shayla left for dance practice, I scraped myself together as best I could under the circumstances. The circumstances being my raging hangover and lack of fucks given to the task at hand.

I finger-brushed my teeth, tied yesterday's hairdo up in a ratty bun, and dumped my destroyed slippers in the trash so I didn't have to look at them. They were just too much of a reminder of last night's whole terrible scene —all three of them.

The fight with Flynn.

Getting scooped up off a street corner by a carload of slimy fuckboys.

And getting rescued from said fuckboys by Johnny O.

*Oh, and don't forget about the blathering, clinging and crying,* Mean Me whispered. She was getting kind of annoying, already. I wasn't sure if I'd be keeping her around.

Then my sister called. Shayla had found my purse, containing my phone and wallet, in her foyer, thank God; I was worried I'd left it in the fuckboys' car.

Apparently, Elle had tried calling me three times today already, before I even turned my ringer on. I picked up, cringing as I wondered if Flynn had mentioned to her what happened last night. "Hey, Elle."

"Angie. Are you okay? Are you at Shayla's?"

"I'm fine. And yes. How'd you know?"

"Because you called me in the middle of the night and said you were going there."

Did I? Damn. I was quite the drunk dialer, historically. Should've probably checked to see if I called anyone else in the middle of my drinking binge. Hopefully not Flynn.

"Sorry. I was a little drunk last night. Hope I didn't wake you up."

"A little drunk? You sounded absolutely wasted."

"I wasn't that wasted." I totally was.

"What happened? You were babbling on about Flynn and something about glitter…?"

"Yeah. Um, we might've gotten into a bit of a fight."

"Oh, Angie…"

"Did you go out after Champagne?" I asked her, suddenly curious if she'd witnessed anything. Had she seen glitter-and-perfume girl? "Was he with you?"

"No. He had the night off."

Crap.

"So… you don't know where he was or who he was with?"

"No, babe. I don't."

I took a breath and asked her in a small voice, "Any chance he might not be your bodyguard anymore?" Kind of couldn't believe I was asking her that. But I needed to ask. Just in case.

In case there was any chance she would take my side on this. And magically make it so I never had to run into him again. She pretty much had that power.

"Angie…" she said regretfully, and I knew what was coming. "You know Flynn has worked with Dirty, with me, for years. He's been loyal and had my back throughout so much. I can't… I mean, it wouldn't be right to fire him over something like this. You know I'm so sorry that things didn't work out between the two of you—"

"Yeah. I know."

"And I'm sure he'll do his best to stay out of your way and try to make it easy on you. You know Flynn."

Yeah. I knew Flynn. He was a professional. Last night aside, he invariably had his shit together.

If anyone was gonna be awkward and emotional about anything and everything, it was me.

"You know I want to support you any way I can," my sister said carefully.

"I know."

"Do you need money?"

"No."

"Well, you know you can come stay with me and Seth—"

"Don't. I don't want your money, Elle. It's humiliating. I'm twenty-eight years old in a few weeks. So please just don't. I'm staying with Shayla for now. I can take care of myself."

"I know you can," she said. Which was generous.

Even I didn't know that.

"Good."

My sister hesitated. "You called me last night for something, Angeline. Tell me how I can support you. What is it you want me to say?"

What I wanted her to say was that she could have Flynn moved somewhere else. He could switch to a different position on Dirty's security team. He could be someone else's bodyguard instead of hers.

But she didn't say that.

"Nothing," I told her.

"I can't punish him, professionally," she said gently. "He's done nothing wrong in that regard. You know that."

She was right. Why should he lose his job? And why should she lose an amazing bodyguard just because I'd fallen in love with him and then failed to be a good girlfriend?

"I've gotta go, okay?"

"Look, I can go by the apartment today," she offered. "Pick up some of your things for you. I can bring it over to you. I'll bring Emma."

"No. That's okay. Really."

Just what I needed; my beloved niece seeing her Auntie Angie looking like last night's drunken ho.

And surely my sister had more important things to do. Between prepping for the upcoming Champagne opening by night and recording Dirty's next album in-studio by day, not to mention being mom to an amazing little girl, her plate was plenty full.

"I don't mind doing it, Angie. You probably shouldn't be over there right now. Give it some space—"

"I'll handle it," I told her, a little more forcefully. "I don't need help right now. Just… let me do it my way, okay?"

My sister fell silent for a moment. I knew it wasn't easy for her, but she said, "Okay. Just let me know if you need anything."

"I will."

"I love you," she said.

"I know. I love you, too. We'll talk later."

I knew she wanted to ask me what I was doing today. *How* I was going to take care of myself. Because the fact was I'd never really done that before.

But she bit her tongue.

"Okay. 'Bye, sweetie."

"'Bye." I hung up. I checked my phone, but mercifully, she was the only one I'd drunk dialed last night. Maybe I'd needed my big sister in the middle of all that chaos. It was instinctual. She'd always been there for me. Protected me.

*You just have to learn when it's time to let go of the ones you don't need anymore.*

Maybe Shayla was right about that in more ways than one. Maybe I needed to stop needing my big sister to rescue me. It wasn't her fault that she was trying to protect me now; she was just doing what I'd always needed her to do.

Damn. My eyes burned and I felt like crying again. How was that even possible? How were there any tears left to cry?

My phone said it was almost ten, and I told myself I was just exhausted and needed to eat something. But when my stomach churned at the mere sight of the food in Shayla's fridge and I almost dry heaved, I instead sipped some more water.

Then I forced myself over to Johnny's place next door to deal with my homelessness head-on.

I walked out the sliding doors off Shayla's designer kitchen and across the back deck, over the strip of grass between the two houses. The yards were pretty much mirror images of one another, though some of the landscaping in Shayla's was less mature and Johnny's backyard featured a gorgeous pool. I stepped onto his back deck—just as he emerged from his gym.

*Barely* holding onto a towel. Which was the only thing he was… "wearing."

It dangled from his hand, over his dick and down between his thighs—covering very fucking little of him. I gaped at his sculpted muscles and the tattoos that enhanced his ridiculously gorgeous body… all that… golden… smooth… skin…

*Holy God,* that was a lot of naked thigh… and hips, abs, and glorious, manly chest for this early in the morning.

Oh, right. It wasn't early.

"Ummm," I said loudly, failing to come up with anything else, and he jerked to a stop, noticing me standing there all man-struck.

*Not a man. Johnny O.*

*Stop staring.*

"Christ," he muttered. "Sneak up on a guy."

"Sorry."

He shut the sliding door behind himself and I stared while he wrapped the towel around his hips, in no particular hurry. His gaze moved down over me, over his shirt, which I was still wearing. His eyes said, *What the fuck do you want?*

His body said, *Look at me all you want.*

As usual, Johnny's mere presence fucked with my head. Which was why I usually avoided it.

Especially if I was alone.

"Hi. Uh, sorry," I repeated. "I'll be quick. I just came to beg you to let me stay at Shayla's place."

He studied me with a slight scowl. "Beg?"

"Yup. Beg, whine, plead. Whatever it takes. I'm desperate here."

"Why?"

I blew out a breath. "Because I absolutely refuse to go crawling to my sister or my parents like I always do. And no way am I going back to my —I mean, my ex-boyfriend's apartment."

His eyes darkened as he took that in. I could not imagine what he was thinking.

Nor did I want to.

"*Why?*" he repeated.

"*Because*, okay? No way am I putting up with a man who bounces from my arms into some glitter wearing skank's the same day we break up and comes home embalmed in her perfume, even to be 'roommates.'" I made vicious air quotes on the word.

Johnny's eyes slid over my face, studying me in a way that made me swallow. "He did that?" I knew the hint of warmth—pity?—I was detecting in his voice was simply because I was one of Shayla's besties, and if I was hurt then Shayla was hurt.

So I tried to ignore it.

"Pretty much."

"You and the bodyguard broke up?"

"His name is Flynn. And let's just skip the part where we totally humiliate me by reliving it, okay? I've had enough humiliation for a lifetime in the last twenty-four hours. So, can I please stay? As I mentioned, I will beg. I have no pride left and very little money but I do need a roof over my head."

His eyes met mine again, briefly. "Stay if you want." Then he walked right past me, toward the patio doors that opened into his kitchen.

"Really?" I scurried after him.

"It's Shayla's house," he said, side-eying me with annoyance as I followed him into his house. That was true. Sort of. But he owned the house, and I was determined to pay my way.

"Don't worry, I'll pay you. Somehow."

"Not necessary."

"Of course it's necessary. This property is worth millions. I'm not freeloading."

He poured himself a water from his fancy water filter tap. "Call it what you want." Then he took a long drink, his throat working—and I glutted myself on the visual of his gym-toned body.

Three years ago, I wouldn't have thought Johnny O'Reilly could get any hotter.

I was wrong.

He'd been doing some seriously intense workouts or something, because over time he'd somehow upgraded from super-hot-older-brother-of-my-best-friend to handed-over-his-eternal-soul-to-Satan-in-exchange-for-that-physique. I could see an alluring vein running down his groin, disappearing under the towel that now swathed his hips, toward the bulge in the front. I could see his abs flexing as he swallowed. I could see his flushed pink nipples.

He really needed to put on some clothes. Or maybe never wear clothes again.

I tried to look him in the eye and only in the eye as he finished drinking and looked at me again.

"It's called freeloading," I repeated.

"So? Then pay some rent."

"I mean, I would, if I could."

He frowned again, like he was already bored with the conversation and really didn't care.

"I can pay you, somehow," I pressed. I knew I was being pathetic and desperate right now. I didn't care.

"I do not need, or want, anything from you," he said carefully, placing his empty glass on the counter.

"Look." I took a breath. "The fact is I don't have a job right now and I'm totally unemployable. So it might take a little while, but I will land on my feet. Meanwhile, I can work for it. I'll pull weeds or something."

"I have a gardener."

"I'll tidy up around here."

"No thanks."

"It could use a tidying." I looked around; the place was, unfortunately, spotless.

"Thanks for the assessment."

"Just let me clean your house in exchange for rent. I'll keep it tidy."

"No."

"Why not?"

He gave a short, silent, non-laugh. "Because Shay would shit. You know that."

"It's just for a tiny bit while I search for a real job. Then I'll pay real rent."

"I have a cleaner."

"Come on, Johnny." I followed him as he headed toward the floating stairs to the second floor. "*Please.*"

He didn't stop.

Ugh. I really was desperate here, because I blurted out, "You're not a total dick, so stop pretending you are."

He shot me a look over his shoulder, like, *Oh, but I am.*

I sighed. "Shayla sometimes admits how much she loves you and stuff, okay? So I know you must have a shred of humanity somewhere in that cold, empty cavern."

He paused at the bottom of the stairs. "Cavern?"

"You know. Your empty chest cavern." My voice faltered as he stared me down. "Where your… heart would be."

"*Would* be?"

"Like, if you actually had one." I cleared my throat.

"You know, you're really winning me over, Angeline."

"I won't get in your way. I'll be as quiet as a mouse."

His eyes held mine, something sinister—or sinful—taking shape in the aquamarine depths for a moment. "Always thought of you as more of a kitten," he said darkly.

And in that darkness…

Kisses. Naked skin. Gasps, moans, screams… and all the other things that usually accompanied my fantasies of him—in the past—but I'd never actually experienced in the flesh. Except for the kissing part.

My stomach clenched.

"I'll be as quiet as a kitten, then," I said evenly, trying to sound like I had no memory of that night, of that kiss, when we both knew I did. I could see it in his eyes.

*Shit.* We really needed to set some boundaries if I was actually going to clean his stupid house and live right next door.

"Um, it's probably better, actually, if I come when you're not here," I suggested. "I can use Shayla's key so you don't even have to let me in."

He gave me a skeptical look. I knew he was hyper vigilant, like paranoid-level, about security and stuff. But come on. He knew Shayla had a key and we were in and out of here all the time when he wasn't here.

"So I'm not in your way, and vice versa," I elaborated. "I'm not some random off the street who's gonna snoop in your music studio and stuff. Believe me. If I wanted to leak the next big hit, I'd snoop in my sister's studio."

The look in his eyes iced over. "Has anyone ever told you how incredibly charming you are, Angeline Delacroix?"

"Yes. What time of day are you not around?"

He glared at me for a long moment. "Mornings. I'm usually gone by now."

Gone where, I didn't ask. I didn't exactly pay attention to his comings and goings when he was in town, even when I hung out at Shayla's. The gym, probably, because having one at home wasn't enough. Breakfast buffet at a strip club. Happy ending massage. Whatever. As long as he was gone.

"Great. How often does your cleaner come?"

He sighed shortly, like he couldn't believe he was even entertaining this conversation. And annoyed, maybe, that he hadn't intimidated me into shutting up and slinking away yet. "Once a week."

"Great," I said brightly. Once a week would leave me plenty of time to look for a real job. "I can start today if you're heading out."

"You'll start tomorrow."

Thank God. Because today I very possibly needed to dry heave, then eat, then puke, then sleep off this hangover. Then repeat, as many times as it took until I could actually keep food down and my skull stopped throbbing.

Johnny had started up the floating stairs. "Wonderful!" I called after him, trying not to stare at his bare, athletic legs. The man was freakin' Adonis. With the soul of Hades. "You won't regret it!"

"You will," he said ominously. "My friends are fucking pigs."

# Chapter Eight

**Angeline**

The next morning, I woke up hungover all over again.

Shayla had dragged me out to a party, that wily bitch. But at least this time I didn't wake up on the floor.

Small wins.

I was in one of Shayla's guest bedrooms, wrapped in her best guest linens; girl knew how to pick out a bedsheet. Unfortunately, I was also in last night's clothes.

I stretched my achy, mildly nauseous body. I really needed to stop drinking. No more booze in this body for at least a week. Though there was the big party at Champagne this weekend…

Okay, no booze until then.

I dragged myself upright, gradually remembering that I had a job to do today. I did not want to clean Johnny's house. However, I did want a job and a home.

Fuck. Adulting sucked.

I forced myself to get up and face the music—meaning my bedraggled self—in the bathroom mirror. Last night's party dress was a now-rumpled little mint-green number edged in sequins that I'd borrowed from Shayla. She always called me Bedroom Barbie when I wore it.

Flynn hated that.

In fact, I wasn't too sure he was much of a fan of Shayla in general.

Damn it. Why was I still thinking about him? All. The. Time.

*Because it's only been two days,* I reminded myself. Felt like so much longer, maybe since the breakup was so imminent for so damn long. It was like going through a car crash in slow motion, one you could see coming from miles away.

Didn't make the impact any less devastating.

I tried to wipe away the worst of last night's raccoon makeup, then dragged myself downstairs for the walk of shame. When I padded into Shayla's kitchen in my bare feet, I found her getting ready for her day, music and coffee on.

"Good morning!" She smirked at last night's dress and last night's face. "You slept in the dress?"

"Yeah. Guess I was too tired to get changed." She'd loaned me a nightie to wear, but maybe I'd forgotten that last night.

I glanced outside, through the big windows along the back of the house. The scene around Johnny's pool, visible through her living room, had snagged my eyes. By the looks of things, he'd had a party last night. There were like dozens of beer bottles, glasses, and assorted crap all over his deck.

Great. *Have fun cleaning that up,* Mean Me taunted. *You seriously begged him to let you clean up after him? Dumbass.*

"Coffee?"

"Hmm?" My eyes snapped back to Shayla. "Sure. Thanks." I was definitely gonna need caffeine to deal with whatever awaited me next door. I slumped onto a stool at the island. "How late did we get home from the bar?"

"Oh, you know, late o'clock." Shayla was in her dance clothes again, no makeup, but looked way more bright-eyed than I felt.

"Dancing today?"

"You know it." She poured a coffee and put it in front of me. "Gotta be in top shape for the video shoot! Rehearsals start next week."

"I can't believe you're gonna be such a star. I love you and I resent you so much right now." I could say that, because she knew I was kidding.

Shayla smiled. "Aw, babe. You're gonna be the next one to make it big. I know you are. Whatever you do, you're gonna kill it."

Of course she thought that. Because that's what friends think.

Even when they're wrong.

"How about the PR thing?" She eyed me over her travel mug. "Danielle Duke's not the only hot shit in town, you know."

"I know."

"Will you start looking at job postings today?" she asked lightly, trying to hide how unenjoyable she found that prospect.

"Yeah. No time like the present, right?"

"Right," she agreed. "You can chill on the couch and send out resumes, line up some interviews…"

"Yup." I didn't even want to break it to her that I didn't have a resume. I figured after I cleaned Johnny's house, I'd get working on that. All I really had to put on it was my internship with Danielle Duke, and the online Public Relations course I'd taken before that.

Maybe I could shamelessly put down Brody Mason, my sister's manager, as a personal reference. Brody was super well-connected. That was sure to get me an interview somewhere, right?

Meanwhile, I wondered how long I could get away with not telling Shayla about cleaning Johnny's house. She'd freak and forbid it, for sure. It would just have to be a tiny little secret for now.

*Like you need more secrets with Johnny O.*

*First a kiss, then… this.*

Hopefully, it was incredibly temporary. There had to be someone else who'd hire me to do… something. If I got crickets when I sent out my resume, I'd just have to start hitting up local cafés and whatever. I wasn't too proud to make lattes for a living, also temporarily.

*Better than cleaning up after Johnny O'Reilly and his "pig" friends.*

Shayla had packed up her things and came around to give me a hug. "Well, good luck. I pulled a bunch of clothes for you, it's all on my bed if you need anything."

"Thank you, for everything. Break a leg and stuff."

She flashed me a delighted grin. "See you later, roomie!" Then she disappeared out the door to the garage. I knew she was excited about us being roommates. I didn't exactly feel the same.

I mean, living with Shayla would be fun as hell. I still felt like a free-loader, though.

*Time to get working.*

I picked up my coffee and headed upstairs, trying to pump myself up to start this new chapter in my life. But instead, I felt flattened. As it turned out, there was getting dumped, getting fired, almost getting molested by a stranger… then a whole other sub-level of low beneath that.

*Johnny O's cleaning lady.*

Shiiiit.

If only yester-me could see me now. You know, the version of me that had a thing for Johnny for *years*. But she was dead and gone now. I'd buried her the night I kissed him behind my boyfriend's back.

And no way was I resurrecting her. That girl was dumb as shit.

Just because Johnny swooped in and saved me the other night like some sexy angel and then grudgingly gave me a place to live and a job, I did not feel a thing for him, and I was never going to.

Other than the hate crush. As much as I liked to pretend it was a thing of the past… it had a way of circling back around. Kind of like the flu; occasionally slipped past your defenses, invaded your system, made you achy and sick until you finally purged it… until the next time it struck.

I headed into Shayla's room, planning to wear something that I could get filthy in. Surely that mess in the backyard was just a glimpse of the horrors that awaited me next door. I still didn't have any of my stuff with me, or any idea when or how I'd be getting it.

But as it turned out, the stuff Shay had pulled for me to wear was… problematic. Unless all I planned to do today was lounge out by Johnny's pool and look good in case a cute FedEx guy dropped by with a package or something. Which, knowing Shayla, was exactly what she hoped I'd really be doing today.

She'd left me not one but three string bikinis.

I dug through the pile of scraps she'd left on her bed for me. Micro mini skirts. Short shorts. There wasn't an actual shirt to be found. And while I wasn't exactly the bustiest girl around, Shayla was thin as a rail; my boobs would never fit into her teeny, tiny bikini tops. The thought of scrubbing Johnny's floors while wearing one, and him walking in on me, made me shiver.

I decided to put his T-shirt back on, with a pair of Shayla's tiny shorts underneath. Because who cared if Johnny's shirt got destroyed. He hadn't asked for it back. And it barely even smelled like him anymore.

I took a little sniff of the soft yellow fabric and my pussy actually contracted. Like, immediately. *Yup, still smells like him.* I made a barfing face at myself in the mirror, trying to convince myself that he grossed me out. I was really leaning into the hate end of that crush. It was the only sensible thing to do.

I used Shayla's stuff to wash my face properly and tied my hair up in a messy knot. I forced myself to eat some breakfast. Then I brushed my teeth with the toothbrush Shay had bought for me on her way home yesterday—seriously; bless her, and to hell with her brother. Shayla O'Reilly was the true angel in my life right now.

Then I headed next door.

As I set out, carrying a bucket loaded with every cleaning supply I could find in Shayla's cupboards and closets, I was feeling pretty desperate to prove my worth here—to my new landlord and worse, to myself. I also promised myself that I'd give it one week, *one* fucking cleaning, and then no matter what happened, I'd have to tell Shayla about this. If I didn't have any job prospects within a week, I'd have to come clean with her before I cleaned her brother's house again.

No roof over my head was worth sneaking around behind my best friend's back.

I knocked on Johnny's back door, but no one answered. I went around and peeked through the window into his garage. His beloved Dodge Hellcat wasn't there, so I knew he was out.

I let myself in through the back door off the kitchen with the spare key that Shayla kept on a big keyring by her back door. Shayla did it all the time, to raid his bar, etcetera. But I'd never been in here alone before, and my heart was already beating in a weird way. It was the adrenaline rush of creeping around in Johnny's house when he wasn't here and no one else was here to see me.

His personal space. His private things.

Rooms where maybe he walked around naked.

And did other stuff naked.

I shivered, in an undeniably sexual way. Because I was a creeper like that.

At least no one was here to know it but me, right?

For the first time, I wondered if Johnny had any cleverly hidden security cameras in his house. I looked around but I didn't see any.

Then the scene of last night's party really hit me. *Whoa.* It was worse than the pool area outside. Bottles, glasses, dishes, half-eaten food… fucking *everywhere*.

Johnny was so neat and tidy about his appearance. Fastidious, even. His house always seemed that way, too. Whenever he was away working, touring, and Shay brought us here to use his pool or the hot tub, everything was clean. His regular cleaner must've been really good.

*He doesn't even need you to do this. It was a pity hire.*

Whatever. He hired me.

I set to work, putting on some angry breakup music in my earbuds, courtesy of Machine Gun Kelly and Halsey, and headed into the guest bathroom on the main floor.

And quickly remembered that I didn't even know how to clean a bathroom.

I'd never actually cleaned one before. Mom and a cleaning service took care of the bathrooms at home, and my parents had paid for the cleaning service to come deep clean the apartment for me and Flynn every other week. Hmm. I supposed Flynn would be cleaning his own toilets now.

Anyway, how hard could cleaning a toilet be?

Then I saw the toilet. There was a condom in it, like someone tried to flush it down and it got stuck.

Welp, that toilet appeared to need a plumber, and I wasn't one. I closed the lid. *My friends are fucking pigs.* Indeed.

It wasn't Johnny's fault or his friends' that I was here, doing this, though. I was the one who begged him for the job. Because unfortunately, it was better than the alternative.

I pictured Flynn's face the other night when he'd come home drunk and stinking of some woman's perfume, lipstick and body glitter smeared on his shirt, his skin. It looked like he'd been mauled by a stripper and he hadn't even taken off his clothes.

*Did you even go home with her?* I'd snapped at him. *Or just fuck her in your car?*

It was the worst fight we'd ever had.

The worst things I'd ever said to him.

The worst night of my life.

*Stop. Thinking. About. It.*

I looked around the bathroom. Shit, it was gonna take me all day to clean this house. I didn't even know how many rooms there were. I was tired already, and I hadn't even started yet.

*Welcome to a grown-ass adult's life,* Mean Me whispered. *It's called work. Get used to it.*

Maybe I needed to start somewhere else?

I wandered out. The whole main floor was a disaster and my hangover wasn't making dealing with it any easier. I glanced up the floating stairs to the second floor.

*I bet upstairs is way less gross.*

Yeah. That's why I wanted to go upstairs so bad.

My nerves crackled with excitement, and I knew I was in trouble. Every time my mind wandered up those floating stairs, I got hit with a sick rush of adrenaline.

I grabbed my bucket and started up the stairs, deciding to give myself just a little peek into Johnny's upstairs rooms. Including his bedroom. Maybe I'd clean the hopefully-not-as-gross upstairs first, then take a break out by the pool for lunch? I wouldn't even look in his underwear drawer or anything. Maybe.

And if I did, I wouldn't touch anything. Much.

Yup. Sounded like a plan.

The house had a similar layout to Shayla's; Johnny had her house built to pretty much match this one. That's what she said. I'd never been upstairs here, but I knew where the master bedroom was. Same as Shayla's—that closed door midway up the hall.

I wondered if Johnny slept in there naked. Men usually slept naked, right?

Flynn sure did.

*Stop. Thinking. About. Him.*

There were a few other doors along the hallway, some of them ajar. An office? Guest rooms for rock star orgies? I nudged open the first one. It was a bedroom. The bed was messed up, covers hanging off the edge. A big wall of blinds blocked out most of the light, but there was a lamp on. And the faint sound of a shower running.

And a man standing by the foot of the bed. Naked.

I knew that tattooed back; the giant, coiled blue serpent with black wings. I'd seen it often from Shayla's windows, out by the pool.

I was staring at Johnny O'Reilly's tight, naked ass as he stood looking down at the phone in his hand. My bucket crashed to the ground, cleaning supplies clattering across the rug as I dropped the whole damn thing.

He startled, looking at me.

My mouth dropped open and my face lit on fire.

"Uh! I haven't…! I didn't…!" I backed up, stammering out a few unfinished protests before bumping against the door frame. "Um, I'll come back!" I darted down to grab the bucket and whatever I could shove back into it, trying not to look at him. He'd turned a bit when I dropped the bucket and *I saw his cock*. "I mean, when you're not here!"

I was blind.

The image of his bare ass and side dick were scorched into my eyeballs and I groped around for the door, fumbling my way out, sweating.

I raced downstairs, heat coursing through me. I ran into the guest bathroom and splashed cold water at my eyes. "No! No no no no no. You didn't."

*Oh, but you did,* said Mean Me. *And it looked goooooooood.*

No.

*No.*

I'd basically spent the last many years of my life avoiding any kind of situation where Johnny O's naked dick and I might make one another's acquaintance.

But Jesus Christ, he had a hot ass. And his soft dick was… thick.

I swallowed the saliva that pooled in my mouth.

*Not happening. Major mistake.*

I'd made mistakes with men my whole damn life, and I wasn't making this one. I didn't even trust myself to get anywhere near that man's dick. It was all about taking care of myself right now, getting my life on track, and Johnny O'Reilly's dick was not on the menu.

Even if he offered it up.

I looked into my eyes in the mirror and saw how flustered I was. I looked hungry. Starving. And sad. And just stupid enough to make another major mistake.

*You know he might offer it up. If you give him even the hint of an opportunity.*

*You have to be strong here, Angie.*

I collected myself and got cleaning the bathroom with determination.

When that was done, I went out to the kitchen. I started cleaning in there.

Then I saw Johnny's naked feet coming down the floating stairs. At least he was dressed now—in nothing but a pair of joggers. They were just thin enough that his dick bounced around under the soft fabric when he walked, and just loose enough that they clung low on his hips and the swell of his muscular ass, showing off the mouthwatering curves and planes of his would-be-illegal-in-some-countries waist/groin area.

It was stunningly obvious that he wasn't wearing underwear.

*Good God.*

When he reached the bottom of the stairs, our eyes met across the open space.

I returned my attention to sorting out the empties that covered the countertops for the recycling bins. A shiver ran down my back as he crossed behind me.

"The layout is different than Shayla's," I said, trying to keep my voice from wavering.

"What?" His voice was rough and raw. Probably how he sounded first thing in the morning. While having morning sex.

"The layout. Of the house. The master bedroom is on the other side."

He cleared his throat a little. "Yup."

"I thought you weren't home. Your car's gone."

When I glanced over, he was taking a glass out of the cupboard and staring at me. I looked away.

"My buddy Shane drove it home last night."

"Oh." I took a deep breath, preparing to force out a quick apology for barging in on him, then vanish into another room until he cleared out, but then a second pair of feet came down the stairs.

*Fucking wonderful.* He wasn't alone up there.

A woman's naked legs appeared. Long, slender legs. Then an enviable butt draped in silky cream fabric. When Johnny's guest reached the bottom of the stairs, she met my eyes, too.

Brianna MacMillan.

She had long, light-brown hair smoothed into a flawless ponytail, the kind of perfect little nose I'd always wished I had, and the figure of a lingerie model in that tiny wisp of a cream sundress layered over a gold bikini.

Just like the first time I'd met her at a party, the woman had "mean girl" written all over her. It was the way her blue-gray eyes scraped over me. Honestly, she might've been my doppelgänger other than the fact that she was taller, wispier, sexier, and achingly prettier than me. I wasn't exactly hideous here, but I'd never been *that* girl.

You know, the girl Johnny O took to bed.

*He would've, if you'd let him,* my memory of that night reminded me. The night he kissed me in the dark with such torment in his eyes.

Brianna's perfect face twisted with a slight sneer in my direction, before she floated over to Johnny. He'd poured a glass of water at his filter tap and took a swig.

I noticed he didn't offer her anything.

She made sure I was watching before her fingers drifted along the waistband of his joggers, where the soft fabric hugged his hip. "What's on the agenda for today?" she asked coyly, like she was inviting him to suck her clit.

*Ugh, don't picture it.*

"A lot," he said flatly.

"Care to take me along?"

He seemed to almost laugh but grimaced instead. "No. I've got work." He stepped away from her as he set his water glass on the counter.

She reconfigured her game plan when flirting didn't work. Her eyes slashed over to me. "Who's the maid? And why's she staring at us?"

That's when I realized she had no idea who I was.

She didn't remember meeting me. She had no idea I was Danielle Duke's intern, or Elle Delacroix's sister. Because she didn't care. Because I didn't even rate with her enough to be memorable, no matter who'd introduced us.

Which meant that she also didn't recognize me as the girl who bought Johnny a drink and sat at his table at the fundraiser, making her jealous and making me lose my job in the first place. What kind of narcissistic A-hole made a stink like that because someone got more attention than she did, and then didn't even care enough to remember that person's face?

When I looked at Johnny, he made a slow, thorough study of his T-shirt on my body. Then my bare legs. Then the rubber gloves I was wearing as I sorted recyclables. Then he said, "She's not 'the maid.'"

"Well, who is she? And why's she in your kitchen?"

"Get out of my house, Brianna."

She bristled but tried to hide it, to save face. "What, right now? Aren't you going to get me a car?"

"Already paid for your Uber back to the hotel," he said evenly, "or back to JC, or wherever. Lamar's waiting outside to see you off."

She stared at him for a long minute, like, *You better fucking say something I want to hear right now.*

He looked right back at her, like, *Keep waiting if you've got time to burn, but I've got better things to do.*

Then she broke the staring contest and left out the front door in a waifish flurry of indignation.

When the door had closed behind her in the distance, I remarked, "She's classy."

Johnny said nothing as I sorted recyclables, but he was still standing there. I could feel him watching me.

"Can totally see why you were 'with' her at that fundraiser, and yet you weren't actually sitting with her. She seems like fun times."

Unnerving silence.

"She's still with JC?" I inquired.

"Last I heard."

"And you… slept with her last night?"

I looked over at him. He was lounging back against the counter, studying me. "A gentleman doesn't kiss and tell, Angeline."

I almost laughed. "I've never thought of you as a gentleman, Johnny."

"No?" He pushed off the counter and sauntered closer. "That's okay." He leaned in as I turned to keep working and murmured in my ear, "Knight in shining armor has a nice ring to it."

"You did not," I protested, shifting away. He was standing way too close to me in those damn pants. "You… Just because you helped me out the other night—"

"Face it." He swiped a strand of my sweaty hair behind my ear. "I saved you the other night. And it bothers you."

I spluttered but no words formed before he was talking again.

"It's okay, Angel," he said in a low, sultry voice. "It can be our little secret."

"I don't want any secrets with you, Johnny. And you're not my savior." And why the hell did he just call me *Angel* like that? Just like he did that night, when he kissed me…

"Uh-huh." His gaze had landed on my boobs. "You're still wearing my shirt."

"I was thinking of cleaning the toilets with it," I told him, deadpan.

His eyes met mine again. "Do what you must." He started away, crossing back to the floating stairs. "And for the record, you really don't have to clean my toilets. But hey, knock yourself out."

He started up the stairs, and I blurted, "Why would you sleep with your lead singer's girlfriend??"

He stopped in his tracks. He looked at me, a darkness in his eyes so deep and so cold, I was suddenly glad as hell that I wasn't JC. "Because, Angeline Delacroix. *Fuck him*."

Then he disappeared up the stairs.

# Chapter Nine

**Johnny**

"Are you fucking serious right now?"

"Really wish I wasn't, brother." Yash's voice came through the AirPods in my ears. I grabbed the towel off the bench next to me and wiped sweat off my face. "Wanted to tell you this shit in person but I'm downtown, so I figured I should head over to Brick House, try to see Trey."

"Fuck," I muttered. I looked up at my buddy, Shane. He was standing next to my weight bench, where he'd been spotting me when Yash called. His eyebrow rose. "What does this mean for the contract?"

"It means we've got a major problem," Yash said nervously. "It's not even the contract. It's Trey. He's not gonna like this. He could pull the deal."

*Fucking Christ.* "Call me after you talk to Trey."

"Will do, brother."

I hung up—and hurled my phone at the wall, where the screen shattered. I heard the sick cracking sound before it hit the floor.

I pressed my face into my hands and sucked in a deep breath.

"What the fuck just happened?" Shane said mildly. It wasn't like me to start breaking shit.

But the all-consuming rage had flooded my system, so fucking fast—just like the other night, with Angeline, in my driveway… it flipped a switch in me that night or something. I'd felt off, weirdly out of control of my own emotions ever since.

No. Not true.

I just wasn't used to having emotions at all. Definitely not ones that had me almost punching strangers and breaking my own damn phone against the wall. What a fucking stupid move.

The doorbell rang through the house. I looked up at Shane. Whoever was at the door, either Lamar had let them in or they had the code to the gate. I couldn't sort it out in my head.

"Did I just break my own fucking phone?"

"Yup." Shane went to pick it up, looking it over. "Still working. But your screen is smashed to shit."

I got to my feet. I walked over to the patio doors, stared blankly through the glass, across the back deck and the pool to the thick trees beyond. We were in my home gym. We were supposed to be working out. Then having a few people over. Maybe barbecue or something.

I wasn't even sure why. A distraction, maybe. Time filler.

Time killer.

While I fucking waited on other people to decide my professional fate, apparently.

"This is such bullshit," I growled.

The doorbell rang again.

"That'll be Lex," Shane said from behind me. "I'll go let him in."

Right; Lex was coming over.

Shane went through the house to get him as I just stood there. I couldn't even process whatever the fuck I was feeling. I didn't know how to. The rage had come on like a flash flood, burning through my system like liquid fire. Then everything jammed up in my head… and I started going numb.

As I stared through the glass in front of me, my vision blurred. Rain ran down the glass, turning to blood.

I blinked the illusion away. There was no rain. It was sunny out.

There was no blood.

I heard Shane and Lex come into the gym.

"I'm losing my shit." That must've been me, because I definitely heard my own voice.

"You're fine," Shane said.

I turned to look at him and Lex. Shane in his workout clothes; lean but ripped, the ghosts of bruises on his face, he looked like the fighter he was. Lex in his usual, a black T-shirt with worn gray-black jeans; his clothes covered his tats so he didn't even look like the biker he was, unless he smiled and his silver canines flashed. He'd left his leather biker vest at home today. He usually didn't wear it unless he was directly working for his motorcycle club. Or looking to pick up, though that was back before he got married.

"What's wrong?" Lex asked, reading the tension in the room.

"Cary Clarke," I said numbly. "He's supposed to produce Breakneck's album. He just pulled out of the project."

"Oh," Lex said. "Shit."

"Which means we just lost his recording studio, too."

Shane looked confused. "But don't you guys have a contract?"

"Yeah. We have a contract. But that contract was for Breakneck. Which means me, JC, Noah and Miles. According to Cary's lawyers, Breakneck is no more, thanks to JC and Miles fucking bailing."

"Well, fuck. I need a drink." Shane went over to the bar fridge and got out a bottle of chilled vodka, pouring it out into glasses along the bar.

"What are you, a savage?" Lex wandered over to the bar as Shane slid a glass his way. "Put some mix in there. Soda and a lime or something, for fuck's sake. It's barely four o'clock." Then he glanced over at me. "Don't tell me you're drinking straight vodka with this lunatic."

"Not yet, but the night is young." Shane smirked at me, nudging a drink my way on the bar.

I knew what my friends were doing. Trying to lighten the mood. It was what they did, and it usually worked. Because shit didn't get to me, in general.

Professionally, I was unshakable. Unbreakable. No matter what came at me, I wouldn't be defeated. From the very beginning, I'd had this *can't stop, won't stop* mindset about my career.

I did not even know how to process all these fucking roadblocks that were suddenly in my path.

No, not roadblocks. No one was blocking my road.

They were drilling the road, leaving fissures, and now they were dynamiting the road, leaving gaping chasms. The road was becoming impassable, and very soon, if I didn't stay ahead of it, it would stop me in my tracks.

"We're going out."

My friends looked over at me. Lex set his drink down. "Oh, fuck."

"I know that look in your eyes, bro," Shane said, but his face split into a grin.

---

Whenever the fuck later, we were at a nightclub downtown. The Ruby. Me, Shane, Lex, and somehow, Dane, who we'd dragged the fuck out by showing up at his office unannounced and putting him in the limo I'd hired.

Unfortunately, the married men had killed my perfectly decent idea of hitting the strip club—"It's for your own good"—so here I was. Getting babysat by a bunch of dudes.

Lamar was with us, but he wasn't drinking. The five of us were wrapped around a table in the VIP section even though it was Monday and the bar was just opening for the night. They'd opened for me, early. One of the perks of being a rock star: bars let me in even when they weren't open.

The manager himself poured us drinks before his staff got in.

"They're fucking me," I announced, after the waitress deposited our latest round of drinks on our table and departed. My friends had kept the conversation on other things—also for my own good, probably—but the more liquor I put back to try to forget, the more it fought its way to the surface.

"They can't fuck you," Lex said easily. "You'll find a way around it. You always do."

I took the drink Shane slid in front of me and put the whole thing back. I didn't even taste it.

"What's the plan?"

I looked at Dane blankly. "What?"

"The plan." He was still wearing his suit from the office, without the jacket, his dark-blond hair neatly in place. He looked way too respectable right now, actually, to be drinking with the rest of us. However, Lex, the biker/criminal, was Dane's own brother, and Shane, the underground fighter and general delinquent, was Dane's best friend. The four of us had been a crew since high school, and maybe we were all too stubborn to change that. And/or loyal. So, here we were. "You always have a plan," Dane pointed out.

I did. That was very true.

But all this shit had blindsided me. It went against all my plans. Yes, I'd had conflict in my band. We'd come to the verge of breaking up before. But none of my bandmates had ever walked out on the band before.

They'd never walked out on *me*.

"My plan," I said, "was to salvage what was left of the band. Me and Noah. Replace the band members we lost, so we can still make good on the record deal. But losing Cary and the studio does not look good. Cary was part of this deal, too. The record company is gonna freak."

"Why?" Shane said. "Who cares if you switch producers? You're the rock star."

"Cary Clarke is more than a star. He's thirty-five and he's already a legend in the music biz. This is gonna hurt us. Bad."

"Why do you think he pulled out?" Lex asked me.

"Because Johnny made out with his wife at a party." That was Shane.

I looked at him. And for the first time since I'd smashed my phone against the wall, then went blank… I actually felt something again. Blistering anger.

"What?" Shane said. "I'm just saying. Food for thought, no?"

"Taylor?" Lex looked entirely confused. "There's no way. Really?"

"She wasn't fucking married to Cary," I grit out. "That was years ago."

"While they were dating or something," Shane supplied.

"They weren't."

"Not what I heard," Shane said. At the look I was giving him, he added, "Devi and I talk. She likes to keep her finger on the pulse of these things. You know, who hooked up with who. Etcetera."

I glanced at Dane, who tossed Shane a mildly annoyed look. Devi was Dane's wife.

"So you're gossiping with the women?" I said.

Shane shrugged. "Beats gossiping with the men. Women know the really interesting shit. Guys don't share like that."

This time when I looked at Dane, he conceded, "True."

"Case in point," Shane said, "Lex didn't even know this dirt about you."

"It's not dirt. Can we get back on track here?"

"How are things with Noah?" Lex changed the subject.

"Good. I talked to him today. He says he's not going anywhere." Unfortunately, it wasn't enough to save us, but it was something.

"Noah's good for it," Shane said supportively. "He'll have your back."

"Why are you assuming this is all on me? It's my fault this is happening?"

Shane and Lex exchanged a look, like, *Who else's fault would it be?*

"Surely Noah has done nothing wrong," I pressed, the anger broiling in my veins.

"I mean, let's be real," Lex said. "Noah's awesome."

"Great guy," Dane agreed.

I took Dane's drink from in front of him and helped myself to it. "You're buying the next round. Fucking billionaire, and I'm buying you drinks."

Shane laughed.

"My wife's calling." Dane pulled out his ringing phone and got up. "Don't be surprised if I don't come back." He slapped me on the shoulder and wandered away to take the call.

"Shit," I muttered. "He's right. I should have a fucking plan." I looked for him across the nearly empty club, but he'd stepped outside, his bodyguard going with him.

Dane was definitely a guy whose opinion I should probably be seeking on this. He ran a multibillion dollar empire and knew how to foster business relationships. But his wife was pregnant. I didn't want to get on Devi's bad side by taking up too much of his time and energy. Devi seemed cool with me these days, but we'd definitely gotten off to a rocky start; she'd gone to high school with all of us and according to her memory, I was a total dick back then. Luckily, she'd wanted things to work with her and Dane enough that she decided to put up with me.

*Fuck.* Did I really alienate people so easily?

Was this shit actually my fault?

"Do you think he's coming back?" I asked, looking to Dane's brother for an answer.

"Fifty-fifty," Lex said.

"Hey, we may not be Dane," Shane said, "but he won't talk to you about your feelings. I mean, you can try. But Dane's shit with that." He slid another drink in front of me. How many was that now? Not enough. "You wanna get something off your chest? Cry? Whatever. I'm your guy."

"Should we leave?" Lex offered dryly, and Lamar grunted in amusement.

"What would you guys do if you were me?" I asked them.

"You could stop being an asshole," Shane suggested.

"Said the asshole."

"You want truth," Lex asked me, "or you want us to massage your ego?"

I sighed. "Truth."

"You're not an asshole through and through," Shane mused. "You're just so focused on what you want, you leave collateral damage by the wayside. And now some of that damage is catching up with you."

"And biting you in the ass," Lex put in.

"Cause and effect," Lamar agreed.

"Can you guys stop agreeing that I deserve this?" My phone buzzed and I glanced at the cracked-to-shit screen, fucking dreading more bad news.

**Shayla:** Are you out?

I picked up the phone. What now?

My sister had been pissing me off, pretty much from the moment she'd said Angeline had a "heart attack" when she woke up thinking she'd spent the night with me. It fucking grated me, replaying in my head about a hundred times since then and fueling my bad mood.

**Me:** No. Not picking up tampons or takeout. Get your own.

**Shayla:** Are you drinking?

**Me:** Jealous?

**Shayla:** Yes. Where's the party?

I grumbled under my breath. I'd tuned out Shane and Lex, or maybe they'd tuned me out as they kept discussing my life problems like a couple of old ladies at a craft circle.

My sister was always looking for the party. Nothing new. But when she asked *me* for the party, good chance she was wondering what dudes she might run into.

I was pretty sure I'd convinced her to back off of JC. But that just left me wondering which of my friends she might have an eye on now.

The only single ones here tonight were Shane and Lamar, and no way was I having that. Or worse, Noah. Last fucking thing I needed was my sister getting involved with another one of my bandmates and causing tension. She had no idea how much drama that shit had caused between JC and me.

**Me:** Who wants to know?

**Shayla:** Me! But I'll bring Angie if it helps.

I stared at her text.

God fucking forbid my sister ever let one of her friends hook up with *me*… which meant she was implying that she'd bring Angeline along for one of my friends.

**Me:** Good night.

I put my phone down.

"Who dat?" Shane lifted his chin at my phone.

"No one. Just my sister."

"She coming out?"

"No."

"Why not?"

"Because I didn't tell her where we are."

Lex laughed. I was too busy taking another swig of my drink to realize why until I saw Shane on his phone. He tossed it on the table when he was done.

"You did not just text my sister."

Shane smiled at me. "Didn't I?"

"Jesus Christ, I hate you sometimes."

Shane just slapped me on the back. He wasn't interested in Shayla, I was pretty sure. But he wasn't above fucking with me for his own amusement. No matter what shape I was in.

Friends. Who needed them, really.

"You need to surround yourself with family when you're in crisis, brother," he said magnanimously.

"Bullshit," I muttered, "coming from the man who hates his family."

"Hate is such a strong word."

"Let's get back on track again," Lex suggested. "We're unpacking Johnny's career issues. I don't have all night."

"I thought we were unpacking his issues with women."

"Let's not get crazy," Lex said. "I definitely don't have all month."

Shane cackled.

"Come to think of it," I muttered at Lex, "kinda hate you, too."

"Let's just tally up all the strikes against him," Shane suggested, like I wasn't fucking here.

"Strikes?" I said doubtfully. "Like what?"

"Are we talking career strikes," Lex asked, "or women?"

"Hmm," Shane said. "I'm thinking they're kinda one and the same right now."

"How?" I demanded.

"Well, let's see." Shane pretended to consider that carefully, like there were so many examples to lead with. The motherfucker was enjoying this way too much. "You made out with Taylor at some party, now Cary doesn't trust you."

"I told you, that was years ago. They weren't even together when that happened."

"You sure about that?"

"I mean, she wasn't wearing a ring. I didn't ask her to disclose her full relationship status before I kissed her. She was into it."

"You screwed your lead singer's girlfriend..." he went on, undeterred.

"That's over now."

"But it's all over the headlines," he pointed out. "Maybe that's why Cary bailed."

"You also married a woman, then completely fucked up that marriage," Lex pointed out, "and then she ended up happily married to one of the most successful musicians in town. That's gotta be bad somehow."

"That was also years ago. A fucking lifetime."

"He's right," Shane agreed. "You have kissed a lot of princesses, Johnny."

"That's three strikes right there, that we know of," Lex pointed out.

"I'm liking you guys so much less than I did this morning."

My friends chuckled, as if I was kidding.

Then a group of girls walked in and headed straight for us across the club. My sister and two of her best friends. Angeline, and Larissa—Trey Jones' little sister.

Fucking great.

When my sister came over, she gave me an I-know-you-don't-want-me-here-but-deal-with-it hug, and I grumbled at her, "Keep her away from me."

"Which one?" She glanced at her friends, confused. They were talking to Shane, who was gathering drink orders. The guy should've just been a fucking bartender already. Serve up drinks, get laid; perfect life for him.

Unfortunately, Shane Madrigal was so good looking, he didn't have to serve up drinks to get laid.

"Trey's sister," I told her. "I'm fucking drunk. Just hang out over there." I gestured across the nightclub.

"Oh-kay," my sister said, dumping her purse on the table.

I stopped her as she went to follow her friends—and Shane—up to the bar.

"And stay away from my friends."

Shayla made an offended noise. "I'm just here for the drinks and the music." She smiled at me, with a warning in her eyes. "But *you* can certainly stay the hell away from mine."

Then she sauntered over to Shane and I watched as he wrapped her in a big, warm hug.

*Dick.*

---

Later, the club was filling up around us. Dane had gone home. Lex was on the verge of leaving. I was pretty sure we'd talked about other things along the way, but somehow my friends were once again discussing all the ways I'd fucked up with women.

Specifically, all the women I'd touched who they seemed to think I shouldn't have.

I didn't realize what experts they were on this subject.

And they didn't even know half the women I'd touched.

My eyes strayed over to Angeline. She was at a table on the other side of the VIP area. The girls could've sat with us, despite my attitude, but Trey Jones had arrived a while ago and they'd joined his table. Trey hung out at the Ruby so much, he should've just bought the place.

I kinda forgot about that when Shane suggested we come here.

Really should've gone to the strippers.

Actually, I probably should've headed over to Trey's table, kissed his ass. According to my friends, I might need to, just a little. Yash had called me back, told me that his chat with Trey had gone "okay." We still had a record deal, but apparently JC was starting to raise a stink about Breakneck continuing on without him. Which meant Yash now wanted us to consult with our legal team about next steps. Meanwhile, Noah said he'd talk to JC, too, see if he could get him to calm down, be reasonable; let Breakneck be Breakneck, even if he didn't want a part in it anymore.

Trey had come by my table to say hi when he arrived, but we didn't get into any business talk in front of our friends. I'd been nice enough, but I definitely wasn't planning on kissing anyone's ass, least of all a record company exec's, no matter what was at stake.

Instead, I found myself thinking about kissing Angeline, three years ago.

That memory was clear now.

I knew the exact night it happened, because it was the night I found out about my mom.

I was a total mess that night. My dad had called to give me the news. But I didn't even remember that call. Or kissing Angeline… until I saw her again at a party and it started to come back to me. I didn't remember a whole chunk of that night. At the time, I attributed that to alcohol, but I'd eventually remembered much of what I'd lost, in therapy.

Localized dissociative amnesia. I'd experienced it exactly two times in my life. And it had nothing to do with drinking.

I'd never told my friends, much less my sister, about what happened that night. About how hard I took the news about my mom. About the memory loss. Or about the kiss. As far as I knew, no one knew about that kiss except Angeline and me.

Maybe I felt guilty about that. That she had to harbor that secret, because of me. I wasn't sure. I felt shitty right now, yes. Generally fucking shitty.

Because I knew what it was like to harbor secrets.

I drank some more, because thinking about those secrets was not something I did. Not if I could help it. And the booze was supposed to help with that. Eventually, it would, as long as I drank enough.

As I drank, I tried not to stare at Angeline. But my eyes kept wandering that way while my buddies joked around, ribbing me whether or not I was listening. She'd seemed so damn pathetic and desperate when she begged me to let her stay at Shayla's and clean my house. And she wasn't looking much better right now. She was wearing my T-shirt again, which looked dirty from cleaning my house yesterday. Her hair looked like it hadn't seen a brush in days, in a blob on top of her head.

I'd never seen her at a bar looking like that. I was surprised Shayla let her out of the house like that, but maybe Shayla didn't get a say in it.

Weird thing was, Angeline Delacroix didn't need makeup or sexy clothes to be attractive. In an oversized, dirty T-shirt and yoga pants with no makeup, zero effort made, she was still beautiful. Soft brown hair. Sweet face. And so much feeling in her eyes…

Maybe it was her eyes that fucked with me so much.

I'd never been good at reading feelings; my own or anyone else's. But Angeline Delacroix's eyes overflowed with emotion whenever she looked at me.

Hatred. That was what I saw.

But also… a lot of other things. If only I could figure out what the fuck they were.

Maybe my friends had a point. Maybe my colleagues were right to think I couldn't be trusted around an attractive woman, much less one I'd already kissed, *tasted*, and couldn't have. A woman I'd been left wanting.

I didn't want Cary Clarke's wife.

I didn't want JC's girlfriend or ex-girlfriend or whatever she was. Not anymore.

But I'd never been left wanting anyone like I wanted Angeline Delacroix.

The match was struck the night I first kissed her… and when I put her to bed the other night and she kissed me, she poured gasoline on that fire.

The temptation of having her in my face, living right next door, wandering around my property? This was the kind of shit that was guaranteed to get me in trouble.

I'd tried to tell her no, though. That she couldn't clean my house. But she *begged*, for fuck's sake.

And then she walked in on me while I was naked.

Because I let her.

I knew she was in the house, coming up the stairs. I didn't exactly lock the door and stop her.

Her eyes met mine through the crowd. She looked away, took a sip of her drink, then glanced my way again. When she found me watching, she turned away and leaned in to talk to Larissa Jones.

Good. She needed to keep away from me. If she wasn't careful, if she gave me the slightest encouragement—when she wasn't wasted—I'd dive right in and glut myself on the juicy distraction from all this band shit that she offered, no matter how off limits to me she was supposed to be.

Fuck limits. I had none. Not when it came to something I'd decided I wanted.

But seeing Trey sitting right over there… I tamped down the urge to find out if I could get Angeline underneath me tonight. His smiling face was a cold reminder that I had a serious problem to deal with, and it wasn't magically going away—no matter how much I drank tonight or who I fucked.

I downed the rest of the drink in front of me and wondered if I should head home, alone, before I somehow made things any worse.

But fuck if I was leaving before Trey Jones did.

---

"You need to somehow rebuild trust with the people you've burned," Lex was saying. "Believe me. I've been there."

I blinked at him. Was he talking to me?

Didn't he go home yet? Last thing I knew, Lamar was walking him out. Wasn't he?

I looked around the table. Shane was sitting next to me. And in between Lex and me, on my other side, was an empty seat where my sister had been, and… Angeline.

Where was Shayla? Washroom? Bar? Making out with some douche in the corner? I looked around, noticing Trey's group was gone.

Larissa; Lamar had walked Larissa out, for Shayla. I looked for Lamar now, and I knew I was fucking wasted when I saw my bodyguard standing a short distance away, his back to the wall, and he shook his head at me. Big, beefy dude, shaking his head at me like a disapproving granny.

He tapped his watch, our signal for *You told me to remind you that you wanted to leave an hour ago.*

"You said Yash mentioned bringing on a publicist…" Lex was saying.

I tried to tune back in. What were we talking about?

"Someone to handle your PR on this mess. What's her name?" Lex asked me. "She works with some big name clients. She works with Elle."

I felt Angeline looking at me.

"Danielle Duke," I supplied.

"No." That was Angeline, and it was so abrupt, we all looked at her. "No, no. No, you don't want Danielle."

"She works with your sister," I pointed out.

"No. She's all wrong for you."

"How do you know?"

"Because I worked for her."

I blinked at her. Elle Delacroix's sister. Sitting at my table, like she did at that fundraiser, talking business with me. Right now, she was only sitting here because of my sister. But the girl had connections, no denying that.

And skills? Maybe. She'd worked with Danielle Duke.

"Fine. Then you can do it."

"What?"

"PR. I need some good PR. Get me out of this mess." I looped my finger in the air. "Clean it up."

"Uh… I—"

"You need a job. I need a publicist. Put together a PR campaign." I was barely making sentences at this point. Too much effort to find the words. But I knew what she could do for me. Why didn't I think of it before? "You'll do it."

Angeline gaped at me. "I'm… I'm not really qualified."

"More qualified for this than cleaning my house. You did a terrible job."

She turned pink. She glanced at my friends, who exchanged a look.

"Elle's sister is cleaning your house?" Lex said.

"I'm not—" she protested, but I cut her off.

"You interned with Danielle Duke. You worked with her clients. You know a lot of people. If you pick up the phone, the media will take your call."

She was growing redder by the minute. I was either embarrassing her or pissing her off. Who could say? Not me. "Because they want a story on my sister."

"So? The point is, they take your call. You tell them you have a better story than Elle Delacroix, they'll be listening."

"And what story is that?" she said. "The story of disgraced rock star Johnny O'Reilly, shaking off the ashes and rising again from the flames of his dumpster fire career?"

I stared at her, unvexed. "I'm sure you can finesse it a little better than that."

"I'm not that experienced," she protested.

I took a slug of my drink, mildly annoyed with her disbelief in herself. No wonder she'd never held down a job, or even gotten one. "Who's Brody Mason?"

"Uh… my sister's manager?"

"He's Dirty's manager and he's the biggest band manager in town. One of the best in the business."

"So?"

"So, you show up at Brody Mason's door, what happens?"

"Um… he invites me in?"

"That's right. You get a seat at his table with his family. Can Danielle Duke do that?" Before she could respond, I went on. "No. She's a legendary publicist, I know. She can probably get into any industry event in this town. But you can get inside people's homes. You have their ear and their advice."

"It's not really that easy."

Fuck, her self-doubt was pissing me off.

"You're not cleaning my goddamn toilets."

We stared at each other.

Shane got up. "Well, that's my cue to get more drinks."

"Not for me." Lex stood and tapped my shoulder. "I'm heading out."

He nodded at Angeline. "Angie. Have a nice night. Lamar will put you in a cab when you're ready."

"Yeah," she said. "Thanks."

He gave me a look, which I ignored. Lex worked security on Dirty's crew. He worked with Angeline's fucking ex-boyfriend, Flynn, actually. It irritated me, that he seemed to think he needed to make sure she was secure when she had me, right here.

*Maybe that's the problem.*

I said nothing, my eyes on her. Then Lex was gone, we were alone, and I was still staring at her.

"What's your problem?" I demanded.

"What's your problem?" she shot back, like a juvenile.

"You. I'm offering you a job. Take it."

"I don't like handouts," she said stubbornly. Then she muttered, "Anymore."

Okay, I actually respected that. "It's not a handout."

"It better not be." She sighed. "I know I could ask a ton of people to help me out financially, or help me land some fancy job. Including my sister, her husband, her manager, and so on. But I'm not doing that. I'm going to pay my own way, do the work, and I'm going to take my clients with me, all the way to the top."

My eyes drifted over her. Her flushed cheeks, her chest heaving in my shirt. Her impassioned little speech was admirable. She almost seemed to believe it.

"Then start with putting out my dumpster fire." I finished my drink. "Whatever Danielle was gonna pay you, I'll match it."

She stared at me, like she didn't dare hope I was serious. Then she leaned in a bit. "Can I still stay at Shayla's?"

"I told you. I don't care."

"She won't like that I'm working as your publicist."

"Then don't tell her."

She looked scandalized. "How the hell will that work?"

"Not my problem." She watched me as I got up. I tried not to sway as I beckoned Lamar over, but fuck was I drunk. "Find my sister," I told him.

Then I pointed at Angeline, who was still staring at me. "And put this one in my car. We're taking her home."

"I guess he hears that one a lot, huh?" Angeline remarked, when Lamar headed off to find Shayla.

I blinked at her. "You probably want to adjust your attitude, now that I'm your landlord and your only client."

She gave me a stormy look with a whole mess of emotions in it, but she bit her tongue.

# Chapter Ten

**Angeline**

When I woke up in the morning, the first thing on my mind was the new opportunity that had steamrolled over me last night. It was like Johnny wouldn't take no for an answer once he decided to hire me to handle his PR campaign.

*What's your problem?*

*You. I'm offering you a job. Take it.*

As I got up to start my day, I was weirdly grateful for his bullheaded certainty about the whole thing.

I would've probably turned him down for a hundred and one different reasons. I wasn't even drinking alcohol last night, which meant I was thinking way too clearly to get roped into anything that meant spending more time with Johnny O'Reilly.

However.

He'd just seemed so damn certain—even if he was drunk—that I was the woman for the job. And as it really sank in—I got a PR job!!—I felt ridiculously amped up about it. A client of my very own! No Danielle Duke! No one but me!

I'd landed my first client.

I mean, he'd kinda landed me. But still.

I now had a reason to get up in the morning.

Not only was I going to put out Johnny's dumpster fire, I was going to go above and beyond his expectations. I only had one client. Least I could do was give him the star treatment. What was it Danielle always said? *Give them what they didn't know they needed and they will love you for it.*

Not that I wanted Johnny to love me or anything. It was a figure of speech. Meaning: wow your client and they will be loyally yours.

I was now a woman on a mission, and that pathetic Angie of yesterday was a distant memory. I had more important shit to do than mope around getting drunk, wearing dirty T-shirts to bars, and feeling bad about my breakup and my lack of direction. I had a direction now.

Straight to the top of the charts with Johnny O.

I was fully dressed—in clothes and makeup borrowed from Shayla—humming to myself as I got the coffee going, when Shayla found me in the kitchen. No matter how late we were out at night, she was so devoted to being in top shape for the video shoot, this was the first morning I was actually up before her.

"Wow," she remarked. "You're up and at 'em early."

"Coffee?" I was already frothing a latte for her.

"I'd love one. Man, I could so get used to having a housewife."

I snickered as she went for the cupboard where she kept her breakfast smoothie mix. "Don't get used to it. I have no intention of following in my mom's footsteps."

"I know. But I love seeing you so… glowing. Do you have to hum Breakneck, though?"

"Oh. Was I?" I totally was. I didn't even love Breakneck's music or anything. I'd been listening to it this morning while I showered though, and "Up in Smoke," which was their biggest hit, had gotten stuck in my head.

"I'll put some music on. Cleanse your brain." She put on Ariana Grande featuring Nicki Minaj, "Side to Side," and started swaying her hips around the kitchen as she mixed her smoothie. I'd never noticed how ode-to-a-bad-boy the lyrics of this song were until they started reminding me of Johnny.

Guilt prickled through me. The fact was, Shayla would support me sneaking around doing just about anything with a bad boy—so long as he wasn't her brother.

When I glanced at her, she was eying me speculatively. "So what's got you up so early, and with that blush-pink eye shimmer blended to perfection? Job interview? Or were you vibing on Shane Madrigal last night…?"

"Shane? No."

"Hmm. Disappointing," she teased. She'd mentioned it before, that she thought I should hook up with Shane, her reasoning being that she would but Johnny would kill her. Plus, I knew she truly thought the best way to get over Flynn was to get under someone else, preferably someone tall, dark and dangerous, and if he was also handsome, all the better.

I hesitated, feeling like a dick, about to ruin her morning and all. It was tempting to let her think I didn't even talk to her brother last night. She knew nothing of the conversation we'd had at his table while she was chatting with some guys at the bar.

But I couldn't do that. I couldn't keep piling on the Johnny secrets. That kiss three years ago was bad enough. It didn't mean anything. It was just a mistake. But working with him behind Shayla's back was bullshit.

I poured her frothed latte carefully into one of her travel mugs. This one said *Hot Ass Ho*. I screwed on the top, handed it to her, and finally looked her in the eye. "You're not going to like this."

She set the mug by her purse and eyed me. "Lay it on me. And if you're moving back in with Flynn, you're right, I don't like it."

"I'm not moving back in with Flynn. But I am going to get my stuff from the apartment later today."

She perked up. "Are you kidding? That's great! I could maybe wrangle Lamar to help you. Or Johnny, if he's not busy."

"No. I'll be fine. I made all the arrangements. Courteney is enlisting Xander's bodyguard, Lucas, to help me. He's bringing his truck. I told Flynn he can keep all the furniture anyway, because it fits just right in the apartment and he paid for most of it. I'm just going to take all my stuff and give him back his keys."

"Babe. I'm so proud of you." Shayla gave me a big hug, which I felt a little guilty taking. "I know this part is not easy."

"Thanks. But that's not the thing you're not gonna like."

"Oh?" She raised a brow at me.

I took a breath and leapt. "I got a client. Someone's hired me to be their publicist. But—"

She gasped, lighting up.

"—that someone is Johnny."

Her sparkle instantly fizzled. "Johnny? You mean my brother, Johnny?"

"Yeah. That Johnny. Please don't be mad."

"I'm not mad. I'm… confused."

"He needs some good PR. His career is in trouble. According to him," I added quickly. "You heard him last night. And I need a client. A job. A fucking life. This is a huge opportunity for me, Shayla. Please see that. As much as you might feel uncomfortable that I'll be working with him… No matter what he says about his career struggles right now, he's still a rock star. Not at Elle's level, but he's getting there, for sure. He's successful. And he's going to be even more successful in the future, if he can, you know, get through this recent mess. I can help. And more than that… he can help me."

She made a little *harumph* sound, frowning. "I mean, I'm sure he can help you. I know how successful he is. But please don't diminish how much you'll be helping him. He's lucky to have someone like you in his corner."

Well, that was a vote of confidence I sorely needed right now. "Then… you're not mad?"

"No. I'm surprised you'd want to work with him, though. I thought you hated him."

"I mean, I'm not saying it would be my first choice. If I had a choice. But… maybe he's the only person I know who needs this enough, right now, to give someone like me a chance. I'm probably lucky I caught him in a moment of weakness."

Shayla raised an eyebrow at me again as she sipped her smoothie. "Weakness?"

"Drunkenness. He seemed pretty sold on my skills and connections last night," I explained. "But the reality is this is my first real gig. It's all on me. I don't have Danielle and her team to support me. I'm flying a bit blind and I'm pretty desperate to make it work."

"Determined," she corrected me. "You're determined to make it work. Change your language, babe. Stop shitting on yourself. And believe me, you'll see, things will start to change for you."

She was right. I knew how powerful word choice could be. I'd put hours into drafting the perfect press releases for Danielle's clients, word by word. I needed to stop undermining myself. "I'm determined to make it work," I said carefully. "Any words of wisdom on how to deal with your brother? Like how to get on his good side and work well with him?"

She gave me a wry smile. "You're not on his good side?"

"Actually, I have no idea."

"Come on, Angie. My brother wouldn't hire you if you weren't in his good books. He doesn't tolerate people he doesn't like."

Hmm. Interesting, considering Johnny had never been all that warm and fuzzy with me. I was half sure he hated me as much as I hated him, he was so chilly around me most of the time.

Other than… well, that kiss was pretty warm. But that was just… madness. A weird, nonsensical blip in the past.

"I'd hate to know what it feels like to be on his bad side, then," I said casually.

"You won't be. You're too cute."

"Brianna's cute," I pointed out. "He got pretty chilly with her."

"Let's not speak of that ho." She sucked back the last of her smoothie and put the cup in the sink. "And allow me to be more specific. There are different kinds of cute. You're cute like… an adorable kitten."

I rolled my eyes.

"What? It's true, okay? Dylan Cope would carry you around in his pocket if he could. The guys all love you."

"I know." This kind of "love" was not the kind I was looking for, unfortunately. "Elle's friends all think I'm a cartoon character."

She laughed. "You do give off Pikachu vibes now and then."

"I truly dislike you sometimes."

"You're a good, sweet person and no decent human wants to hurt you," she amended. "And if my brother does, you tell me." She gave me a sharp look and scooped up her things. "I'm outta here. Enjoy your day… *cringe*… working with my brother. And don't you dare say I didn't warn you, if it all goes to shit."

"I won't."

"Good. And don't wear anything sexy. Like, anything sexier than that." She eyeballed the leggings and long, flowy tank she'd loaned to me, after I pointed out to her that I needed actual clothes to wear around, not just lingerie disguised as clothes. She frowned. "My brother's got a one track mind. And that bra makes your boobs look *really* nice."

"Relax. It's not like that."

She wasn't really listening, too busy examining my shirt like she was searching for signs of translucency. "If you bend over and he gets an eyeful of the girls… Actually, you should really put on a sweater."

"I'm not here for the eye candy. I'm not going to bend over. And it's hardly sweater weather, Shay."

"Babe. He starts giving you eyes or something, you're telling me you've got it in you to resist?" She stared me down, actually waiting on an answer to that.

"Yes, Mom. I can resist the attractive man. I may even be able to keep my clothes on and refrain from having sexual intercourse with him while we have a work related conversation."

"Are you sure?"

I gave her a look. "I hate him, remember?"

"Hate sex is the new workplace quickie. Hasn't anyone told you?"

I laughed and gave her a little shove toward the door. "Get out of here. I'll remain fully dressed and I won't even think sexy thoughts."

"*Babe*," she admonished me, "now I know you're lying to me."

"Have a great day!"

"You, too. I guess." The door to the garage swung shut behind her as she appeared to be thinking way too much about this. Then she popped her head back in. "And don't take any meetings in his bedroom!"

I almost spilled the latte I was making for myself. "How stupid do you think I am?"

She grinned at me, then left.

I shook my head, laughing under my breath. It wasn't like she was wrong to be concerned, though. Her brother, my new client, was seriously hot, and I was seriously into that about him, for a long, long time. She and I both knew it. As much as I'd sworn to her up and down over the years that I didn't like him, she knew I'd had a crush on him, once upon a time. And that I still found him stupidly, annoyingly attractive.

That he was… well, exactly my type. At least, in a fantasy sense.

*Maybe I should put on a sweater.*

I sipped my latte, marveling over how smoothly that went. I was shocked, actually, that Shayla didn't have more of a problem with me working with her brother. Her only concern seemed to be about me actually spending time with her brother. Alone time. Wherein I might remember how hot he was and jump his bones.

*Nope. Not doing that.*

I made the promise to myself and sealed it with a solemn vow to my best friend; I sent her a text in words that I knew would touch her heart.

*Chicks before dicks. Always.*

*Lil Brats Forever.*

---

After breakfast, I got all set up to work at Shayla's laptop on the kitchen island. I really did need to go over to the apartment—*Flynn's apartment*; it was his apartment now—and get my things. Bring them over here. Unpack. Settle in. Wear something that actually belonged to me.

But first, I needed to start unpacking Johnny's dumpster fire. Even as successful as he was, something told me there would be a lot to unpack.

Shayla had given me her password to log onto the laptop and I went straight to the internet, logged into my Google account. Step One in my client intake process: educate myself on my client. Only after that could I start putting together a whole PR plan for Johnny and start writing his new story, so to speak.

For now I was calling this story *Reinventing Johnny*. I opened a new document and typed that into the document title. Had a nice ring to it.

Dude seriously needed a reinvention.

I got to work researching Johnny's public image. I started searching through all the recent and most popular media topics I could find on him. As it turned out, “Breakneck,” “tattoos,” and “nude” were the hottest web searches associated with the name Johnny O’Reilly. (There were no nude pics, but people were definitely hoping to find them.)

I read through all his career highlights and major reviews of his albums with Breakneck.

While I worked, I checked my phone a thousand times for a message from Johnny. No dice. His words to me last night, just before him and Lamar drove me and Shayla home were *We’ll get started tomorrow.* Then, while Shayla wasn’t looking, he’d had me put my number in his phone—which was challenging since the screen was weirdly smashed to shit—and send a text to myself so I’d have his.

I messaged him mid-morning to let him know I was available anytime, but he hadn’t replied.

After a quick lunch break, I pored over the bio some former publicist of his had written, which was lackluster and generic. *No wonder he wanted a new publicist.* The bio could’ve been describing any rock star. And Johnny O’Reilly was not any rock star. He had his own thing going on.

We just had to sell that to the world in a way that was a little more… palatable. At least, more palatable than it had been lately.

I searched out those Tweets about Johnny at the fundraiser, the ones Danielle had told me about. I’d avoided doing it so far. My sister had schooled me on ignoring gossip online, even if it was about me. It never was, anyway. I’d had a few cursory mentions here or there, odd times I’d appeared in public with my sister, but nothing that amounted to gossip. Because who was interested in me? It was usually just some photo caption; *Elle Delacroix and sister arrive at charity event.* That kind of thing. I rarely even got named.

When I found the Tweets, I saw that they focused on Johnny anyway. There were a couple of photos of me and him talking at his table, and they did refer to me as “mystery sweetheart.” But no one had circled back to name me.

I wondered if someone who disliked Brianna had taken the pics? Trying to hurt her or something? Because if it wasn’t for Brianna—or, more likely, her people, since she didn’t even seem to know who the hell

I was—complaining to Danielle, I'd never even know about those Tweets.

Then I read through a bunch of articles about the whole Johnny/Brianna/JC scandal. They all regurgitated the same information and the same quotes from some anonymous source.

Johnny fucked his lead singer's girlfriend. JC then dumped her; apparently that part happened two days ago—the day I'd met her in Johnny's kitchen. Poor Brianna was a starry-eyed victim of two alpha males both trying to play her for their own gain. That was the gist of it. By the way the articles painted Brianna as a successful model who was above the men who'd drawn her into this web of betrayals, I was going to assume that the "anonymous source" came from within her camp.

Smart, though. The best thing Brianna's publicist—Danielle Duke—could do right now was get ahead of the story; get coverage circulating that painted Johnny, the lover who'd rejected her, as a womanizer, and JC, the boyfriend who'd dumped her, as a coldhearted status climber. Whatever established Brianna as the better person in the situation.

After spending hours poring over news articles and entertainment gossip sites that painted my client as an asshole, I really needed a palate cleanser.

And finally I found it—during an image search, of all things.

There were plenty of public images of Johnny O to choose from, between red carpet photos, concert photos, paparazzi images and fan pics, and even a few editorials. But there was one that really stood out. It was the same image I'd seen on the wall at Champagne.

The image was from Lollapalooza, ten years ago.

I quickly did a fact check to make sure my calculations were correct, and confirmed that the photo was taken two years before Breakneck formed. With a little more digging, I figured out that at the time of the photo, Johnny had been playing with another band on his then-record label, on a temporary contract while their guitarist recovered from a surgery. Lollapalooza was a major highlight from that brief stint, and very possibly the largest show Johnny had ever played.

I studied the photo. There was something so raw and powerful about it. Gritty black-and-white, it showed Johnny onstage in black jeans and no shirt, his guitar strapped on—but he wasn't playing. His left hand curled around the neck of the guitar, his fingers still ghosting a chord, but his right hand had moved up to his face. His thumb was pressed to his full bottom lip, like he was holding back a smile, but his eyes were lit up as he looked out over the crowd. He seemed to be focused on something specific in the audience. Something that delighted him.

It felt like an intimate moment; his reaction to the crowd's reaction to him.

He also looked young. He would've been only twenty then. Less tattoos, his blond hair a little longer, sweat-damp strands reaching his jaw. There was a boy who became a rock star in that picture—and was caught marveling at the fact. That was no egocentric god looking down on the masses with unerring confidence. Just a young man standing at a cross-roads between where he'd come from and where he might go.

I realized, I'd never heard of Johnny O'Reilly until he was with Break-neck, and I didn't meet him in person until a couple of years after the band was formed.

I never really knew who he was before.

I saved the photo, knowing there was magic in it. I even inserted it into my *Reinventing Johnny* document, where I'd been taking notes and saving links, as inspiration. And a reminder to myself, maybe, of that guy he once was, the guy who set out to be a rock star.

A guy I'd never met.

# Chapter Eleven

**Angeline**

Mid-afternoon, Johnny finally sent me a text asking me to come over to his house.

I left the laptop behind so I could give my client my full attention, bringing along my phone just in case I needed to write anything down. Step Two in my client intake process: meet with the client.

When I tapped on the glass doors off his deck, he answered the door in shorts and a tank top, sweat gleaming on his sculpted arms and shoulders.

Great. Fantastic. Not attractive at all.

I hugged Shayla's sweater around myself.

"Cold?" He eyed me strangely as I stepped inside.

"Oh, you know. Air conditioning." God, he smelled incredible. Like sweaty man, but in the best way. "Working out?"

"Air conditioning's not on." He slid the glass door shut behind me. "And I was shooting hoops with Lamar."

"Right. I'm just…" *Weird. He's staring at you right now because you're being weird.* "I had a chill earlier." I cleared my throat and wandered toward his kitchen trying to get his smell out of my nostrils.

"Are you getting sick or something?"

"No. Don't worry."

"Okay… Well, I thought we could just squeeze this in. I don't have much time."

I turned to look at him. Standing there in his sweaty athletic clothes, like he had zero interest in a conversation about his career or his public image right now, even to bother to get properly dressed.

"Is this a bad time?" I asked, confused. "You asked me to come over." *And now you're acting like you don't want either of us to be here.* "I'm not sick, really."

"Uh, look. I don't want to be a dick or anything," he said, basically telling me he was about to be a dick. "But apparently, I hired you to be my publicist last night?"

"Why are you asking me, like that's a question?"

"Because I don't exactly remember doing it."

I stared at him. What the fuck?

"Shane told me this morning," he explained. "I remember talking to you about Danielle Duke and stuff, but…"

"Are you fucking *kidding* me?"

"Not kidding. Drinking. A lot. But since, as Shane explained it, I really talked you into it…" He looked dubious about that—like *I'd* convinced *him* to hire me, and his own friend was lying to him about it? "I'm willing to give you a chance."

"Oh. Well, lucky me," I said, with exaggerated glee.

"Yeah, well. I need to shower, then I have plans. So…" *So… don't waste my time.* I could hear the unspoken end of that sentence.

"Plans," I echoed evenly.

"Yup."

I really hoped his "plans" didn't involve another high-profile mean girl. But maybe I'd slip that in later. We were not starting off on the best foot. He'd just told me, basically, that this meeting was unimportant to him. However, I knew that saving his career was important to him. Therefore, translation: *I don't believe you can actually do anything of value for me.*

"I won't waste your time," I promised him.

"Good."

He headed into the kitchen, around the big island, and I pulled a stool up to it. While he wasn't looking, I quickly peeled off Shayla's sweater. It really was too warm for it. When he glanced over at me, his eyes went straight to my chest.

Damn, maybe this bra did make the girls look nice.

"You want a drink?"

"Uh…" Shit. *Think.*

Ordinarily, I'd go with the vibe the client set for a meeting, assuming it was appropriate. A drink in the afternoon while meeting with a rock star seemed appropriate. Doing it while alone with him in his house, when his band had just imploded over a sex-related scandal, not so much.

Also, my meeting with Danielle Duke was still scorched painfully into my squishy red matter. It hurt me when she said all those things about me. I did not need to blur the line between professional and personal here. I did not need to do anything that could be viewed as inappropriate by my client. A man who had, apparently, monopolized my attention at a public event during said sex scandal, presumably to make his date jealous, or because he was just fucking bored?

Who even knew what the man considered appropriate.

I swallowed.

Johnny was looking at me expectantly; the open fridge was probably freezing his balls.

"Uh… no. Thanks. Sparkling water?"

He pulled two bottles out of the fridge, strolled over to the island and slid one across to me. "Glass? Ice?"

I cracked the bottle open. Some fancy brand with a gold label, probably owned by a rapper. "No, thanks."

"Lime wedge? Anything?"

"No. Thank you."

He leaned on one hip against the island, looking at me, like he had no idea what to do about me. He seemed out of sorts somehow. Because I didn't want anything?

"You don't need to do anything for me," I told him.

"I'm not used to a woman being in my house and not expecting anything," he said bluntly. As if that had anything to do with me.

"Like… what? And don't say sex things. I get it."

A dismissive look flashed over his face like, *Yeah, I wasn't gonna go there.* "Like anything. Drinks. Coke. Pool. The steam room—"

"You have cocaine?" I glanced around, suddenly looking for white powder trails and mirrored trays. I didn't see any.

"I'm not a D-Boy, Angeline. I have friends."

Right. Friends who brought the coke over at a moment's notice if his mean girl du jour requested it.

"That's good to hear. And I said no sex things, remember?"

He sipped his drink, his eyes staying on me. "Using a steam room can be non-sexual."

"I'm sure. Let's talk about your career."

"Let's."

"Oh, and by the way. You're not going to like this conversation. So you might want to prepare yourself for that, because we are having it."

"What makes you think I won't like it?"

"I read many articles online where you're quoted expressing distaste for a lot of things the media says about you."

"So? You're not the media."

"But I will be speaking to them for you. And putting things out there for them to publicize. About you."

"Things I expect you to handle appropriately."

"Of course. That's the whole point. So. Why don't we start with Breakneck? No one seems to know where the band is at, publicly, so that's good. For now. But rumors will fly, bad and wrong information may spread at any time, with the speed and adaptability of a super virus, as you know. And other people may start talking to the press about it first. Nothing we can do about that. But we can control your version of events. Only you speak for Johnny O. And, well, me. So what are we saying?"

"Nothing, yet."

"Oh."

"We're in negotiations. Through our lawyers," he added with distaste.

"Okay. To what end?"

"The goal is to come to an amicable arrangement without anyone suing anyone else. That's what I'm told."

"But once you get lawyers involved…"

"I'd rather not get lawyers involved, but as of this morning, JC has started threatening to take the band. Take the name. Take everything. Yash said it was best to start talking through the lawyers."

I made a mental note to talk to Yash, if appropriate. But first we needed to wade through some muddy ground.

"Okay. So for now, no comment on the band situation, specifically."

"Right. Anything about Breakneck needs to stay quiet. Until we're clear to talk about it."

"No problem. We can keep our narrative about you, how excited you are about upcoming projects. You are excited, right?"

"Sure, if I had something to be excited about. Feels like the rug got pulled on that. Now that I have no band."

"But that's just a temporary situation, right?"

"Right."

"Is there anything else you think I should know? About your future career, your ambitions, goals?"

"I can't really see past this fucking mess right now. So right now it's about trying to recover from the bad press while we get this shit sorted with Breakneck, so me and Noah can carry on."

"So Noah's still with you?"

"So he says."

"Are you worried he might leave, too?"

He hesitated. It was the first time since we started talking that he didn't have a quick answer at the ready. "No. I know Noah's in this like I am. For life."

"That's good. We can talk about that, publicly, when the time comes. It could really help. Noah has… how do I put this? A much better reputation than you do, publicly." Okay, so I was going with brutal honesty.

"Wow. Thanks for that."

"You're welcome. And I'm sorry. If you want me to sugarcoat things for you…" I thought about how Danielle always said our job was to sugarcoat our clients' behavior for mass consumption.

I disagreed.

I'd rather find the things in Johnny that didn't need to be sugarcoated, and make them shine. That was my goal. And I only realized it right now, having this conversation. It was already the most serious, in-depth conversation I'd ever had with him. It was one of few one-on-one conversations I'd ever had with him. And he was actually speaking to me like a colleague. And not just because I was working for Danielle Duke.

Had to admit, I was loving it. My adrenaline was pumping.

*Screw you and your shitty world view, Danielle Duke.*

"How about your personal life?" I asked him.

"What about my personal life?"

"Look, Johnny. See this?" I laid my phone on the island between us, screen down. "This is in everyone's pocket. And what do we find on it? Pretty much anything we want to find. I just spent the day researching what is publicly findable about you on the internet. And there was as much about your personal life as there was about your music."

"So? There's nothing I can do about that. That's just how it is when you're in the public eye."

"Yes. And no. Some celebrities are very good at keeping their personal lives out of headlines and off the internet. Celebrities who are way more famous than you. You know how they do that? Great publicists, for one. But mainly, they generally don't do salacious stuff in public for people to talk about."

"If you're talking about the Brianna thing…"

"Yes. Let's talk about this 'Brianna thing.' The media is calling it a love triangle—"

"Because three people were involved, and they're not creative enough to come up with anything else."

"Were? Meaning you're no longer involved?"

"With Brianna? No. With JC? No."

"That's good news. I mean, in regard to Brianna. How long did the affair last?"

"It was hardly an affair. She wasn't his wife. They were seeing each other on and off for a while. Whatever he says about his relationship with Brianna or about me in the media, the fact is he was also seeing other women during that time. Including my sister, as you know."

"Uh-huh. And how long was the affair?" I pressed.

He sighed. "Like, a week."

*Was it worth it?* I really wanted to ask him. Because no way could it be worth it, no matter how pretty she was.

But I didn't ask. I wasn't here to attack him or put him on the defensive. Just morbidly curious, when I really shouldn't be.

"How did you leave your relationship with JC? I mean, personally."

"I don't know. Neutral."

"Neutral? As in…"

"As in our relationship doesn't exist anymore."

"That doesn't sound neutral."

"Call it what you want."

Okay; moving on. "Any other affairs I should know about? Of a recent or highly inflammatory nature?"

He just stared at me. I could tell I was irritating him. Putting him through what he probably felt was an inquisition, in his own kitchen. He hadn't even sat down, just stood across the island from me like he wasn't relaxed enough to sit down.

He was on guard. I couldn't blame him.

I was being rather nosey.

"I'm not your little sister's friend right now, okay?" I told him. "And I'm really not that much younger than you, if it makes you feel better. I'm your publicist. Get used to me asking you questions. I'm not pulling any punches because you're my best friend's brother. You're my client, and you need to know you can trust me with your private business. At least, any of it that I should know. And I'd like to be informed if you're keeping a bunch of rotting skeletons stuffed in the closet that could be unearthed at any moment."

"No skeletons," he said flatly. "Not a serial killer either, just so you know."

"Great. So, no other affairs?"

"Has anyone ever told you that you talk too much?"

"I talk when I have something to say." I took a sip of my water, giving him a moment, but he still didn't answer the question. "Oh, I'm sorry. Do you prefer women who just sit around looking pretty and saying nothing at all?"

"Yeah," he muttered, taking a sip of his water. "Maybe."

"Well, there's a word for that. It's called furniture. I'm a sentient being with a mouth. Get used to it."

His aquamarine gaze went straight to my mouth.

I quickly kept talking. "So, affairs?"

"No."

"Specific people you've perhaps wronged or had major issues with in the past, who may be looking to kick you, publicly, while you're down?"

I half-expected him to say, *Where do I start?*

But instead he just said, "None that I can think of. Why?"

"Helps me to know who and what to look out for. On that note, any long buried arrests, convictions, lawsuits, or secret babies I should know about?"

"And why would you need to know about that?"

"Damage control. These things, celebrity scandals, have a way of blowing up. Escalating. First, a scandal breaks, then another blemish on the celebrity's past comes to light, then another, and before you know it, skeletons pouring out everywhere. Plus, I'm sure Shayla would want to know if she's a secret auntie." I kept a straight face, waiting for his response to that.

He replied with a similarly straight face. "No criminal record and no babies. That I know of."

"Great. Any other dark secrets from your past?"

He looked away so quickly I couldn't even read the expression in his eyes. When he met mine again, his face was carefully blank.

But he didn't answer me.

"What?" I said. "That's the last question. Oh, also, do you have any favorite snacks or drinks or anything? I like to bring clients coffee and feel-good gift baskets when we meet."

He sighed inaudibly. "Dark roast coffee."

"But no dark secrets?"

"No."

"Wonderful. Cream and sugar?"

"Cream, no sugar. And I only drink organic."

"Of course you do. Do you mind if I talk to Yash?"

He took a slow sip of his water, contemplating me—and maybe the pain in his ass I was rapidly becoming. "Go ahead."

"We'd be talking about you. How do you feel about that?"

"What, are you my therapist now?"

"Do you have one?"

"Surely that's personal, Angeline."

*I'll take that as a yes.*

"Your media coverage gets plenty personal. If you have any diagnosed personality disorders or anything, might be nice for me to know, since your public image is now my domain."

"Any 'diagnoses' or whatever I discuss with my therapist is none of your business. Or anyone else's."

"Of course it isn't. But what if it becomes public business? As it does for some celebrities?"

"And how would that happen?"

"Usually, because the celebrity in question overdoses on prescription pills."

He stared at me. I stared back.

"Thanks for the warning," he said, deadpan. "For the record, I don't give a fuck if you and Yash talk about me."

That was a lie, I was pretty sure.

"That's good. Because I'd love to get his perspective on you, on where you've been and where you're headed, career wise. But, for the record, I'm not going to ask Shayla a single thing about you, so you don't need to worry about that."

He frowned a little, like that took him by surprise. "Why wouldn't you?"

"Because that might lead to tension between us, and there's literally a zero—no, a sub-zero-times-infinity chance that I'd ever let the likes of you come between my girl and me."

"Let me guess. That last part was my sister's friend talking, not my publicist."

"Correct. But I will be speaking to Yash as your publicist, and same goes for anyone else I speak to about you publicly, of course."

"You have questions about me that you think I can't answer myself?"

I considered how to put it, then went with honesty. "I'm trying to decide if you're being honest with me or not. And if you're giving me all the information I need to do my job to the best of my ability or not. The only way to know that is with time, and more information sources."

"So basically, you're going to dig around and fact check everything I say?"

"Yes. Pretty much."

"And this is standard when taking on a client?"

"I don't know. Probably not. But you're my first one. And my only one, so far. So, I've got time to burn, shit to prove, and considering my general life situation right now, major motivation to make sure this year is the best year of your entire career."

Okay, that definitely took him by surprise.

"Then we have a common goal," he said after a moment.

"Great." I hopped off the bar stool. "Thank you for the expensive water. I'll start putting together a press release introducing myself to the media as your new publicist and I'll be sure to no-comment on your band situation. You'll have a chance to read it over and approve before it goes out, and we'll discuss the timing of it, of course."

"Of course," he said, though I knew he'd thought of none of this. It wasn't his job to think of this.

"I hope I can take the burden of having to care about any of this off of you. So you can focus on what you do best."

"Which is?"

I shrugged. "Playing that rock 'n' roll the way the girls like it."

"You know," he said dryly, "sometimes the guys like it, too."

I looked him over briefly in his tank top and shorts, all lean muscles and tattoos and sex appeal. "Sure they do." I turned on my heel and headed for the glass doors to the deck, before my eyes got any ideas about checking him out any more.

"You have a lot of confidence," he said behind me.

I paused. "I don't have a lot of confidence, actually. But I am confident about you." That was true. "And in case no one's ever told you…" I turned, jolting a little when I found him directly behind me. "Uh, sex appeal sells." I eased back as he reached to open the door for me. I watched his beautiful arm flex as he slid it open.

Then our eyes crashed together. "Does it?"

I frowned. "You know it does. And so does a beautiful face and a six pack. And I will shamelessly play the beauty card if it gets you positive attention. No one can credibly attack your musical skills. You have talent. So, there's absolutely no shame in letting the world enjoy your pretty face, too. No one can call Johnny O a pretty boy or a talentless mimbo with any authority."

"Mimbo," he repeated.

"It's a male bimbo."

"Yeah, I get it."

"Point being, keep doing those workouts." I patted his abs, which flexed under my hand. "The cameras will be coming for you, I guarantee it. But you might want to think about purging all the mean girls from your social calendar." There; slipped it right in and turned to dodge out the door before he could—

"Mean girls?"

I stopped in my tracks. *Damn*; not fast enough.

"Yeah. You know. Brianna types." I forced myself to meet his eyes again. "It would help me do my job, like a thousand percent, if you took care to only show up in public with lovely, classy women with either non-existent or pristine public profiles, from now on. Oh, and who are not dating any of your bandmates."

His jaw clenched.

"You get the picture. Now, I really have to go pick up all my worldly belongings from my ex's apartment. Before he decides to, I don't know, burn it all or something." I patted his six pack again, because I had absolutely no reason to, then awkwardly jetted out of there.

# Chapter Twelve

**Angeline**

My worldly belongings, which Courteney and her husband's bodyguard helped me pick up from Flynn's place while he wasn't there—his choice—sat in boxes for all of the next day and the next as I worked on my laptop around Shayla's house and on her back deck while listening to Breakneck songs.

I was getting more acquainted with Breakneck's music, memorizing the albums and the song names, who wrote which songs, and learning the lyrics. I wanted to know my client and his body of work as well as any fan. As of the official press release I'd be putting out soon, I was Johnny's publicist. Which meant that anyone, at any time, might ask me something about him, and I did not want to be caught without an answer. Or at least an understanding of what they were referring to.

I had a video call with Yash, who seemed cautiously optimistic about having me onboard. My last name—Elle's last name—seemed to have currency with him, as it did for most people I'd met in the music industry.

Mostly, I fussed over the press release, trying to paint my client in the best light possible. He was a passionate, talented rock star with legions of fans, and he couldn't wait to put out his next album. That part was true enough. We'd address what was going on behind the scenes in more detail as it became appropriate to do so.

But without some kind of splashy hook, big news or an event to go with the release, I knew it wouldn't get any play. I was hoping we could figure out what our hook might be, but since we couldn't yet talk about Johnny's band situation, that made it extra challenging.

On Thursday evening, when I was tired of staring at my laptop screen, tweaking words, and Shayla had gone out with some dancer friends, I finally faced the pile of boxes looming in my new bedroom. I put my hair up in a ponytail and dove in, unpacking my things. With every item I unpacked, it felt like I was letting go of my life with Flynn just a little more. Cosmetics, clothes, jewelry. Some books, travel keepsakes; I still had some things in storage at my mom and dad's house, but pretty much everything I owned was in these boxes.

Once I'd unpacked enough of my own clothes to pull a comfy outfit together—soft, marshmallow-pink cutoff sweats and a cropped shirt with a unicorn on it, because I unabashedly loved me some pastels and a unicorn—I changed into them, relieved to be back in my own clothes. I put the clothes Shayla had generously loaned to me in the laundry. Then I filled my new closet and dresser, turning Shayla's guest room into my own, neatly hanging my clothes and organizing my things. When Shayla's clothes were clean, I folded them and left them on her bed for her.

When I drifted into the kitchen for a glass of water, tapped out and ready to sleep, I saw Johnny out by his pool. He was lying on a lounge chair—wearing some very small swim trunks, from what I could tell.

I stared.

He was looking down at his phone, the dusk sky above him all these amazing aqua/pink hues toward the west. The soft lights around the edges of the deck glowed, and with Johnny center stage, practically naked, it looked like a photo spread.

We'd definitely need to do a fresh photo shoot for his press kit at some point. No one could deny Johnny O's sex appeal. Any way you wanted to look at it, his physical attractiveness, his magnetism, were a core part of his story.

I just had to make sure that was a good thing, not a negative.

As I watched, the glow of the phone in his hand lit up his face. So like that night… his face lit up by the flame of his lighter. I could remember that moment, so sharply. His eyes meeting mine. Whatever the hell was in his eyes in that moment, though… that *torment*… I never saw it again.

Johnny could be arrogant and cold, but there was something more going on with him. I'd been on the periphery of his life for long enough to know: he wasn't that simple. He didn't show his feelings much, but that didn't mean he didn't have them.

I knew I could make people love him.

I knew there had to be something to love.

Not just his music. Not just his looks. His peers knew about those things and still had issues with him. There was something else. Other things, inside of him, that he kept hidden. Carefully guarded.

Walled up.

I was sure of it.

There was way more to Johnny O'Reilly than met the eye.

Maybe I'd always suspected that.

Maybe that was why I'd crushed on him so hard.

Maybe that was why, when he kissed me that night, I turned and ran the other way. Straight into my boyfriend's arms. And never allowed myself to look back.

After watching him for a long moment, I went back up to my room.

There was one final box sitting beside the closet, and I picked it up and put it on the bed, opening the flaps and forcing myself to look inside. It was all the stuff from the drawers of my bedside table.

Little notes from Flynn, things he'd left on the fridge for me. *Have a good day.* Simple stuff like that; the man was never flowery with his words.

My sexy lingerie, which I did not see myself wearing for anyone anytime soon. I dug gently through it, lifting out each piece and laying them in a dresser drawer. *Here's hoping.*

In the bottom of the box, I found my collection of sex toys. I dug idly through those, too, wondering if I should pull any out. They all seemed tainted with bad memories now. I cringed when I saw the big purple dildo, remembering how I'd told Flynn when we moved in together that I'd named it Dylan.

Major mistake. What made me think a guy would ever want to hear that?

*He asked!* Mean Me whispered.

I lifted the purple dildo out of the box. "Welp. Goodbye, dear Dylan. We had some good times, didn't we?" Then I tossed him—it—out. It made a sad, dejected thud in the bathroom wastebasket.

In the end, I upended the whole box over the wastebasket. I threw them all out, feeling bad about how my desire for something Flynn didn't give me made him feel bad.

---

"Why did you and the bodyguard break up?"

I was sitting at Johnny's kitchen island again, while he made a stir fry, because apparently he couldn't just sit down while we had a meeting. I had no idea he could cook, but then again I'd never really been over to his house much; at least not while he was here.

I looked up from my laptop, where I was making notes while I went over the press release with him. He was tossing things in his wok—looked and smelled pretty good—while the wok hissed, steam plumed in the air and the hood fan hummed.

But that question was not on the agenda.

"Are you even listening to me?"

"Yup."

"Then why did you just interrupt me with a personal question? Which is, by the way, not your business."

"You asked all about my personal business."

"I asked about things that could cause problems with your public image. Because it affects how I do my job."

"Uh-huh. Well, your personal problems could become part of my public image, like everything else in my life. I should know the story there too."

Hmm. Arguably a valid point. By a stretch.

"I do not have 'problems.'" I did, but so what? "My personal life is not my clients' business."

He tossed me a glance. "Even if it's scandalous?"

"There is no scandal in my life. Unless any paparazzi were stalking me at the mall today. 'Sister of rock star Elle Delacroix buys a vibrator.' Major headlines."

I looked up again as the wok sizzled angrily. Johnny, who was staring at me, righted it just before it upended and all the vegetables slid off.

"Did you just almost drop your dinner because I said vibrator?"

"I thought your personal life was none of my business."

"It was a joke."

"So you did buy a vibrator, or you didn't?"

"Really not answering that." I fixed a typo on my document. "Yes, I bought a vibrator. Why is this newsworthy? No one saw me."

"I didn't say it was newsworthy."

"Now you're just creeping."

He laughed shortly. "You offered up the information. I'm not supposed to get a mental image?"

"Of me taking a vibe to the cashier and pulling out my sad, low-limit credit card?"

"Yeah. That's exactly what a guy pictures when you say you bought a vibrator." He eyed me briefly. "How naïve are you?"

"I was kidding and trying to deflect to a more savory conversation topic."

"I can't have a publicist that naïve working for me."

"I am not naïve. Can we focus here? Maybe if you actually listened to what I had to say, you'd realize that I actually know what I'm talking about." Yeah, my assertiveness on this was growing exponentially, like every time this guy made me push to prove why I should be doing this job for him.

He was a real jerk that way.

However, it was really spurring my conviction that I could do this.

At least, it was until my realization this afternoon…

"So, talk," he said.

"As I was saying. I've got this all written up and ready to go, more or less. But we still don't have anything newsworthy to put in it. There's no story here. I made a freaking spreadsheet to brainstorm ideas. I talked to Yash. But…"

"But?"

*Alrighty, here comes the hard part.*

*Just say it.*

I took a breath and admitted, "I've realized… that I'm not really sure you actually need a publicist right now."

There. Said it.

He gave me a look. "What, are you trying to fire yourself now?"

"Kind of?"

He scowled, like I made no sense. "Why?"

"Because the more I go over it… Yes, there's this scandal in the media. There's Brianna's side of it. And maybe soon we'll hear JC's. You can put yours out there, too. But honestly… it's not your public or media persona that matters here, ultimately. It's not the public that has an issue with you."

He was listening, so that was something. Even if I'd just sort of fired myself.

"Keep talking," he ordered.

"Okay. Your PR, in this case, really needs to start, and maybe even end, at home. Literally here in Vancouver. We're not having this conversation right now because you're struggling to sell records, or because listeners don't like you or your music and you're trying to get more positive album reviews and interviews in magazines. We're talking because your colleagues are jumping ship right now and that's a problem for you, right? It's your colleagues you need to concern yourself with. If you can get your next album out there, the fans will buy it."

"If?"

"When. When you get your next album out there. But right now, you're getting doors slammed in your face at the industry level, right here, among your peers."

"So, maybe I go back to Toronto. I've recorded there before. Or L.A.. Or somewhere else. I can pull together the band anywhere and record."

"First of all, your problems go where you go." *I would know.* "These problems will follow you until you address them. You think Cary Clarke and JC, and whoever else doesn't want to work with you tomorrow, doesn't have reach beyond Vancouver? And second… you really want to leave your home, what you've built here, Shayla, everything… because of other people's opinions of you?"

Okay, that got to him. I could see it. The gears were turning in his head.

"This is your home, Johnny. You've put a lot of money and work into building this, for you and your sister, and for your future. Vancouver real estate is a smart investment. Owning two homes where you can live with your sister, build family and community, is smart. Lean into that. What's not smart is running away."

He pushed stir fry onto a plate and put it in front of me. "Who says I'm running?"

"Everyone in the industry, if you leave Vancouver now in the midst of this mounting shitstorm."

He handed me a fork.

"Thank you."

"You're welcome." He made himself a plate, sat down across the island from me and started eating.

"You want to make a big deal, publicly, out of Cary Clarke pulling out of your project?" I went on. "You leave town, you just made it into a headline. Right now, it's pretty buried. Producers change projects all the time. It's mildly interesting music news, but it's inconclusive of anything. You leave town and suddenly people start connecting dots. And who comes out looking good in that story? Cary. The producer who jumped ship because of your 'love triangle' scandal and your playboy reputation. He's a family man. And he's a fellow rock star. One who overcame a huge loss, publicly, to be where he is. He's a hero, Johnny, in the public eye and among his peers. Your peers. Which, I'm sorry to inform you, makes you the villain."

He took that in.

I tasted my stir fry. "This is freaking delicious."

"I'm the villain," he said, as maybe it sank in.

"In this story right now, yes. Which is why we need to change the story. For you, like I said, that needs to happen at home. Right at the root of the problem."

"How?"

"Well…"

Now, that was the hard part. And one I didn't exactly have an answer for.

If I knew how to change people's personal opinions of others, I'd make it so people stopped seeing me as a cartoon kitten lapping ice cream or whatever, and took me more seriously.

I didn't say that, though. I'd already potentially fired myself here. I didn't need to make it any worse.

"People in the industry know anything in the media can be bullshit anyway," I said, thinking it through. "And a lot of them know you. At least, you up until now. And you can't change yesterday. So, it's how they perceive you in real life, from here on in, that matters. Personal interactions. Working relationships. You can't necessarily change how someone feels about you, thinks about you, or behaves toward you. But you can change how you relate to people, maybe, and that will have an effect, over time."

"I'm not changing who I am just to please other people, Angeline."

"I wouldn't ask you to. It's not about changing who you are. I know you're a decent person, Johnny. How close am I with Shayla? *Close.* I know the good, the bad and the ugly about you. At least, from Shayla's point of view."

He frowned.

"And believe me, there is a whole lot of good." Yup; totally turned that around on him. "Don't look so surprised. She loves you. A lot. Shayla likes the good life, as you know…"

He sort of snorted an agreement.

"But she wouldn't be caught dead living with you, like this, if she didn't adore you. She has… men… she could live with."

He stopped eating. "Come again?"

"Not something you want to hear, I'm sure. But she has options, that's all I'm gonna say."

He considered that. "What about JC?"

"You never asked her?"

"We don't talk about that kind of thing. We just… argue."

Yeah. I could attest to that. "She's not that into JC anymore. Ever since Brianna."

"Oh."

"Anyway…" I said tentatively. "As I said, you don't need to change who you are. But if you actually want me to keep working with you…"

"I do," he said, with conviction, before I could go on.

"But I thought—"

"Stop talking, okay? You just said a whole lot of useful, thoughtful shit, Angeline. Don't ruin it. You have a good perspective on this. I have no idea if you can help me with any of this, but I'll take what I can get. You put out whatever press release you think is necessary, whenever. You coordinate with Yash. And I'll do whatever else you guys think I should do. Meanwhile, I need to keep working on music. I've got songs to write. I lost half my band. I also lost half of the new songs, the ones JC wrote. And potentially all of them. I want to be ready when this shit all gets sorted out."

"Right. Of course. Well… I'd suggest, then, that you get writing, and you let me find opportunities for you to work on your interactions with your peers. Win them over. In other words, let me handle your social calendar." He'd resumed eating, but his eyes clashed with mine. "You know, while coordinating with Yash."

"You're talking again."

"I know you have a lot of work to do." I kept talking. "Music to make. But we should be getting you out to every event we can. From red carpet events like the Champagne opening this weekend to house parties, where you can mingle with the right people, make an impression. The *right* impression. And start making up for lost time." *Or, ruined time.*

Johnny studied me. "Is that the advice you'd give Elle if she was facing a career crisis?"

"I'm not my sister's publicist. If you've hired me just so you can get intel on my sister's career, you've come to the wrong place."

"If you're here to party with me," he countered, "you've come to the wrong place. I'm not looking for a party planner." His eyes moved over me. Some guys just had a talent for stripping you naked with their eyes, and Johnny had that talent, in spades. It actually made me squirm. "Or a date," he grunted.

"Oh my God. Please." I shut my laptop and put my fork down, suddenly losing my appetite. Heat was flushing through me, and I told myself it was anger. "I am not here to date you."

"Then who's going to these parties with me?"

What the hell…?

Did he really think my desire to schedule up his social calendar was part of some ploy to trick him into being my boyfriend?

Jeez. The ego on this guy.

*Your client. Be polite.*

*But not too polite.*

"Whoever you want to go to these parties with you," I answered him carefully. "And I recommend someone who's actually single."

He gave me an unamused look. "Tread carefully, Angeline. I didn't hire you to be my good conscience."

*Do you have one?* I wanted to ask, but I bit my tongue.

*You wanted him to give you a chance. He's giving you a chance. Suck it up.*

"Look, if you want to talk about Elle," I said, "I can tell you, she got her start by getting out there. Brody was relentless too, getting Zane and Jesse out to every party and show they could in the early days. Before they even had a solid band. Before they found Elle and Dylan and formed Dirty. That was *how* they found Elle and Dylan."

"So?"

"So, the way I see it, this is a rebirth, Johnny O. You need to start over. At least in terms of how you relate to your peers."

"I am never apologizing to JC. In case that's where you're going with this."

I could see it in his eyes. He meant that.

"Whatever has gone down between you and JC," I told him, "is water under the bridge. And I'm sure that's a two-way river. But it's done. Let it go and move on. Some people aren't meant to stay friends, and that's okay. Just don't let it eat you."

"Who says it's eating me?"

I didn't answer that. I could tell it was eating him. I could feel it.

It was the way he tensed up whenever JC's name came up.

He was staring at me, and I tried to finish my stir fry. It really was good. "You never answered the question," he said.

"What question?"

"Why did you and the bodyguard break up?"

I sighed quietly. "He has a name. It's Flynn. You can start using it."

"Okay. Why did you and Flynn—"

"Actually, don't. Let's not talk about him."

"Why? You've got something to hide?"

I eyed him. Why was he being so nosey about this?

As if he even cared about my breakup?

"Flynn and I broke up," I told him evenly, "because he told me he doesn't want to have kids."

He said nothing to that. He didn't ask any more questions.

I wanted to extend trust, to earn trust. But of course, that answer was not the full truth. And in omitting the truth, I realized I wasn't comfortable enough with Johnny to be honest enough to earn his trust anyway. Not on a personal level.

If I was honest with him, he'd know too much.

It would serve neither of us for him to know why Flynn really broke up with me. Or for him to know how much I'd crushed on him when I was young and stupid.

*It wasn't that long ago,* Mean Angie reminded me.

I told her to shut up.

# Chapter Thirteen

**Angeline**

That evening, I ended up at the mall for the second time in one day. With Courteney.

Because along with realizing that I was not comfortable enough with Johnny to be honest with him, personally, I'd also realized that tossing away my entire collection of personal pleasure devices, if I was going to be meeting with him on any kind of regular basis, was a giant mistake.

Courteney followed me through the small adult store with the blacked-out front window, looking at the items on display with mild curiosity. And mild confusion. We were in the same adult store I'd already bought a new vibe at today. Clearly, I had a problem.

"Does this really feel good?" Courteney asked me, picking up a small, smooth vibe shaped like a computer mouse.

"Never know 'til you try it." I tossed one in my basket.

"I guess I'd have to try it," she said distractedly, but she wandered onward. "Is that your new life motto or something?" She smirked a little. "'Never know 'til you try it'?"

"In the bedroom, mostly. And for your information, it's not new."

"Oh." She looked intrigued. "Really?"

"I told Flynn I'd try anything once. I meant it."

"Ohh." I could see Courteney's imagination working overtime on that one. "Wow. Lucky guy."

"He didn't seem to think so."

She followed me in silence to the next display. "So, you guys really weren't very compatible that way, huh?"

"Nope." I dropped a cock ring in my basket. No idea why, since I didn't have a cock to put it on. But it was on sale.

Besides, Flynn never would've put a cock ring on for me. For some reason, that was annoying me right now.

I really should've taken my own advice: *It's water under the bridge. Just let it go.*

I sighed. "Okay, can I just say it? Flynn and I were not compatible lovers. We weren't. And I tried to sugarcoat that pill to make it go down easier for a long, long time."

Courteney listened, looking like she felt very sorry for me and my sad sex life. Because of course, she and her husband were like feral rabbits. Their sex life was so hot, Courteney blushed when she talked about it.

"The idea that men are always horny," I went on, "always high testosterone, always hard and ready, and always thrilled with a woman who has a super high sex drive, is not true. Not for all men. Clearly. And the idea that only women use sex as an emotional weapon? Also bullshit. Believe me."

"He really, uh, did a number on you about that, huh?"

"Yeah. He did. I let him." I turned to her. "Look, Flynn is an amazing guy. You know I don't want to trash talk him. He's got a good heart. And he's going to make some woman really happy. He's a super solid, steadfast type, and someone will adore him for it. He's just not… my type."

"I know," she said sadly. She'd heard it all before. I really didn't need to explain it all to her. But sometimes, I did need to vent.

"But I'm done now," I went on. "We're done. And I need to find Angie again." I looked at some fuzzy handcuffs, then moved on. Really, who was gonna lock me up in them? "Ugh. This is weirdly depressing." I tossed the cock ring back on a shelf. "What am I even doing?"

"You're shopping," she said firmly, putting the cock ring back in my basket. "And you're having fun. With your B.O.B.."

She meant Bestie of Besties. That was what Courteney called us; I was her Bestie of Besties, she was mine.

"You realize BOB stands for battery operated boyfriend, right?"

She frowned. "Oh. Right."

I laughed a little.

I felt bad, actually, when I thought about how much we'd kind of drifted apart from one another. Not on purpose, but when she'd gotten so tight with Xander, and they got married, and they were so often away on tour… I'd toured with them, with Flynn and my sister, sometimes. Dirty and the Players toured together a lot. But when I was home, maybe it was natural that I'd gravitated toward Shayla, my single bestie—instead of my blissfully married one. The one who was always up for a party, always game to distract me from my problems.

Until those problems became so insurmountable that they could no longer be ignored.

I watched Court perusing the shelves, trying so hard to be my winglady on this when she had no need to be here, and it made me all warm. She really was my first-ever Bestie of Besties.

She caught me watching her. "Come on. Keep having fun." She hooked her arm through mine to urge me along.

I pulled her toward the back of the store, where the really good stuff was, eying my pretty best friend sidelong, with all her luscious blond hair and the generous boobs. I had no idea she was not that well versed in sex toys. Courteney was six years younger than me, but her husband was a fuck-hot drummer. She wasn't innocent. "Courteney Clarke. Have you never used a vibrator?"

"I've never used any of these things." She looked around us at the graphic items on the shelves. "I mean, you know Xander's my only sexual partner, ever." She glanced at a giant dildo on display. "I did try a dildo once…"

"And?"

"It felt weird. Rubbery. Not like skin."

"What about skin with a condom over it? You get used to that."

"Xander and I don't use condoms anymore."

"Maybe you could experiment. Try a few things, see what you like."

"I just don't think I'm that into them." She shrugged, disinterested. "Xander is like a whole toy shop."

I sighed, slightly exasperated. "Well, gee, we don't all have a real life, man sized, rock-star-sex-god to fuck with anytime we feel like it. Some of us have intense sexual desire and want to get pounded on the daily but we don't because we're single. So excuse us while we try to satisfy ourselves with well-designed toys."

Courteney's hazel eyes widened. "Uh… sorry."

"*Shit.* I know. I just overreacted." I blew out a breath. "I'm a little tense."

"Flynn?" she asked gently.

"No. Not exactly. Just… everything."

"It's a lot of change in a short time," she said sympathetically. "You've never really been on your own before. Trying to keep a roof over your head and start up your career… it's hard. There's a lot at stake and it's not easy, even if you're you."

I gave her a questioning look. "Me?"

"You know. *Us.* The Lil Brats. Kid sisters of rock stars." She tossed her arm around me. "You have more doors open for you, sure. You have a leg up on getting started with your life, more so than the average girl. Maybe. But… you also have crushing expectations on your shoulders, right out of the gate. You'll never not be Elle's little sister, before you even walk in a room. You know I know what that's like."

"Your brother *is* amazing…"

"I know. That's what I mean. It took a long time to fight my way out of that shadow."

"And now look at you. Bestselling author."

She swiped that away, looking embarrassed, like she did whenever that particular accolade came up. "Only because I wrote a book about a famous person. Who I only knew because of my brother."

I stopped dead and looked her in the eye. "You wrote a fabulous book, Courteney. It was a beautiful story, about a beautiful person, very well told."

"Thank you," she said quietly. Her eyes shone a little, like they usually did whenever Gabe, the subject of her book, came up in conversation.

"You're welcome." I gave her a hug.

Then I continued browsing and she followed, and I could feel her watching me. "What about Johnny?" she asked me. "Is he any of the reason for your… tension?"

I glanced at her and she raised an eyebrow. As my OG Bestie of Besties, Courteney was the only person who knew the full extent of my secret longings for Johnny.

*In the past*, I reminded myself.

"You mean, my client?"

"Right. You were crushing on him for ages. That whole 'I hate him but I want to lick him all over' thing you had going on…"

"It's called a hate crush, and it's long dead."

"Is it? I mean… is there any desire there these days, at all? Of the licking variety?"

I looked her in the eye, and I couldn't lie. "Okay, tons." She frowned. "But that doesn't mean I have to act on it."

"Right." She hesitated. "I am sorry that Cary pulled out of his project." She sighed softly. "I feel torn about it. I mean, he's Shayla's brother, and now he's your client… I'm sure once this whole mess settles and Johnny works things out with his band, my brother would consider working with him again someday. I mean, don't tell Johnny I said that. I don't want to speak for Cary or get involved."

"I won't. Believe me. We are not getting in the middle of some male pissing match, or whatever it is."

"Yeah. Just… be careful with him, okay?" Courteney's pretty eyes filled with worry, for me. "I know what Shayla says about him and that he's not terrible. Xander likes him okay. But… I know what everyone else says about him, too."

"Don't worry. Really. I know who I'm dealing with."

"Good. And hey, if you ever forget, Shay will be happy to remind you."

I groaned. "I know." As much as Shayla loved her brother, she knew he was not a happily-ever-after type of guy. And I was a seeking-happily-ever-after type of girl. Bottom line, she did not want to see my heart smashed again.

I would not be smashed.

I would not get derailed in my mission to land on my feet. And that was what Johnny would be to me if I kept touching his abs: a massive derailment.

*You really need to stop touching his abs.*

I did it again, today, as I was leaving his place. Like a horny sex maniac. This time, I made it seem like an accident as we both reached for the door at the same time.

It wasn't an accident.

*Because you are a sex maniac.*

On that note, I probably needed to make things crystal clear with him. And with myself. The conversation today probed around it a bit. But I needed him to know, I wasn't crushing on him. I wasn't hooking up with him.

There would be no getting personally involved. Naked or otherwise.

I picked up a wicked looking black thing from the shelf. *The Avenging Angel.* Huh; dark. It had a phallic end and then two horned prongs that were obviously for the clit.

"Yup," I muttered, "you sure look like a Johnny."

I glanced at Courteney, remembering she could hear me. She tried really hard not to make a grossed out face, but I knew her too well.

"Hmm. Or maybe I'll call it Xander…"

She laughed. "Oh my God! Do not!"

I grinned and stashed the Avenging Angel in my basket.

"Holy shit. Johnny's expensive." Courteney showed me the price tag. "Can you afford such an expensive Battery Operated Boyfriend? I'm sure there's a BOB in the clearance bin that can show you a good time."

I snickered. "Well, I'm trying to be confident here. If I can prove my worth to Johnny, maybe he'll keep me on longterm."

Courteney eyed me. "I ask you this with love. Do you think you're going to last a month as his publicist if you start pleasuring yourself with a sex toy you named after him?"

I placed my basket on the counter, smiling at the cashier. "Girl's gotta blow off steam somehow."

"Hmm. All that steam," Court mused. "Do you think he's feeling the heat?"

"I doubt it. Wherever he goes, that man is fire." I sighed. "I probably don't even rate as a wisp of smoke on his radar."

# Chapter Fourteen

**Johnny**

I rang my sister's doorbell. I was dressed sharp, in black trousers and a white-on-black paisley print shirt, no tie. The shirt was unbuttoned halfway, the sleeves rolled up to show off my neck, chest and arm tats.

It was nine o'clock, the night of Champagne nightclub's grand pre-opening VIP-only party. The limo was already waiting in the driveway. And I wondered idly what I was in for getting Shayla, Angeline and my date, Maxine, all in one car.

Drama, no doubt.

My sister never got along with the women I dated, for one. And throwing Angeline into the mix was a giant question mark. I had no idea what she'd make of Maxine or if she'd approve of her for my "rebirth." I could easily picture my sister getting scrappy, though, and Angeline trying to mediate.

Women fighting over me was hardly a new scene, but it wasn't one I particularly enjoyed, even when it was mildly entertaining for the ego.

When the giant smoked-glass slab of a front door—which I'd forked over an uncomfortable amount of money for because Shayla loved it—swept open, Angeline appeared. In a sleek black long-sleeved mini dress, black pantyhose and black sneakers. I had no idea pantyhose and sneakers were a thing, but she made it work. Her hair was slicked back in a ponytail, and her smoky, jagged eye makeup and glossy red lips had a vaguely eighties vibe.

The sneakers made sense for her, but the rest of it reeked of my sister's influence. Last fucking thing I needed: my sister's attitude rubbing off on my new publicist.

I looked her outfit over, slowly. "No kittens, sparkles, or faces of ex-boyfriends?"

"Shayla!" she called over her shoulder. "Your asshat brother is here!"

"Your client is here," I corrected her.

"My mistake." She faked a smile, stepping back with an impressed gasp, like she'd just noticed me standing here. "Johnny! You look dashing."

My eyes drifted over her tits for the third time. The dress was a slinky, tight-fitting knit and moved alluringly with her body. The sheen of her silky bra was visible through the knit at certain angles. "You look like one of those hot chicks pretending to play instruments in that Robert Palmer video."

She scowled. "That's how you talk to your publicist?"

"I'm confused on the etiquette. Who are we to each other tonight?" I stepped past her, into the foyer.

"And who's Robert Palmer?"

"How old are you?"

I could feel her bristling as she shut the door behind me. "Two years younger than you. Don't get imperious."

"And yet, so young."

"What does that even mean?"

"Also, you're closer to three years younger than me."

"Big difference."

"Quick quiz. Who's Gordon Sumner?"

"You mean that famous chef?"

"What's a whammy bar?"

"Who cares."

"What year was *Appetite for Destruction* released?"

"What is that, a bad horror movie?"

"It's the top selling debut album of all time, and you should read more."

"You should get bent. Hi!" She fake-smiled again as my sister came down the stairs.

"Hey!" Shayla greeted us. "You guys look great."

"So do you," I said, my eyes on my new, non-shattered phone. I was reading the text that had just come in from Maxine.

*Can't make it. Have fun.*

It seemed like a brush off.

"*So what* if I don't know everything about the music industry since the beginning of time," Angeline was huffing next to me. "That doesn't mean I can't kick ass as your publicist."

"Shit," I muttered. I sent a quick text to a couple of girls I thought might be game to come to the party tonight, last minute. Ever since that fucking love triangle thing broke in the media, people had been bailing on me left and right. Women included.

"What's wrong?" Shayla asked.

When I looked up, I tried not to react when I actually saw what my sister was wearing. Which was a few strips of black vinyl with matching boots and not much else. "My date cancelled."

"So? She's a ho."

"Uh-huh. The S&M dungeon called. They want their wardrobe back."

Shayla tossed me a dirty look from where she was bent over her hall table, applying a thick veneer of lipgloss in the mirror. "She's a cuntwaffle. Just forget her."

"You think every woman I date is a 'cuntwaffle.'" My phone buzzed and I glanced at it.

"Maybe you should stop dating cuntwaffles."

"Guys," Angeline said half-heartedly, like she knew how ineffectual her attempts to get my sister to shut up would be.

I slipped my phone into my pocket. "And what exactly makes a woman a cuntwaffle, in your estimation?"

"Let's see," Shayla said. "She called me Sheila. She expected me to wait on her like I was your freakin' serving staff. And she told me, unsolicited, that I'd really benefit from a nose job."

Oh. "Why the hell didn't you tell me that?"

"As if it would make a diff? You wanted to fuck her. I know how it goes." My sister turned to me. "I can handle that shit. But the last one you brought home, you know, *Brianna*"—she said the name with exaggerated distaste—"was a total bitch to my girl." She looped her arm through Angeline's and Angeline suddenly found the ceiling light fixture incredibly interesting. She wouldn't meet my eyes. But obviously, she'd filled Shayla in on her little run-in with Brianna in my kitchen. "And seriously," Shayla went on, "who fucks a member of their boyfriend's band behind his back? Cunt. Waffle."

"Let's just head out, shall we?" Angeline drew the front door open.

"This wouldn't have anything to do with the fact that you have a thing for JC?"

"*Had.* If you don't know that you can do better than Brianna MacMillan and all that love triangle drama, dear brother, I'm here to tell you. You can do better."

"The limo's waiting," Angeline tried again, gesturing out at the driveway.

"You guys have fun." I headed for the door.

"Aren't you coming with us?" Shayla sighed impatiently and I paused. "I'm sorry I called your date a cuntwaffle, okay?"

"I'm not going without a date," I informed my sister.

She tossed a look at Angeline, like, *See, what'd I tell you about him.*

I hated that look.

I nodded a good night at Angeline as I walked out the door she was still holding open. "Enjoy the limo."

I heard some hushed whispering and then someone following me. "Why?" Angeline's sneakers padded on the stone path behind me as I headed back over to my house. "Why aren't you coming?"

"Because I don't do that."

"Do what?" She followed me, right into my house. "What, exactly, do you not do, Johnny O'Reilly?"

I turned to her. "I don't show up at parties without a date."

"Why not?" She squinted up at me. "I call bullshit."

I rubbed the bridge of my nose. *Here we go.* Nothing was simple with this girl. She just had to keep talking.

And sending fucking gift baskets.

She'd sent me two already; one with gourmet coffee stuff and one loaded with organic energy drinks. With little notes about "staying positive" in the face of adversity, with sparkles on them. The thought of her buying that shit for me on her "low-limit credit card" just pissed me off.

"What's bullshit? I said I'm not going."

"Why are you being difficult? I've seen you show up at parties like a jillion times without a date."

"First, I have no idea how many times is a 'jillion' because it doesn't exist. I hope you plan on being a little more clear when writing press releases. Second, I'm not showing up at a nightclub opening without a hot date. Especially when that nightclub is owned by Dylan Cope, Summer Sorensen, and your sister."

"Because…?"

"I'm not going." I tossed my keys on the hall table for effect.

She stood back a bit, taking me in. "You're jealous."

"Of what?"

"Of their success."

I headed into the kitchen.

She followed me. "Can't you just get a replacement date?"

"No."

She made a skeptical sound. "Because she was *that* special?"

"Because," I said, slipping my phone from my pocket and thumbing through messages, "let's see. Girl one already has plans, girl two said she can't make it for no reason at all, and girl three hasn't replied."

"Maybe if you stopped calling them by numbers and remembered their names."

"I know their names." I stashed my phone in my pocket again. "Didn't think you'd care for the details." I headed for the fridge.

"You won't go to the party because it's a big night celebrating your peers' success, and you feel shitty if you walk in without a flashy date."

That didn't sound like a question so I ignored it, fixing myself a drink while she hovered.

"You feel like it puts you in their shadow and you hate that."

"You done yet?"

"I'm right." She shook her head when I tipped the bottle toward her in offering. "I know I'm right, because I know exactly how you feel."

"Uh-huh." I tossed a lime wedge into my vodka soda and took a sip.

"You can show up alone, you know." She followed me again as I went into the living room. "Come on. You're Johnny O! No one even notices the girl you're with, believe me."

I threw her a look as I flopped onto the sectional. "They noticed Brianna. Or did you not read the headlines?"

"Because she's a semi-famous model *and she was dating your lead singer.*"

I flicked on the TV. It was on mute and I started scrolling through the offerings.

"Johnny." Angeline put her hands on her hips, which was hilarious, because the girl couldn't get stern with a mosquito. "Trust me, okay? When you walk into a room, people see *you*. Period."

"And you know this because…?"

She sighed shortly. "Because I'm often in that room when you walk in."

I kept my eyes fixed on the TV, resisting the urge to gloat that she'd just admitted that she ever noticed me that way. "So? You're a woman."

"So!?"

"Of course you notice me. Not everyone sees what you see, Angeline."

"Wow. You just managed to take arrogant and condescending to a whole new level."

I looked her in the eye. "Tell me how you really know people notice me, and not my date, when I walk into a room."

She sighed again, her hands dropping from her hips. "Because I'm about as invisible next to my sister as those girls are next to you. And about as replaceable."

"That's what you think?"

"That the women you date are replaceable? Uh, yeah." She threw her arms out, indicating my home, where no trace of any of the women I'd dated remained.

"I meant," I said, setting my drink aside, "you really think that you, next to your sister, are replaceable?"

"Uh, let's see. To anyone who notices her first, which is everyone, I might as well not be there. So yes. I could be anyone or no one. No one cares."

I clicked the TV off and got to my feet, walking over to her. "That's what you think?"

"That's what I know."

I stood in front of her, studying her for a moment. "Then why would you want to show up with me?"

"I don't. But since you're my client, I highly recommend that you get over yourself and go to this party with your sister."

"I'm not going alone."

"So you're saying she is invisible, next to you."

"That's not what I said."

"Then go with Shayla!"

"She's my sister. She's not a date."

Angeline groaned, looking exasperated. "Just come with us, Johnny."

"Us?"

Her eyes darted away.

"You're asking me on a date now?"

"*No.*" She seemed to force herself to look at me. Her cheeks looked suddenly flushed. "We can go as friends. That is a thing, you know."

"I didn't know we were friends."

"We're not. But we can make nice in public. It's a skill set you could use some practice with, actually. So, practice taking me, your pretend friend, to a party."

"I don't do that, either."

"What, go with a friend to a party?"

"Go with a female friend to a party."

"For a rock star, you have a lot of rules."

"Yeah, maybe I do."

"Stupid ones."

"That's subjective."

"Well, maybe it's time to break your subjectively stupid rules. What you've been doing hasn't been working so well, remember?"

Yeah. I remembered. "Look, maybe you don't realize this, Angeline. But showing up to this kind of high-profile event with a female friend is lame. It means either you couldn't get a date, or you want to fuck your friend but she's friend-zoned you and you're still hoping there's a chance."

"Really. Those are the only two options?"

"Yes. In summary, it's what losers do."

"Then I guess tonight you're a loser who's going to this party with me. Better than a loser who sits at home watching TV because he's too stubborn to show up at a party where someone might get more attention than him. That doesn't sound like a loser to me. It sounds like a big giant baby. And we are not friends. I'm your publicist. Now put your man pants on and take me to the goddamn party."

Huh. Maybe I was wrong about her. That was fairly stern. "My pants are on."

She'd stalked into the front hall and now picked up my keys, tossing them at me. "Then grab your keys and let's go."

I twirled my finger at the area in front of me, where she'd just reamed me out. "Where'd all that come from?"

She blew out a breath. "Mean Angie. I need to go change my bra, it's digging into me and making me squizzy. Meet us outside in five minutes."

With that, she vanished out the front door.

---

Ten minutes later, we were in the back of the limo. Angeline, me and Lamar. Shayla was up front with the driver. Her choice, but yeah, I'd maybe pointed out to her that he looked amenable to chitchat and she took the bait. He looked pretty but basic, the kind of guy who, when he wasn't driving a limo, would probably be smoking a bong in his parents' basement in between acting auditions that he never got hired for.

In other words, my sister's type.

I wasn't the only one in this family who could probably aim a little higher.

Angeline, staring out the window next to me, hadn't said a word to me.

Lamar was reading a book, some self help thing about a winning mindset or mastering negotiations, which was what he did when I was with a woman and he was pretending he wasn't here.

I'd been staring at my phone, mostly. Girl three had finally gotten back to me. She wasn't single anymore. Or so she said.

Finally, I broke the silence. "What the hell is squizzy?"

"What?" Angeline looked at me, distracted.

"You said your uncomfortable bra was making you 'squizzy.'"

"Oh. It's just a word."

"No, it's not."

She bristled. "Then I guess I made it up."

"You should really stop making up words."

She rolled her eyes.

"Why did you just roll your eyes at me?"

"Because I didn't ask you for your critique on my word choice or anything else. Why are you trying to tell me what to do?" Her eyes gleamed. She was getting riled up again.

"Are you asking as my sister's friend, or as my publicist right now?"

"Sister's friend."

"Because I feel it's my right."

She balked. "Your *right*?"

"Yes. I tell my sister what to do all the time. I'm like a father figure to her—"

She cut me off with a laugh. "Excuse me? You're her brother."

"I'm her half-brother. She wasn't even born until I was seven. When she was six and going into first grade, I was thirteen. She was barely hitting puberty when I became a man."

"And that makes you her daddy?"

"It makes me more mature, more experienced and able to offer advice, guidance, support and protection. Like a father figure."

Angeline shook her head at me, like she was astonished at my ego. I was getting pretty used to that look by now. "Okay, let's put aside how wrong that may be—"

"It's not."

"But what the hell does that have to do with me? You're not my daddy or my brother."

"You're her close friend and roommate. You came dragging around after getting dumped and fired and ending up homeless and broke—"

"That's not—"

"It's only natural that I would try to help you out. With advice, guidance, support… and protection."

Her mouth snapped shut.

"Unless you prefer that I don't." I paused, wondering if she'd actually ask me to butt out of her life, when she so clearly needed me in her life right now. "Admit it. Your life has improved since you started spending more time with me."

"You are stunning, Johnny O."

"Thank you."

"I can't believe how conceited you are."

I glanced out the window, pretending to be more interested in the passing traffic than the conversation. "You know, it's rude to disrespect your elders."

"Gross. You're two years older than me, asshat."

"Three."

"Not even."

I looked at her again. Sitting next to me in her black dress, she looked a lot like a woman I might show up at an event like this with, on an actual date. Pretty. Sexy.

I'd given it a solid try to not think of Angeline Delacroix as sexy, but that had gone out the window the moment she stripped off that giant T-shirt in front of me—and I got an eyeful of her in her little panties and bra.

I'd taken off my own shirt and told her to put it on, to try to kill any ideas I might get about seeing her like that. But no matter how much of a sad disaster she was that night, I couldn't stop replaying it in my mind.

The way she clung to me. The things she said.

Drunk and emotional Angeline was very loose with her words.

Maybe I got a glimpse of how she really felt about me that night. Maybe I didn't. But the possibility was enough to make me wonder.

Make me want to try to expose her emotions again.

For some reason, her emotions fucking fascinated me.

Maybe because they were so damn foreign to me.

Not only did I not particularly have any, I tended not to keep women around who did. I had no real competency with emotions. Generally, they repelled me because they confused me. They made me uneasy, sometimes triggering rash responses, because I just couldn't deal. It was like an allergy. You didn't get a pet cat if you were allergic to cats.

And you didn't let yourself fall for the cute stray kitten that appeared on your doorstep and bring it into your bed.

I had no idea why I'd invited her into my life. Did I really need a publicist / social calendar organizer / cheerleader person / pain in my ass, any more than I just needed a new band and to keep moving forward?

"I find our relationship confusing," I told her. "When are you my publicist and when are you my sister's annoying friend?"

*And when are you that girl I can't stop thinking about, the one who needed me that night?*

"Well, that depends." She gave me a fake smile. "If whatever just came out of my mouth is about to get me fired as your publicist, then I'm your sister's friend. And when I'm telling you what to do, I'm your publicist."

"So, basically, you say and do whatever you want, you tell *me* what to do, I swallow it and shut up?"

She pretended to consider that carefully. "Uh-huh. Yeah… that sounds real good to me."

"Yeah, real good. Except for when you're making piss-poor decisions… like trailing home a bunch of horny frat boys, and you need me to save you."

"I don't need you."

"You needed me."

"They would've left." She muttered, "Eventually."

"You couldn't climb the stairs."

"Shayla would've come home."

"You thanked me. You clung to me like a baby monkey, crying all over me."

"I was crazy drunk!"

"You hugged me when I tucked you into bed."

She fumed. “Is it so uncomfortable for you to have someone, a woman, your sister’s annoying friend, helping you, and for you to not have the upper hand? Is that it? It makes you feel like a ‘loser’ to need something from me, so you keep trying to drag me into your well of shame? I am not ashamed of needing help that night. But I don’t need you. Fire me if you want. I’ll be okay.” She turned to look out the window.

“I know you will.”

“You’d be fine without me, too. You don’t need me. You just refuse to fix your shit yourself, so you want to pay someone else to do it.”

“That may be true.”

She turned back to me, looking stunned that I’d agreed with her.

After a moment, she went on. “I can’t fix you, Johnny. You have to do the work. I can lead a rock star to water, but I can’t make him drink. And I definitely can’t make people forget all the slutty, arrogant, selfish shit you’ve done. Not if you don’t stop doing it.”

My gaze drifted down to her lip, where she bit down a little, like she was suddenly nervous I’d be mad. And maybe fire her for it. “Tell me how you really feel.”

“That is how I feel,” she said in a small voice.

No. That’s wasn’t all of it.

But it was a start.

“I hope you’re a better publicist than you are a liar,” I told her. Then I reached into the bar compartment for the Champagne and poured us both a drink.

# Chapter Fifteen

**Johnny**

When the limo driver opened the door for us in front of Champagne nightclub, my sister was already talking to some people she knew on the sidewalk. I followed Angeline out of the limo and walked her in past the velvet rope, up the short red carpet that had been rolled out.

Jude Grayson, Dirty's head of security, stood near the door with a group of guys; an imposing figure, even among all the bouncers. Jude was a biker, a member of Lex's motorcycle club, the West Coast Kings. When I caught his eye, he lifted his chin to me and offered his hand. "Johnny."

"Jude. Nice place," I remarked, though I hadn't seen the inside yet. The grand entrance had been renovated, and the bouncers wore pressed black slacks and collared black shirts with the embroidered club logo, setting the tone for the dress code. I could already hear the music thumping. No doubt Summer, a former DJ herself, would've had a top DJ booked. I really didn't have to step inside to know what I was in for. "Dylan and Elle have outdone themselves."

"They have." Jude's dark gaze slid to the woman at my side. "Angeline."

"Hey, Jude." I watched as they hugged each other. Not only was Jude in charge of Dirty's security, which meant Elle's, he was Flynn's boss. I wondered what he thought of Elle's sister standing next to me. And if Flynn was gonna hear about it, the second our backs were turned. "Is my sister here?" she asked him.

"She's here, darlin'." Jude's dark gaze slid back to me, assessing.

"Great. See you inside!" Angeline turned to head inside, and I followed with a parting nod at Jude, my hand settling on her lower back.

"He does not like you showing up with me," I said in her ear.

"Well, good thing he's not my daddy, either." She smiled prettily at me, just as Shayla suddenly caught up to us, grabbed on to her and tore her away. The next thing I knew, they were gone. Disappeared into the crowded club.

When I tracked down Angeline, like half an hour later, I pulled her aside. I'd been mingling, and while there were easily a dozen tables where I knew people and could've sat down, I was already sick to death of the tone of conversation. Everyone either wanted to commiserate over my recent "loss" or casually probe me for the inside dirt on my band breakup. And whether or not Brianna and I were now an item.

The Johnny/Brianna/JC love triangle headlines seemed to have suckered a lot of people in. Even people who should've known better. Not only was there no love between Brianna and me, according to what I'd heard—from Noah, not the media—she and JC had parted ways, too.

I leaned into Angeline, even as she tried to keep her body a respectable distance from mine. Hard to have a private conversation, even in a loud nightclub. "I thought we were attending this event together. You know, you being my not-friend, not-date, publicist person."

"We are. We attended. You said you weren't showing up alone. You didn't. Objective achieved."

"Literally, one person saw us arrive together."

"Who, Jude? Oh, he'll be telling my sister," she noted grimly. "Don't worry."

"Let's go say hi to whoever we need to and get out of here."

She frowned. "Why? What's the rush?"

"If you didn't notice, I'm slightly the hot topic of gossip and scandal right now. Which is why I don't read the news or hang out on social media. I hate that shit. I'd rather not have to experience it right in my face." More than a few people were sending looks our way, trying to read the exchange between us, and I wasn't loving it.

"Well, as I've explained to you, the only way to silence a scandal is to replace it with a new conversation."

"Yeah, and I don't have an album in the works or a new lead singer to announce. That's the only thing anyone wants to talk about."

She frowned at me again, but at least there was a shred of what I took to be empathy in it, or something. "I'm sure it's not like that."

"Oh, it is."

She saw something past my shoulder and brightened. "Let's go say hi to Seth. He's with Zane."

Yeah. Fucking great idea. Just who I wanted to talk to. Seth Brothers, her brother-in-law, rhythm guitarist in Vancouver's most beloved band, Dirty. And worse, Zane Traynor, Dirty's lead singer and the reigning local god of rock 'n' roll. Most successful vocalist to come out of this city in the last decade, at least. And a guy I'd never really gotten along with all that well, historically. "How about let's not."

"Why? You played that show with Zane and Wet Blanket, what was that, like, six months ago?"

"Eight. And just because I stepped in as a guest at a small local show for his side project charity band doesn't make us best buds. We respect each other as musicians."

"Okay. So, he respects you as a musician. Do you hear yourself? You've gotta give people a chance to *feel* for you, Johnny. If he can feel respect for you, he can feel empathy for what you're going through, too. Your colleagues are your peers. They could be your friends. If you stopped seeing them as competition all the damn time."

"They are competition."

"*Colleagues,*" she corrected me. "Dirty and the Players are super tight friends. They tour together all the time, support each other. They share the same management. You need to shed that chip on your shoulder, the one dedicated to anyone who has more than you."

I took a sip of my drink. "I don't have a chip on my shoulder."

She scoffed. "Tell me what you think of Zane Traynor, *honestly*, Johnny. No bullshit."

I glanced around to make sure no one was hearing this over the music. "Why?"

"The first things that come to mind," she pressed. "Don't go reaching for insults or criticism just because you can. What do you actually think of him?"

I stared at her. What was it about this girl that made me put up with her, even when she fucking irritated me?

Still hadn't decided if this whole working with her thing was a stroke of genius or an exercise in madness. She made an exceptional point or two, now and then. She also pissed me off in a way that nothing and no one had pissed me off in a long damn time.

And talked way too fucking much.

I drew closer to her, making sure I had her ear, and hers alone. "I think he's incredibly talented, okay? And despite not being able to play an instrument other than a harmonica, he's one of the most naturally gifted musicians I've ever met. I also think he's underrated, mainly because of the genre he sings, and maybe because he's been known to be an alcoholic, unpredictable, erratic and have an overly sexualized public image."

Angeline blinked at me, taking that in. Surprised or impressed, maybe, that I'd given it that much thought. When literally, this shit was all I thought about. She had no idea the depths of my competitiveness.

"Well," she said carefully, "wouldn't it be nice if people judged us on our work alone, and not on our image or the gossip that surrounds our personal behavior?"

"Yeah. Real nice."

"So, if that's what you think of him, speak to him like that's how you think of him. Genuinely. It'll go a long way to smoothing things out between you. It's okay to admire people. Pretending you don't is just… douchy." She took me by the arm and started tugging me across the room.

"I didn't say I wanted to go talk to him," I grumbled, but I went with her. Mostly because she was touching me, and I didn't particularly want her not to.

"It's called making new friends, Johnny. You should try it once in a while. All your besties are like, rich-boy high school bros, right?"

"Don't knock my friends. You don't even know them."

She stopped. "Oh, I know them. Dane, Lex and Shane, right? They'd kill for you, just like you would for them, 'til death do us part, right? But what the hell do they really know about *you*?" She jabbed me in the chest, just like she did that night when she was wasted. "They aren't musicians, much less famous musicians. They don't know that part of your life, intimately. They don't know what it's like to be you. But guess what?" She indicated Seth and Zane with a sweep of her arm. "Those guys do."

Before I could say anything else to stall her, she grabbed my arm again and dragged me right over to Seth and Zane. They were standing by a big booth full of people, flanked by some big dudes from Dirty's security team. "Hey, Seth," Angeline said, interrupting their conversation. They didn't seem to mind. "Hey, Zane." She gave Seth a hug, then hugged Zane as he greeted her.

"Heyyy." Zane looked her over in her little black dress. "Looking scorching, Little Elle."

I stepped closer to her, not loving the way he looked at her. Zane was married, happily from what I'd heard, but the man was a flirt without even trying. He was hot as hell, according to every female I'd ever met, and the way his ice-blue eyes slid over her… I wondered if he'd ever tried anything with Angeline, and my stomach tightened into a hot, irritated fist.

"He calls you 'Little Elle'?" I said in her ear.

"Be nice," she hissed at me. Then she said to them, "This is my friend, Johnny." She gave me a pointed look, like she was willing me to behave. "Johnny, this is my brother-in-law, Seth. And this is Zane. They play in this band called Dirty."

Zane smirked and Seth raised an eyebrow, probably wondering why Angeline was being weird. We weren't strangers.

But then again, this was my "rebirth," right?

"Hey, Johnny." Zane offered me a hand and I went in for a hug. Mostly so Angeline couldn't complain later that I didn't make an effort. Had to shut her up somehow.

By the time I'd greeted Seth, she'd slipped away. She stood a few tables away, sipping her drink, and I caught her eye. She flashed me a smile and turned her back to me.

Sly.

I put in some small talk with Zane and Seth about their forthcoming album. Then I said hi to another member of Dirty, Jesse Mayes, and his wife, Katie, who'd stopped by the booth. I made sure to congratulate Katie on her gorgeous paintings, which were all over the walls—along with large black-and-white photographs of local musicians, which I suspected were the work of Amber Cope.

My ex-wife.

Who was definitely on the list of people I didn't particularly want to run into tonight.

I said hi to Brody Mason, manager of Dirty and the Players, and his wife, Jessa, when they came by. And wondered if I should clear out of here before my luck ran out and Amber showed up with her husband.

Then I spotted Dane. He'd just walked in with his wife, Devi, and I made a beeline for them. Hanging with some of *my* friends at this event was a definite necessity. I could count on them, at least, not to ask about my band bullshit.

Lex and his wife, Talia, joined us shortly after, and as I got talking to them, I noticed Angeline come over and say hi to Devi. When I caught her arm and tugged her over—same way she'd done to me—to try to introduce her to Talia, she and Talia hugged, and I realized they were already girlfriends. I didn't know that, but I probably should've. Talia had worked for Dirty's management team before she worked for the Players', and everyone on Dirty's team seemed to love Angeline.

Apparently, she made friends way the hell easier than I did.

She was right. My best friends were my buddies from high school. It never occurred to me before, though, that that might be lame somehow.

They were all cool guys.

It wasn't like I *couldn't* make new friends.

When I headed over to the bar with Lex and Dane, I could see Talia and Devi and a few other girls rallying around Angeline, some of them shooting me looks. Probably asking her what the fuck she was doing here with me. I had no idea which people in this room already knew she was my publicist.

But even if they knew… they were probably asking her what the fuck she was doing here with me.

Then I noticed Flynn. He was hanging out by a table in the corner where Elle sat with a group of women, keeping a watchful eye over the crowd. I watched him for a few minutes. But even when Elle got up to go talk to her sister, and he followed, he stayed away from Angeline and she stayed away from him.

After I got a fresh drink, I wandered over to say hi to Elle. "Congrats on your big night, Elle."

"Thank you, Johnny." She smiled politely and gave me a hug. I liked to think that Elle liked me a little better than her male bandmates had over the years, but that was probably wishful thinking. In reality, she probably just wasn't as vocal about her issues with me. "What do you think of the club?" She seemed to genuinely want my opinion.

"It's hot." I looked her over; she was looking pretty hot herself in her slinky, silver sequined dress. "I like the decor."

I didn't even have to look at Angeline to know she was probably rolling her eyes. Probably thought I was treating her sister like "furniture." But I was just being honest.

Elle slipped an arm around her sister. "Well, thank you for contributing to it." She raised her chin a little, like she was indicating something behind me.

I turned to look, and discovered that one of the huge black-and-white portraits was of *me*. It was a photo of me onstage at Lollapalooza from years ago. Before Breakneck was even formed.

"Hey, my pleasure," I said cooly. "Didn't realize I'd made the cut."

"Oh, you made the cut." Elle smirked. "We went with the most popular images from Amber's gallery tour. You're a fine art masterpiece, Johnny O."

Angeline cocked her head, studying the image.

"Excuse me," Elle said apologetically; she was getting pulled away by her assistant. "We'll talk later, okay?" She gave Angeline a sharp look that probably didn't bode too well for me.

Did Angeline tell her sister she was working for me yet?

I had no idea.

I studied Angeline as she studied my photo, shifting closer to her once

Elle was gone. "See," she mused, "now that's the Johnny O we need more of."

I glanced at the photo again. "Too bad there's no more. That band was a temporary gig."

"So?" She assessed me with her pretty, suddenly sharp blue-gray eyes. "You're still that man. We could definitely use some good photo ops, and someone like Amber behind the lens. Maybe she'd even photograph you again."

"I don't think so."

"Why not?"

"She's my ex-wife."

"Oh. Right." She frowned, like that was just another strike against me that she'd have to contend with; my failed marriage to a beloved member of the Dirty family. "I totally forgot you were married."

"Most people do. It was a long time ago, and it only lasted sixteen days. But that photo was taken when we were dating, before we got married."

Angeline looked up at it again. "It's an incredible photo."

"She's talented," I admitted. The other photos on the wall said as much. There was one of Zane from Dirty's last tour that was epic. Onstage, he was gleaming with sweat, shirtless, loose jeans around his hips and blond hair falling over his eyes, laughing as he lifted his microphone into the air. I'd seen it on a magazine cover, and later, all over the place. Posters, mugs, phone cases. I couldn't get away from it.

"She is," Angeline agreed. "She's taken some pretty incredible photos of my sister." She eyed me. "Maybe we could ask her if she'd photograph you, as part of your whole rebirth thing."

"I think she's probably got better things to do."

Angeline looked annoyed with me, yet again. "Just because she photographs Dirty all the time doesn't mean you're not worthy of her camera. You've got to get that out of your head. You're just as worthy a musician as my sister and her bandmates. You've worked just as hard. I know you have."

"It's not that I'm not worthy," I told her. "It's just probably not on Amber's bucket list to do a photo shoot with her ex-husband."

"Why not?" she pressed.

Seriously? Could we not just leave it at that?

"Because maybe she hates him."

"Maybe she doesn't."

"Maybe not. But either way, I'm not sure her husband would be too keen on the idea."

"Who, Dylan?" Angeline immediately turned to gaze across the room at Dirty's drummer. I saw him now; hard to miss in any crowd, between his height and the wavy auburn hair. Angeline knew exactly where he was standing, and those wide eyes of hers told me all too much. "Dylan would never… He's such a sweetheart," she gushed.

I studied her, and the wide-open admiration on her face. *Jesus Christ.* She had a thing for Dylan Cope.

It was brutally obvious.

A hot, sickening surge of… something… flared in my gut. The fist was back, squeezing, hard and tight.

"Let me guess. You had a crush on him."

Angeline squinted at me. "It's not a 'crush' if it lasts for, like, ten years."

"Is that a rule?"

"Yes."

I held her gaze. We were inches apart, and I wanted to keep her eyes on me. Not on Dylan. The ferocity with which I did not want her to look at him was kinda nauseating.

"How long did you crush on me?" I asked her, point blank.

"Only as long as the acid trip lasted. Then I sobered up and realized you weren't cartoon Justin Bieber."

I smirked. Colorful lie.

She'd crushed on me. She'd told me as much when she was drunk. Even if she wouldn't admit it right now.

"Here's an idea," I suggested. "Why don't we go say hi to Danielle Duke?"

Angeline's sweet face frosted right over. For sure, she knew her former almost-boss was here. If I'd noticed her, Angeline sure as hell had. "Sure," she said. "Right after we say hi to Dylan."

"Right."

She grabbed my arm again and tried to drag me toward him. "Come on."

"Angeline." I dug my heels in. "Can you just accept that there are some people who hate me, and that's never gonna change?"

She glared at me. "Yes. Because I hate you." Her hand dropped from my arm. "And that is never going to change."

She said it with such passionate conviction… I almost believed her.

Maybe she almost believed it, too.

# Chapter Sixteen

**Johnny**

"Dylan Cope doesn't want to see me," I informed Angeline. We were still in a standoff. She wanted me to go chat with my ex-wife's husband, maybe congratulate him on his hot new nightclub and his general success, and I wanted to do something more fun, like maybe put a drill bit through my hand. "I don't particularly want to see him either."

"Why not?" she demanded, glancing across the club at him again. "What did you do?"

"Maybe it was what he did."

"Right." She half-laughed, like there was no way her precious Dylan could ever possibly do wrong.

"I'm gonna go get another drink."

She caught my arm again. "What did he do?" She couldn't even stop herself from rolling her eyes, pre-rejecting whatever I was about to say.

"Okay. You really want to know? He clocked me at a bar in L.A.."

"Clocked you. Like… hit you?""

"Like sucker punched me for no reason."

Angeline scrutinized me. "I don't believe it. If Dylan hit you, you did something."

"Yeah. I had a conversation with my ex-wife, his girlfriend at the time, that turned into an argument with his bodyguard. And then my bodyguard got involved, they started brawling and I tried to yank Amber out of the way. A bunch of people were pushing and shoving, and Dylan punched me. In the face. And yes, it was on purpose."

"Well." She crossed her arms. "You must've done something to deserve it."

"Right. God forbid Dylan Cope makes a mistake."

She considered that, maybe. I had no doubt Dylan's pristine reputation was still intact in her mind. Though she was probably liking me less as the night went on. *Story of my life.*

"You're talking to him," she decided. "This is exactly the kind of thing you need to get past."

"I'm past it. It's fine. I just don't need to see him *right now*."

"You mean, now that your career is imploding?"

"It's far from imploding."

It wasn't, really.

She narrowed her eyes at me. "Is that why you went all Kung Fu Panda? Because he punched you?"

"Huh?"

"That's what Shay calls you when you do your martial arts stuff. KFP."

"It's MMA," I informed her. "I train with Shane. He's a fighter. And yeah, maybe the fact that I got cold-cocked by a guy I would never have expected it from was a wake up call. I've usually got security when I go out, but sometimes a man has to look out for himself."

"You mean, because you have so many enemies?"

"I mean because I'm famous and who knows what awaits around any given corner. People are always coming at me, for one reason or another. If this place wasn't filled with VIPs and security, and it was just a regular night at the bar, and I was just standing here like this with you… I'd have people all over me right now."

"I know," she said with distaste. She glanced aside, and only then did I notice the group of women who were checking me out from a nearby table.

Angeline met my eyes again, and I knew that she did know. Because Elle. I couldn't imagine being a woman in this position, actually. It was impressive that her sister ever left the house. But then again, Elle probably never left the house without Flynn, or Seth's bodyguard, or a whole fleet of Dirty's security team; whatever the situation called for.

It must've been weird as hell being the sister of a hot female rock star.

Angeline said she got overlooked all the time because of it. But Zane Traynor sure as shit wasn't overlooking her in her little black dress. I wondered how many times she'd been hit on or harassed by guys because she was with Elle. Yet she didn't have her own bodyguard.

Suddenly, that fucking bothered me.

"Do Elle or Jude ever assign you security?"

She wrinkled her nose a little. "No. Why would they?"

"Because maybe they should. Especially if you're gonna be wandering the streets picking up groups of dudes in your slippers."

She grit her teeth. "This, again. It was one stupid time."

"Was it? What happens in a situation like that if the guys actually realize who you are, who your sister is? Do they get nicer? Or do they get more grabby?"

"I don't need a bodyguard, Johnny. If I need security, there's coverage everywhere my sister goes. They all look out for me."

"Like Flynn?" I noticed how she tensed up at her ex-boyfriend's name. And the grim look that overtook her pretty face. "Your ex is gonna watch your ass now? Is that a good idea?"

"Why are you dissecting my life right now? It's none of your business. This night isn't about me. It's about you."

"I can't take an interest in my publicist's security?"

"You're deflecting." She glanced over at Dylan again. "Let's just go over."

"Let's get a drink."

"Let's go over, then get a drink."

"No."

"Johnny, you can't have everything your way," she said, exasperated. "Your way got you into trouble, remember?"

"So we'll do it your way. After we get a drink."

"You can keep fighting with me, but you're not gonna win. I'm your publicist. You have to do what I say on this, remember?"

"I never agreed to that."

I kind of did. But either way, I won.

Or did I?

After debating back and forth a few more times, we got a drink… at the bar near where Dylan was hanging out.

I knew what Angeline was up to.

Sure enough, soon as I'd bought her a drink, she wormed her way over to Dylan through the crowd and touched his arm. The path she'd cleared led straight to me and when he turned, he saw her and smiled; then he saw me over her shoulder and the smile cooled a fraction.

I inwardly rolled my eyes and went over. Angeline smiled at me. Fake or not, the girl was too cute to be pissed at for very long. Another thing that was annoying about her.

Amber was with Dylan, of course. I hadn't seen her through the crowd. But at least she was turned away, talking to someone else.

"Dylan," Angeline said gravely as I joined them, "this is my friend, Kung Fu Panda."

"Hey," I said, and we shook hands.

"Hey," Dylan greeted me with a half-smirk. "Kung Fu…?"

"It's a nickname. You know… little sisters." I knew he had a few.

"Right," Dylan said. "Thanks for coming." No attitude. He was actually… friendly. He always had been, more or less, when I'd run into him.

Other than that one time when his fist met my face.

Although… considering how fast I'd almost punched a guy for touching Angeline, when she wasn't even my girlfriend… maybe I did deserve it? From Dylan's point of view, in that moment, I had my hands on his woman. Even if I was trying to help her out of the fray.

And anyway, that shit was years ago now.

"You guys did a great job," I told him. "This place was due for a reno."

"Thanks, man. It was all Summer, really. Woman's a force of nature. Elle and I just hang on for the ride."

"Right." I smiled a bit, and it wasn't even fake. Unfortunately, Angeline was right about Dylan. He had the kind of likable-guy reputation, well earned, that an asshole like myself could only dream of.

No one would ever guess that *he* punched *me* in the face, once upon a time, and not the other way around.

"It's gonna be the hottest club in town, by miles," Angeline gushed. She looked at Dylan like a cartoon puppy who'd just eaten a bag of magic mushrooms. If dopamine was airborne, we'd all be high right now.

Strangely, I couldn't remember ever being so viscerally jealous of a guy over a woman. Ever.

I tried to ignore it, but the irritated fist was clenching in my gut again, a hot, nauseating ball of something like fury.

And I wasn't even dating this woman. Or fucking her.

"I'm coming here," she gushed on, "like, every weekend."

Dylan smiled at her, then shot a look at me. Like, *With who?*

"Me, too," I said casually. "When I'm not on tour."

"How's that going?" he asked. "You're going into the studio on the new album soon, huh?" The way he asked, kind of cautiously, I knew he'd heard all the gossip.

But I had to be prepared for this.

People would never stop asking, so unless I wanted to bury my head in the sand and never speak to another human until my next album was in the bag, I had to have an answer for this question. Angeline and I had gone over it.

*Remember what we rehearsed*, her eyes seemed to say.

"Soon," I said. "JC and Miles just moved on from Breakneck, so we're regrouping." That was Angeline's buzz word. *Regrouping.* As in, I don't have a group, so I need to regroup. She said it had a positive, deliberate spin. Like it was a conscious choice. We didn't break up. JC and Miles moved on. And now, *regrouping*.

Hopefully into something better than before.

"Ah, shit," Dylan sympathized. "I heard that. Well, hey it happens. Look what happened with the Players, though. Whatever you put together next could go big, even bigger than before."

"I fucking hope so."

Amber suddenly noticed us and turned around. "Hey. Johnny," she said carefully, as Dylan slid an arm around her.

"Amber. You look beautiful," I told her. She did. But I also figured it was the appropriate thing to say to one's ex-wife when running into her at a formal event. Which I had done, from time to time, over the years. Every time, we'd been civil. And every time, she just looked better.

Life as the wife of Dylan Cope agreed with her.

She wore a champagne-gold beaded dress tonight, kind of bohemian glam, which was very Amber, her wavy caramel hair loose, a beaded silk flower on one side.

"Thank you," she said, kissing Angeline on the cheek when Angeline went in for a hug. They exchanged a quick word I couldn't hear, and I noticed the way they held onto one another's arms as they spoke, before letting each other go. They were friendly. Of course.

For the first time, I wondered what delightful things my ex-wife might've said about me over the years, to whomever. Like maybe to the girls.

Not that I particularly cared. Until right this moment.

I drew Angeline gently back to my side as Dylan brought Amber up to speed on the conversation. Amber seemed friendly enough, yet guarded as she listened, eying me with her pale green eyes.

"You're rebuilding your band, then?" she asked me politely. "Ashley went through something similar, with the Players. Maybe it will work out for the best?"

Very polite.

"Yeah. Thank you," I forced the politeness back. How soon could I get out of this conversation?

"I hear Coop's still looking for something permanent," Dylan offered, referring to Ashley Player's ex-bassist. I hadn't thought of Andy Cooper, but he'd probably be a step up from Miles.

"Really? I'll keep that in mind."

"He might even be willing to play on the album and see how that goes. If you need someone in-studio, quick."

"Yeah. Thanks." The recommendation was kind of Dylan. I didn't really know what else to say. Felt weirdly like anything I might say could be taken the wrong way, given the audience.

Luckily, I didn't have to force conversation much longer because Summer swept in. After I'd congratulated her on the club, she nudged

Dylan aside to introduce him to some people, Amber went with them, and I managed to slip away with Angeline.

Who apparently wanted me to talk to like a hundred more people before the night was finally through. According to her, we were just getting started.

I could see she was getting an adrenaline charge out of all of this. Her eyes were sparkling, her cheeks flushed.

Gave me an idea of how she might look if we'd just made out in the washroom.

But it wasn't enough to keep me around. I went along with it as long as I could stand, but she really had no idea, apparently, how shit this night was for me.

"You're doing fine," she said to me, once, after she left me to use the ladies' room and I told her I'd come within an inch of ditching out the back door while she was gone. "Making friends, remember? There's no time like the present to make a new friend."

I couldn't even stop the roll of my eyes. The woman was a living Care Bear.

I was not like her.

I wasn't warm, sweet, cute or, apparently, likable. I had no idea how to open my life or my heart to people. I really didn't know how to put myself out there to try to win people back over, either.

I was used to running the other way when people ran out on me. Even a hint of rejection or disappointment in another human sent me jetting. What the hell did I need that for?

Problem was, when you just kept disappointing people, and all you did was turn your back on them in return… the number of people you could turn to just got smaller and smaller.

Angeline was wrong when she said I didn't really need her. But that didn't mean I enjoyed being in this position.

Far from it.

I finally managed to drag her over to Shayla so we could head home. But my sister wasn't ready to leave. She tried to shoo me away, but I just stood there with Lamar while the two of them had girl talk, assuming they'd be done soon. Wrong.

Then I actually overheard what they were talking about.

"I've been going about it all wrong," Angeline was saying. "The thing with Flynn…" Then something about "it's time to finally move on." At least, that was what I thought she said.

But then I realized that maybe she actually said, "it's time to finally move on what I want."

I leaned in closer to eavesdrop, and Lamar shook his head at me. The girls barely noticed I was there.

"… always thought he was so hot," Angeline was gushing. "I just thought he was out of my league."

*What the fuck…*

Was she talking about Dylan Cope? The hot fist clenched in my gut.

"… he's single, though," I heard her say. *Not Dylan, then.* "What have I got to lose?"

Who the fuck was she talking about?

"He's not out of your league," my sister encouraged her.

They both turned, and I followed their line of sight to the dude sprawled at a nearby table. Shaggy hair, grossly tight jeans, and enough bloated ego to crowd every other rock star out of the room.

Jesus, no.

"Go talk to him," I heard my sister say.

"*No.*"

They both looked at me.

"Excuse me?" Angeline said. She blinked at me, and I realized the sparkle in her glossy eyes wasn't just social adrenaline. She was getting drunk.

"What are you still doing here?" Shayla demanded. Like they thought I'd left? I was right fucking here, the whole time.

I looked deep into Angeline's eyes. "Preventing you from making a giant mistake. You're not hitting on Dean Fucking Slater. The man is pond scum when it comes to women."

"You don't know," she said.

I laughed. Oh yes, I knew. I'd toured with one of Dean's bands. He was currently without a band, yet again, because no one could stand to work with him for more than a tour or two.

There was a reason he was known as Dickhead Dean. The guy was nice enough, maybe, but the little head did all the thinking for him. And there wasn't much thinking going on.

"I'm going over there," Angeline said.

"You go over there," I growled, slow and deliberate, so she heard every word, "I'm going with you. You go on a date with him, I'm going with you. He tries to touch you, I break something on his body."

Her mouth tumbled open. "Are you kidding me?"

"I'm not kidding."

"Ugh. He's not." Shayla actually didn't fight me on this, which was rare. "He's cockblocked my dates before. Don't tempt him."

Angeline gaped at me. "You have no right to stalk me. I'm a grown woman and I'm not your baby sister."

"And yet, I'll do it. Easiest way to ensure it never happens is to promise me, right now, that you'll never go near Dean Slater or his dirty disease dick."

"Ew," Shayla said.

Angeline made a disgusted face. "Fine. I promise. You just ruined it, anyway."

"I will never not hear 'dirty disease dick' when I look at him now," Shayla agreed sadly.

I smiled. For the first time tonight, I actually full-on smiled. "Let's go."

"Fuck that," my sister said.

"It's time to go," I growled at my publicist. "We have business to discuss."

Angeline scowled at me, like, *We do?*

Shayla sighed. "Then I'll see you guys later." And with that, my sister gave Angeline a kiss on the cheek, gave me a kiss on the cheek, and bolted into the crowd before me or Lamar could corral her into the car.

"Well." I smiled at Angeline. "Guess it's just you and me for the ride home." I was actually semi-enjoying my night right now.

Maybe because Angeline looked so annoyed with me, yet so turned off by Dean Slater at the same time.

---

In the limo, I fell quiet. But predictably, Angeline wouldn't shut up.

She kept going over every conversation of the night, dissecting every interaction between me and another human, how well she thought it all went. Because all she could see was the positive spin, how successfully we were going to rebuild my broken relationship with the rest of the human race, one conversation at a time.

She was weirdly over the fucking moon about the whole event. You would've thought I'd just played Wembley Stadium to a sold out crowd or something.

Then I realized why she was buzzing—when she started going on about Dylan again. "Isn't he the best?" she gushed. "Suggesting you call Andy Cooper about joining your band? He's so nice. Amber's so lucky."

Yeah. That was why Angeline liked him. Sure.

Because he was nice.

Had nothing to do with the fact that besides owning the hottest new nightclub in town he was a ripped underwear model in his spare time, a successful, six-foot-plus drummer, and she'd probably wanted to climb that for years.

"Guess you missed your chance," I muttered.

"Huh?"

"He's married. Unless you go in for married guys."

Her jaw dropped. "Of course not."

"You do, if you're crushing on Dylan Cope." First Dylan, then Dean Slater… How many rock stars did this woman want in her bed, anyway?

"I just like him," she said, sounding wounded. "There's no law against that. I like his wife, too." She withdrew into the corner of the seat, finally shutting up. "He's one of my sister's best friends," she added after a moment. "So don't make it into something it's not. I'm not trying to bang him."

"No?" I met her eyes. "Who are you trying to bang?"

She blinked at me. "What does that mean? Just because I was considering going over to talk to Dean…"

"Right. Just to talk." I pulled out my phone and started scrolling.

"You think I'm trying to fuck you?" Her voice was disturbingly quiet and completely devoid of the happy buzz she'd been exuding just moments ago.

I looked at her. "Are you?"

She shook her head slowly.

Lamar gave me a look across the limo, like, *Really, bro? Couldn't you save this drama for when I'm not here?*

"You think…" Angeline said, "that I want to fuck you so bad… that I made my boyfriend break up with me, made my boss fire me, made up this whole elaborate ruse that I wanted to clean your house in exchange for a roof over my head, and then that I wanted to be your publicist so I could start building my career while helping you with yours, and meanwhile keep that roof over my head and maybe grow some self-reliance and self-respect… all so I could fuck you?" Her voice had gone eerily shrill, even as it remained quiet, and I wasn't even sure if her fierce denial was evidence that she did want to fuck me or that she did not. Hard to tell.

Either way, she was pissed.

"It was just a question, Angeline."

"You know what, Johnny? Go to hell." She spun as far away from me as she could in the corner of the seat and stared out the window.

"Pretty sure I'm headed there already, Angel."

She gave me a strange, questioning look, then fell silent again.

When the limo dropped us at home, I walked Angeline up to Shayla's door. She gave me an irritated, slightly creeped out look over her shoulder, like I was stalking her.

"Good night," she said, unlocking the door.

"Good night." I stood on the front step, watching her as she went into the house. "Thank you for taking me to the party."

The smoked-glass slab slid closed, but just before it shut completely, she swung it back open a foot. She peered out at me.

"*You* took *me* to the party," she corrected me.

"Whatever you say."

She looked me up and down. "Well, don't just stand there like a hungry puppy on the door step. Go home, for God's sake."

"I will."

Her face twisted with annoyance. "What are you doing, Johnny?"

"I'm waiting until you're safely home."

"I'm home."

"The door's still open."

"So, I'll close it."

"Okay."

"Good night."

"Good night, Angel."

She huffed quietly, holding the door open. "Why do you call me Angel?"

"Because it suits you."

"Because I'm innocent and holy? I'm not that good."

"Because you're miraculous and I don't have a better word for you."

She stared at me. "I'm… miraculous?" The door slipped open a bit more.

"You're a divine phenomenon. I've never met a woman like you."

"Like… *what?*"

There were a lot of things I could've said to explain what I meant.

*Someone who makes me think about things the way you do.*

*Someone who makes me feel the way you do.*

*Someone who makes me* feel.

Instead I said, "Like someone who's willing to put up with me long enough to try to help me. Also, it's the first five letters of your first name."

Her face had softened. "Why do you do that? Why are you such a massive jerk, and then you're so kind? And then just when you're kind, you're dismissive about it."

"Am I?"

She looked away. "I'm really closing the door now."

"Angeline?"

She met my eyes like she'd rather not. Like she was bracing herself for however I was about to ruin her night next.

"You told me the other night, when you were wasted, that I was your hero."

"I did not."

"You really did."

"Door's closing." The door started to slide and she disappeared from view. "In three, two, one—" The door settled into place.

"Actually," I said to the slab of smoked glass, "you told me you had a crush on me for four years."

Then I went home alone.

# Chapter Seventeen

**Angeline**

When Shayla let us into Johnny's house the next morning to "borrow"—in other words steal—some flour because she wanted to make pancakes, I could hear a guitar in the distance. Acoustic, very faint.

It was Sunday morning and I'd promised Shayla we'd do brunch, then go shopping to pick out something special for her to wear to rehearsals this week. They had a wardrobe for her to wear for the video shoot—she'd already had a fitting—and she definitely had a ton of dance clothes, but she said she wanted to show up in something "just right."

But I hesitated to follow her as she headed back out of Johnny's kitchen.

When I told her I was going to go "check in with my client" she frowned like the entire concept of Johnny and I, alone together, taking up rent in her brain was intolerable. "Have zero fun," she said warningly. "And don't let the pancakes get cold."

"I won't. I'll just be a minute."

She plucked an apple from the fruit bowl on the counter like that was Johnny's payment for stealing my time from her, and headed back over to her place.

I followed the sound of the acoustic guitar, downstairs, where Johnny had a music studio. He was playing an old song I recognized but couldn't name. I'd heard him playing the same song before, other times when Shayla had dragged me over here to barge in on him for one reason or another. Her dishwasher broke, she was out of milk, she needed cash to tip her cab driver. Whatever she needed, he'd always handed it over.

As I walked up to the open studio door and listened to him play, I realized how envious I was of Shayla and Johnny's relationship. Of having a brother, especially a brother like him. Not because he did everything for her that she asked. Because he fucking loved her.

Which meant that he'd look out for her, protect her, for the rest of their lives.

Who wouldn't want a relationship like that? It was a big part of what made Shayla who she was, which was a girl who loved herself.

"What song is that?"

Johnny startled, the rhythm of the song ending on a broken chord when he looked up.

"Hi," I said softly, suddenly self-conscious about barging in on him. He seemed to startle easily. How many times had I snuck up on him lately, on his own property?

Several.

"You'd make a terrible bodyguard." I tried to make a joke. "You're very jumpy."

He frowned. Not in the mood for jokes, then.

I hesitated awkwardly on the threshold. Was this bad etiquette? The door was open, but he didn't seem like he was in the mood for company. It was evident in the tension in his body, even before he knew I was here.

He uncurled from his position around the guitar and set it aside.

"Sorry. I didn't mean to sneak up on you. I've heard you play that song before. What is it?"

"It's nothing. How did you get in here?"

"Oh. Shayla let me in. She needed flour for pancakes. Do you want to have brunch with us?"

The invitation seemed to take him by surprise. He looked distracted, like I'd pulled him out of deep focus. I knew what that was about. I'd been around enough musicians over the past decade and a half, throughout my sister's career.

"I don't mean to interrupt. If you were working."

"I wasn't working." He got slowly to his feet. "But I can't do brunch. I'm heading over to Noah's in a bit. He's back in town, and we're gonna talk over some things. Probably have lunch."

"Oh. That's good." I was glad he and Noah, his drummer, seemed close. Everything I'd heard about Noah from people in passing, including my sister, was positive. Also, he was super hot. He and Johnny made a good team.

"Yeah." Johnny looked tense. He didn't offer anything else. Maybe he was still pulling himself out of deep focus.

Or maybe last night was more uncomfortable for him than I'd realized, and his tension was about that?

When we'd said good night, I'd been irritated about the way he'd given me so much static about Dean. Not to mention his attitude about Dylan. I'd thought he'd done really well at the party, overall. But seeing him react to all the other rock stars in the room the way he did, so guarded, even when he was playing nice, with that chip firmly in place on his shoulder… and getting his back up about Dylan and Dean like that… maybe it really sank in for me how much work needed to be done here.

And how much more patient, maybe, I needed to be. Rome wasn't built in a day and you didn't transform someone's relationship with his peers overnight.

Not that I expected that kind of outcome from one party. But maybe I just had no clue, going in, how it really was between him and his peers. His relationship with them was just so different than my sister's was. People in the music industry generally respected Elle, welcomed her wherever she went. Thanks to last night, I was just beginning to really understand what it would be like to not have that kind of warm reception. For most of your colleagues to be so guarded around you, and vice versa.

What it would be like to be Johnny O.

"You did well last night," I told him, trying to be gentle about it. "I realize it was maybe awkward. Your band is… struggling… while my sister's is on top of the world. Not to mention the Players… It must be incredibly hard not to compare yourself to where they're at. But you handled it well." He did. Mostly. "You were gracious and professional."

"Yeah?" He didn't seem to take that too well. "Is that what you decided? Or is that what other people told you?"

"Uh, it matters what other people think, in this case. Since we're trying to fix your broken relationship to the world outside these doors."

"I'm not living to please everyone else. I already told you that."

"I'm not saying you should."

He crossed his arms over his chest, his gaze sweeping over me. "That's what this is really about, right? What people think of *you*, showing up with me. You're a people pleaser."

That caught me off guard.

Why was he turning this around on me?

And was that what he really thought? That I was concerned about my own reputation? It wasn't like I was running up to all his peers and shouting *Don't worry, I'm just his publicist!* all night. I'd introduced him to people as my friend.

Let people think what they'd think about me. *His* reputation and his career were my first concerns at that party.

"What, you're gonna deny it?" he pressed. "You're gonna pretend you don't care what your sister and Seth and your friends thought of you showing up with me?"

"I didn't really think about that at all."

I didn't. Until I ran into so many of my girlfriends, they all demanded to know what was going on, and I found myself swearing to them up and down that Johnny and I were not "together." I was his publicist and nothing more.

But that wasn't because I was worried about what they'd think of *me* if I was messing around with him or something. I just didn't want them to immediately jump on hating him because they thought he was bad for me. I could feel that vibe; that everyone instinctively wanted to protect me from him.

"What about Flynn?" he said.

"I didn't think about Flynn, either."

"That's hard to believe."

It was the truth, though. I'd seen Flynn at the party. He saw me. We didn't speak to each other. I really didn't think about what he might think seeing me with Johnny. We weren't even on a date. We were working.

Yet here Johnny was, accusing me of… I wasn't even sure what.

"So, which is it?" I asked him. "Am I worried what people will think, seeing me with you? Or am I trying to be seen with you, to help my social status?"

"You tell me."

"You know what? You're your own worst enemy, Johnny O'Reilly."

"I have enough enemies. What I need are more people on my team."

"Well, then maybe you need a reality check. You're gonna need to do more than just force yourself to be nice to people to make them want to work with you. And I'll tell you something else. You've probably missed the cues, from plenty of people, who were willing to be on your team."

"And where do you get that from?" he said flatly.

"Watching you. Listening to you talk to people. Zane. Seth. Dylan. My sister. They're all way more willing to let you in than you think they are. You don't *let* people let you in."

He rolled his eyes just slightly as he looked away.

"You're doing it right now."

"And now she's my therapist again."

"It's true. You know what your problem is?"

"I'm my own worst enemy," he reiterated, sounding bored.

"You need to learn how to be nice to people, genuinely nice, when they actually stick around. It's called a relationship."

His eyes met mine, but he didn't argue. Maybe he knew I was right.

"Nothing to say to that one?" I challenged.

"I have relationships."

"Yeah. Noah likes you, it seems. You have friends. How did that magically happen? I'll tell you how," I answered for him. "Because the few people you call friends are people you chose to let in. And I'd bet every last dollar I have that you treat them way the hell better than you treat the women you sleep with. Or date. Or whatever it is you actually do with the women in your life. And I'd bet you're also way more kind and generous with your friends than you are with your colleagues, your potential friends. Because you're so stuck in this competitive mindset of yours."

He stared at me, and his tongue ran over his bottom lip. He looked like he was biting back whatever he wanted to say. Something ugly, I was pretty sure.

"I thought you were broke," he said finally.

"So you can see how much I mean it. I desperately need those last dollars."

"So what do you propose? Charm school?"

"You don't need charm school. I can teach you how to be nice and have healthy relationships."

He laughed.

And Mean Angie got mad.

"Look, no one likes you, okay?"

There. I said it.

But… *oof.* The look in his eyes. It was just a brief glimpse, but I'd swear to God I saw it: pain. It flashed through those aquamarine depths like a heart attack. Then it was gone, replaced with a dark wall.

"Sorry," I said quickly. "That was Mean Me. It's this new thing I've been practicing. Just in my head. I've got the opposite problem as you do. I'm too nice."

"Uh-huh."

"I mean… usually. Not right now, I guess. But just hear me out on this, okay? People like me."

"Like who?" he challenged. "Like the boyfriend who just broke up with you, or the boss who fired you?"

I took a deep breath. I probably deserved that one. "Okay, so besides those two people, people like me. And technically she didn't fire me, she just never hired me. But that's not the point. You know why people like me?"

Johnny stared at me blankly. "Again, I'm not sure what people we're talking about."

"How about your sister, for one?"

"Yeah, well, she likes me too. Are we really trusting her judgment?"

"I'm nice, but I'm not fake about it," I pressed on. I knew my good qualities, so it wasn't hard. "I listen. I care, genuinely. I treat people with kindness and respect—"

"And this has *what* to do with me?"

I blew out a breath. The man was stubborn as shit. "I'm taking you to a dinner. Tomorrow night."

"What dinner?"

"Social calendar, remember? I organize, you show up and be nice?"

"I never said I'd be nice."

"Yeah. Honestly, I really should've realized that you needed more… practice… before I set you loose at that party last night. That was kind of like setting a panther free in a den of lions and expecting him to make friends."

He didn't say anything as he stared me down, which I took as progress of a kind.

"It's just a little dinner with a couple of VIPs, okay?"

"Who?"

"Not important. Just like in your daily life as a famous person, you should be prepared for anything. And to be nice about it."

"If it's Dylan and Amber Cope—"

"What? No. I would never blindside you like that."

His deep, aquamarine eyes bore into me, silently assessing.

Then he said, "Okay."

"Really?"

"What have I got to lose. You fuck up, you're fired. You don't fuck up and you actually help me…" He shrugged. "Then it's worth the pain."

Pain? "Uh, you're telling me being nice to people is going to be painful?"

"Depends on the people. And how nice we're talking. And how much I have to censor myself to get through this."

Okay, that was fair. I'd hate to have to force myself to be nice to absolutely everyone in any given situation. But if he really wanted to improve his "asshole" reputation…

"It'll be great. Not painful at all. You're going to be sincere and have pleasant conversation, and resist every urge you have to act like a dick.

And I'll be there to help you along, keep things flowing. Easy peasy, right?"

"Right." He said it grudgingly, but I couldn't help it—it warmed me that he was going along with my ideas. That he was trusting me.

That he was giving me a chance to do what I was pretty sure I did best.

*Raw kitten power.*

I needed my own pastel superhero cape or something. If I couldn't make people like Johnny O, it would be the death of me. I was going to live and die on this sword.

My first client, my first success story.

"Uh, Angeline?"

"Hmm?"

"Where'd you go there?"

"Oh. Um, I was picturing myself as a pastel superhero."

His eyebrow crept up.

"Never mind. Thank you. You won't regret this. It'll be… fun…" I faded off, swallowing as he slowly stalked over to me.

Kind of like a panther in heat approaching his female victim… uh, mate.

He'd stopped in front of me, looking down into my eyes. The man was so delicious up close, it rendered me momentarily dumbstruck.

I'd only survived last night because it was darkish in the club. Right now, with the morning light pouring through the windows of his studio, he was vividly gorgeous. The bright blond of his hair, the deep blue-green of his eyes, his dark eyebrows and the stubble across his jaw… the tattoo creeping up his neck.

His soft shirt was unbuttoned so low, his tattooed chest so close to my mouth…

"What should I wear to this dinner?" he said, in a sinfully low voice… like he was asking me where I wanted to lick first. I actually had to struggle to compute what he'd really just said.

"Whatever you want to wear." Then I remembered some of the things I'd seen him wear, like a very small towel draped over his dick, and squeezed out, "Something professional."

When his heated gaze dropped to my chest for one mind-fucking heartbeat, I blurted, “And we are not getting involved.”

His eyes met mine.

“It’s just a dinner. It’s not a date. My body is not available. And neither is my… uh… my heart,” I whispered. I suddenly felt parched. I needed water or something.

Then he said the most unexpected thing.

“I wouldn’t know what to do with it if it was, Angeline.”

It was entirely fucked up that that statement actually turned me on.

I liked dangerous, messed up men. I knew that. I was drawn to them like a bumbling bee to a honey trap. I knew I’d be vulnerable to this man and all his wicked charms if I let him get under my skin in any way. I’d get horny and weak.

I was already horny.

There were just too many years of longing for him in my past, and too many signals that his system sent crashing into mine, flipping switches and pressing buttons, whenever he got close to me.

I couldn’t let that happen. I couldn’t let him get that close.

I took a careful step back.

“I’ll see you tomorrow for dinner. I’ll let you know what time to be ready.”

“You do that,” he said, the panther-in-heat look in his eyes lingering on my face.

I stuck out my hand. “Have a nice day, Johnny.”

He stared at me, like, *Really?*

“Consider it practice. You know, manners?” I prompted.

He slipped his hand slowly into mine and squeezed. Bad idea. It was the most sexually arousing handshake in history, as that warm squeeze sent a rush of heat and lust straight between my legs and my clit hummed with want.

I broke eye contact—because no way was I looking him in the eyes while my pussy flipped out at his touch—and snatched my hand back.

*Professional relationship only.*

*No touching.*

“I have to go. Pancakes.”

Then I darted out of his studio, my heart pounding.

# Chapter Eighteen

### Johnny

"Johnny!" Vivian threw the door open wide, and her arms with it. As always, she seemed delighted to see me, as if my habit of dropping into her home with no notice, anytime I felt like it, wasn't the least bit annoying or off-putting.

I hugged her and wondered, not for the first time, how many other strays her husband had picked up over the years and if they ever dropped in like this.

She smiled up at me like an old lady cherub in her floral-print kaftan, her pale white-blonde hair in soft wisps around her face. This woman was the loving grandmother I'd never had. My own grandmother was chilly and acerbic, the other one had died when I was three, and my step-grandmother was uncomfortably conservative. So, I'd adopted Vivian as my de facto grandma after we'd met at least a few dozen times and I finally decided to trust her.

Her husband was another story. I'd met Rory hundreds of times, spent hours in his office, talking to him, not talking to him, hating and resenting and fighting him. Then chasing him to keep talking to me, years after his retirement from his career as a child and adolescent psychiatrist.

When he'd explained to me that he couldn't keep treating me because he no longer practiced and I got over the perceived rejection, I'd found creative ways to keep our conversation going. In retirement, the man had taken up endless creative hobbies, so I'd given him guitar lessons. After that, I'd come learn about shaping his bonsai trees with him or let him teach me how to paint, whatever it took.

Last year, after the cancer diagnosis and treatment, he got deeply interested in longevity and I brought him for a tour of my home gym. When he kept coming back to use the hot-cold circuit, I finally sent him a cold plunge bath of his own. He already had a sauna.

"Is he using the cold plunge?" I asked Viv as I stepped into the house and she shut the door. I glanced into the living room, but didn't see Rory.

"Almost every day." When I turned back to Vivian, she flattened her hands on my chest and looked up into my eyes. "Johnny. You've got to stop sending him gifts. All he wants is time with you."

"It goes with the sauna, though," I said lightly. "It's a circuit. Hot, cold. You can't have one without the other." I knew Rory could afford to buy it on his own, but I'd taken care of it, paid to have it installed. I'd come by a few weeks ago to make sure the installers did a good job, but Viv wasn't home at the time.

I'd told myself I was giving him the best kind of gift, something he wanted but might never get around to doing for himself. But when Viv looked into my eyes, I knew why I really did it. Rory had called me on it in our talks, many times; my habit of trying to buy people's loyalty, because I didn't know how to get it any other way. Or so I'd come to believe, according to him.

I knew he was right, because I still had this lingering expectation, even after all these years, that one day he'd tell me to stop coming to see him.

"I'm just taking care of his health, Viv. That's good for both of us, right?"

She frowned and seemed to stubbornly accept the explanation. I kissed her on the head.

"Would you like some privacy?" she offered. "I can bring in lunch."

"I'm not hungry. Privacy would be good."

"You go on, then. He's in with his babies today."

That could mean anything from some new craft Rory had picked up to more cats. At last count he had five of them, all former strays. I headed deeper into the sprawling art deco house, through the study in back that opened up to a lush rainforest-like courtyard. A bird, probably a new pet, was chirping somewhere.

I found Rory wearing a men's kaftan, similar to his wife's but in a natural cotton color, tending to what had to be two-dozen identical plants lined on a table.

"You look like a hippie," I greeted him.

He glanced at me over his glasses, looking even less surprised than his wife did that I'd dropped in out of nowhere.

"I am a hippie. The sixties were good years. They don't make bands like they did back then."

"Spoken like an old man," I teased him.

"Did you know I'm turning seventy-nine at the end of the year?"

Yeah. I knew. The thought of it was giving me a mental ulcer. The idea of Rory getting old, too old to talk to me about my problems anymore, had been eating a hole in me for years. The day this man died was gonna wreck me in a way I wasn't sure I'd ever come back from.

I'd never told him that, of course. Last thing he needed was worrying about me falling apart over losing him. He'd call me codependent or something and tell me to go back to therapy.

I watched him lovingly wiping invisible dust from the long emerald-green leaves of the plants, while he watched me.

"Your latest obsession?" I inquired. The plants weren't here last time I came by.

"I prefer hobby."

"It's not a hobby if it keeps you up at night. And you know you were up all night, misting them or something."

He neither confirmed nor denied as he continued dusting leaves.

I walked around the table. "So what is this, a grow op?"

"I'm sure you know what a marijuana plant looks like," he said mildly, "and this isn't it."

"I wouldn't put it past you to cultivate some new psychotropic wondershrub."

He didn't laugh. "Now there's an idea." He eyed me over the rims of his glasses again. It seemed to me he'd shrunk over the years, though I'd been twelve when I met him. He seemed much larger then. "Spathiphyllum."

"What was that, a sneeze?"

"Peace lilies." He indicted the plant he was caressing. "Did you know they filter harmful toxins from the air? And if you give them the right care, they can bloom all year long. They're beautiful, hardy plants."

"I didn't know that," I said genially. As if there was any chance I might know that.

"I'll give you one to take home."

"Thank you."

"Did Lamar drive you here?"

"He did."

"I'll give him one, too. Are you driving much lately?"

And so it began. Every time we met, Rory checked in with me on various points of concern. Was I driving? Was I sleeping? What was I eating? Was I going to therapy? And so on.

"Define 'much'?"

He eyed me. "As much as you want to."

"Yes. I drive when I want to."

"Have you been exercising?"

"I always exercise."

"Going to therapy?"

"Yes and no. I don't like the new doc."

He *tsk*ed, like this was expected. "You rarely do."

"None of them are you. You left impossible shoes to fill."

"You bonded to me when you were young and in need of guidance," he said lightly, downplaying his role in saving my life. "You need to give them a chance."

"Which is why you never let me tell you who I'm seeing," I poked. Rory refused to let me utter the name of any mental health professionals I saw. He had bad opinions of many of them and didn't want that to taint my experience, he said.

"Whoever it is," he said mildly, "give it time. It took you a damn long time to listen to me."

"I remember."

"How are you sleeping?"

"About as well as you are." Ever since chemo last year, the man barely slept. It was like he didn't want to sleep anymore, now that he'd been face to face with his mortality. Maybe he didn't want to miss anything.

I couldn't say I blamed him.

My own sleep issues were something else, though.

"Are you avoiding it?"

I knew what he meant; he wanted to know if I'd been avoiding sleep to avoid the nightmares. But I deflected. "Are you?"

He gave me a disapproving look. He'd been much more tolerant of my backtalk in therapy. As a kid, he'd let me get away with a lot of shit in the name of trying to help me. But that look said we both knew my attitude should've improved by now.

"Are the dreams getting any better?"

I wandered over to the sitting area, one of the cushioned chairs arranged under a fluttering array of dreamcatchers, and sat down. "They never get better. You know that. They only get less frequent."

"Last time I saw you—what was it, a few weeks ago? You were doing well. But last week on the phone you sounded… detached. Distant."

"I was probably playing guitar."

"It concerned me."

"You don't need to be concerned. Should I be concerned that you're not sleeping? You look like shit."

"So do you." He eyed me. "What have you been up to lately?"

Subtle. He'd probably already read the rumors about my band falling apart.

I hesitated to answer. I wasn't sure what he'd make of it, which made me hesitate to tell him what was on my mind. Because he'd be able to make of it things I couldn't. He saw patterns, saw reasons and answers, cause and effect, in so many ways that I never could.

But there she was, on my mind. No matter how I tried to focus on other things.

"I hired a woman to be my new publicist and I'm pretty sure I'm about to sleep with her."

He eyed me again, in that way only someone who knew much better than you did—about everything—could. "You think that's a good idea?"

"Which part?" Before he could answer, I forced it out. "I lost my record producer. The recording studio. And JC and Miles are gone. It's official. And now the lawyers are in on it, negotiating. Hopefully not making everything worse."

Rory had completely stopped caressing leaves to study me.

"Aren't you going to ask me how I feel about that?" I asked him, semi-sarcastically.

"I would, but we both already know how you feel about it. Do you want to talk about it?"

"I don't know."

I knew he was reading things I wasn't saying. There was a shit ton he could see, even when I wasn't talking. I'd hated it when I was a kid. Now, it was a relief and kind of a curse, being in his presence. You couldn't hide much from Rory. But he never forced me to talk about things when I wasn't ready, either.

I was here because I wanted to be. I'd talk when I wanted to.

He'd talk back because he wanted to. If he didn't, he would've kicked me out long ago, cut me off. I knew that much.

"Have you thought about telling her?" he asked me.

"She knows." I rubbed my hand over my face. "She knows what's going on inside my career." Unfortunately, she knew too much. Already.

All that shit she'd said about me being my own worst enemy? About no one liking me? About me wanting to hire her to fix my shit because I wasn't doing it myself?

Way too fucking accurate.

I wasn't prepared for her to see all that shit. Or for what happened last night; getting all fucking jealous and possessive when I saw her admiring other guys… I wasn't prepared.

I didn't know how to handle a relationship, on any level. Having Angeline in my space, all up in my shit when I was at my worst…

*No. Not your worst.*

*It gets much worse than that.*

"I wasn't referring to your career," Rory said, with his usual infinite patience. "I was referring to the fortress." He waited until I met his eyes again. "Do you feel like you want to tell her?"

I didn't even know how to answer that.

It was not something he asked casually. He'd rarely asked. Which meant that something about her, something about *me*, had tipped him off that she might by important to me somehow.

Even though I was here for that—for his insight—it bothered me when he saw things I didn't want him to see. And it was a relief. Because if he saw it first, I didn't have to say it myself. I could waste time denying it instead. Then he'd waste time trying to get through to me. It was a game I played, and he knew it; making him work for it. Making him prove that he cared enough to help.

I couldn't stop doing it. After all these years, I still couldn't stop. Trying to make him, just like everyone else in my life, prove to me that they cared.

Because deep down, I never believed them.

"Why would I want to tell her?" It bothered me, the implication—that she was someone important enough, someone who deserved to be told. How the hell could he know that, when I'd barely said two words about her?

I wasn't even sure how important she was to me.

I wasn't ready for anyone to be important to me.

My sister, sure. My dad. My stepmom.

A few of my friends.

My band—what a fucking joke. They were supposed to be important. Like family.

And yet half of them had fucking bailed on me.

Rory kept tending to his plants, almost unconsciously. I could tell all his focus was now on me, no matter what he was doing with his hands, as I got up and started pacing around the courtyard.

"Do you remember, long ago, when you told me?" he asked me, watching me pace. "It was one of our early sessions."

"Yeah. I remember."

"Why do you think you remember?"

"Because it stands out."

"How many people have you told, over the years?"

He knew the answer to that. "I find it irritating when you do that."

"When I do what?"

"Ask me questions you already know the answer to. It makes me feel like a child."

"In many ways, Johnny, you still are a child. We've discussed that. We can discuss it again."

"Not right now." I didn't come here to discuss the fucking fortress. I came here to talk about JC. Or my career going into tailspin. Or something.

"I'm asking," Rory said, "because the answer is meaningful and it might be a good idea to keep it front of mind."

I grit my teeth. But finally, I answered the question. "The answer is one. I've told one person."

"Me."

"Yes."

"Not your beloved sister."

"Why would I tell her? I can't tell her."

"Do you still feel you're protecting her by not telling her?"

"Yes. Of course."

"What about your stepmother?"

"No. My dad wouldn't want that. Even if I wanted to."

"You don't think she could provide a measure of support?"

"It would upset my dad."

"What about your closest friends?"

I laughed bitterly. "By your estimation, I don't have any close friends."

"Closeness requires some transparency. Trust. Tell me, Johnny. How can a friend get past the wall?"

We both knew exactly what was meant by that.

The wall was high, a fortress in my mind. It was already there when we'd met, but Rory had helped me to envision it, to put words to it.

I was inside this fortress.

But I wasn't a king in a tower. I was a small boy, sitting in a ball in the center, in a silent clearing. Alone.

"There's no getting past the wall."

"What if there was a way?" he asked me.

"There's no way," I said. Then I corrected myself. "I don't know a way."

"It's safe inside the wall," he said compassionately.

I didn't say anything. We'd already had this conversation, so many times.

Why was he bringing it up now?

"You remember, I used to encourage you to envision yourself as a man inside that fortress," he said. "I hoped you would, and that one day we might get you to take a step outside the wall. But over time we came to realize, together, that the wall was too crucial to you. It was your survival mechanism. So, we took some time nurturing the wall. Fortifying it in your mind. It seemed a healthy exercise, for a while. It seemed to carry you through a great many difficult times."

I waited, listening. Rory didn't talk a whole lot. When he talked a lot, it was time to listen. It usually meant he'd been thinking on something for a long time, and I *should* listen.

"We've talked about how your father did the best he could for you," he went on. "That the decisions he made came from a place of love, and you've recognized that. He was younger than you are now when you were born. He did what he knew how to do as a father, which was try to protect his son. Those were your words."

"Yeah." I rubbed my jaw, getting more and more uncomfortable with this conversation. "I know."

"He was the first builder of the wall."

I sucked in a breath. Rory had never said anything like that before.

But the truth of it resonated in a place so deep, I recognized it as fact. It left me speechless.

I stopped pacing and sat down.

"You didn't know it," he kept going, "because you were too young to know it. But it was your father who led you into that quiet clearing, and he laid the first stones. He built the wall for you because you couldn't. You were just a boy. He kept laying stones and even though you didn't know what he was building, you watched him lay the foundation. You watched him build the fortress around you, until one day you were strong enough to take over. You continued building the wall yourself, just as your father had done before you."

I was listening, and I could see the fortress. Not from the outside. As always, I was inside. I was the boy. And the wall was so high around me, I couldn't see the sky anymore.

"Is there anyone inside the wall with you now?" Rory's voice came from somewhere outside. Like I was asleep and he was awake, somewhere beyond. I'd shut my eyes. The fortress was all I could see.

"No."

"Your father doesn't come there anymore."

"No. He doesn't." I started to cry, but my eyes were closed. I pushed my thumbs into my eyes until the wall of the fortress turned red.

"He used to visit. Didn't he. In the early days. Long ago."

"Yeah. He did."

"I know it's painful." Rory's voice lowered gently. "The pain is where you have to go. You need to walk into it. Otherwise, you just keep running. You keep building the wall. And the really tragic part, Johnny, is that that boy never becomes a man."

I opened my eyes, blinking the tears away. Rory had come to sit down, on a chair across from me.

"Have you ever asked yourself," he said gently, "really asked yourself, do you want to be alone in the fortress?"

"No. Of course I don't want to be alone. But it's impossible."

"Ask yourself now," he said. "How did your father get inside the wall?"

"What do you mean?"

"Well, he was the original architect. He loves you. How would he come to visit the son he loves inside the fortress?"

I didn't know what to say. The fortress was nothing but a wall of stone that went on forever.

"You've told me many times about the great lengths he took to protect you," Rory said. "Maybe he hasn't been back in a long while, because that place is too painful for him, too. But you do believe that he loves you."

Rory waited, like that was a question, so I forced out an answer.

"Yes."

"Then wouldn't he have built you a door, Johnny?"

# Chapter Nineteen

**Johnny**

We all have nightmares, sometimes.

Mine is in the backseat of a car.

There's a dark street. The sound of the windshield wipers, beating back the weather, a slow, monotonous thud, as the rain on the glass turns to blood. There's an old rock song playing on the car radio.

And a stranger in the front seat.

There's cold, hard metal in my hand with a terrible weight to it. I know it to be the weight of death.

I've carried it with me for a long time now.

And in this nightmare, there's a sound so loud it breaks apart everything else and leaves only silence in its wake.

Afterwards, I can't speak for days.

Maybe in some ways, I still can't.

# Chapter Twenty

**Angeline**

The next time I saw Johnny, I was taking him to dinner.

Actually, he took me, in his car, which made it feel way more like a date, the two of us cruising through the city and over the Lions Gate Bridge into West Vancouver in his rumbling Hellcat. Lamar didn't even come with us.

Along the drive, I'd been trying to focus on how not-a-date this was by peppering my client with niceness advice—like how to encourage others to talk about themselves and really listen to them, to try to get out of his own head and be genuinely present with people… But when we turned into our dinner hosts' driveway, my stream of advice ground to a halt.

There was a car in the driveway that belonged to…

"Uh-oh." It fell out of my mouth before I could think.

"What?" Johnny looked over at me just as my eyes found the man standing in the shadows beyond the car, smoking a cigarette.

"Flynn," I breathed.

"Elle is here?"

"Elle and I, uh, grew up here. I had no idea she'd be here tonight, though. This is my parents' house," I confessed sheepishly. I still hadn't told Johnny who our dinner hosts were, until now. I'd told him to be prepared for anything; however, I was the one who'd failed to prepare. For this.

I wasn't prepared for anything but a nice dinner with my parents—the two nicest people I'd ever known. I'd come relaxed, or at least as relaxed as I could be with Johnny at my side, looking scrumptious in a pair of fitted jeans that accentuated his muscular thighs and a snug, collared shirt with the sleeves rolled up and the top few buttons casually undone, his tattoos and golden skin and glorious toned physique all on display.

But of course, my sister was as welcome at dinner with our parents as I was. She might've warned me about Flynn, though.

Before I could recover my wits, Johnny had stepped smoothly out of the car, come around to my door and opened it for me. He even offered me a hand. I took it, gliding out of the low car with his help, in my cute dress. Fitted, pale pink, cut just above the knee. I'd done my hair in pretty waves.

I'd felt pretty, confident, when Johnny picked me up at Shayla's and walked me to his waiting car in the driveway. But suddenly I felt self-conscious.

Did I look like I was on a date?

Why did I care?

Flynn had seen us, obviously, and put out his cigarette. Johnny shut my door and put his hand lightly on the small of my back to guide me up the driveway, and Flynn wandered over to intercept us. Johnny's touch sent tingles skittering all over my body, just like it did when he'd put his hand on my back or my arm at Champagne the other night. I had no idea if my ex-boyfriend had noticed Johnny's hand on me that night, but he was definitely noticing now and it was extra uncomfortable.

"Angie," Flynn greeted me neutrally. He had the stoic bodyguard routine down, even with me. "I was just dropping Elle off," he explained. As if I thought he was hanging out in my parents' driveway hoping to catch a random glimpse of me?

His watchful eyes flicked from me to Johnny and back.

"Hi, Flynn." I tried to keep my voice unemotional but polite. You know, setting an example for my client. When what I kinda really wanted to do was ask him how glitter-and-perfume girl was doing. "I don't know if you heard. I have a client." I gestured at Johnny.

Flynn looked at him again.

"Publicity," I added, when that didn't seem to compute. "I'm Johnny's publicist."

Understanding seemed to dawn. "Right. Flynn," he introduced himself, also neutrally, as he offered Johnny his hand. "I'm not sure we've officially met."

Johnny shook his hand, and whatever he was thinking, he behaved himself. "Nice to see you," he said, whether it was or not. Even I believed him. *Well done.*

"Well, we should get inside," I prompted when the two of them just stared each other down. "Mom probably has hors d'oeuvres coming out of the oven. I don't want to stress her out if they get cold."

Flynn nodded, moving aside to let us pass, though it wasn't really necessary. There was plenty of room. "Enjoy your dinner."

"Thank you. Have a nice evening."

As Johnny followed me up to the door, Flynn got into his car and reversed out of the driveway. Johnny leaned into me. "If being 'nice' means being fake polite to an ex like that, I'll pass."

"You were polite to Amber Cope the other night," I pointed out.

"No, I was honest with Amber. I told her she looked good and she did. You can find something honest to say or don't bother."

Hmm. "That's a solid point. However, I'm afraid me and my ex aren't quite there yet. It's been mere days since we had our last tearful, drunken fight. How long has it been since Amber broke your heart?"

He did not look impressed that I'd also made a solid point. "Like a decade," he muttered. "And I see your point. However, she didn't break my heart."

"So then, you broke hers?" I studied him, but he just gave me one of his cool, dark-wall looks. He was being incredibly cool about the fact that I'd sprung dinner with my parents on him, and he wasn't even complaining that I was wasting his time. I mean, I'd told him we were dining with VIPs tonight; he'd probably expected something a little more… glamorous. My parents were fairly wealthy and they had a beautiful home, but they didn't have anything to do with the music biz other than having a rock star daughter.

Johnny wasn't giving me static about it, and I wasn't even sure why.

Maybe he was just tolerating this whole night to shut me up about his niceness issues.

He reached for the doorbell, but I swatted his hand away. He raised an eyebrow at me when I pulled out my keys and let us in.

"You have a key to your parents' house?"

"Well, I lived here all my life. I only moved out a year ago to move in with Flynn. And whenever we had a fight… I'd come here." I felt embarrassed saying that to a grown man and kinda winced. "I probably do that too much. Run to my parents."

Actually, I was starting to rethink this whole plan. Bringing someone to dinner with my parents was natural for me. Especially anyone new in my life who I wanted to get to know better.

Was that what this really was?

No. *Professional relationship.*

"You two fight a lot?" Johnny's dark eyebrows had twisted together over his eyes.

"What? No. Not like *that*."

He made a growly noise. "I don't like him."

"Why?" I tried to read between the lines of the testosterone fueled vibe he was giving off. Much like the other night; that whole scene over Dean Slater. "Because he fucked me for almost four years?" Guys were so weirdly territorial about that, even with girls they had no right to be territorial over. Like, *You're talking to me right now, don't talk to him.*

"Yes," he said bluntly. "And he broke your heart."

I looked away, slipping off my heels, trying to ignore the way my heart was pounding. And the way his neck muscles were straining under his tattoos. Why was he getting all protective again? Just like he did at Champagne…

It was really fucking hot.

This hate crush was getting more annoying by the minute. I kept trying to lean into the hate part, yet I kept getting sucked back in the other direction whenever he did sexy stuff. Which, unfortunately for me, was way too often.

Johnny O'Reilly was one of those rare guys who was sexy even when he was being a dick.

*Maybe this is why Shayla keeps warning you about him.*

"Take off your shoes, okay? Mom is obsessive about her floors." I watched as he removed his Fendi low-tops. "And if you must know… I kinda broke his heart first. It's complicated. Most relationships are."

Johnny stood to his full height and looked down at me, his eyes dark and penetrating. "What, like the ones that don't work out?"

"Yeah. I'm sure you know a lot about those."

I turned to head into the house.

He caught my arm, stopping me in my tracks in the entryway. "You broke it off with him?"

"How is it your business," I asked him, squirming out of his grasp, "who hurt whom in my relationship, and you won't answer the same question about your ex-wife?"

He stared me down. I stared right back.

"I didn't break her heart."

Bullshit. Definitely not what I'd heard.

My sister didn't trade in gossip, so even though she and Dylan were tight, she'd never dished to me about his wife's ex-husband—even though she'd probably heard some things. However. I'd definitely heard from several of my girlfriends, including Talia—Johnny's buddy Lex's wife—who'd heard from Amber herself, that Johnny had done a number on her. Something about cheating.

Big surprise.

I startled out of the eye contact vortex that Johnny had somehow sucked me into when I heard someone coming. The entry hall lights that I hadn't even noticed were off flicked on. We'd been standing, bickering, in the near-dark. Like some grouchy couple.

"Well, look who I found whispering in the dark," my mom said, with obvious intrigue, looking from me to Johnny.

I scrambled for words, feeling weirdly defensive. Like my mom had barged in on me while I was watching porn or something. "Mom. I told you I was bringing a…" Wait. What did I tell her? "Um, Shayla's brother."

"Yes! Johnny, right? Come on in." My mom ushered us in, giving me a hug. "What a pretty dress! Your hair looks so beautiful." She ran her fingers over my loose curls. I tolerated it like a cat who didn't really like being touched but secretly enjoyed the attention and fucking loved being fed. "Did you curl it?"

"Well, tiny cartoon birds didn't spring forth from the depths of my closet to curl it for me. So, yes."

Mom laughed like she truly appreciated my humor. "Is she this sarcastic with you?" She turned to Johnny.

I looked at Johnny too, willing him to be nice. Even if he'd rather be honest.

"All the time." The way he said it, with a charming smile for my mom, it felt like a compliment.

Hmm. Wasn't so sure how much I liked him being nice. Not if it meant charming the shit out of my mom so damn fast. The man was knock-your-panties-off gorgeous when he smiled. He really didn't do it enough.

"Johnny is my client," I blurted out, before Mom could get any ideas; I saw the way her eyes dipped over his tight jeans, the tattoos and all the gorgeousness. "My first client, on my own. You know, because of Shayla. He's taken me on to do some publicity work for him."

"Oh!" Mom looked genuinely excited, which she was. "How lovely!"

"Your daughter's being modest," he told her. "I hired her *despite* my sister."

My mom laughed again, charmed. She loved all the rock stars and roadies who'd come into my sister's life. Many of them treated her like a mom figure because she was, honestly, an awesome mom. But many of them flirted with her, too. My mom was a beautiful woman.

"I can't wait to hear all about it over dinner," she said, her eyes meeting mine. My mom wore A-line dresses on a daily basis, with cutesy aprons when she was in the kitchen, and never had a hair out of place, like she was in some 1950s ad for baking products. But once upon a time, she'd hitchhiked down the west coast with my dad to hang out on the beach and go to rock shows on the Sunset Strip for an entire summer, even though her parents tried to forbid it. Back then, she had teased bangs and wore dramatic eyeliner, lacy gloves and corsets à la Madonna's *Like a*

*Virgin* album cover. I'd seen my parents' photo albums; Felicia Delacroix wasn't half as innocent as she looked now.

She wasn't naïve, either.

I could tell, she thought Johnny O'Reilly was hot as hell. And probably a heap of trouble. She was giving me that subtle, probably unconscious look that said she'd never understand my taste in men. And that she didn't believe for a minute that he was just my client.

But then again, she did love Flynn. She probably wasn't ready to meet any new guy I might bring home, for any reason.

"Thank you for having me," Johnny said politely.

"You two head on into the dining room. Your father's in there," she told me, lightly rubbing my back like she did when I was a little girl and I was overly excited about something—as if I looked like I needed soothing right now. Did I? "Thomas!" she called up the hall. "Get them some wine, will you? I have canapés coming!" Then she disappeared into the kitchen.

I glanced at Johnny as I led him deeper into the house; I could hear my niece's tiny, adorable voice, chatting away with her grandpa and her daddy in the dining room.

"You get used to it," I told him.

"Used to what?"

"Felicia Delacroix's over-the-top 'awesome mom' thing. Believe it or not, it's genuine."

"She's very nice," he said politely. Maybe practicing his manners as per my tips in the car.

"She's like a greeting card come to life," I said under my breath.

"She seems to adore you."

"What can I say? I'm freaking adorable."

I expected him to roll his eyes or something. Instead he just looked at me. We were doing that extended eye contact thing again and I wasn't sure why. We were also standing in a dark hallway again, alone, paused just outside the dining room.

I tore my gaze away when it was clear Johnny was never planning to. Sheesh. I tugged discreetly at the neckline of my dress to get air. It was fucking hot as hell in here, with his eyes on me like that.

Where did he get off, looking at me like that?

*Oh, God. Don't think about him getting off.*

When we walked into the dining room my dad was standing by the bar in the corner, and he was indeed pouring us wine. Elle and Seth were standing nearby, and everyone looked at us. I waved at Dad.

Emma squealed when she saw me and launched herself at my legs. "Annie Angie!" That was what she called me, because she hadn't quite gotten the knack of pronouncing "Auntie" yet.

"Hey, peanut." I gave her a squeeze. My niece had just turned four and she looked cute as ever in a little velvet jumper, her blonde hair in wild curls.

I met my sister's eyes. "You couldn't warn me that my ex-boyfriend was in the driveway?" was the first thing I said to her, in front of everyone.

"I did. Check your phone."

I dug it out of my purse as Johnny went to shake hands with Seth and my dad. There was a text from my sister on my phone. *We're coming to dinner. Flynn is dropping us off. See you soon. XO*

Oh.

Elle had come over and gave me a hug. "You okay?" she asked me. Her eyes said, *And why are you bringing Johnny O'Reilly to dinner with our parents?*

"I'm fine." I glanced over at Johnny, who was now chatting with my dad and my brother-in-law. Weird.

Suddenly, this whole thing did feel like a date. Like I'd brought home a guy I liked, and he was trying to impress my family. We both were. I'd worn a pretty dress because my mom liked me in dresses.

But this wasn't a date.

This was just a practice dinner. A trial run, for future social occasions where the stakes would be much higher. And honestly, maybe it was a test, of sorts. I didn't tell Johnny that. But I really needed to observe him in action, socially, so I could try to figure out where the problems lay. And how *much* work this was going to be.

I was no therapist, nor did I want to be his—despite his accusations to that effect—but I was a decent judge of character and I knew a troubled human when I saw one. I hoped Johnny could get past his troubles to pull his shit together, as soon as possible, so he could get on with his career.

But if he couldn't win over Tom and Felicia Delacroix, nicest humans on Earth… I'd know we had a long-ass, mountainous road ahead of us.

"Are you sure about this?" Elle asked me, following my gaze across the room.

"About what?"

She sighed. "I don't know. Whatever the hell this is, Angie."

I turned to my sister and looked her in the eye. "This is my first big girl job. I don't really know why he hired me, but he hired me. So just don't ruin it for me, okay?"

"Ruin it?" Elle looked taken aback. "Why would I do that? I'm on your team, Angie. Always. Do you seriously think I'm not?"

"I seriously think you don't trust him with your little sister," I told her, "on any level. But I've known Johnny for years, as Shayla's brother. I have my own relationship with him. Just trust me, okay?"

"I do trust you."

"Then believe me when I say I know what I'm doing."

My sister actually looked moved by my conviction, and much more sold on it than I was. Did I know what I was doing? Fuck, no. But it was mine to figure out.

"I believe you," Elle said gently. "I only want the best for you, you know."

"I know." I gave her a quick hug.

Then Seth strolled over. In his casual T-shirt and jeans, my sister's rock star husband looked even better than he did all dressed up at the nightclub the other night. He swiped his brown hair casually out of his face, looking like the DILF he was. He'd been growing it out again; it now touched his chin and that meant the dreamy waves were coming back.

"Angeline." He smiled wryly at me, his grayish-green eyes crinkling. If he was also wondering why I was showing up to family dinner with Johnny O, he was way cooler about it than my sister.

"Hey, bro." I gave him a hug, sucking in the comforting scent of him. Seth Brothers was a slice of heavenly maleness on Earth. Ever since he'd made a baby with my sister, though, I'd made a concerted effort to stop drooling whenever I saw him. But I could still appreciate the hugs and the scenery.

And I definitely appreciated the fact that Seth had been an amazing brother-in-law to me.

"You want a drink?" he offered, as Elle got pulled away by Emma. Seth was drinking coffee, his go to, no matter what time of night it was.

I glanced over at the bar, where Johnny and my dad appeared to be bonding over their wine. "Not tonight. I've had enough this past week. You don't even want to know what happened the night Flynn and I broke up."

"We've all been there, Angie," he said easily, sympathetically. "Don't sweat it." He didn't ask any questions. Which was why it was always so easy to be honest with Seth.

He didn't pry like my sister did.

Seth was the closest thing to a big brother I'd ever had. My best friends all had older brothers, but those guys—Courteney's brother, Cary, Larissa's brother, Trey, and of course, Johnny (shudder)—had never felt like brothers to me. Maybe because they all made me nervous on some level?

Not Seth. Seth put me at ease.

Plus, as a recovered addict—recovering? Whatever it was properly called—Seth had been there, for sure. Probably nothing I could tell him would faze him. Worry him, maybe. But he was way easier to talk to than my sister most of the time. Less reactive. The downside was that he'd probably tell my sister whatever we talked about. And I wouldn't exactly ask him not to. I knew he wasn't into that. It was a recovery thing. Harboring secrets was not cool, from his wife especially.

"I'm okay," I said, to his unasked question. I hadn't really talked to him, one on one, since the breakup.

"Well, even if you're not. You don't need to be." He glanced over at Elle and Emma. "You can still call us, anytime. Even if we're away, on tour. We're always here for you, Angie."

"I know." I knew he meant that. Because he cared about me, sure. But mostly because he was that devoted to Elle, and anything that was important to her. "So, hey," I asked him, awkward-yet-casual, "when you know something is bad for you, but you just can't stop doing it… that's an addiction, right?"

If the question concerned him, like it would concern my sister, Seth didn't show it. "I think that could be a lot of things." He studied me for a moment. "You worried you're drinking too much?"

"No. Other than this week. But that's just a breakup thing."

"You want to talk about it?"

I wasn't sure if he was referring to the breakup, or to that thing I couldn't stop doing. But either way… "Not really. But you don't need to worry about me having a drinking problem or anything. I promise. It's more of a… a man problem."

Seth's eyebrows drew together and I could feel his response to that one, a very big-brother response. Like, *What man is causing you problems?* "You sure you're okay?"

"Not that kind of problem. Not *a* man. Just men in general. I mean, me and men. Actually…" I made a kind of sigh-groan. "I'm the problem."

"Oh. I see." His lips quirked a little, amused. Seth had fine lips. Full and pouty like Brad Pitt.

"Your daughter's lucky," I muttered. "She got your lips. And my sister's stubbornness, actually. So, good luck with that."

His eyebrow lifted.

Then his eyes drifted over to Johnny. "So… you been spending a lot of time with Johnny O?" The question was casual. Too casual.

"You know, you're not as cool as you think, Seth Brothers."

He was. He was way cooler than he thought. That was what made Seth so cool. He wasn't full of himself, when he really could be.

He laughed, a soft, smoky laugh. "Neither are you, Angeline Delacroix."

I tried not to smile. It felt like a compliment, coming from Seth.

"He's nice," I told him, feeling kind of defensive of my client.

"That's what I hear," Seth said, deadpan. He was eying Johnny again.

We both knew he'd heard no such thing.

---

As the night progressed, I really started to question what the hell I was doing here.

Just like my sister was questioning it. I could see it all over her face.

Yes, I wanted to help Johnny save his career. I'd explained that to her already, to prepare her for seeing me show up at the Champagne opening with him; I figured I owed her that much.

But there were so many other ways I could help him as his publicist or even as his friend, if I wanted to be his friend, other than bringing him to dinner at my parents' house.

For his part, Johnny was on his best behavior. Not fake, which would've come off entirely wrong in front of Elle and Seth, who'd known him for a long time professionally and socially. But more like the nicest version of himself.

By the time we were finished dinner and I decided we should cut and run before anything went sideways, Johnny had really won over my parents. Clearly, they thought he was a great guy. Why wouldn't they? All the other rock stars my sister brought to dinner were great guys. She'd married a great guy. Why would my charming client be any different?

I made sure our goodbyes were quick, and I gave Seth puppy dog eyes so he'd hopefully get the message and prevent my sister from following us outside, where she could get nosey. He slung an arm around her when we walked out the door and I knew it was killing her to not go look out the window, see if we came in the same car and if Johnny opened my door for me or what.

He did.

But just as I was about to get in, Flynn's car pulled into the driveway. He was barely in park when he got out, his eyes locked on me. "Can I talk to you for a minute?"

Jesus. What did my sister do, text him the second I said we'd be leaving soon, so he could confront me in the driveway for her?

"Okay." I tried to smile at Johnny when he shot me a questioning look. "Can you wait for me in the car?"

"Sure." His hand lingered on my back a beat longer than necessary. Then he gave Flynn a look. It was a man to man *I've got my eye on you* look. That hyper vigilant mode of Johnny's had switched on again; the one I'd glimpsed the other night when he caught me crushing on Dean. And when he'd saved me from that carload of guys.

Flynn gave him a stoic yet icy look right back.

Johnny got in the car as I drifted away from it, though my door was still open. Flynn walked with me for a few steps, then said quietly, "Be careful with that one."

I turned to face him. "Are you serious?" I dropped my voice, hoping Johnny wouldn't overhear us. "That's what you pulled me aside to say? As if you have a right?"

"I have a right to care, Angie. We were together for over three years. You think I want to see you hurt?"

I raised my chin. "He won't hurt me."

"I hope not," Flynn said. He held my eyes for a long moment.

I knew he wasn't dense about Johnny. Flynn was extremely observant. He'd probably seen Johnny out at clubs and parties with many, many girls over the years, if he'd been paying any attention. Flynn never knew about that secret kiss between me and Johnny, or about my crush on him, exactly. At least, not that I'd ever admitted to him. Though he'd definitely accused me of being attracted to him, among other men.

Which just made me feel worse about what was happening right now.

I'd never told him, never admitted the truth, even though he'd obviously picked up on… *something*. And now here I was with Johnny, just days after our breakup. And yes, I was wildly attracted to him. I always had been. Weirdly, I was acutely aware of just how much I was attracted to him, standing here with my ex-boyfriend's eyes on me. I felt exposed, like I'd been caught red-handed doing something terrible.

"You deserve a man who will treat you right, Angeline," he said.

I felt my chin give the slightest shake. I looked away.

He'd treated me right. We both knew that.

But I'd wanted more.

I'd wanted… something else.

That hurt us both. But I had every right to go on with my life and try again. With whoever I wanted to.

Just like he did.

"He's my client," I said firmly. "And my best friend's brother. He won't hurt me." When Flynn didn't say anything, I met his eyes again.

"If he does," he said grimly, "you can call me."

A sick, disturbed feeling churned in my gut.

What the hell did that even mean? If Johnny hurt me, Flynn would come running to the rescue? Or take me back? Or let me cry on his shoulder or something?

Fucking no, on all counts.

"Why, so you can hurt him for me?" I said.

Flynn's jaw spasmed. I knew it bothered him, that I wasn't his to protect anymore. But that was his problem, not mine.

He broke up with me.

"You're Elle's bodyguard," I reminded him. "Not mine."

I got in the car, and as we backed out of the driveway I tried not to look at Flynn. He leaned back against his car to wait for Elle and Seth. He didn't look at me, either. He looked at the ground in front of him, his posture casual but his soul wound tight. So tight… I'd never really been able to get at whatever lay within.

It made me feel both better and worse knowing that this breakup had been as hard for him as it was for me.

"Everything okay?" Johnny asked me after a minute or two.

"Yes."

"You okay with seeing him?"

"Yes. I have to be." I sighed, trying to let go of the tension that seeing Flynn had caused. "He's working for my sister until the end of time. Goes wherever she goes. Travels with her. Will be an honorary uncle to her children. Etcetera." I tried not to sound bitter when I laughed a small laugh. "He's part of the family now."

"He didn't get invited to dinner," Johnny pointed out.

"Not this time. Because we were there. But trust me, he's invited to plenty of family functions. Even now that we've broken up, he'll be around. My parents love him." I almost bit my tongue. I felt bad I'd blurted that out, as if Johnny was my new boyfriend and that might make him feel like shit. I cleared my throat. "They like you, too."

"They seem to like everyone." He glanced at me, and I wasn't sure how to read that look. "Especially Elle."

"Yup."

"Why do you downplay yourself?"

"Huh? I don't."

"You do, actually. You all talk about Elle like she's the only one in the family with talent. Like there isn't enough to go around or something?"

I thought about that.

Did I do that? Did they do that?

I watched Johnny as he drove, his eyes trained on the road ahead. He didn't take his eyes off the road much. He seemed like an unusually tense driver, actually, which was curious since he'd insisted on driving tonight.

"Well," I said, "Elle just had it, you know? *It.* She always had it, from a really young age." I shrugged. "I could never catch up."

"Says who?"

I laughed. "Says my eighth grade music teacher. He was so fucking disappointed when I turned out not to sound anything like my sister. It was comical."

Johnny scowled, his eyes still on the road, like he didn't believe I found that funny at all. "You don't think you can play an instrument?"

"Nope."

"Elle's a strong vocalist. She's sensational on bass. I have a hard time believing her sister has no affinity whatsoever for music."

"Well, I don't."

"Because you never bothered?" he pressed.

"I bothered. I played a little piano as a kid. I liked to sing."

"You have a good voice?"

"I'm okay."

"Is that what people told you?"

"I mean, you can hardly blame them. They hear Elle sing. And then they hear me sing… Mom and Dad didn't mean to single her out and make me feel lesser than. I know they didn't. But it was kind of impossible for them not to. She was so good, and she went so far with it so young. There was a lot they had to do in the early days to support her so she could become who she is today. It was a priority in our house, supporting Elle's talent. I was just…" I shrugged again. "Average."

*Wow.* That seemed to really annoy him or something. His jaw ticked as he drove.

"That's what you think of yourself? Average?"

"There's nothing wrong with being average, Johnny O'Reilly," I told him simply. But I still felt a little raw about it, deep inside—that there was nothing I could ever do to be as special as my sister because I just wasn't born that way. Maybe I'd always feel raw about it. "We can't all be rock stars."

---

When we got home, Johnny walked me to Shayla's front door. Same as last time, when he walked me here after Champagne. But this time it felt even more awkward.

Because I really wasn't sure where I stood with him.

I'd set out on this night sure of where I stood. As his publicist.

Now I was… confused.

Seeing my family's reactions to us together… they all seemed to think there was something between us. Something more than we were letting on.

So did Flynn.

And now I found myself wanting to know, badly, what Johnny thought about all of it. What he thought of *me*.

It sucked.

When we reached the door, I turned to him, resolved to say a professional *good night* and *thank you*. I met his eyes, that deep aquamarine-blue looking extra dark as his gaze drifted down to my lips.

"Well, good night. Thank you for accompanying me to dinner." I sounded nervous, even to myself, and not at all professional and composed. "I hope it was helpful. I think you did well." Was it my imagination, or was he drifting closer to me? "You got along well with my dad. I mean, everyone gets along with my dad. He's in sales. It's kind of his thing." Was I drifting closer to him? "But he liked you. I could tell. Which means you either put on a great act or you're really coming around. You know, when you learn to listen to people instead of—"

His lips met mine and for a long, breathless moment, we fused together in a molten hot kiss that felt like it lifted me right off the ground.

Oh, *shit*.

I wasn't even sure who instigated it. It just… happened.

When our lips dragged apart and I sucked on his bottom lip a little harder than necessary, I felt the warm, tender inside like wet, silky heaven, and my pussy throbbed.

I sucked in a shaky breath.

His eyes, darker than an inky night sky now, burned down on me in silence, his face still so close to mine.

Neither of us backed away.

I'd tried to avoid getting involved with him, I really did. I wasn't trying to date him. Or fuck him.

But when our lips touched just now… I just wanted it too badly.

Because I was weak. Weak when it came to my own lustful responses to certain men. At least I knew this about myself. Everything in me screamed *yes*, except that small part of me that feared the outcome of getting involved with Johnny O'Reilly…

Pain.

Most of my parts, very insistent parts, were telling me that there was nothing that would help me move on from my breakup with Flynn like the all-consuming intensity of a hot and heavy fling with a man like the one standing in front of me. That maybe it was time for a passionate, nonsensical affair with someone who made my toes curl without even touching me, like Johnny was doing right now.

Then his hand touched the side of my face and my brain melted into a glob of throbbing mush, like all the rest of my vital organs. "Uh…" I breathed, as he smoothed my hair back from my cheek with his thumb, sending a tide of shivers through my body, one cascading over the other.

*Holy. Christ.*

This was way better than the first time he kissed me.

It was *worse*.

Because I had no real reason to stop him this time.

Shayla… Shayla would get over it, right? And so would my sister.

I could not think rationally right now, and I knew it. But I wanted this. Desperately.

"I'm sorry," he murmured. "Were you trying to make a point?"

"Uh, yeah. I was. I was rambling, I know." I could feel my face heating as he brushed his thumb gently back and forth over my cheek, the warmth of his hand lightly cupping my jaw.

"Please. Go on."

"Uh… I can't remember. Manners. You had good manners tonight," I managed to force out.

"Great," he said softly. "I hope I passed your test on how to treat a 'nice' woman in front of her family."

Right. So he knew I was kinda testing him tonight. "Um… you did okay."

He'd been a total gentleman tonight, and he knew it.

I wondered if it was calculated or real.

The butterflies freaking out inside me felt real. His hand was still touching me, his thumb caressing my cheek. It was hypnotic, as his eyes traced the curves of my face.

"Am I fucking this up already," he asked me in a low, soft voice, "by trying to make it into something it's not instead of letting you just do your job?"

Jesus. Right now, hearing him say that… *Trying to make it into something…* on the heels of that kiss? I didn't know what to say. My heart was thudding and my panties were on fire. But I was afraid of making it into something it wasn't, too.

Maybe he felt my thudding heart and read my fear. Because when I said nothing, his hand dropped away. "What happens now, Angel?" he asked, his eyes holding mine. "This is your lesson."

I tried to ignore the way his low, husky voice made my heart trip when he called me Angel. "L-lesson?"

"You're teaching me how to be nice."

"Oh. Right." I floundered, caught between wanting him to be nice and wanting him to be a raging asshole and drag me into the bushes to bend me over, right the fuck now. "Well… what would you do now, at the end of a real dinner date?"

His gaze dropped to my lips again. "Assuming I liked her?"

"Uh… would you go on a date with someone you didn't like?"

"No."

"So, then…"

"So, then I'd take her inside."

My breath caught as our eyes locked for an uncomfortably long heartbeat, then two, three. Oh, God. Was he taking me inside?

"Lucky for you, we're not on a date," he said gently.

"Yeah." I laughed nervously. "Lucky me."

"Good night, Angeline," he said, then he started to turn away.

And the fact that he was trying to be a gentleman right now? For my sake? Because I advised him to be nice tonight? It just turned me on even more. Because I knew, a gentleman he was not.

Then he paused. "Maybe you're right. Maybe I am my own worst enemy." His eyes drifted briefly down my body.

Then he turned and disappeared into his house.

## Chapter Twenty-One

**Johnny**

I couldn't go to sleep. There was no fucking way.

From my phone, I turned on the ambient lights in my bedroom, so they were already on when I walked in; the ones that glowed behind the headboard of the bed and along the floor where it stepped down into the sitting area. I flicked on the fake fireplace too, the slab of glass on the wall that shimmered like the Northern Lights; instead of green and purple hues, the light that danced across the slab was scarlet and gold.

The whole room was warm and luxurious.

It felt empty tonight.

I paced the length of the room, fighting down the urge to go next door and talk to Angeline.

And say what?

*There's nothing for you to say that won't ruin it.*

*You already said enough.*

With another app on my phone, I slid open the glass doors to the patio to let in the fresh night air. Every detail of the house had been seen to by a top designer, to meet my exacting needs and preferences. I'd spent the most time planning out the bedroom.

Maybe because it was the room where I knew I'd be entertaining women the most. And there was something hotel-like about it, wasn't there? *Come in, maybe awe at the amenities, enjoy yourself knowing you won't have to clean up afterwards, and get the fuck out in the morning if not sooner. Someone else will be checking in soon enough.*

I wanted it to feel that way.

Weirdly, I didn't want it to feel that way for Angeline. I knew that, because I was actually wondering what she thought of this room. She'd been in here when she cleaned my house, but she really did do a terrible job. From the looks of things, she'd skipped cleaning this room entirely. Couldn't really blame her for that, after she saw Brianna stroll out of it.

I had no idea how I was ever going to make Angeline feel safe enough with me to walk in here again.

What was she doing right now?

Was she pacing, thinking about me?

Was she sleeping?

There were security feeds from the cameras in Shayla's house I could've looked at on my phone, windows I could've looked through, to try to get a glimpse of her. I had keys. I could call her phone. I could get to her in any number of ways, and yet… I couldn't. Not if I wanted to respect the line she'd drawn between us.

Did I want to respect it?

I wasn't even sure, and it was driving me crazy.

She'd kissed me back tonight, practically sucked my lip off, but I knew she didn't trust me. She told me she hated me, like two nights ago.

But she didn't really know me, did she. She just knew certain things.

Maybe she didn't want to know me.

As I paced around the room, I felt… uneven. That was the only way I knew how to describe it. After all the years of talking to Rory and close to a dozen other therapists, I still didn't have language to connect words to my feelings.

I didn't have feelings.

They told me I did. That most of my emotions were just buried, deep.

If you were Rory, you told me I'd locked them inside the fortress with the boy.

If you were another therapist, you said I used alcohol or drugs to avoid them, that I was self-medicating with liquor or sex or music, or that I was a sex addict, or that I was codependent or self-loathing or self-sabotaging, or that I had anxiety or insomnia. None of their diagnoses ever seemed to agree with one another.

If I went to a medical doctor, he wanted to prescribe pills. If I went to a talk therapist, he wanted to talk. If I went to group therapy, they wanted me to talk to other survivors. People, even professionals, only saw what they were trained to see.

Any way you wanted to look at it, though, I was disconnected from my feelings. So disconnected, I didn't know how to influence them on my own most of the time, control them. Or even access them. That was what Rory said. And the other therapists I'd seen over the years generally agreed with that, at least.

But no one had ever really understood me like Rory did. Or maybe no one had ever been able to get through to me like Rory did; maybe that was all it was.

I couldn't exactly call Rory in the middle of the night, though. Even if he might be awake anyway. I had to respect his life, his marriage, his health. There had to be boundaries.

I went to him too much as it was.

So all I knew in moments like these, alone, with no one to talk to, was that I felt uneven. Unsettled. Unbalanced.

I used to combat this loss of equilibrium by staying up around the clock doing lines of coke. Disturbing my thought processes until I was no longer aware of the unevenness.

But nurturing a cocaine habit wasn't exactly the course of therapy any doctors prescribed.

Anyway, the first time Shayla saw me doing blow, when she was fifteen, was the very last time I did it. I didn't want her thinking that shit was okay, for her or for any guy she brought into her life. I didn't like being a bad influence on her, or a bad role model, and I knew I was, in so many ways.

Now, when I felt uneven, I'd drink, maybe. Alcohol just made me more uneven, usually, but at least it helped me forget the details. Drinking was a distraction more than a pleasure.

Or, I'd use sex as a distraction. A mood lifter.

That sometimes worked, on a biological level. But not for very long.

Or, I'd smoke pot. Sativa, not indica, to keep my mind active. I'd play guitar. Reading or watching TV or even listening to music was too passive. I needed to do something with my hands, stimulate my brain in a certain way, to switch my focus away from that unevenness.

But the last thing, the very worst thing I could do was go to sleep.

If I slept in this state, the nightmare would find me.

I thumbed through my phone. A few people had dropped me a text about going out tonight. Shane. Noah. Even Yash. But I didn't like being around my friends when I was this uneven—unless I wanted to get immediately, extremely wasted.

I didn't want to get wasted right now. And anyway, Shane and Lex had given me enough flack the last time I brought my problems to them. The night I'd hired Angeline to be my publicist… because I couldn't stop looking at her across the bar, thinking about her.

That was what this was about, right? I didn't really hire her to be my publicist. I hired her because I wanted her around, even when I didn't want her around.

She irritated me and she fucking fascinated me.

I could've easily spent the rest of the night with her, even if nothing happened between us tonight. We could've had a drink. Talked. Watched fucking Netflix for all I cared. We were both alone. According to the alarm system on Shayla's house, also connected to my phone, my sister wasn't home.

But maybe Angeline just wasn't interested. She already regretted that kiss, and tomorrow she'd tell me she hated me all over again.

I finally stopped pacing and got undressed, maybe to convince myself I wasn't going next door. I picked up the wooden box on my nightstand, walked naked out onto the patio in the dark. I settled onto a lounge chair and opened the box, taking out some weed and rolling papers. Rolled myself a blunt, then laid back and smoked, looking up at the night sky.

Then my phone lit up with a notification. When I picked it up, I saw her name on the screen.

**Angeline:** You didn't fuck anything up. You did well. It was a nice night.

As I was reading the text she'd sent me, another one came in.

**Angeline:** And a nice kiss.

I texted her back, because *what the fuck.*

**Me:** Nice?

I sent her an eye roll emoji. And a thumbs down emoji. And a vomiting emoji.

She sent back a laughing emoji.

**Angeline:** You were a gentleman. Let's leave it at that.

**Me:** I'm not a gentleman.

**Angeline:** I know.

I let that hang for a minute while I smoked, wondering what she was thinking.

And what she really felt about me.

Because the girl felt every fucking thing. All you had to do was look at her to know it. It was in her eyes. Maybe I couldn't tell *what* she felt, but whatever she really felt about me… hatred wasn't it.

I tried to remember all the shit she'd said to me about relationships in her little lectures. Listening to people… Genuinely caring…

Letting people in.

That last bit wasn't something I was used to doing with anyone, women included. Flirting, sure. But that wasn't the same thing. Flirting could be a wall as much as it was a door.

Actually opening up to make space for someone close to me, to let them get close to me, was something else entirely. Something I'd never really known how to do.

**Me:** I'm not good at boundaries. Just tell me if I'm treading over the line.

I wondered if she was still awake as I waited for her response.

**Angeline:** Why aren't you good at boundaries?

**Me:** Maybe I have a hard time sensing where yours are at.

**Angeline:** Why?

I finished my smoke, then finally responded.

**Me:** Because I'm so focused on keeping my own locked down tight.

**Angeline:** Well it goes both ways. You can tell me if I'm overstepping too.

**Me:** You're always overstepping.

Another laughing emoji came at me.

I smiled. It occurred to me that we'd just covered more ground, personally, in this text conversation than we had in days. Or possibly ever.

**Me:** Maybe it's easier if we test the boundaries here. Then you know I won't try to kiss you again.

*Yet.*

**Angeline:** Okay…

**Me:** First rule. You have to be honest.

**Angeline:** Great. Rules again. You have too many of those you know.

**Me:** That's the only rule. Also if you say something that might be misinterpreted and you want to make it clear we're not arguing… punctuate it with an appropriate emoji.

**Angeline:** I thought guys hated emojis.

**Me:** You use so many superlatives and made up words I need to know if you're being sarcastic or what. I have a hard enough time reading emotions in person.

**Angeline:** Okay. So you go first. Test my boundaries.

No emoji.

Was she kidding? Or flirting?

Did she mean that as sexually as I read it?

I considered carefully. She'd kissed me back tonight, but then she didn't seem to want me to take her inside. But then she texted me to tell me it was a "nice kiss."

And now she wanted me to test her boundaries.

From a safe distance.

I tried to think of something that might push the envelope but still keep that safe distance intact for her.

**Me:** I've seen you on my security cams.

**Angeline:** What security cams?

**Me:** The ones all over the house.

**Angeline:** You have cameras all over your house? (Mind blown emoji.)

Okay; she'd used an emoji. So… she wanted me to know that she was blown away by that information, rather than mad?

Which encouraged me to keep going.

**Me:** In almost every room. I saw you when you came over to clean. I saw you coming upstairs. (Two eyeballs emoji.)

**Angeline:** For real? (Dead emoji.)

Hmm. Did that mean "I'm dead" like "I'm astonished"… or did she now want me dead?

**Me:** I was watching you on my phone. (Happy tears emoji.)

**Angeline:** When I walked in on you naked?? (Scream of horror emoji.)

**Me:** Yes.

**Angeline:** You could've put some pants on. (Face plant emoji.)

**Me:** I could've. But then you wouldn't have seen me naked. (Drooling emoji. Eggplant emoji.)

**Angeline:** (Angry swearing face emoji.)

*Shit.*

Her name popped up as my phone rang and I answered casually. "Ms. Delacroix. What can I do for you this evening?"

"Where are you?" she demanded.

"On the patio off my bedroom. Naked and slightly high."

"That emoji thing was stupid. Were you saying I was drooling because I saw you naked, or were *you* drooling because I saw you naked?"

"Does it matter?"

"Yes."

"Can't it be both?"

"No. Maybe. I don't know."

"What's wrong?"

"I'm annoyed."

"About what?"

"Your stupid games."

"I'm not playing games. I'm trying to talk to you. You don't make it easy."

She huffed a little and went silent.

"What are you thinking?"

"Are you really naked?" she asked softly, kinda shyly, and my dick throbbed. I was half-hard already, just phone flirting with her.

"Yes."

"What are *you* thinking about?"

I took a breath. *Push that envelope a little further...* "The window in the guest room next to my bedroom. The one that looks into your room."

"You can see me?"

"No. Not yet. Do you want me to look?"

I hadn't looked. Yet. Not like it hadn't crossed my mind, though. I knew what room she'd be staying in; Shayla's largest guest room, the fully furnished one.

The worst she could do was say no. Message received, right? It was just a question.

But as usual, Angeline didn't respond the way I hoped she would—with a clean and tidy yes or no. Instead she said, "What is it you want to see?"

Now, was this a minefield or what? I say the wrong thing, I'm a creep. I'm not taking her seriously as my publicist. She starts questioning every interaction we've ever had and my every motive. And on and on.

I say the right thing, maybe we both get something we want.

"You can keep thinking about it," she said, "but fair warning, I might fall asleep."

"I want to see you safe in your bed. I want to see what you sleep in."

I wondered if that surprised her, that I didn't go straight to something purely sexual.

Either way, her voice sounded breathy and turned on when she said, "I'm not wearing it yet."

"Then I want to see you put it on."

Again, I waited for her to tell me to fuck off. Or invite me to come look at her, in whatever way she'd let me.

"It's embarrassing," she said.

"All the better."

"Why?"

"Because you can trust me with whatever it is. That night I put you to bed, you trusted me."

"So?"

I sucked in a slow breath between my teeth, trying to open up. Be transparent. It wasn't easy. "So… I've never been so drawn to someone in my life."

There was a long silence on the phone line.

Then Angeline said softly, "That's not true."

"It is true."

"If that's true, if you felt *that* drawn to me…" She hesitated. "There's no way you didn't either try something, or go home and take matters into your own hand."

Well, she was right about that.

"First of all, I didn't try anything. You were so fucking drunk you told me I was sooooo gorgeous and you liked my eyes."

"Ugh. Exactly my point. If I was giving you green lights all over the place—"

"I wouldn't call them green lights. You said a ton of shit you'd never said to me before, drunk or sober. Taking that as a green light when you could barely stand is called assault. Which is why I did the second thing."

"You're telling me you went home and jerked off after you tucked me into bed?"

"Yes."

"But you're a rock star."

I sighed inaudibly. "So I can't fantasize about you?"

"No."

"You have some seriously warped self-opinion, sweetheart."

"Tell me one thing that was a turn on about me that night," she demanded, "instead of being pathetic."

"Your eyes."

"What about my eyes?"

"The way you looked at me. You have this way of looking at me like you're hypnotized. And hungry. But only if I catch you looking when you think I don't notice. You did it openly that night. And I promise you, it was really, really hard not to kiss you back when you kissed me."

"I kissed you!?" She sounded mortified. Or something. Shocked? I wasn't sure.

"Just a little soft kiss on the lips when we said good night."

"Oh my God." I could practically hear her cringing through the phone.

"Also, your breasts were pretty amazing," I added casually.

"You've never seen them," she said, sounding unsure. "Unless you've been spying on me through that window."

"You wore a lace bra that night. It was see through. And little panties." She groaned a little. "I can picture it, anytime."

"Like right now?" she whispered.

"Yeah. Right now. But… I could also enjoy a new picture."

I could. This conversation and the memories of that night had my cock standing on end. A little more, whatever she might show me… I wasn't gonna say no to that.

"You want to see me?"

"Yes."

"You… you want me?" She sounded breathless and shy again, uncertain.

"Yes."

"Show me."

I swallowed. She really didn't believe that I wanted her? That she turned me on?

"You want me to come to the window?" *Or come over there?*

"No. Just… send me a pic?"

"Really? You want that?"

"Yes."

"Okay, then. I will." I agreed without even thinking about it, without considering the privacy aspect. As in, I was protective of mine.

Which was interesting on its own. I'd had other girls ask me for pictures. Like, a lot. I'd never sent one before.

I got up and went into my bedroom, laid back on my bed. I didn't have to do anything to get ready for it. I sent her a photo, up close and personal of my rock hard cock, via text.

"There you go," I told her, bringing the phone back up to my ear. When she was utterly silent, I confessed, "Believe it or not, I've never sent a photo of my dick to a woman before."

"Why?" she breathed. "You're not shy." Presuming, again, that she knew way more about me than she did.

"Not really. But I'm private. And fairly famous."

"So why would you send it to me but not anyone else?"

"Trust."

After a moment, she said softly, "More. Please."

A warm shiver ran through me at her words. "Okay. What do you want?"

"I… I want to listen to you. While you touch yourself."

Shiiit. This was getting way too hot. Somehow, the knowledge that she was right next door but I couldn't just go touch her—because she hadn't said I could—just made it hotter. "You're killing me…"

"Please."

I groaned. Now she was begging?

Killing. Me.

"A visual would help," I told her.

I really didn't need a visual. But I'd take one if she was willing.

"Of what?"

"Your breasts." Naked, clothed, playing with her nipples… Whatever she was willing to share, I'd leave that up to her.

She sent me back a pic of her naked breasts peeking out from under her top. *My fucking yellow T-shirt.*

Was that what she wore to bed?

The adrenaline rush shot straight to my groin. My cock flexed and I smoothed my palm along the shaft. My eyes dragged over the photo, my shirt against her naked skin, the fabric pushed up to show her perfect tits… the creamy-soft handfuls tipped with gorgeous pink nipples I could've sucked on all fucking night.

I ran my fingertips up and down my shaft, stroking, then squeezing the head, coaxing out a bead of pre-come.

"Are you…" she said shyly, "are you touching yourself?"

It took me a breathless minute to respond to that. "Yes. Do you like that?" My voice was weirdly gravelly but I tried to sound calm, totally cool, so she wouldn't think I was judging her or anything. I wasn't judging. I was losing my mind.

"Yes." It was just a whisper, and in that one word, I heard the unspoken question. *Is that okay?*

I swallowed thickly. "You just want to listen?"

"Yeah."

My pulse was thudding so hard through my entire body I wasn't sure I should trust my ears. "Are you sure?"

"Yes."

"Just… tell me to stop and I'll stop. If there's anything you don't like. Or if you change your mind."

"Okay."

"Promise me."

"I promise."

"There's no way this ends up making you hate me."

"I already hate you."

I kinda choked out a laugh. Stubborn girl.

"Then tell me what you want from this guy you hate," I said roughly.

"I want to hear you get off on me."

Well, that was pretty fucking clear. No shyness now.

"I can do that." My voice was thick with lust as I stroked my cock. I was so turned on hearing about her turned on, I had no idea if this was gonna live up to her fantasies. Did she want it to be fast and furious? Or did she want it to last…?

I put the call on speaker, then set the phone down on a pillow next to me so I could free up my hands. As I ran my fingers up and down my shaft, my cock stood up tall, fucking grateful.

"Tell me what you hear right now."

"You," she said, her voice taking on that slightly self-conscious, shy note again, and it slayed me.

I was starting to understand her vibe, though. She knew what she wanted—major turn-on. She was just unsure how to ask for it. I wasn't sure if she was nervous about it, afraid of rejection or judgment, or just unpracticed, but whatever it was, I couldn't remember the last time I was this fucking hard. My entire body was into it, the ache spreading with every hungry throb through my veins.

But I tried to hold back, tried not to rush it.

Maybe I could help make her feel more comfortable about asking?

"What do you want to hear, Angel? Tell me."

"You," she breathed. "Making yourself come for me."

I squeezed out the words as my heart thumped its hungry rhythm. "I'm going to."

"And if you're actually watching porn or something," she added, "that is cheating. And you're missing the point."

"This isn't a game," I reminded her, "and I'm not cheating. I'm not missing the point. The point is you're listening, and I'm doing this for you."

She laughed a little. "I'm sure the orgasm won't be a hardship on you."

"The orgasm will be better because you're here."

"I'm not there."

"But you're listening." I kept jacking myself slowly, fingers only, stroking my shaft, my cock standing stiff in the air… The simple knowledge that she could hear my breathing was ramping up my excitement, so fast. "And talking to me. Your voice is gonna make me come."

She could probably hear it in my voice; I was falling apart already. I was breathing heavier even as I tried to relax.

"Is it?" she teased. "I didn't know you liked my voice so much."

Oh, I liked. Every time she spoke, my cock spasmed. I rode the waves of those spasms, my fingers following the rhythm. Building toward that climax she'd requested.

"I love your voice," I told her, mine sounding drunk with arousal.

She didn't say anything to that.

I wanted her to tell me she liked this.

I wanted her to tell me she liked *me*.

I wanted her to tell me how fucking hot this was.

But for some reason, it all got stuck in my throat. Maybe, in a way, I wasn't so used to asking for what I wanted, either.

Bossing around some chick I just met in bed, taking control of the sexual act, being dominant, alpha, whatever. I could do that.

But *asking…* that was different. Especially asking for something meaningful from someone you cared about.

Especially when you didn't know if the answer would be no.

Was this what vulnerability felt like?

The fact was, I didn't usually care enough to get vulnerable with women.

I wasn't shy. I wasn't self-conscious. But with Angeline… I didn't want to mess up. I didn't want her to think this was just about me getting off, or about using her. This was about what I told her it was about in the beginning: trust.

So instead I said, "Say my name." I couldn't believe how desperate I sounded.

I half-expected her to laugh.

"Johnny."

My ass clenched and my dick shuddered as I ran my fingers up and down. "Fuck. I'm not gonna last, Angel."

"Try," she breathed, and I could hear the lust in her voice. The fact that this was turning her on was making it so much more fucking intense.

"I can't. Not with you listening." *And sounding like you love it.*

"You've come for me like this before?" she pressed.

"Yes."

"Then come for me."

Christ, just her telling me to come was a rush. "Fuck. I'm gonna come…"

"*Oh,*" she gasped, like she couldn't believe I got there so fast. Her pleasured surprise made it even more erotic.

Intimate.

"You want it?" I gasped, squeezing my cock in my fist now, trying to hold it back until she said so.

"Yeah…"

"Angeline…" I groaned her name as the ecstasy surged, letting go. My cock convulsed in my fist and I ejaculated for her. Hot come spurt onto my abs. I smeared my free hand over it, then used it to jack myself off in long, greedy pulls. I spurt for her a few more times, moaning, mindless. "Angie. Angie… fuck."

She was silent, but breathing softly.

I kept stroking, root to tip and back again, as I softened a little. My head spun. The occasional spasm racked through me and my hips flexed a little. I just rode it out, panting, trying to give her what she asked for.

I could hear her breathing softly, but she still didn't say anything. I figured maybe she was embarrassed. Or, dare to dream… busy touching herself?

"It's okay," I told her, still stroking myself. "It's okay to like it." I thought maybe that was what she needed to hear.

"Did that feel good?" she finally whispered.

"Yes."

It did. The peak of that orgasm was soul-splitting. But the high faded fast. It was weirdly anticlimactic, not being able to see her, touch her, taste her. I wanted more of her.

I wanted *her*.

"Are you touching yourself?" I asked her, picking up the phone and bringing it to my ear.

"Yes."

"Baby," I said, softly, because suddenly she felt ridiculously precious to me. I wanted to hold her right now, which was bizarre. I felt drunk on the need to touch her. "Tell me what you're feeling."

"I'm so turned on," she gushed.

"Tell me what you're doing. I want to hear you."

"I got this big dildo," she said, all trace of shyness gone, replaced by a desperate desire. "It has soft horns for the clit. It looks demonic."

I swallowed. "Is it inside you?"

"Yeah."

"You're fucking yourself right now?"

"Yes."

Holy Christ. *Don't fuck this up.* "Good, baby," I said gently. "Keep going. Make yourself feel good."

"I don't know how this feels," she practically sobbed, her voice smeared with lust. "I don't know how it feels to trust you."

"It's okay. You're safe, Angeline." I closed my eyes and pictured her face. I tried to picture her in ecstasy. Unfortunately, I'd never seen her like that before. "You're so pretty. I just want to kiss you."

"Johnny," she sobbed.

"Yeah. Say my name while you fuck yourself, Angel."

"Johnny. Johnny…"

My body flushed with heat as she said my name.

"I want to kiss you while you come. I want to suck on your pussy."

"Oh, God."

"Come for me, baby. You're so fucking sweet. I want to hear you come."

"Johnny… I don't know…"

"It's okay." I took a breath, trying to slow down. "It's just you and me. You have no idea how good it felt, having you right here with me. I want you to feel good like that, too."

"Okay…"

"What can I do?"

"Just… talk to me."

"Okay, sweetheart. Keep fucking yourself for me, nice and deep." I tried to think of something specific that might rev things up for her. She'd asked for that picture of my cock. And she seemed to want me to come for her pretty badly… "Imagine it's my cock filling you."

That was rewarded with a little mewl of pleasure.

I imagined that big dildo, slick with her juices, sliding in and out of her tight pussy. But she needed more. She needed me?

Fuck, just that thought turned me on, made me want to touch her so fucking badly, get my hands all over her body…

"Close your eyes and picture that orgasm I just had," I told her. "Can you see me coming?"

"Yeah…"

"It's happening deep inside you, right now. I'm coming inside you, so hard."

She gasped, then made a shuddery, unintelligible sound. Then I heard my name again. "Johnny!"

"Come, baby."

"*Yeah*. I'm coming..."

"*Angel.*" I listened to her soft cries and moans. "Keep coming. You're so beautiful." I lay there just listening, my hand idly squeezing my half-hard cock, as she came... so close to my ear but so fucking far away. Too far.

"Johnny. Oh my God." She sighed when she was satisfied. "That was... I don't think I can ever look you in the eye again."

"Fuck that. I'm coming over there." I sat up.

"No, you're not." Her tone was firm. Forceful.

"Angeline. For fuck's sake."

"Do not."

I collapsed back into the pillows. "You're looking me in the eye in the morning," I told her, just as firmly. "I'm coming over there to make breakfast."

"And then what?"

I sighed. "In a perfect world? You let me explore your naked body and make love to you all day long as I figure out every single touch that drives you crazy, so I can do it again any time you'll let me. But I guess that's up to you."

She sucked in a soft breath. Silence stretched for a long moment.

"Can I think about that?" The self-consciousness had returned. A wariness. About me, about this, about what just happened. Whatever it was, I hated it.

But I couldn't exactly push her on it. Not over a fucking phone.

"Of course."

"Good night, Johnny," she breathed.

I grit my teeth for a moment as I fought back all the things I would've rather said to her right now to try to keep her on the phone.

*It's not about what you want,* I told myself. *It's about trust.*

"Good night, Angel," I said softly. "I'm here if you change your mind."

"About what?"

"About sleeping in my bed tonight."

I held my breath as she went silent again for a few heartbeats.

"I'll see you at breakfast," she said softly. Then she hung up.

# Chapter Twenty-Two

**Angeline**

The next day was… torturous.

Johnny showed up to make breakfast, as promised, but whether or not he'd banked on Shayla being there was anyone's guess. When he walked in, both of us were in the kitchen, though we'd just gotten up and started making coffee.

If Shayla thought anything was unusual about her brother strolling in to make us breakfast on a Tuesday morning, she didn't say so. She actually seemed quite happy to see him and frothed him a latte. It was her second day of rehearsals for the Players video shoot, so maybe she thought that was why he was here, to wish her well?

Maybe he partly was?

He did make a point of meeting my eyes when she wasn't looking. She was getting ingredients out of the fridge and his eyes crashed into mine. I stared as he dragged his teeth over his lip and my insides lit on fire, while Shayla babbled excitedly about her day.

Then the two of them got talking about the upcoming video shoot while he cooked. I just watched him, trying to read him while I sat quietly at the island. But he wasn't giving much away.

He'd come over like he said he would.

But after last night… I wasn't even sure what the fuck to say around him. Especially in front of Shayla. Were we lovers now? Were we a thing?

Would we have to tell her? Soon?

Did he really mean all that stuff about exploring my body and "making love" to me anytime I'd let him?

I wanted to believe it, desperately.

But the man was a player, after all. It was hard to know what might be a line, ego-stroking attention seeking, or just plain fun and games.

Was I a calculated conquest?

Or did he actually like me?

It was already kinda bothering me how much I was hoping for the latter. Because last night was… unexpected. And wildly fucking exciting. I'd be flat-out lying if I said I wasn't dying to find out what happened the next time we were alone together.

I'd felt safe over the phone.

But it was also a terrible tease. The thought of experiencing it again, this time in the flesh…

With his hands on me…

I felt desperate to make him come—while looking in his eyes, so I could get a better sense of what the fuck was really going on here. So I'd know how the fuck to feel about it.

That, and I just really fucking wanted him. There was really no reason to pretend otherwise now.

Now that he'd opened that door… and I'd gone tumbling through, dildo in hand.

I tried to be careful not to check him out when Shayla was looking at me. But luckily Shayla's mind was elsewhere, which gave me plenty of opportunity to ogle.

Johnny was wearing a snug white tank top that showed off his mouth-watering physique, his artful, sexy tattoos… and those fucking joggers again.

This time, he appeared to be wearing supportive underwear beneath. For his sister's benefit?

I thought about how he'd confessed that he knew I was about to walk in on him when he was naked that day in his bedroom. Which meant that he also likely knew I was still in the house when he came downstairs, bouncing around all commando in his sweatpants.

I flushed hot just trying to put it all together. Had he been trying to seduce me all along? Or was he just seizing an opportunity when I came into his house?

Was he seizing an opportunity last night, because I texted?

Or did he feel safe over the phone, like I did?

Was he being deeply, openly honest with everything he said to me?

*This isn't a game, and I'm not cheating.*

*I've never been so drawn to someone in my life.*

We ate at the island while Shayla did most of the talking; she was obviously excited about her dance rehearsals, learning the choreography for the video. Johnny had made us egg white omelettes, which were just as good as his stir fry, along with a freshly blended berry and yogurt smoothie.

But then he up and left, before we'd even finished our smoothies. He said he had "a lot of shit" to do today and took his smoothie with him, wishing us both a great day before vanishing out the back door.

"Well, that was nice," I said to Shayla once we were alone. "Your brother coming over here to make breakfast."

"Oh. Yeah, he does that sometimes." She eyed me with amusement. "Maybe your niceness coaching is rubbing off?" I'd told her I was taking Johnny to dinner with my parents last night, because I wanted to teach him how to be nicer to people and he needed to practice on some easy targets.

She'd laughed hysterically.

I mean, it was pretty ridiculous, for various reasons.

Although the outcome was… incredible.

"I didn't know there were security cams all over your house," I said casually as she finished her smoothie.

"What?"

"Johnny mentioned there are cameras all over the house. I think he meant your house and his?"

"Oh. Yeah. There are more in his. He's freakish about security, as you know."

I did know, kind of. He had a live-in bodyguard, for one. Even my sister didn't have Flynn live right on her property or even in her neighborhood, and she was way more famous.

"So… the camera feeds go to Lamar?"

"Ew. No." Shayla winced dramatically. "You think Lamar wants to watch whatever's going down in Johnny's house? It goes to Johnny's phone."

"So… everything that happens in your house goes to your brother's phone too?"

She cackled. "Oh my God. Are you kidding? Can you imagine?"

"Oh. Uh, good." I laughed nervously. "That's what I thought. Just wanted to be sure."

"*No.* There's only a cam at my front door and back door. Johnny has one in like every room of his house. I half think it's for purposes other than security, you know what I mean?" She hiked up a brow and went to put her dishes in the dishwasher.

"Right…" I got up to help her clean up.

Once Shayla headed out to rehearsals, I went up to my room, where I worked on my laptop with the window open. Since my room faced Johnny's house, I'd learned that I could hear the Hellcat coming and going from my window.

About a half hour later, I heard it pulling out of his garage.

When I went to the window, I could see the car easing up to the gate. It turned right onto the street and I glimpsed Johnny in the passenger seat, which meant Lamar was driving.

I still wasn't totally sure what Johnny did with his days. I knew he did MMA training with Shane, though I had no idea how often. Shayla had also mentioned at some point that Johnny had a personal trainer and a voice coach, though I had no idea if those people did house calls or what. He might have a meeting with Yash. Now that Noah was back in town, he might be meeting up with him again.

Other than that… no clue.

I didn't like sitting around wondering. I knew this wasn't a professional curiosity, either. It felt grossly girlfriend-like, my desire to know where he was going, what he'd be doing and with whom.

And what he was thinking.

It didn't escape me that while I'd become utterly preoccupied with thoughts of Johnny… I'd completely stopped thinking about Flynn.

Maybe that was why I was letting myself get so sucked into this. So carried away with what this could be. Because it could be a hot as hell fling to help me get over my breakup.

And if that was the case… I didn't want it to be just a one time, phone sex, because-he-was-bored-and-alone thing. I wanted more.

Much more.

But since Johnny hadn't said a word about last night, electronically or in person, I wasn't going to say it first.

I sent him a text, though.

**Me:** Anything I can help with today?

He answered about an hour later.

**Johnny:** No, Angel.

That was it.

Those two tiny words drove me crazy for the rest of the day. One, because he told me no. But two, because he called me Angel.

---

I woke to the throaty purr of the Hellcat rolling into the driveway. I was instantly, groggily awake. My laptop said it was just past midnight.

I wasn't even sure if midnight was an early or a late Tuesday night for Johnny O'Reilly.

I'd fallen asleep curled around my laptop, watching some rom com. It was still playing, and I closed it. I lay in bed, listening to the sounds of the Hellcat rumbling into Johnny's garage and the garage closing. By the time silence fell, I was vividly awake… and replaying last night in my mind just like I had all day, like a thousand times.

Including the things he'd said.

*I've seen you on my security cams.*

I thought about what he said when I asked him to send me an intimate pic; that he'd never sent one to a woman before. And when I'd asked him why he sent it to me…

*Trust.*

And that other thing he said… about watching me come upstairs on his phone when he was naked. And when I told him that he could've put some pants on…

*I could've. But then you wouldn't have seen me naked.*

It felt like a puzzle. There was a message in it, wasn't there? An invitation.

*I like looking at you. I want you to like looking at me.*

Something like that?

He'd asked me to tell him if he was treading over the line. He was very careful, gentle with me last night. But maybe I wanted him to tread over the line. Way over.

I wanted badly to know, if I'd given him the green light, asked him to come over, would he have fucked me last night?

Would he be inside me right now?

I was so aroused, I couldn't rest. I couldn't even get comfortable in my bed. I kept looking at my phone, at the graphic pic he'd sent me… his hard cock erect… swollen… so fucking hot… and all I knew for sure was I wanted it.

I wanted *him*. Inside me.

I wanted more of the man who'd played with me over the phone last night. That hot, careful, but willing guy. The one who unabashedly tested the boundaries with me.

And called me Angel.

*You're safe, Angeline.*

*I want to kiss you while you come.*

*You're so beautiful.*

I couldn't get his voice out of my head.

Did he really think I was beautiful?

Was he really drawn to me, like he said?

I wanted to know. I wanted to take the boundaries down… and see what happened.

So, I slipped open my bedside drawer and took out Johnny, the sleek toy version. He was cold and hard and somehow that felt weirdly appropriate. But I didn't slip him between my legs and go to town.

My whole body throbbing with anticipation, I slipped on Johnny's T-shirt, feeling like an absolute ho—and loving it—as I snuck out of the house.

*See, this is why Flynn broke up with you. Because you're out of control.*

I didn't care. I was so horny, I didn't fucking care. I'd been horny all fucking day.

There was only so much a girl could take.

And if I didn't think I'd be well-received, I wouldn't do this. But after last night… I knew the door was open, so to speak.

At least, I fucking hoped it was.

And I knew, as my heart pounded in my chest, that I was fucking kidding myself if I wanted to believe this was just about wanting to get over Flynn.

This was about wanting to get under Johnny.

I'd never had a guy do erotic stuff with me like that right out of the gate. Sexy photos, phone sex… I mean, surely it wouldn't be hard to find some random guy who would. But I didn't want a random guy. This guy I'd known, lusted after, for years. And last night, he said all the right things. He told me it was about trust. He was right.

But that wasn't all it was about.

I'd trusted Flynn, but he'd never taken a risk like that with me, even after years together. He'd never fully tapped into that kinky, curious, sex-hungry part of me.

Even when I begged him to.

Phone sex? Naked pictures? No. Those were too risky. Because what if it got overheard or leaked somehow. You didn't take risks like that.

Flynn never understood that sometimes the risk was the point.

And the turn-on.

So I crept over to Johnny's house, allowing myself to freely fantasize about him like I had all day. Given the circumstances, my fantasies focused on catching him in the act. What act, I wasn't sure. I'd take anything. I just hoped he was naked while he was doing it. Jerking off, showering, making a fucking sandwich. I wanted to see that mouthwatering dick of his again.

Maybe he'd show it to me again if I asked? In person this time?

I swallowed, picturing Johnny taking out his dick while I fucked myself with my sex toy until I came, desperate and hungry at his feet. And then he laughed at me and said something brutal like *That's my dirty little good girl* with adoration in his eyes and jacked off on me. I wanted him to make a mess all over me. After, maybe, he tied me down? I had a helplessness kink. And a shame kink. And a praise kink. So many kinks all rolled into one, I probably didn't even know what they were all called.

Largely because I'd never really had an opportunity to explore them with a man.

All I knew was my juices were running down the insides of my thighs just thinking about doing very dirty things with Johnny O'Reilly. Best friend's brother? Client? Who cared. What I got a taste of last night was not to be passed up, if there was any chance it might happen again.

So long as he was going to be nice about it.

And calling me *sweetheart*, *baby*, and *Angel* the whole time and telling me I was safe? I was addicted, my mouth literally watering. Already.

I let myself into his house with Shayla's key, for the second time, and stole in through the back door. Only when I saw the glow on the alarm panel in the dark did it occur to me to think about the alarm. Luckily, it wasn't activated. My heart was beating up in my throat and I swallowed thickly. The rush of adrenalin—the thought of getting caught; call that another kink—just made me hotter. My hands were shaking, I was so aroused as I shut the door behind me.

I stood in the dark, listening, as my pulse thrummed through my body, spurring me on.

Silence.

I eased into the kitchen. A strip of lighting under the upper cupboards cast a soft glow across the countertops. I stole across to the floating stairs at the edge of the living room and peered up. Dim light. Silence. He was up in his bedroom, for sure.

*What if he has someone up there?*

Typical; Mean Me had reared her annoying head, trying to ruin this for me. I was divorcing her for sure. *I don't need you anymore,* I told her. *Niceness for the win.*

No. He didn't have someone up there.

He said it was about trust.

*So, trust him.*

I looked around. I wanted to spread myself over his kitchen island and go to town.

But that seemed especially unsanitary.

Actually, I wanted to creep upstairs and peep through the crack in his door, watching as he played with his dick for like an hour. I wanted to watch him stroke himself slowly until he came, jacking into the air. Then I wanted to crawl in there and lick it off his body.

The idea of creeping up there and finding him touching himself made me quiver with excitement.

I tiptoed into the sunken living room instead and went searching for the security camera. Now that I knew there was one, it wasn't hard to spot. In the corner, next to one of his sleek speakers. It seemed to be aimed directly into the middle of the room, where the big sectional sofa was.

I peeled off his T-shirt. I listened again. There was no sound from upstairs.

The sectional smelled faintly of him as I sank onto it; cologne and his warm male musk, like sex and scotch and coffee and his cedar sauna all rolled into one. It made me melt. I laid his shirt down to protect the sofa in case I gushed like a waterfall—I would—and laid back on it, naked.

My heart was pounding out of my chest. It was all I could hear in my ears, my own raging heartbeat. I was naked on Johnny's couch, right in front of his camera, and I was so worked up about it… by the time I actually touched myself, my pussy was swollen and hypersensitive.

Would he get a notification that the camera had picked up movement or something?

God, I hoped so.

*And dear God, Shayla, please be right about Lamar.*

I did a little prayer that Johnny's bodyguard wasn't the one watching this right now.

Then I went to town with Johnny, the toy version. I took my time, trying to vividly imagine Johnny—the real version—jacking himself off, bringing himself to orgasm while he thought about me, as I panted, pleasuring myself—

"Angeline."

I stopped, still panting audibly, as I opened my eyes. Johnny had walked into the room, and he'd definitely caught me in the act.

There was the instinctual urge to jump out of my skin and cover myself, of course—I wasn't a total lunatic—but what I actually did was freeze and start praying that he strode over and told me I was a naughty, dirty little slut while his eyes told me to keep going.

My face flushed with heat as I did nothing. I just lay there, with my legs spread and my big black pleasure toy lodged deep, breathing heavily and sweating.

"What are you doing?" he said softy, but his voice said he already knew. He already saw. He floated closer, his eyes caressing my body in the semi-dark. By the time he'd reached the sofa, I'd slipped the toy out and started to scramble up.

"I'm sorry," I said, but I wasn't. I crawled up on my knees, kneeling naked on the sofa in front of him. I peered up at him, hoping he wanted what he saw.

My eyes dragged over him, hungrily. He wore satiny-soft pajama pants slung low on his hips and nothing else, and his dick looked big, semi-hard, draped in the fabric. His sculpted abs were right in my face. I wanted to lick him.

I wanted to fuck him.

I knew I wasn't supposed to. I wasn't supposed to lust after him like that. It was Lil Brat rules, and I was breaking them.

I couldn't stop myself.

I confessed, "I'm a sexual deviant." I chewed my lip.

His eyes slid all over me, slowly. "Tell me what you were doing," he said, his voice low and rough.

"I was fucking myself."

"On my couch."

"Yes."

"You wanted me to catch you?"

I swallowed. "I just… like it."

"Like what?"

*Being in your house.*

*Doing something I'm not supposed to do.*

*Everything.*

I didn't say anything.

When he waited, I finally forced out again, "I'm sorry. I just lose control sometimes. I can't help it."

"Lose control…"

"So horny," I squeaked out, "I can't think."

Of course, I'd never actually lost control like this in front of anyone but my own boyfriend before… but he just made me feel so damn safe last night. So… wanted.

*Please, let this not be a giant, horrifying mistake.*

His eyes drifted over me again. "You're shaking."

I was. Because I was so aroused. I was naked. I was dripping. And he was looking at me.

"You like it," he observed.

"Uh-huh." My voice shook.

His eyes seemed to darken with knowing as they met mine again and held. "Are you a bad girl, Angeline?"

When I didn't speak, he touched a finger to my chin and tipped my face up, making me hold his gaze. "No," he said, his voice like warm, heated silk. "You're a good girl. My naughty, sweet, good girl."

*My.*

I kind of whimpered my agreement.

Like he knew he was getting close to hitting the mark as I quivered, he elaborated. "Does my good girl want to come?"

I nodded.

His thumb drifted along my jaw. "Of course you do. You want a nice, juicy come?" It was like we were both hypnotized by the idea. His dark, heated gaze dropped to my mouth. "You want me to watch you have an orgasm, Angel?"

"Uh-huh," I said in a daze, my mouth opening like an invitation. I was entranced by his touch on my skin as his thumb stroked back and forth. Then his thumb sank into my mouth.

I bit down on it a little, watching his eyes flare, then sucked.

"You want me to taste it?" he said gruffly.

My brain broke.

"You want me to lick it up?"

*Oh God.*

"Of course you do," he answered. "Because you're so naughty… and so damn sweet." Then he leaned down and murmured in my ear, "I bet you're even sweeter with whipped cream." He pulled his thumb out of my mouth and I almost sobbed.

Whipped cream…

What?

My whole body was so fucking hot, I could barely think in a straight line. I felt wobbly and drunk.

Was this really happening?

*Yes, because you're a deviant.*

God, Shayla was gonna be mad…

When he stood back up, he was untying his pants. He pulled the drawstring right out, then pushed them down over his hips and let them drop to his ankles. He stepped out of them. He was gloriously naked in the near-dark, a mouth-watering display of virility and danger, all sculpted physique and dark tattoos. His dick was right in front of me, standing straight up, and I stared.

Holy Christ, it was even more gorgeous in person.

"Look at me."

I looked up at Johnny's eyes. He took my wrists and tied them gently with the silky drawstring, while I did nothing but kneel in front of him, staring at his eyes.

When my wrists were bound, he nudged me back, laying me down on the sofa with my arms above my head. "Don't move, Angel," he said, holding my eyes.

Why would I move? This was fucking amazing.

I watched him, his gorgeous naked ass and tattooed back, as he walked into the kitchen and disappeared beyond the island. He took something out of the fridge and walked back over. He was holding a can of whipped cream.

My whole body throbbed with excitement so excruciating, I was afraid I might come as soon as he touched my skin.

Maybe he sensed that, because instead of touching me, he eased into it —by dispensing a cool dollop of whipped cream onto each of my nipples, then onto my clit. While I squirmed, my brain blown. Was this happening?

I couldn't even rationalize anymore. I no longer even registered that this was… risky or whatever. It was purely sexual, and it was happening. We both wanted it to happen.

"Tell me I'm a good girl again," I whispered as he put the whipped cream can aside. "Tell me you like it that I'm sweet."

Johnny looked down at me, ran his tongue over his lip and said, "So good, sweet girl, I'm gonna eat you…"

Then he sank onto his knees on the couch, lowering himself over me, and proceeded to eat the whipped cream off, very fucking slowly, as I writhed in pleasure beneath him, panting. Trying not to lose it too fast…

He took his time sucking the whipped cream off my nipples, then kissed his way down my belly with his wicked mouth. While he gently ate whipped cream off my clit, I completely lost my shit.

*Yes!*

This was what I'd always wanted with a lover. Someone who took the reins from me when I made the first move and drove us to a place even beyond my own imagination. Creativity. Enthusiasm.

*Hunger.*

Someone who gave back as good as he got. *Better.*

This was so good… I didn't even want to come. Not yet.

"Tell me," he said darkly, while he played his tongue over my clit, like my body was a dessert all its own. "Tell me what you want me to do to my sweet, deviant girl."

There it was again. *My.*

"I w-want you to fuck me," I said hoarsely.

In response, he spread my legs wider and pushed my knees up, splitting me wide open, and went to town on my pussy, delving his tongue inside me as I spoke. Fucking me with his tongue.

"I… I want you to put me on my knees at your feet and stroke your cock while you watch me touch myself, and call me your sweet girl while you come on my face. I want you to come all over me. I want you to fuck my mouth and groan while you come down my throat and call me your good girl. I want… so many… fucking… things…" My body pulsed with heat as he ate me out and I wondered what he was thinking. "Am I being too greedy?" I asked, with hope in my breathless voice.

"So greedy," he said roughly, but I could hear how much he liked it. He suckled my clit, gently, teasing, making me squirm.

"Johnny…" I groaned, agonized. "Make me come…"

"Yeah, Angel. You're gonna come in my mouth. Because you can't help it, can you?"

"Call me your horny little slut," I blurted out.

Oh shit. Did I just say that?

He couldn't seem to believe it, either. His eyes met mine, burning with heat. He licked up over my clit. Then he spread me open with his thumbs and played at my clit with his tongue, making me convulse. I was so close to tumbling over the edge…

"I think my horny little slut is hungry," he murmured darkly, his breath caressing my wet clit.

*My.*

Maybe that was another kink, then. *Possession.*

His kink or mine?

Both?

I'd never had a guy say possessive stuff like that the first time he saw me naked. It was sending me into meltdown.

"You're gonna come for me," he said roughly, then went at my clit again.

*Lick.*

*Suck.*

*Kiss.*

"You know you want to." He flicked my clit with his tongue, once, twice, and I came, screaming raggedly as my core convulsed. "Good, baby," he rewarded me, lavishing my clit with kisses and slow, deep sucks between his words, "Mmmm. That's a good girl. Keep coming. Gush on my face, my pretty little slut…"

The devil was between my legs and I loved it.

My head was spinning as my core clenched again, so damn hungry and empty… as he flicked and sucked, it was like sweet, heavenly torture, and we were both loving it. I could hear it in his deep, hungry breaths.

When he stopped and looked up at me, his face was slick with my juices and his lips were flushed. I collapsed back on the sofa.

"That better, Angel?" he whispered, wiping a hand over his mouth. "You feel better?"

I nodded, panting.

"Tell me." He prowled up over me and his eyes burned into mine. "Tell me the truth. Trust, remember?"

"I… I need more," I gushed, shakily.

A slow, deviant smile crept across his gorgeous face. "More?"

"Yeah. More."

"What do you need?"

"I need your cock. Please. I want you to fuck me."

"Hard?"

I nodded eagerly.

He traced a finger down the curve of my cheek. "And come on your sweet face?"

I made a strangled, desperate sound. "On my face. Make it messy. Be loud," I told him as he shifted, and he fumbled getting his hard cock lined up. Was he as excited as I was? "I want to hear you. I love your voice…"

I spread my legs wide, my knees up by my shoulders, as he pushed in. We both watched as he filled me. He groaned, low and hungry. His eyes hit mine. "Keep watching," he ordered.

He eased in, and I grabbed at his ass, trying to pull him deeper. God, he was big. He didn't look this big when he was soft. But he was thick as fuck.

"Fuck, Angeline." He groaned again as he withdrew a bit, then sank into me again. I was so wet, we made slippery noises together. He pounded into me, hard, just like I asked, and he grunted and groaned with pleasure.

Holy God, this was epic. Every fantasy I'd ever had, he was nailing every one of them, willingly and fast. Plus, he was so damn hot. Watching his body working over mine was mind-bending erotic.

"Tell me," he groaned, as he drilled into me with a desperate need. "Tell me how it feels. Good?"

"Fuck," I panted, so turned on that he was turned on. By *me*. "You feel so hard and so fucking big."

"You just can't get enough, can you? My horny little cock slut—" His voice broke as he pounded into me and I gasped and moaned beneath him, spreading my legs as far as I could. He took the cue and grabbed my ankles, hoisting them onto his shoulders and pressing his hips against me, sinking deeper. He groaned with the pleasure, then grunted every time he slammed in. We were going at it like rutting beasts and it was the hottest thing I'd ever experienced.

"Don't stop," I begged. "Don't come yet. Keep pounding me."

"Yeah? You like that sweet pussy pounded…?"

"Yeah."

"Good. I'm gonna feed that hungry little pussy until it chokes."

Oh, God. My eyes rolled back in my head. He was good at dirty talk, too.

"Keep talking," I begged as my core muscles clenched around him. He made a strangled, pleasured sound as he kept pounding.

"Fuck. You're so pretty. You love this, don't you."

"Yes."

"You want my cock…"

"I want it so bad. Give me more."

He picked up the pace a bit, slamming into me a little faster as his chest pressed against my legs and he stretched me wide.

"God… so good…" I managed.

"Angel…"

"God, I'm so horny…" I moaned, aching.

He shifted to support himself with one hand on the sofa above me, and ran his other hand over my body, squeezing my breasts, a greedy, possessive touch. "Baby. I'll give you all the cock you want."

"Yeah. More…" I was in a daze, a lust stricken daze, as he pounded into me, so deep. "Fill me up, like that…"

"Such a good girl," he murmured. "Taking my cock… so good."

He pressed against my thighs. I relaxed my muscles, just welcoming the pounding. Delirious with the bliss of this.

"Look at me."

I met his eyes again. I gasped, my core clenching on him again, spasming. The look in his eyes was all-consuming intense, a dark need sucking me in as he held my gaze.

"You're gonna come again. Look at my eyes when you come."

"Yes…"

"Say my name."

"Johnny," I whispered.

"That's right. Who's fucking you right now?"

"Johnny."

"Whose dick are you gonna come on?"

"Yours."

"That's right, baby. Now tell me who's making you feel so fucking good right now."

"You are."

"Tell me what you want," he ordered.

"I want to see you come all over me."

"Yeah? You like my dick?"

"I love your dick," I gushed.

"You wanna taste it?"

"Yeah."

"You want my cock in that sweet mouth, Angel?"

"Yeah. Yeah, it's so hot. When I saw you naked… I couldn't stop thinking about it," I confessed. "I kept dreaming about you…"

He shuddered, losing his rhythm as he pounded into me. I could feel his stomach muscles bunching, clenching against me.

Holy Christ, he was losing his mind, too.

"Oh, God," I writhed beneath him, bearing down. "Your cock feels perfect inside me. You're perfect."

His eyes rolled closed. "No. I'm no good."

"You are good. No one has ever fucked me so good." It wasn't a lie. "That beautiful cock…"

His eyes flew open. "Fuck, baby, you've gotta come."

I didn't dare look away. My core clenched on his hard length.

"Good girl, squeeze me…" he moaned, slamming into me again and again.

I shuddered, convulsing on him, and I knew he could feel it as I screeched, "Oh God, oh God, you fuck so fucking good… I'm coming." He made me come so hard, I was in a bliss on another level.

He hissed out a breath between his teeth as he suddenly locked up, his body rigid. I fucked him mercilessly, riding his cock, until he grit out, "Baby, I can't…" Then he ripped his cock out, kneeled up over me, and with one hand on his dick, shoved his length into my waiting mouth.

With his other hand, he shoved between my spread legs and thrust a couple of fingers into me, rubbing against my core with his whole hand as my orgasm kept shuddering through me.

He groaned as his cock spasmed, and I felt the first hot spurt of his climax on my tongue. "Good girl," he groaned, "suck me off." I sucked and licked. Then I wrapped my hands around his shaft, pulled him from my mouth and let him blow the rest on my face. "God, yeah," he groaned as his cream spurt on my lips and cheek and I pulled on his cock, wanting more.

His hand slid into my hair almost affectionately as his hips rocked in rhythm with my pulls. I sucked on the plump head of his cock, savoring every last drop, until he shuddered.

As he collapsed back on the sofa and his fingers slid from inside me, I lay back with my legs still spread wide. He reached to tug on the silky drawstring that bound my hands, freeing them, as his eyes dragged over me.

As he watched, I smeared his come on my face, my lips, and smeared it into my mouth, sucked it off my fingers. While my other hand stole down to my clit. Johnny's eyes widened as he watched me rub my clit in swift, aggressive circles as I feasted on my fingers, tasting him. I saw it his eyes—appreciation. Hunger, for sure. Curiosity.

"Beautiful," he murmured. "Make yourself come again, Angel. I want to watch." He idly stroked his softening dick as I did what he said.

He watched as my body convulsed again. I rubbed my clit as I came, whimpering with pleasure and near exhaustion, still desperate for more. I rubbed and kneaded as the spasms rippled through me. He looked mesmerized, his eyes dancing between my pussy and my open mouth, my dazed eyes, my spread thighs, my busy hand.

Then I collapsed.

"You feel better now?" I could hear the satisfied pleasure in his voice. He liked that.

My lust didn't make him feel threatened.

I could've cried as that realization washed over me.

I nodded, still panting, blinking back the emotion.

I was better. For now. But that was so good, I'd be fantasizing about it for the rest of my life and probably horny again in like an hour.

And then of course there was the guilt and the *holy God what did I just do* that was bound to kick in when the hormone rush faded. But oh well. Right now, I couldn't give a fuck.

Johnny couldn't either, clearly.

"So, what was that?" he panted in a daze, as he lay sprawled next to me on the sofa. His hand drifted slowly up my thigh. There was a touch of amusement in his voice, but I saw the heat in his dark gaze as it roamed over my body.

"That was sex," I said softly, feeling almost painfully exposed as our eyes locked, but there was really nowhere to hide. "The way I like it."

# Chapter Twenty-Three

**Johnny**

I stepped out into the twilit evening, checking my phone. Angeline's text from five minutes ago said: *Meet you outside in 5.* But there was no sign of her on the path that connected Shayla's front door with mine.

I was dressed up and ready, had a gift bag with a bottle of Peach Schnapps for Lex's wife; Talia was obsessed with this stuff. Angeline had informed me when we'd "reviewed my social calendar" today—meaning she'd emailed Yash a list of upcoming events she expected me to attend—that I was to make an appearance at Lex and Talia's housewarming party tonight.

That wasn't why I was going. I was going for Lex. But I'd asked Angeline, by text, if she wanted to go with me. She was already going anyway, apparently, but I'd half-expected her to say no.

I wasn't sure how she'd feel about showing up at a party with me so soon after things had… shifted… between us.

To my surprise, she actually accepted my invitation.

*As long as it's not a date,* she'd said.

*Why would it be a date?* I'd replied, lobbing that ball right back into her court. Maybe it irked me just a bit that she could beg me to come on her face but God forbid she go on a date with me where other humans might glimpse us together.

She didn't reply.

I hadn't seen her since last night, on my couch. Even though I'd spent half the day lounging on my back deck and I was pretty sure she was home, working. For me, her lone client. She'd been fussing over my social media profiles for days—the ones Yash had some virtual assistant run for us—and sending notes to Yash on wording that should be tweaked, stuff like that.

I headed over to my car. Lamar had already pulled it out of the garage for me and stood waiting next to his car. He'd follow us to the party. Mainly because I didn't do backseats, and I didn't want Lamar in mine; I wanted to drive Angeline myself, and after last night I wanted her alone.

Last time I saw her, she was wearing my T-shirt, yet again, and backing out of my living room, acting way too cool about the fact that I'd just eaten whipped cream off her most sensitive body parts, then fucked her until her eyes rolled back in her head while she begged me to do it. I'd made her come, she'd made herself come. Then she'd insisted that she was exhausted and wanted nothing more than to go back to my sister's place and crash.

She even forced a yawn.

I wasn't dense. No matter how much the sex had knocked her out, more than she wanted sleep she wanted the hell out of there.

I'd almost dragged her up to my shower to wash her off and tuck her into bed, but something told me that would only make her more uncomfortable. As soon as she'd stopped panting and begging and come down from the hormone high and started looking so uneasy, I wasn't really sure what to do or say around her.

I'd never been awkward with a girl after sex. Never.

But I'd never actually worried about completely freaking a girl out after sex, either. Something told me that if I did the wrong thing, she wouldn't be coming back for another round.

After waiting for a few minutes, I wondered if I should go ring Shayla's doorbell, or go back into the house with Lamar and chill. He raised an eyebrow at me but said nothing, probably trying to recall the last time I waited anywhere for a woman—never—other than my sister.

Finally, Angeline burst out the front door of Shayla's house and hurried down the driveway toward me in a fluster. She wore pale blue jeans with rips in the knees, cute sneakers and a soft blue T-shirt that hugged her perfect tits. It had a rainbow print of a butterfly on it. Her brown hair was like ribbons of velvet around her shoulders, long, soft waves, the front pieces pinned back off her face. Pretty. The girl was so pretty.

Her blue-gray eyes met mine and I mobilized to open the passenger door for her. She flashed me a tight smile. "Hello, Johnny."

I held her eyes as she sank into her seat, then shut the door for her.

Right. So that's how it was gonna be. My publicist was on duty tonight. We were going with rigidly, awkwardly formal. At least, she was. I was totally fine, as long as she didn't give me some crap about last night being a one time thing.

It was not a one time thing.

I sauntered around to the driver's side and got in. As I backed us out of the driveway and we took off up the street, I wondered which one of us would bring up what happened last night first.

"Last night was… weird." *Her.*

"Don't gush on me too much at once. It'll go to my head."

"Not bad weird. Just…" A long silence ensued, like she was digging deep for the right words. "I didn't expect that to happen."

"Really. You figured when I found a naked intruder on my couch going to town on herself, I'd just turn around and go back to bed?"

Our eyes met briefly before she looked away. "I mean, you could've called the cops."

"If you were a stranger, I would have." When she was uncomfortably silent, I added, "But you're not a stranger."

"Look, I know it's weird, okay? I just got sex brain and lost it."

"Lost what?"

"You know. Common sense."

"And common sense tells you…"

"Not to break into your next door neighbor's house and fuck yourself on his couch because his smell turns you on and the thought of masturbating in his house where he might catch you on his security cams makes you wet."

I took that in, my pulse quickening… floored at her words, in so many directions… "So that's what I am now? Your neighbor?" I glanced at her, the streetlights sliding over her pretty face.

"No. You're more than that."

"Your client."

"Yeah. That just makes it worse, though."

"Makes what worse?"

"That I couldn't control myself."

My hands tightened on the wheel. Blood was thumping through my body, making my cock throb. "Did it ever occur to you, Angeline, that maybe you don't need to control yourself?"

She made a little *tsssht* sound that sounded annoyingly like my sister. "Of course I do."

"Not around me, you don't."

When she was dead silent, I glanced at her to find her watching me.

I trained my eyes on the road, wondering if this was the best conversation to have while I was driving. But she seemed embarrassed or regretful or something. I did not want to walk into this party, filled with friends and colleagues—and *her* friends—while she was in any way uncomfortable with me.

Angeline showed her emotions pretty freely. And just because I had a hard time reading what they were didn't mean that other people would. I knew that much. What would her friends see her feeling tonight when they saw her with me? Attraction? Discomfort?

Both?

Even though I'd sensed that she was hot for me in the past—or maybe just wanted to believe that I did—I'd ignored it, mostly for my sister's benefit. But also because I knew I couldn't exactly indulge it. Not without dropping a bomb into the calm waters of my relationship with Elle Delacroix and her band, and every other industry contact Elle had wrapped around her finger in this town. Simply put, I fucked Angeline Delacroix and a whole bunch of people got their shit in a knot, from her sister to my sister and a whole lot of people in between. I knew I'd get grief over it.

But those waters weren't exactly calm anymore. Maybe they never really were, right beneath the surface. So what the hell was I trying to protect anyway? Some moral code that was never my own to begin with?

Angeline was the sweet, quirky, lovely girl everyone adored and I was the asshole everyone tolerated, for the most part. I knew how it was.

Things ended with her boyfriend the bodyguard and everyone still loved him. He still had his job as Elle's trusted protector. If Angeline ended things with me after a few fucks? I'd end up the bad guy everyone hated for it.

Been there before, a few too many times.

Thing was, now that we'd fucked, I wasn't gonna let her convince herself it was a one time mistake or something to be ashamed of. I didn't want her to feel bad about it.

"Are you on birth control?" I asked her. I didn't come inside her, but still. We'd both trusted each other enough, hopefully, that neither of us was gonna have to worry about what we did last night without protection.

"I am. Are you clean? Please tell me you're careful with that."

"I am."

"Do you wrap it? Like, with other girls?"

"Yes."

"With Brianna?"

"Yes."

"Then why didn't you with me?"

"I don't know." That was the truth. Maybe because she didn't ask me to? "Are you okay with that?"

"I was last night. I think I still am."

"It wasn't a mistake, Angeline. You wanted it. So did I. It doesn't have to be complicated."

"That's the thing, Johnny. What if it is complicated?"

I considered that. "Then it's complicated. Deal with it."

She made a soft, exasperated noise, like I wasn't getting it or something. "Be honest. Did I weird you out?"

"What?" I tried not to take my eyes off the road, but I had to glance at her. "No."

"Not at all?" she pressed. "Not afterwards, when you went to bed, got some sleep, had time to digest what happened?"

"No. Why would you think that?" She said nothing, and I realized the probable answer to that. "You've 'weirded out' other guys?"

"Maybe."

I was getting the picture. "Just because some guys are freaked out by your enthusiasm, babe, doesn't say a thing about you. That's on them."

She sighed a little. "I didn't shock you?"

"No," I said automatically, but then I wondered if that was true. It wasn't that the sex shocked me or anything. It was Angeline that surprised me.

Now that I knew she was so… sexually exuberant… I was even more fascinated by her. I'd rarely met a woman who I was that sexually compatible with right off the bat.

I glanced at her again, sitting there like she was unavailable to me, even after what we did last night. She was hiding from me now, closing up.

"It makes you uncomfortable. It doesn't have to."

"What, that we had sex? I'm a big girl. I chose to have sex with you. There's nothing to be uncomfortable about."

"Then you're not uncomfortable that I now know you're a super freak?"

She laughed abruptly. "Stop it."

"You're a penile enthusiast, Angeline. Just embrace it. Nothing to be embarrassed about."

I actually heard her jaw drop open. She made a sputtery, flabbergasted sound.

"It's a beautiful thing, really."

"Stop it!" She smacked my arm, but I could hear her trying not to laugh.

"It's inspiring to meet a woman who's so into cock."

"Just—" She choked on a laugh. "Don't, okay? Don't make fun of me."

I gave the road ahead the most serious look I could as I drove. "I'm not making fun of you."

"You are."

"I'm totally not. You liked getting fucked. I liked fucking you. It was mutually beneficial."

"Uh-huh."

"And you liked all the other stuff that happened, too."

She cleared her throat quietly but didn't respond.

"You liked it when I caught you in my living room."

"You liked catching me in your living room," she retorted.

"Yeah. I did. I liked that you made the next move. That you opened that door." When she said nothing, I went on. "I don't know how fast I would have."

"You wouldn't?"

"I wasn't sure if you really wanted me to."

"But… you wanted to?"

"Yeah. I wanted to." I glanced at her. She was still watching me, and her eyes searched mine.

"We're almost there, aren't we," she said when my gaze returned to the road.

"Yeah. Almost."

"Can you pull off somewhere? I need to tell you something."

I glanced at her again. She swallowed and looked away.

"Sure."

At the next light, I pulled off the street we were on and wound through the residential neighborhood. Found a dark spot between the street lights to pull up to the curb, in front of a big hedge. Private. I put the car in park and gave her my attention. "You okay?"

She blinked at me. "Johnny…"

"Yeah." My heart was thudding in my chest, too damn hard.

Angeline shifted toward me a little, then reached for my lap—and slid her hand over the package in my jeans. My breath caught in my throat.

She squeezed me a little, her eyes on mine.

A groan of appreciation slipped from my throat as I thickened in her hand, stiffening. I shifted my hips a bit, trying to make room in my jeans.

I turned off the car.

She leaned in, pressing up against me. Her mouth hovered near mine, and I resisted the urge to push my hands into her hair and pull her to me. I didn't want to scare her off. We didn't even kiss last night, in the middle of all that smoldering sex. I wasn't sure if she felt uneasy about what happened, or even what didn't. So I just let her lead.

"Johnny," she whispered again, her hand now squeezing my rock hard length.

"Angeline," I choked out.

Then she kissed me, her mouth slanting over mine, her tongue sliding over my lip, and I thrust my tongue into her mouth in response, unable to hold back. I moaned into our kiss as she pulled at my jeans, opening them. She slid her hand inside my underwear and squeezed my naked shaft. I flexed in her hand, eager and throbbing.

As she broke our kiss to lean down into my lap, obviously to suck me off, I breathed in bliss, "What are you doing to me?"

"I've been thinking about this all day," she said in a kind of hungered agony as she pulled my underwear aside, freeing my dick. She peeked up, her eyes hitting mine, like she was making sure this was okay. She jacked me slowly, working her tight fist up and down. Felt so good I wanted to close my eyes. But I never wanted to look away from her.

I wanted to watch.

I held her eyes as I gathered her soft hair back from her face into a handful at the nape of her neck. She turned her face downward and I felt her hot breath on my cock. Her little tongue flickered out to taste the wet slit in my cockhead, and I sank back into the seat. "That's it, Angel…" My voice was hoarse with longing as she lavished the head of my cock with soft licks, even as I tried to relax.

She'd been thinking about this all day? That made two of us.

"Tell me what to do," she whispered. I could feel the restless energy in her body. She was holding herself back. Waiting for my commands. Dirty talk excited her. Last night, it made her gush.

I wondered how wet she was already, but she didn't ask me to touch her. She liked instigating, too. She was trembling right now with restrained excitement.

"Suck, sweetheart."

She wrapped her wet mouth around the crown of my cock and sucked. I groaned as my balls tightened.

"Deeper."

She drove her mouth down on my dick. Hot, wet heaven engulfed me.

"Fuck me with that pretty mouth…" I muttered, barely able to breathe as she followed my command. She sucked me deep, using her tight fist to cover what her mouth couldn't. My shaft flexed in her mouth.

Then I tensed, startled by a movement outside the car.

"Stop. Stay there." I held her there by her hair. "Someone's walking by." I watched the couple strolling by with their dog, talking. They stopped to wait as the dog nosed around in the bush. They didn't even look my way as I sat pressed against the seat, my heart thudding, cock pulsing, buried in Angeline's mouth, the root of my shaft wrapped in her hand.

She moaned a little as my cock spasmed in her mouth, wriggling in her seat. Excitement. She liked getting caught, too, maybe. Like last night, on my couch.

This girl was a sweet conundrum of desires and kinks, and I planned to strip them all bare and indulge them all.

But I didn't plan on letting anyone else see her like this. This was *mine*.

"Shh, Angel," I soothed her, even as I tried to catch my breath.

She sucked on me, teasing me, keeping her head down.

I wrapped my hand around hers at the base of my cock, squeezing, trying to hold back. I didn't want to come like this. She squeezed her fist in rhythm with the pulsating sucks, driving me fucking crazy as the couple and their dog finally drifted past, taking way too fucking long.

I exhaled a harsh breath. "They're gone."

She slid back to the tip again. Then her head started bobbing slowly up and down as she slid her mouth over me again and again, sucking each time she withdrew.

"God. You want me to come…?" The words were rough and desperate. I dug my hand into her hair, gripping the back of her neck.

She made a hungry, guttural moan and kept sucking.

"Fuck," I groaned. "Yeah. Take what you want, Angel…"

I tried to relax and just let her take it. My balls were so tight, my dick so impossibly hard, everything was rushing together. I was so fucking turned on by how bad she wanted this.

*I've been thinking about this all day.*

It felt so fucking good I could barely sit still. I slammed my hand on the window, the other one still gripping her neck. She sucked in long, rhythmic pulls, and I could feel the heat and the strain of her arousal coming off her. It was steaming up the car. The sight of her head in my lap was almost too much. I couldn't even see my cock disappearing into her mouth. I could only *feel*. Her arousal and mine, entwined together as I rushed toward the finish. Her hot, wet mouth guiding the way.

"That's it, Angel," I forced out, my voice gruff. "Make me come, hard."

She sucked again, hand and mouth stroking me root to tip, slow. I felt the spasm hit deep in my ass before it ran right up through me. My balls seized. "Fuck, Angie, you're making me come…" My cock convulsed deep in her silky soft mouth and I growled, slamming my head back against the seat as the climax rocked me. I released into her in hot, wrenching pulses.

I felt her swallow, a couple of times, as she made hungry, breathless noises.

I groaned helplessly, completely lost in the pleasure she was giving me. The pleasure she was taking from my body as my cock pulsed in her mouth.

*I've been thinking about this all day.*

Fuck, that made me hot.

Angeline, thinking about me. About this.

I blinked at her head in my lap, fucking feasting on my dick as I finished. She switched from sucking to licking, practically purring as she savored my taste. I shuddered and rasped out her name. "Angeline."

She gave me one more thorough lick, twirling her tongue all around my cockhead, before letting go. She sat up, and as I released her neck, her eyes hit mine, wild with lust. Her shirt was pushed up over her bra and one of her breasts, bared, jutted out over her bra. Her fingers were on her nipple, squeezing.

She'd been playing with her nipple while she sucked me off. That discovery shot straight between my legs and my semi-hard dick spasmed.

She dove on me, straddling me in the tight space, shoving her chest at my mouth as she clawed at her bra, making both tits pop out in my face. Our hands entangled as we both grabbed her breasts to guide them to my mouth. One firm, super soft nipple grazed my lip and she gasped as I groaned, sucking her nipple into my mouth. I sucked her gently, teasing as she panted, then went from one to the other, back and forth, licking and sucking languidly.

"Fuck, you're so pretty," I told her, kissing her soft breasts as we both clutched at them.

She made a sound of agonized pleasure as I sucked deeply. "Johnny," she gasped. I looked up at her face. Her eyes were wide and dark, and her tongue slid restlessly across her lower lip. "Oh, God," she rasped as I twirled my tongue around her nipple.

"What's the matter, Angel?" I teased the pink bud with the tip of my tongue, slowly.

She made another anguished sound of lust, her hips wriggling, grinding in my lap. My bare dick was hard again, pressed against her jeans, her warm ass.

I squeezed her breasts, giving a wet kiss to one blushing nipple, then the other, as she squirmed hotly. "So pretty… I could suck on your tits all night."

"Johnny… I'm so jacked up right now, I'm gonna die if you don't fuck me."

My heart thudding, I slid my hand around the back of her neck and pulled her face close to mine. With my lips teasing hers, I told her, "I'm not gonna fuck you. I'm gonna take you to this house party…" I slid my mouth across her jaw to her ear, and let my lips tease her lobe as I whispered in her ear. "I'm gonna make you wait, Angel. I'm gonna find someplace to get you alone. And then I'm gonna savor your pussy like it's my last meal. When you come for me, I'm going to watch you tremble and shake and gush for me."

I kissed her lips again, and when our eyes met, I told her, "I'm going to make you beg for it, and I'm going to savor that, too. "

# Chapter Twenty-Four

**Johnny**

When we pulled up to Lex's block, the residential street was parked up with cars. There were a few bikers outside the house, members of Lex's motorcycle club, the West Coast Kings; they directed us to where we could park, where they had some guys keeping an eye on the cars along the street. Lot of nice rides. The party would be filled with VIPs, which meant tight security.

I walked Angeline up to the house, my hand on the small of her back, as Lamar shadowed us. Lex and Talia's house was one of the few on this block with a fence around the whole yard. The fence was new, and as we entered through the gate, I saw Angeline looking around. She seemed tense. No one was out front but the few big security dudes we saw, a combo of Kings and guys from both Dirty and the Players' security crews. I knew Angeline went to parties like this all the time, so she probably wasn't nervous about that.

I would've liked to think she was nervous-excited about what I told her would be happening later, when I got her alone. But I suspected she was maybe still uncomfortable about walking into this party with me.

"Have you been here before?" I asked her. Lex and Talia had bought the old house with the help of one of the Kings, a friend of Lex's named

Maddox, who was now their roommate; they'd been doing renovations for months, but the house was finally finished. I'd been over a few times to check out the progress, but the final result was impressive.

"Just once, when they first bought it. Talia had a bunch of the girls over."

"They did a lot of work on it."

"I heard," she said tightly. "It looks nice."

Yeah, she was uncomfortable.

"You know everyone here, I'm sure." She probably knew more people than I did at some industry parties, given that her sister was Elle Delacroix, superstar. I had no doubt that most of the Dirty family as well as the Players' would be here tonight, since Lex and Talia worked with the bands.

"Yeah," Angeline said distractedly as we climbed the front porch. "Probably."

"Don't worry." I stopped her, touching her chin with my knuckle to tip her face up to mine. I looked deep into her eyes. "Anyone ruins your night, I'll kiss it better."

She laughed a little, uncomfortably. I didn't kiss her, though. I led her into the party, as one of the on-duty security guys opened the front door for us.

It was the second time we were walking into a party together and people might have opinions about that fact, not that I particularly cared, but this time, she definitely seemed to.

As it turned out, my friends didn't seem all that surprised to see me with her.

Hers did.

From the moment we arrived, they made it pretty clear that I was not supposed to be with their girl. When we walked in, there were a bunch of girls, along with Ashley Player, gathered around Talia on the couch. Some of them looked over at us, and the rest followed suit, openly staring at us while one of Lex's club brothers greeted me. When Talia's jaw dropped at the sight of us, I glanced over my shoulder to find Angeline subtly flipping her the finger.

I smiled to myself. Mean Angie was out tonight. I liked her, actually, as much as I liked regular Angie. But that finger made me wonder how much grief her friends had been giving her since she'd started "working" with me.

"Don't let them get to you," I told her.

"They're my friends," she said defensively. "They're not trying to get to me." *They just hate you*, her eyes seemed to say. She was avoiding eye contact with me again.

"So? They're your friends, so that gives them the right to judge?"

"They're not judging." Her gray-blue eyes, soft with a self-consciousness that made me slightly hate her friends right back, met mine. "They're looking out for me."

Talia and Maggie, Zane Traynor's wife, appeared next to us. Talia took Angeline's hand. "Can we talk to you?"

"Uh, sure." Angeline glanced at me uncertainly.

"Go nuts," I told them. I handed Talia the bottle of peach liqueur and leaned in to kiss her cheek. "The house looks great, Tal."

"Johnny," she said, belatedly. "Thanks for coming." Her eyes said, *But why'd you have to come with such a nice girl?*

I tamped down the urge to roll my eyes as I wandered into the house in search of Lex.

And that was pretty much how it went all night.

My buddies saw me with Angeline, they slapped me on the back when she wasn't looking. *She's cute*, they said. *She's sweet as hell*, they said. *What'd you do to get with that?* That was Shane.

Every time we ran across some of Angeline's friends, they nudged her aside, probably to ask her what the hell she was doing with me, if she was drunk or high, if she was safe, if she needed a ride home. Because God forbid I was actually looking out for her.

Pissed me off, actually.

By the fifth time or so it happened, I interrupted her chat with Summer, took her hand in mine, and walked away with her. "Uh, bye, Summer! Catch you later!" Angeline called over her shoulder. "Where are we going?"

"Nowhere," I said, leading her out onto the back patio where people were hanging out under the stars. "But you're with me for the rest of the night."

"Okay." She discreetly took her hand back, like she was worried someone might see. "Why?"

I looked her in the eye. "Because everyone thinks you shouldn't be."

She glanced around, then drew closer to me, lowering her voice. "I'm confused now. Am I your publicist or your sister's friend right now?"

"Neither. You're the woman who's going to climax for me soon."

Her eyes hazed over a little as they held mine, her face flushing a soft pink that reminded me of how she looked when she climaxed. Like an angel in ecstasy.

She smiled a little, hesitantly, like she wasn't sure what to make of that.

"You want a drink," I told her.

She stared up at me with wide eyes, looking beautifully aroused. "Okay."

I took her over to the patio bar and got her a drink. Then I stayed by her side for the rest of the night.

---

"I see you've got a new toy."

Summer had walked up to me while Angeline slipped away to use the washroom. It was past midnight and the party was thinning out a little. I was heading inside through the back door, about to go find Angeline and corner her to deliver on my promise in the car, when Summer stepped into my path.

I quickly did the math; Summer was Elle's best friend. Elle wasn't here.

I feigned ignorance. "Toy?"

"You know the toy I speak of. Just don't break it, okay?"

"If you're referring to Angeline, you can say her name. Or at least not talk about her like an inanimate object with no free will." I looked Summer over. Thick, dark hair, curves accentuated in a purple halter top and sleek black pants with studs up the sides. "You look good, Summer. You wear rock star as well as you wore DJ."

Her blue eyes narrowed, distrusting. I wasn't flirting though, or kissing ass. I was being honest. Why was it so hard for people to believe me when I was being honest?

"That girl is precious," she informed me.

"I know."

"She's beloved," she pressed on, like I hadn't spoken. "To Elle, to me, and a whole lot of people, Johnny. And we can all see what's going on."

"Yeah? What's going on?"

I shifted aside as a couple of people brushed past, heading outside.

When we were alone again, Summer said, "She's always been into you, okay? You've got her wrapped around your finger, already. Or at least your…" She glanced down, briefly, making her point. Her eyes met mine again, with force. "Don't use her, okay? I'm sure you can find someone else if that's what you're after."

"Why would you assume I'm using her?"

"You've hired her to be your publicist and she's not even a publicist."

"She's learning. I gave her an opportunity."

"I'm sure."

"Nice seeing you, Summer." I went to brush past her, but she stepped in front of me.

"Look, Johnny. Elle won't say these things to your face because she doesn't want to embarrass Angeline. I have no such filter. I'd rather embarrass her than have her ripped apart by a man who has zero respect for women."

Instantly, my blood went hot. "Back off, Summer. You don't know shit about me or my life."

"I know you use women, cheat on them and toss them away, and it's not okay with me if you do that to her. She deserves better. She just went through a breakup. She's vulnerable and if you prey on that just to get your dick wet, you can kiss any chance of working with my band or Elle's goodbye. I mean it, Johnny."

Yeah. I could see that.

Was that how Cary felt, too? And all her other bandmates?

"So, you're threatening me now."

"I'm telling you how it is."

"I see how it is. You can't make her stay away from me, and that pisses you off."

She drew back a bit. Her husband, Ronan, the Players' head of security, suddenly joined us, looming next to her. He read his wife's mood and looked hard at me. "Everything okay?"

I ignored him. "She's a grown woman, Summer. She'll do what she wants."

"Yes, she is. That doesn't mean I can't look out for her. You treat her like the angel she is, or we have a problem."

I took a breath, assessing her. What first felt like an attack on me now struck me as what it really was. Summer had her claws out to protect Angeline. She saw me as a threat.

But I wasn't a threat.

"I appreciate you looking out for her. You don't need to worry about me, though. I know what an angel she is."

Summer looked mildly shocked, no retort for that one.

"Have a nice night, Summer. Say hi to Cary for me." I nodded at her husband and brushed past.

I headed upstairs, looking for Angeline, when I didn't find her in the living room. I found her on the second floor, talking to Talia and Devi. I wasn't sure if that was a good thing or not; the wives of two of my best friends having a girl-to-girl with her.

Judging by the way they both looked at me, with marked suspicion, I was thinking not. Talia and Devi had both tolerated me, welcomed me into their homes; they'd been friendly, even. But it seemed the warm welcome had evaporated when I showed up in one of their homes with one of their esteemed girl crew.

"Hey, Johnny," Angeline said softly. They'd all stopped their conversation as I approached.

"Hey, Angel. You find the washroom?"

"Yeah. It's back there." She gestured toward the end of the hall, where a door to a dark room stood ajar.

"Great." I headed toward it, taking her by surprise when I caught her arm and pulled her with me. She followed me into the bathroom, where I flipped on a light and locked the door behind us.

"People… listening…" she stammered, already breathless as I pushed her back against the door.

"They can't hear anything," I muttered against her skin as I kissed her throat. "Music."

"But, they know…"

"They know nothing." I slid my hand into her hair at the back of her head and tugged, looking into her eyes. "Are Talia and Devi close with Shayla? Are they gonna tell?"

She swallowed. "No. No, they wouldn't do that. They barely know her."

I searched her eyes for that desperate, hungry look she gave me last night. And tonight, in my car, after she sucked me off. "Beg me."

She shuddered with arousal, her hands digging into my chest. "Beg you…?"

"Beg me for what you want, Angeline."

"Oh…"

I tipped her jaw up with my thumb and kissed her neck again, sucking a path down to her collarbone.

"Johnny… *Yeah*. I… I want you to make me come," she whispered.

The fact that she wanted this, but now she was being fucking shy about it all over again? Turned me on more than I would've thought possible. I was so fucking hard, my cock already straining in my jeans, flexing at every soft, needy sound she made as I ran my tongue along the hollow of her collarbone. I grabbed her breast and squeezed through her shirt, finding the hard bud of her nipple and plucking gently.

"You want to come, Angel?"

She wriggled against the door. "I like coming for you." Again, she sounded shy about it, but there was nothing shy about her fingers clawing at my chest muscles and suddenly gripping my nipples.

I bit the soft spot between her neck and shoulder gently and she squirmed, gasping. My cock shuddered.

After that little run-in with Summer, I wanted to fuck the hell out of her just to prove to myself that I could. To show Angeline that I would, no matter what her friends thought. But now that I had her alone, in my hands, in my mouth… all I wanted was the high and the satisfaction of watching her come.

I ran my hands down her curves to her jeans and undid them. "Off," I ordered. She helped me push them down, then stepped out of them. "Panties, too." She slipped them off obediently. "Now sit on the sink."

She hopped up on the smooth countertop in front of the sink. There were a few inches of surface, enough for her to get comfy on if I helped her out. I got down on my knees in front of her and tossed her legs over my shoulders, making her fall back. She caught herself, hands propped on either side of the sink. She was breathing heavily, looking flushed and beautiful and so hungry for this.

"Let me see you…" My eyes drifted down her chest, and she used one hand to pull her shirt up. She tugged her bra up too, letting her breasts fall out beneath, baring them to me. "Don't touch."

She settled back on her hands, watching me, waiting, her chest rising and falling with shaky breaths. The torture of anticipation.

I licked alongside her pussy, that super soft skin that she'd cleared of hair. She had none but a little strip above her clit, the same silky soft light-brown as the hair on her head, trimmed into a small triangle like an arrow pointing the way to paradise.

I licked again on the other side as she melted, her thighs sinking into my shoulders.

"I don't hear you begging."

"Oh… *Please.*"

I drifted a fingertip over the opening of her pussy, the slick wetness on her lips. I rubbed it around, gently, just barely touching her, and she squirmed.

"Oh, God. Yeah, do that." Her eyes met mine. "Please," she added hastily.

I caressed her opening, dipping my fingertip inside, making her mouth fall open. "You like that?"

"Uh-huh."

I increased the pressure, rubbing her opening with teasing sweeps of my finger, dipping in just slightly, drawing out the slick wetness and massaging her with it. "Can you come like this?"

"I don't think so."

"No? What if I don't touch your clit at all, and I make you come?"

"Uhh…"

Her ability to speak fled as I slipped the length of my finger into her. I curled it up into her front wall, stroking her. Her mouth dropped open again, but no words came.

"You like that?" I knew she did.

"Yeah. *More.*"

I slipped a second finger in and rubbed both against her front wall. She started shaking, quivering when it felt good.

"God, yeah. More, Johnny. Please…" She twisted her hips, trying to get more pressure.

"Relax," I told her, kissing the soft skin next to her pussy. "Don't move, Angel. Just feel. Feel what I'm doing to you."

She sighed raggedly, then whimpered when I slipped in a third finger. I moved them together, shoving them in deep, then curling them, undulating into the tissues of her front wall.

She shuddered. "Johnny…"

"Yeah. Say my name."

She panted my name, again and again, as I fucked her with my fingers and rubbed her inside in a deep rhythm, not too fast. Her body shook and shivered, and she sobbed a little when my fingers pressed up into her front wall again.

I pulsated them against her wet flesh, just figuring out what she liked best. That elicited a little cry and her head fell back.

"Shh, Angel, it's okay."

"I think I'm gonna…"

"You're gonna come." I kissed her soft flesh again, nuzzling into the soft hollow between her thigh and her pussy. I drifted my mouth over to the other side, skipping right over her pussy, letting her feel nothing there but my warm breath.

"Oh, please, yes…" She kept pleading, as I kept urging her closer to orgasm. I knew she'd get there.

"Just try to relax," I soothed her.

"God…" She heaved a sigh and looked at me. Her eyes were wet with unshed tears. "It feels so good…"

"I know, Angel. I'm gonna make you feel so good."

I pressed a kiss to her smooth skin again, then kissed her closer to her opening. She moaned. I drifted my tongue over her flesh, teasing her opening as I kept fucking her with my fingers… and something about that combo—my tongue teasing her delicate opening and the deep, massaging thrusts—sent her over. Her cunt bore down on my hand, rippling around me as she climaxed. I kept licking, kept rubbing her inside as she shuddered and shook, her pussy spasming around me in deep, shuddering pulses.

"Oh fuck, don't stop," she begged, and I kept going until she seemed to be floating back down, catching her breath.

Her eyes met mine and she gave me a slow smile, looking flushed.

Then her smile melted into molten ecstasy as I closed my lips over her neglected clit, sucking. I lashed it with my tongue, then sucked in deep, hungry pulls, pressing against her front wall with the fingers that were still buried inside her.

"*Ohhh…* Johnny," she gasped, and her hips jerked a little, her body shuddering as she came again—fucking hard. Her hand slapped the counter, the other one clawing into my hair as the spasms ripped through her and she moaned in delirium, her back arching.

I sucked, then licked, then kissed, until she was safely back to her senses and could support herself on the counter. Just barely. My fingers slid out of her and her legs fell from my shoulders as I got to my feet. I stood between her legs and gathered her to me. She was limp and hot, and gazed up at me with lust in her eyes.

"You," I told her, before she could say anything, "are an angel."

She tilted her head slightly, studying me like she wasn't sure where such sweet words came from, or what she'd done to deserve them. I smoothed her hair back from her pretty face and kissed her lips softly.

When I drew back to meet her eyes again, she whispered, "Fuck me. Please."

The fact that she wanted me to, so fucking badly, was making me so hard it was brutal torture. But there were more important things than my dick right now.

"No." I kissed her forehead.

"Why not?"

I didn't want to tell her about the conversation with her sister's best friend, but it was still clinging to me, like the echoes of a bad dream. "Can you come again?"

She dropped her gaze. "Yeah. Um, probably."

"Look at me."

Her eyes found mine again. I leaned in and kissed her, slow and wet, sucking softly on her bottom lip. I slid my tongue languidly through her mouth, stroking hers.

"This is mine," I told her, seized with a need to mark this. Watching her come, making her come, feeling her come… *All mine.* In her eyes, I saw the first flash of apprehension since she got in my car tonight, and clarified, "You don't come for anyone but me, Angel. Your pleasure is mine."

She let out a shuddery breath. Relieved, maybe, that the claim I was staking was only sexual. That I wasn't asking for more than that.

At least, not out loud.

"Okay," she agreed softly.

"I'm the only one who makes you come. When you need someone to touch you, to undress you, to suck on your pretty tits and play with your pussy, eat that sweet little clit, you come to me." She shivered as I ran my finger down the center of her body, from between her breasts to just above her clit. "Anytime you need a dick to play with… you need to be teased… you need to beg for a come… you need to be driven to climax again and again until you can't walk… you need a hard cock in your beautiful body… you need a good, hard fuck, Angeline, whatever you need, you come to me."

"Okay. Yes. But… don't you want to?" She glanced down at my cock, straining hard in my jeans. "Right now?"

"Yes, I want to."

She watched me, looking disoriented as I helped her off the sink and helped her get dressed. I washed my hands, running them under ice-cold water, not looking at her for a minute so I could calm down enough to lose the erection, so we could go say our goodbyes.

"You're not going to?" she asked behind me, sounding confused and maybe a little rejected.

"Not here," I said. "Not now." Then I kissed her so deeply she couldn't possibly believe I was rejecting her in any way. I held her face and looked in her eyes. "But you want cock, Angeline, I've got all the cock you'll ever need."

"When we get home," she whispered as we slipped out of the bathroom together.

But I didn't answer. The things Summer said were still in my head, louder now that I didn't have the distraction of pleasuring Angeline. And they were both intoxicating me and pissing me off.

*You've got her wrapped around your finger, already. Or at least your...*

And that other thing she said, which I knew was true, and all of Angeline's friends knew, too.

*She deserves better.*

# Chapter Twenty-Five

**Angeline**

On the drive home from the party, Johnny was quiet. Reserved. He didn't say much, just one word answers to my questions in a smooth, controlled voice.

I wasn't sure if this was him pulling away, or… something else. Whatever it was, there was something on his mind, preoccupying him. Making him outwardly cool and tense.

I hoped it was his impatience to fuck me as soon as he got me home. But I wasn't sure.

Lamar tailed us home, which I didn't totally understand—why couldn't he just drive with us to the party in the first place? But then I remembered: blowjob. I'd instigated it, sure. But that didn't mean Johnny wasn't anticipating something happening.

As both cars pulled into Johnny's driveway, I glanced at Johnny, but his focus was on driving; he always seemed tense when he was behind the wheel. Now, I had no idea if any of that tension was about me or not.

I eyed Shayla's house. The usual combo of lights were on, the ones that stayed on for security when she wasn't home in the evening. I sent her a text, and by the time she replied we'd parked in the garage. Johnny was doing something on his phone anyway, so I read the text, then looked over at him. He was watching me.

"Shayla's not home," I told him. "She's out with Larissa tonight."

Johnny didn't say a word. He got out of the car, and I watched as he came around to open my door for me. I noticed that Lamar had already disappeared into the house, heading off to his suite. Johnny gave me his hand and when I took it, he drew me out of the car—and out of the garage into the night. I went where he led, up the path that disappeared into the dark between the two houses.

In the shadows, he suddenly pulled me up against him, falling back against the wall of the house and kissing me. Fire erupted in my belly as I sank against him. God, this man's kisses… He kissed me possessively, like he had every right to… his hands on my face and digging in my hair, holding me close, like there was nothing else in the world but this kiss.

When it ended, a strange ache throbbed in my chest.

Johnny shifted to dig something out of his back pocket. A slim cigarette case, from which he extracted a nicely rolled joint. His eyes never left mine as he lit up, and that flash of fire on his face in the dark… I wondered if he was remembering that night, when I found him in the shadows, smoking, and he kissed me.

He took the joint from between his lips and offered it to me, his eyes dropping to my mouth as I took a tiny puff.

Then he smoked, studying my face. He offered it to me again, but I shook my head, *no thanks*.

"I thought you smoked," he said. Because of course he'd probably seen me smoking up with Shayla by his pool plenty of times over the years.

"Yeah. Chilling with friends, it's okay. It's different when I'm—" I almost said, *when I'm on a date*. "With a man."

"How so?"

"Uh, hard to explain."

He took another drag and blew the sweet, musky smoke in the air between us. I liked the smell of it and breathed it in with the fresh night air. I also liked the idea that maybe it was making him relax. Johnny didn't really do relaxed, as far as I'd ever witnessed. He did cool. He projected laid back and careless, but he was anything but. The man always seemed so tightly locked down. On guard.

For what, I had no idea. He had security up the ass. His property was locked down tight, between Lamar, the security gate, the high fence, the cameras, and who knew what else.

"Does it make you relax?" I decided to ask him.

"It'll make me last. So I can fuck you longer."

"Oh." Well, shit. I was thinking something along those lines about myself, but not in a good way. *Maybe it isn't so hard to explain.* "I don't mind pot, but honestly it makes me spacey, hard to focus. And… it makes it really hard to come."

I swore I saw flames leap to life in the depths of his eyes. Challenge accepted?

I shivered deliciously as he pulled me tight against him and I slid my arms up around his neck.

"Is that what it's like for you?" I asked him.

"No. Nothing could keep me from coming with you."

I laughed. "Uh, you kept yourself from coming when we were in the bathroom at the party."

"Temporarily."

"Why?"

"Because your pleasure is more important."

Heat seeped through me at his words, and I could feel my panties getting soaked. Because my body knew exactly what was coming.

*Pleasure.*

Mine and his. Though he was taking his damn time getting to it.

"Says who?" I challenged.

"I just did." He smoked as I waited for his next move, slow pulls that burned the joint down to a stub between his fingers. He had control of the both of us right now—of the entire situation, as I leaned on him waiting for him to touch me—and maybe he knew it. But I'd instigated that blowjob in the car, and he'd held himself back from fucking me in that bathroom. I wanted him to take control of whatever was about to happen.

Waiting for it was both maddening and maddeningly arousing.

"Also," he said, "I wanted to fuck you much longer than you'd probably want me to in that bathroom. And you might've had trouble walking out of there without everyone knowing how long I fucked you."

"Oh, he's impressed with his own talents."

He licked his bottom lip slowly. "Not nearly as impressed as you are." The blunt had expired and I watched as he flicked what was left of it into the bushes. But he still didn't make a move.

Then he said, "Come with me," in a commanding tone. Soft but dominant... The pang of desire through my body was immediate, and when he turned for me to follow, reaching to touch my hand with his, the electricity where our fingers met made my heart leap.

I followed as he held my hand loosely and led me toward the back of his house. Then up the exterior stairs to the patio off his bedroom.

Along the way, he said nothing.

But he did stop after a few stairs to peel off my shirt. And my bra. Then he made me walk in front of him, as I felt the heat of his gaze all over me. A few steps later, he sat me down on a stair to take off my shoes. A few more steps and he stopped us to peel off my jeans. By the time we reached the patio up top, I was shaking with desire and anticipation.

He slipped a hand around my waist, stopping me. He pressed up against me from behind, his heat consuming me as his body connected with mine. His hard cock pressed against my ass. His warm breath and his lips teased my neck. "Panties off, Angel."

Then he stood back, presumably to watch me obey that command.

I did, slipping off my last item of clothing.

When I turned to see where he'd gone, he was standing back near the railing, the dark night sky spread moodily above him. His eyes were on mine. "Now take off my clothes."

I did as he told me to, as he watched me under hooded eyes. He didn't help at all, except to step out of his jeans and boxer briefs when I needed him to. His words kept replaying in my head, intoxicating me like a delicious drug, making my whole body thud with anticipation. *Your pleasure is more important.*

When he was naked before me, I ran my hands greedily down his muscled chest and abs. When I looked at his hard cock, my mouth watered.

"Did I say you could touch?" That same low, soft, dominant tone came at me, sending a prickle down my spine, and I took my hands back.

"Um… no?"

He flicked his chin toward the lounge chair next to us. "Get down on all fours, Angeline."

I swallowed thickly—pure, drooling lust—as arousal coursed through me. I got on my knees on the long, padded lounge chair. As I dropped forward onto my hands, I felt Johnny walking slowly around me, barefoot and silent. I thought I felt him stop behind me and the heat of his gaze warming my skin.

The next command came just as softly, yet just as impossible to refuse. "On your elbows."

I complied, feeling utterly naked, utterly sexual, as he prowled around me. Watching.

"Wh-what are you doing?" My voice wavered, soft in the night.

"Figuring out what you like."

I laughed nervously, a breathless sound that totally gave me away. "You already know what I like."

"I know some things you like," he corrected me. "I want to know all. Spread your knees." His warm hand landed gently but possessively on my ass, then smoothed upwards to my waist. My body responded automatically, my back arching, tipping my ass up like an offering, as I obeyed and spread my knees.

My body shook, which was the only thing that actually kind of embarrassed me. That lack of control over myself. But I couldn't help it. I felt lightheaded, in the best way. I wasn't sure I'd ever been as turned on as I was with Johnny O'Reilly ordering me to get down on all fours naked in front of him, right out on his patio with the night air all over my skin, while he contemplated fucking me.

I fucking hoped that's what he was contemplating.

"Maybe smoking that pot wasn't such a good idea," I teased nervously, wondering if he knew how long he was making me wait. If I'd just smoked a whole blunt to myself, I'd be reeling, lose all track of time.

But he seemed to have no such problem with focus. His second hand deliberately joined the first, gently squeezing my waist as he moved in close. I peeked back to see him standing behind me, straddling the lounge chair.

"Head down," he commanded smoothly.

I rested my head on my forearms, sucking in a breath as I braced for his possession. Would it be fast? Hard? Slow and teasing…?

After a long, breathless moment, he said, "Breathe, Angel."

I released the breath I'd been holding, and as I relaxed, I felt the head of his cock at my entrance. Sweet longing gripped me when he hesitated, making me wait again.

"God, you're a tease," I gushed.

Maybe I half-expected some kind of punishment or further teasing in response to that statement. Instead, he pushed into me in a deep, controlled stroke that made my entire body snap to attention, every bit of me, inside and out, tuning in to his possession. He filled me, hot and bare, and I'd never felt anything more fucking exquisite.

"Johnny," I gasped in utter, delirious pleasure.

"That what you wanted, Angeline?"

God, the husky, horny way he said my name. That I could command such desire from him… it was heady magic.

"I wanted you to want me," I whispered.

He pulled out, slowly, until the head of his cock was stretching my opening, then fed me the whole shaft again… until his body pressed tight to mine. I could feel him stretching my channel open, the restrained power in his hips against me, the possessive bite of his fingers around my hips and waist. I felt wide open to him, filled by him, and all I wanted was more. Again and again and again.

But he remained still until I squirmed with hunger.

His hands slid down my ass, his thumbs seeking the flesh between my legs. He drew me open, gently, and slowly, so slowly, began to fuck me. Just a few times, until I groaned. Then he seated himself deep again, going still. I felt his cock spasm inside me and I wondered if this was torturing him as much as it was me.

"Feel me inside you, Angel?" His voice was growing raspy now, but no less demanding.

"Yes."

"Say my name."

"Johnny," I breathed. He pulled out again and then eased back in, and it felt like my brain was gradually being rewired, every time he possessed me—no matter how he did it—and made me utter his name. Made me acknowledge who was driving me wild like this.

"Johnny," I gasped, as he pumped into me, a little faster, harder, rocking me. I pushed back against him, taking his thrusts as the intensity ramped up; both the controlled power of his thrusts and my reaction to them. Arousal swept through my body at dizzying speed, making me flush all over.

"*Johnny.*" I bore down on him, wanting every sensation I could feel as he battered into me, brutal now, but still not fast, making every nerve hyper-tuned to his next move… ever inch, every beat of his rhythm, felt all the way down to my curling toes.

He groaned above me, squeezing my ass cheeks as he controlled the depth of his thrusts, controlled me completely as he fucked into me. "Does my cock slut need more?" The words were spoken with desire and affection, and molten heat washed through me like a drug through my veins. *My.* It was the *my* in that sentence, as much as the dirty words, that floored me.

*This is mine.*

*You don't come for anyone but me, Angel.*

*Your pleasure is mine…*

I moaned, feeling desperate and so split open, so naked for him, that it was making the whole world spin.

"Tell me you need it," he rasped, sounding hungry and needy himself.

"I need this. Please, give it to me."

He did, fucking me faster, still deep, sending that flush of heat through me again.

"Bear down on me," he ordered.

I did, squeezing his invading cock as hard as I could.

He moaned and suddenly his hands left my ass. He grabbed me and pulled me up, holding me against his hard, hot body, my back to his front. He locked a possessive arm around my waist and kept fucking me. But the angle had changed. The depth.

Suddenly, his cockhead was rubbing into my front wall, hitting that glorious, engorged g-spot. In my experience, there was no spot; it was much better than that. That whole area, when touched the right way, at the right time, sent my whole core into inside-out meltdown. When he slid his other hand between my legs and pinched the tip of my clit between his fingers, I detonated with a scream.

My body shook, my core spasming around him as he fucked me, my clit pulsing under his fingers and all around his invading cock. I could feel his heat and the restrained lust in his body, tense against me, as he teased out my orgasm… and the feeling that he was savoring it just made me come harder.

The arm around my waist slid upwards, his hand slipping around my throat. He squeezed gently, possessively, as his other hand rubbed between my legs and the explosions rippled through me.

It wasn't until my head had unscrambled and I remembered where I was that the horror hit me. I twisted out of his arms and detached myself from his cock, falling back on the lounge chair. I panted, blinking up at him.

He looked like a literal sex god kneeling over me, Eros incarnate, his muscles sculpted in the moonlight, his body glistening with sweat.

"You made me scream," I rasped. "What if Shayla heard?"

"You said she's not home." He leaned down over me and kissed away the rest of my complaints and protests, until I was soft and pliant under him once more.

"I need to make you come," I gushed as soon as he let me speak again.

Johnny nuzzled my neck, kissing my throat. "We're getting to that," he rasped against my skin. "Your pleasure is more important, remember?"

"I didn't agree to that."

He just looked at me, heat smoldering in his eyes.

I didn't argue any further. I didn't need him to give me pleasure in order for me to get turned on. Just looking at him turned me on. But the way he savored my pleasure was delectable. The way he took his time seeking out my pleasure was awe-inspiring. But it turned me on so much, it just made me want him even more.

Vicious cycle.

I reached for his cock, but he caught my arms and pinned them down at my sides and gave me a slow, wicked smile.

"Please," I panted.

"Please what?" He was teasing me. Toying with me.

My fault, probably, for giving him that killer blowjob in the car. Between that and the pot making him "last longer," maybe he'd tease me all damn night now.

"I want to make you come."

"You'll make me come when I say you can make me come."

We stared into each other's eyes. Then he licked my bottom lip and kissed me again. Somehow, he'd already figured out that teasing me and giving me sexy orders turned my bones to mush and any pathetic resolve I might have to ashes and smoke. So unfair.

"Something wrong?" he said, cool and controlled, when I squirmed.

"You're stupid."

He laughed shortly.

"I'd do anything to make you come right now. Stop torturing me."

He dipped down and drifted his lips up my throat. "Just making it last, sweetheart." His voice was a soft, sexy purr against my skin. "How bad do you want it?"

"Punch you in the eye bad," I panted.

Johnny chuckled under his breath and plunged his tongue into my mouth, silencing me with a ferocious kiss that had me burning up with lust all over again. But I could feel the restrained hunger in him, still. His thick erection jabbed against my thigh. He wanted this as much as I did.

He kissed his way down my throat to my chest, and when his tongue drifted over my peaked nipple, he said softly, "You're getting cold."

Before I could respond, he'd lifted me up in his arms and carried me down the stairs.

# Chapter Twenty-Six

**Angeline**

Johnny set me on my feet in front of the sliding doors into his gym. He punched in a code to the security pad and let us in. I really wasn't all that cold, but I wasn't about to complain if he wanted to bend me over in his cedar sauna now or something.

He didn't take me into the sauna. He took me into the dimly-lit steam room, which smelled faintly of eucalyptus. I was instantly invigorated, breathing in the steaming, fragrant air.

"You just keep it hot all the time, in case some babe stops by for a steam?" I inquired, trying to sound casual about it but seriously wondering.

"I turned it on when we got here." His dry tone said I was being a smart ass. "From my phone."

"Well, aren't you fancy." Secretly, it thrilled me that he'd planned ahead. That he wanted to bring me in here.

He tugged me against his body. "I also verified that Shayla wasn't home. Security system."

"You give Big Brother a whole new meaning."

"What can I say. I like to have eyes all over the place." His hands slid suggestively over my curves, like they were replacing his eyes. The only lighting was a soft strip of light near the ceiling, and I could barely see him in the mist.

He took me by the hand, led me over to a bench and sat down, pulling me onto his lap. Facing him, so I could straddle him on my knees. I felt the thick towel he'd sat us down on as I got into position; very thoughtful.

Then I took his hard length inside me, immediately and hungrily, when he angled himself so I could. I started riding him with hungered abandon, but realized quickly that wouldn't fly in a steam room. It was way too fucking hot, the air too thick.

"There's no rush, sweetheart," Johnny murmured, rubbing my shoulders with his strong hands. "And you don't want to exert yourself, it's too hot." He kneaded the muscles of my back as his words and the steam soothed me, and I turned limp, riding him languidly.

"This is gonna be… the laziest lay of your life," I said dreamily, slumping against him.

I felt him smile as he kissed my neck.

"How am I gonna make you come…?" I complained drunkenly.

"It really won't take much."

"No…?"

"Just be you."

Ugh. The things this guy said. I didn't even care if they were lines. They fucking worked.

"Was that a line?" I tried to be mad about it, but I was melting too fast. Goddamn, it was steamy in here.

Johnny's hand slid up my back to knead the back of my neck, and if I'd let my mouth fall open I'd be drooling all over him. "It's not a line if it's sincere, Angel," he whispered in my ear. "All you have to do to get me off is be you," he repeated.

"Why are you so delicious?" My mouth smashed into his before he could answer as I attacked him with a slow, delirious kiss. We melted into a steamy, gyrating mass of pleasure, until suddenly he broke the kiss.

"Stop," he warned.

"Why?"

"Don't make me come."

"Why not? I'm on birth control." I looked into his eyes as well as I could, but it was so steamy and dark in here, it was like we were smoldering in a volcano. "It's about trust, remember?"

"I trust you. I just don't want you to feel…"

"I know what I want to feel." I kept riding him, driving him to the edge.

"Just… slow down, baby…" he panted, his hands sliding up and down my back. I knew he wanted to make it last.

I didn't listen. In my opinion, he was done giving the commands. For now.

I tightened my arms around him, kissing him deep—but my hips sped up. I fucked him in fast, shallow swallows, my pussy gorging on his cock, giving him no chance to resist…

"Slow," he panted against my mouth.

"Nope. Not slowing. Not stopping. Unless you wanna toss me off…"

Too late.

I knew it was too late when he tensed, groaned, and yanked me against him, tight. His hips snapped up. The length of his hard cock flexed inside me as he started to ejaculate. "Fuck, Angel." He moaned as he lost it, helpless to the climax I'd unleashed as he jerked inside me, loading me with cream, and I fucking reveled in it. I moved my hips in an undulating rhythm, getting him off completely as he groaned and growled in bliss… then gradually slowing as he relaxed.

"You weren't supposed to make me come so fast," he panted, his words slurring with sated pleasure against my sweaty skin as he kissed my neck. He actually had the nerve to complain to me after that fabulous orgasm.

"Are you kidding? You fought that off for hours."

He ran his hands gently up and down my curves, sending delicious tingles through me. "Could've kept going for hours."

Fuck, I could barely even see the man through all the steam and he was so damn sexy.

"*I* couldn't have." I kissed him, then wriggled uncomfortably, too hot to actually get up. "Shit, it's way too hot in here now," I complained. "I'm gonna faint." In response, he gripped my ass with strong hands and lifted me against him as he got to his feet. How he managed that without passing out, I'd never know. "Are you human?"

"Unfortunately. Being your personal sex robot would be a good gig."

I giggled, our sweaty bodies slipping as he carried me out of the steam room and into the showers. Good thing he was strong. I just climbed him and held on.

"I'm not even gonna try to imagine why there are like five shower heads in here," I mused as he set me carefully on my feet.

Johnny gazed down at me as he got one of the shower heads running for us, then steered me into the warm water. "Multiple people can use the pool at once."

"And shower together afterwards?" I inquired.

"You assume this showering happens in a naked free-for-all."

"There are no partitions for privacy, so yeah, I'm gonna assume."

I turned slowly under the wide stream of warm water, letting it soak me completely, while Johnny loaded up his palms with body wash. Then he smoothed it all over my curves, concentrating on my thighs like he was taking care to wash me free of any of his come that had gushed out. It was rather sweet.

Until I imagined him doing the same thing to other girls he'd brought in here, and jealousy prickled in my gut.

Strange…

I'd become so accustomed to watching other girls get with the guys I'd wanted from afar, over the years, that jealousy wasn't really a big thing for me. I knew there were prettier girls, girls there was no point competing with. Girls like my sister. I'd learned to accept it, and in accepting it came a kind of peace and self-assurance of its own. If a man didn't want me for me, why put myself through the pain and turmoil of trying and losing out?

But. Standing here in Johnny's multi-person shower did something strange to my insides. I felt peeled inside-out. Exposed and raw. I didn't like thinking of him spending a whole evening with me doing what we just did—all the kisses, all the deep eye contact, all his focused attention on me, never mind the explosive sex—and then him turning around and doing it all over again with someone else.

The thought made me feel quite sick, actually.

*No point running from it if it's gonna happen*, I told myself. *Better to face it head on.* If there was one thing I'd learned from my long, slow breakup with Flynn, it was that heartbreak would be better in fast forward. Why draw out that inevitable hurt?

*Just get it the fuck over with.*

When Johnny didn't say another word, instead just watching me shower with hooded eyes, I forced out, "Okay, I'll just ask you. Why are there five shower heads in here?"

His eyes, in their slow travel over my body, met mine. When that deep, dark aquamarine locked onto me, I felt helpless. Like whatever he would say… it wouldn't change a thing. I wasn't sure why that didn't scare me more.

"If I said it was for orgies, would it change how you view me?"

"No. Because I already assumed it was for orgies."

His expression turned thoughtful. "How many people does it take to constitute an orgy?"

"Don't get cute about it. Five definitely constitutes."

"When I designed the house," he said carefully, "I anticipated multiple people wanting to shower at once. If my friends want to have an orgy in here, I'd prefer they shower afterwards."

I laughed. "That explanation is so seamless, I almost bought it."

"It's true."

"It may be. But you're omitting."

"Omitting what?"

"Past sexual behavior of your own. Because you think I'll judge you."

"I don't think you'll judge." His arms slid around me possessively, protectively, holding us both under the warm water together.

I stared up into his eyes, reading between the lines of that response.

Something else, then. Something was holding him back from being transparent with me. I didn't exactly ask for numbers. *How many women have you screwed? How many women have you cheated on? How many women have you hurt?* Because the numbers didn't matter to me. Fact was, I knew he'd done all those things. Screwed. Cheated. Hurt.

In the past.

What mattered to me was how he treated women—including me—from this point on.

People could grow. And I didn't feel an uncaring, hurtful person wrapping himself around me right now.

But whatever was holding him back, he was afraid it would drive me away. I could feel that in his hesitation to answer my direct question with a direct answer.

"Am I invited to one of these orgies?" I prodded.

His arms tightened around me. "Any of my friends invites you to an orgy," he said in a low, possessive voice, "you telling me you don't know the answer?"

I blinked innocently. "'Ask Johnny'?"

"Johnny says no," he growled.

"I meant, am I invited next time you have a party?" Our eyes were locked, tension thick in the steam around us. We both knew what I was really asking.

*Are you planning to have steam room sex followed by an intimate shower with any other women anytime soon?*

"The only party here," he said darkly, "is in my pants, and you're the only one invited."

"You're not wearing any pants," I said innocently. "But thank you. I appreciate you calling off the orgies."

"How would I have an orgy?" He shut off the shower, then started walking me backwards out of the room, predatory, his body steering mine where he wanted it. "You're so hungry for my cock, none of the other girls would get any."

"Poor girls," I said sarcastically.

Then he kissed me. Hard and demanding, until I kissed him back as passionately and thoroughly as he was kissing me. He held me against him, hot and wet, naked flesh to naked flesh, easing me slowly backwards out of the gym the entire time. We stood on the back deck, the night air cool on my wet skin as he kissed me, hot and slow, like he could kiss me all night.

Then, suddenly, he lifted me up—and tossed me in the pool. My body crashed into the water, and after the steam room and the hot shower it felt fucking cold. Naturally, I screamed.

"You asshole!"

He'd jumped in after me, and as soon as he emerged I splashed water in his face.

"What?" He wiped water from his eyes. "You told me to toss you, in the steam room. I thought you were into that."

"Nice try." I splashed him again as he circled like a shark. "Don't make me scream like that. What if Shayla came home?"

"She didn't." He grabbed me and pulled me against him, clearly pleased with himself. "And you already screamed up the backyard. What's one more scream?" He dragged me with him to the shallow end, where he held me, wrapping my legs around his waist.

"Don't you dare even think about making me scream again. I'm spent." *Hmm.* As the words came out of my mouth, I realized I'd never said those words to a man before.

I'd never actually been with a man who satisfied me so thoroughly that he actually wore me out. I wasn't even sure if that was a little sad, or just fucking awesome that I'd finally found one who did. Both, maybe.

"What?" Johnny smoothed my hair back off my face, then cupped my head in his hand and tugged my face close to his. "What are you thinking?"

"I'm thinking… I need to sleep off this sex binge. I can't keep up with the sex robot."

He laughed softly, then kissed me again. I shivered as his hot body kept me warm, the comparatively cool water lapping against my skin.

I didn't really want to say good night and go to sleep.

Couldn't we just make out in his pool all night and pretend nothing else existed, like our careers and people who didn't approve of "us" and all responsibilities whatsoever? It seemed so grossly unfair that I'd finally met my sexual match and I was basically forbidden from being with him, by both of our sisters.

Johnny broke the kiss, suddenly, his body going rigid. It was like watching a bloodhound catch a sent. That hyper vigilant thing of his kicked into overdrive; I could feel it. In a split second the air changed and the sudden tension in him had me looking around into the shadows of the yard.

"What?" I breathed.

"You hear that?"

"No…"

His eyes locked with mine. "Shayla's home." His arms tightened around me like a steel brace when I instinctively tried to back away from him.

"Are you sure?"

"I heard the front gate. That's the garage door."

I probably wouldn't have noticed it if he didn't point it out, the distant rumble was that faint. I tried to stay calm so I wouldn't freak him out. But internally, I was freaking out.

What if Shayla saw us like this?

Just the idea that she might feel betrayed… Or even for a moment, that she might think I was one of *those* girls. There'd been so many of them over the years: girls who'd used her to try to get access to her brother.

*No.*

Johnny just held me tighter, maybe sensing my tension or my urge to flee. His eyes held mine, cool and calm. "Are you gonna tell her?"

I sighed raggedly. I really, really didn't want to hurt Shayla or our friendship. But… "Eventually. I have to. I mean, if this…" I failed to come up with any words to describe *this*, or to quantify it. "If this is… lasting… for any length of time…"

Johnny's gaze dropped to my lips, and then he kissed me again. Soft and decisive. "Stay with me tonight." It was a husky whisper in the night, and I knew the invitation was genuine.

"I can't. She'd find out. And I'm not gonna blurt it out to her right now. It's the middle of the night and I've got your sex juices all over me." I pushed him away playfully, but he got the message and let me go. I was running scared, panicked with the idea that Shayla might see us out here. Together. Naked.

Before I had a chance to explain it to her.

As if I could've explained it…

*So, hey, me and your brother have picked up this new hobby. Turns out*

*I love making him come, and vice versa. Oh, and when he calls me his little cock slut while he fucks me, it's about the hottest thing I've ever experienced. I probably couldn't stop fucking him if you held a gun to my head and ordered me to stop. Cool, huh?*

Brutal. I mean, I knew she didn't need the details, but the girl wasn't exactly inexperienced, and she knew her brother. She also knew me. Incredibly well. So as soon as she heard the words "me and your brother..." out of my mouth, her vivid imagination would fill in the blanks.

Yup. She was gonna murder me.

"Well," I told him as we got out of the pool and he started toweling me off, "it's been nice knowing you. Occasionally."

Johnny gave me a faint, charming smile.

Lights were coming on in Shayla's house and I grabbed the towel, cinching it tight around myself. "Don't be surprised if you never see me alive again," I squeaked out. "Sorry I might have to miss that meeting with Yash tomorrow. Please ask Harry Styles to come sing 'Sign of the Times' at my funeral. I'm sure if you and my sister chipped in, you could afford it."

While I spoke, the slight smile had vanished and Johnny's expression darkened. "What are you talking about?"

"Your sister. My murder. Please don't be mad at her. And cover it up, okay? Make it look like a burglary gone awry or something. She shouldn't have to spend the rest of her life in prison because we're horny." With that, I tried to dart toward her house, but Johnny caught me by the arm with an iron grip. He spun me back toward him and planted another kiss on my lips. Hot, slow, and deadly.

My knees went rubbery at the warning in that kiss: *This has nothing to do with being horny.*

"Do not," he said in a low voice that made a shiver run through me, "joke about dying."

"But it was just a joke. Kind of."

"Not funny."

"Johnny... I'm sorry, okay? I need to go."

He released me again as I tugged away. I hurried my ass over to Shayla's house before she could poke a head outside or something. I had no idea if our voices would carry, if she'd hear us through some open window, and I was flipping out.

"What about your clothes?" Johnny's projected whisper behind me made me spin and shush him.

"Keep them!" I whispered back. "Burn them! I don't care."

"Or you could just pick them up tomorrow," he said dryly.

"Shh!" I crept up Shayla's back deck, heart drumming. I was already forming the excuse in my mind: I'd gone for a late night swim to clear my head. Alone. For all she knew, I was wearing a bikini under this towel, right?

I glanced back to find Johnny standing on his poolside deck, watching me. Naked in the night, like the apparition of some god caught between worlds. Because how the hell did a being that fine belong in this one?

I'd never met a man who could command such a sexual response from me, even at such a distance. I couldn't even see his eyes, but I could feel them on me. It was as unnerving as it was intoxicating, when I paused to think about it.

I watched him towel himself off at a leisurely pace, and the ferocity of my irritation with him nearly equalled my lust for him.

"Go!" I hissed quietly. "Get your hot ass in the house!"

"Yes, ma'am." His voice was soft in the night as the shadows of his eyes burned into mine across the distance.

I swallowed, and watched him walk his hot, naked ass up the stairs to the upper patio. He picked up my clothes along the way and when he caught me watching him, he tossed me a heated smile that set fire to my insides.

"Damn it, Shayla," I muttered under my breath. "It's your fault for having such a stupid, sexy brother." Then I headed into her house, marinating in guilt and lust.

# Chapter Twenty-Seven

**Johnny**

"I want you so bad right now," Angeline purred next to me, "I can't see straight."

I glanced at her as I drove, and now *I* couldn't see straight. Not when she was sitting so close to me, exuding rainbows and lust.

God, she was pretty when she was aroused.

I refocused on the road.

I was really trying to use some restraint here. Take the time, learn where Angeline's boundaries were. Learn what she liked, what she wanted, what made her purr.

I was also trying to show her I wasn't just using her for sex. I didn't want her to see me like Summer so clearly did.

I was trying to make sure I gave much more than I took.

So, this morning, I'd taken her over to Yash's place. We'd had a video call with my lawyer that I'd let her listen in on. Currently, we were waiting on the lawyers to finish doing their thing. Back and forth discussion. Paperwork. Since JC was, apparently, still spewing bullshit about taking Breakneck—the name, the songs, everything—our side, mine and Noah's, was doing what could be done to explain to his side that that was never fucking happening.

I wasn't worried about it. JC was losing his mind if he thought that shit would fly.

I'd formed Breakneck myself. Came up with the name, co-wrote all the songs. Was arguably the most famous member of the band; not a small feat for anyone other than a lead singer to pull off. I knew I had rights, and a legal team to back them.

Yash was similarly confident about our position.

So, I was just trying to be patient and trust our team to do their part, so I could get on with my fucking life.

After that video call, we'd ordered in lunch and had a long meeting with Yash. I thought it would be good if Yash and Angeline had a talk in person, but it turned out to be the best meeting I'd had with Yash in a long time—thanks to Angeline charming the ever-loving hell out of him. Both of them had fed off one another, getting so genuinely excited about my future career that it was actually inspiring to behold.

Apparently, having a professional chat with my manager got Angeline all charged up. As we drove home from the meeting she was oozing so much joy, even I could tell what she was feeling. She felt respected. Spoken to like a peer by Yash and me. And that made her feel confident.

Actually, it turned her on.

Why the hell didn't I get Lamar to drive us? Serious mistake.

I had this thing about never driving in dangerous conditions. I didn't even drive in the rain, and I didn't do distracted driving.

So I was really trying not to get derailed by Angeline's excitement.

When I didn't respond to her, she said, "I'm aching for you," in that soft, beautiful voice of hers, like sex in a cloud of cotton candy.

I gripped the wheel, trying to focus on the road and not on the beautiful woman throbbing heat at me from two feet away.

"My panties are wet." When her words didn't get the reaction she wanted, she went on. "Wouldn't it be fun if you came in my mouth right now? Or my—"

"How about we turn up the music."

She laughed. It was a soft, throaty laugh, and I could hear how horny she was. She picked up my phone and switched songs. On the way to Yash's, she'd amused herself by invading my music collection, and now she put on DJ Khaled featuring Drake, "For Free." I knew the song, thanks to Shayla.

"Really?"

"What?" she said innocently.

"I just don't think a dude should tell you his music is 'the best' at the start of every single song he produces."

"Uh, have you heard a single rap or hip-hop song in your life? That's how they roll."

"Uh-huh." I was just glad for the topic change; I'd listen to whatever she wanted. All I listened to was heavy hip-hop, alt-rock, hard rock and dirty R&B. I liked soul, blood and sex in my music. But DJ Khaled and Drake annoyed me. "Let's just say there's confidence, and then there's something else."

"But this song is for you," she said, extra innocently. "You shouldn't have to do it for free. Last night on your patio? That was gooood." When I glanced over at her, she was grinning at me, her cheeks flushed. She turned up the music, which sounded pretty boss on my sound system, and maybe it would at least keep her occupied.

Wrong.

Halfway through the song, she turned it back down and purred, "But wouldn't it feel good? Coming in me right now?" She sounded drunk with lust, like she'd been thinking about it for way too long already.

Then she said a whole lot of alluring shit that made it almost impossible to see the road ahead of me. Stuff that involved a lot of *licking*, *biting* and *sucking*. I tried to ignore it, but it was fucking futile.

"I'm a little busy," I told her. "You'll have to wait."

"But I'm begging for a come," she teased.

"*Your* come. You're supposed to beg for your come."

"What if I want to beg for yours?"

I cleared my throat, trying to clear my head of the arousal that was clogging up the pathways to my brain. The ones I needed for driving.

Next time I drove anywhere with Angeline, Lamar was definitely taking the wheel.

"I like begging for your come."

"I'm driving."

"Let me suck on your cock."

"Not happening."

"You're so hard, though."

She was right. I was so damn hard.

"No."

"Why not?" I could hear her fake-pouting.

"Because I'm driving."

"So? Don't tell me you never let a girl suck you off while you were driving before."

I tossed her a look. "Have you? Sucked a guy off while he was…?"

"No. You just seemed like a guy I could do that with."

"Wrong."

"Huh. How disappointing. What happened to 'Anytime you need a dick to play with…'"

"I'm driving you home. Your life is in my hands right now. Why do you think I didn't drink at the party last night? You don't let someone get in your car unless you're committed to getting them home safe."

"But it would feel so good."

"No."

"Just a little taste…" she begged, maybe because she'd figured out that her begging was a serious hot spot for me.

"No, Angeline."

"I'll be gentle."

"I said no."

But by the time she'd been begging for two fucking DJ Khaled songs, I caved.

"Fine. You want to play with my dick? Take it out. Touching only. No mouth and no happy ending."

She laughed a little. But she reached over and carefully unbuttoned and unzipped, freeing me. My cock flexed helplessly in her grip when she slid her warm, soft hand around my shaft.

"Fuck. Do not touch me with your mouth right now. Promise me."

She giggled with nervous restraint. Her hand was shaking. "Okay."

"How are you so turned on right now?" It was amazing, really. We'd just parted ways with Yash. She'd gone from business to bedroom eyes in seconds flat.

"Johnny. Don't ask me stupid questions."

When I glanced at her, her eyes were blown wide as she drank me in.

I gripped the wheel tighter.

"Stroke," I commanded. "Gently. And don't go fast."

She did as she was told. Mostly.

"I said slow," I groaned. "*Slowly*, Angel."

"I love it when you call me Angel. Call me your Angel while I touch you."

I groaned quietly. "Slow down."

"This is slow. If I wanted to make you come, I'd really bust that dick."

"Stop talking," I grit out.

She laughed again, softly. That, and her warm hand sliding up and down my shaft, stroking me in a slow rhythm because she couldn't even wait until we got home, almost did me in.

I blew out a breath, staring into traffic. Refusing to look at her.

"Feel good?" she purred.

"Stop."

"You want me to stop stroking your bare cock with my hand?" she teased indulgently.

"*Stop talking.* And slow down."

"If you came right now," she wondered aloud, "do you think you could just keep driving while you ejaculated?"

"You make me come," I growled, "and I'm crashing this car for sure."

She seemed to take that as a delicious challenge. I saw her licking her lips gratuitously out of the corner of my eye. "Mmm. Then I better not make you come."

"Angeline." I swallowed, my throat tight. "Do not make me put my dick away."

"Relax," she said, a soft glee in her voice. She rubbed her thumb over the wet slit in my cockhead, smearing my pre-come around. "I'll be gentle, Johnny. I promise."

"No coming."

"No, I won't make you come. I mean, if you climax because you just can't help it—"

"Angie." My teeth ground on her name.

"I just want to touch you." Her voice softened. "You don't know how hot I am for you…"

I groaned again.

"You have a beautiful dick," she said shyly.

My cock flexed and I growled in my throat.

"Ohh, shit," she whispered, swallowing down the lust she was trying to contain. "You like that…"

"Stop."

"You're so big," she indulged me. "And so thick."

"No."

"Your cock is gorgeous."

"Don't," I rasped. "Do not make my eyes roll back in my head. I need to see the road."

"Look at that plump, thick head," she gushed.

"Shut your mouth."

"You're so beautiful. I love all your tattoos…"

"Nope. Please." I was starting to sweat, and the muscles in my arms jumped as I tightened my grip on the wheel.

"Your beautiful muscles flexing when you fuck me—"

"Angeline, I'm begging you. And I don't beg."

She bit her tongue and didn't say another thing, though her hand eased slowly up and down my shaft for the rest of the drive home, while my heart beat like thunder in my chest.

---

We'd barely made it into my kitchen before Angeline was tearing her clothes off. Her shirt went first, then her little skirt. "I want to be naked with you," she gushed.

So I tossed my keys on the counter and helped her strip off her bra. Her panties dropped to the floor, then she was on her knees before I could react, tearing at my belt. She snapped it open, tore open my jeans… and then looked up at me. Her lust glazed eyes were big and round, and she dragged her teeth slowly over her flushed bottom lip.

I wasn't sure why she'd stopped. She clung to my jeans, holding them open, but didn't dig inside. My underwear was still in place, my hard dick jutting in her face.

"You okay?" I asked her as she swallowed, gazing up at me. I cupped her face and slid my fingers into her hair.

"Mm-hmm." She nodded a little, licking her lip. "Is this okay?"

I studied her face. "What is it you're shy about, Angel?" I studied her face as she bit her lip again. I could feel her desire burning her up. She stirred at my feet, exuding barely restrained energy. "Your hunger?"

She nodded.

I took out my cock. Swollen, hard. Her eyes darkened with lust as she looked at it. Like I told her, I wasn't shy. I'd never been unsure about myself in that way. Not like I was with her.

I wanted her to be sure. I wanted her to like everything we did together.

"You want that?"

She nodded.

"Tell me."

I wanted to hear her say it, like she did in the car. Beg for it. Her words turned me on more than she could ever know. Her desire.

Her need.

If I felt like she actually needed me, that would be the ultimate drug. I'd probably come on the spot.

"Can I…" She gazed up at me shyly, her face flushing. "Can I tie you up?"

I stared at her. Not at all what I'd expected her to say.

The girl just blew my damn mind. Again.

I wasn't sure if it excited me or scared me more, that she always did shit I did not see coming. I didn't even know what all these sensations were that were creeping up out of the dark whenever I was with her.

But my cock was a lot more clear on things than I was. Excited. According to my cock, I was definitely excited.

My hand smeared over my face and I pitched forward, suddenly needing to hold onto the counter. I leaned there, with Angeline on her knees beneath me, my dick out and so hard it was sweet torture.

"Angeline. Where the hell have you been all my life?"

A sweet smile spread across her face. "Right in front of you, I think."

"Then I must be a damn idiot."

"Is that a yes?"

"It's a yes."

"Come here." She got to her feet and took my hand. Then she led me up the stairs to my bedroom like she owned the place. Naked.

I followed obediently.

Whatever the fuck she had in mind, I was there for it. Naked, hard, and willing.

Except I wasn't naked. Not yet. She brought me to stand beside my bed and then stood naked in front of me and warned me, "Don't touch," kinda like I told her last night on the patio. Then she took her sweet time slipping my belt from the belt loops in my jeans, one by one. When she looked up into my eyes, she smiled at me.

I was starting to sweat again. If she didn't undress me soon, I'd tear off my own clothes. My dick was the only thing out, and the rest of me wanted to follow suit.

But somehow, having just my cock out made me feel more naked.

Did she know what she was doing to me?

I watched as she played with my belt, wrapping it tentatively around her wrist. The way she went about things made it feel like this was her first time. Like everything we did together was her first time. But she also had all these ideas…

I swallowed. I wasn't sure if I wanted to know how experienced she was. Or wasn't.

Or with fucking whom.

I just wanted this, *this* time, to be the one she remembered.

And came back for again.

So I waited, trying to be patient, while she fussed with the belt. Then she placed it carefully on the bed. I blew out a breath, trying to keep calm as she slid my shirt up and dragged it off over my head.

Then she took the belt and wrapped it around my wrists in a sort of figure eight, buckled it and cinched it fairly tight. I could still get some play. I could maybe pull out of it, with some effort. But when she stood back to check out her work, I just let my bound arms hang in front of me.

"Raise your arms over your head."

I did as I was told and her eyes moved appreciatively over my body, from my bound hands, to my face, to my mouth, where I licked my lip hungrily. And down my chest, down my abs, to my unzipped jeans, where my cock stood straight up, aching for her attention.

My eyes dragged over her too, completely naked in front of me.

"Holy…" She faded off, swallowing. "You are so sexy."

I groaned. "Angeline."

Her eyes met mine. I still couldn't fucking tell if this was calculated or not. If she knew she was slowly driving me crazy.

"Can you take off my pants and fuck me, for fuck's sake?"

Her cheeks went pink. "Oh. I just got distracted…" She drifted her fingertips down my abs.

"This isn't payback for last night?"

"Um, no. But it could be." Her eyes flashed with mischief and I groaned.

So, not calculated. She was savoring. Exploring. Playing with me. Going with whatever felt good, for both of us.

That thought made my heart thud, a heavy, hot rhythm that put me strangely at ease.

Safe. I felt safe with her.

I wasn't sure I'd ever felt unsafe in a sexual situation before, but there it was. Angeline made me feel safe. And it was like a drug coursing through my veins, languid, warm, making me melt into this.

She moved to push my jeans down, then nudged me to sit down on the bed so she could slip them, and my underwear, off.

"Lie back on the bed."

I did what she told me to do, lying on my back. She arranged the pillows, propping my head up a bit. Then she arranged my arms above my head, resting on the pillows, too.

Her eyes met mine while she was still leaning over me. "Don't be a jerk and pull out of it, even if you can."

"I'm your prisoner," I promised her solemnly, lying obediently where she placed me.

She groaned softly in her throat as she stood back, looking down over me. "Is it wrong that that turns me on?"

"Nothing is wrong that turns you on."

She blinked at me. Then her eyes filled with such single-minded focus, such unmistakable lust, that my cock flexed, standing straight up.

She looked at it. "Oh! Wow. I have something."

Then she ran out of the room.

"Angie?"

"Don't move!!" she called out, as she left me there.

I waited for her, lying on my bed with my wrists bound. For way too long.

I thought about getting up. Going after her. But I didn't. I stayed where she told me to, trying to just breathe. My dick growing semi-soft.

Then I heard her coming back up the stairs. She hurried into the room, looking flushed. She held up a black, rubber-looking ring.

"See?" she said breathlessly.

"Is that a cock ring?"

"Uh-huh."

"You just ran next door for that? Naked?"

"Of course not. I wrapped up in a kitchen towel."

I groaned. "Be careful," I reminded her. Did she even check to make sure Shayla wasn't home? I knew she'd be upset if Shayla found out about this, especially like *this*. And Shayla… I knew she'd be pissed. At me.

I hadn't quite figured out how to handle that yet. I was just trying not to think about it.

"Can I put it on you?"

I actually didn't answer for a moment. I blinked at Angeline, standing over me naked, holding a cock ring. I'd never put on a cock ring before. But my dick was definitely hard again.

"Uh… you ever use that with anyone else?"

She frowned. "Hell, no."

"You ever put a cock ring on a guy before?"

"No."

My dick throbbed. “Then go for it.”

“Okay. Um. I’m not sure of the technique, so…”

“I think you need lube—” My words cut off with a pleasured hiss as she leaned down and swallowed my cock. The sweet shock of her hot, slippery mouth sliding down over me had me speechless. She took me deep, lavishing me with her tongue, and when I was all wet, she slid her mouth off and slid the cock ring on. All the way down to the base of my shaft.

“Well. That was easy.”

“Because I’m so fucking hard,” I grit out. My cock was throbbing, squeezed by the ring, and I wasn’t gonna say it was a bad feeling. “Now what?” My eyes met hers in challenge.

“Hmm. Is it okay if I just think about it for a minute?”

“This is your rodeo, babe.” I was trying to play it cool, which was probably ridiculous. My dick was probably harder than it had ever been in my life. And she was staring at it.

She sank onto the bed next to me on her knees.

“You’re so big…” she said, like she was hypnotized. Her eyes dragged over my naked body. “You’re so beautiful, Johnny.”

Jesus. Was this what she had planned? Tie me up and stare at me and tell me how hot she thought I was?

I was probably gonna come into thin air if she kept that up for long.

But she didn’t go on, even as her eyes moved over me, glazing over with desire.

I groaned, desperate to hear more, even as my gaze dragged over her body. Her naked, perky breasts, her hard, rosy-pink nipples. “Tell me.”

“I love your gorgeous muscles. Your beautiful skin…” She started running her hands over my body, and my muscles rippled under her fingertips. “Your hard chest. Your sexy ass.” My cock bounced as I clenched involuntarily. Her words turned me the fuck on. Her soft voice. The appreciation in her eyes.

My nipples hardened as she drifted her fingers over them, and she played with them a little, studying my reactions with glazed eyes.

She bit her lip. “You’re a work of art, Johnny.”

I groaned again, my dick throbbing. She didn’t miss it.

"Look at that beautiful cock." Her eyes caressed it. "Look how hard it is. So hard and thick…" Her eyes met mine. She looked turned on because she was talking dirty to me, lavishing me with praise—and I was eating it up. It made her feel bolder, maybe.

I wanted to encourage that.

"Tell me. Tell me what it's like when I fuck you."

"You're so big. I have to spread so wide for you."

God. I was so hard. Her eyes fell to my dick again as she reached out to touch it. She drifted her fingertips up my shaft and down again, sending warm shivers of desire through me.

I couldn't remember ever being so fucking turned on. Wanting someone so badly.

"You like my cock…?" I forced out. My voice was ragged, my breathing labored.

"So hot…" she gushed. Then her fingers drifted down over my ball sac. She squeezed gently, and I groaned. "I like this, too. I love how swollen you get." She touched her finger to the tip of my cock and smeared the bead of slick juice around. "You're leaking, baby. You're so turned on…"

"Don't stop…" I loved watching her explore my body.

I loved watching her look at me like that.

"So hard," she murmured, stroking her fingers gently up and down my shaft.

"How you like it…?"

"Just how I like it." She swallowed, and I watched her shiver. Her nipples were so hard. She was so turned on, it was killing me. Angeline, aroused, made me fucking delirious. "I can't wait for you to come," she said, gently stroking my dick like it was her new favorite pet. "You're so hard, all over."

God, yeah. I was so fucking hard and ready, I was gonna blow just listening to her get horny while looking at me and describing what she saw.

"Come feast on me, baby," I practically begged her. I was trying to keep it together here, but I was unraveling, quick. "Put that sweet mouth on me."

She met my eyes. “Where?”

“Every-fucking-where. Kiss all the places you like.”

She leaned over me and started kissing and licking her way up my abs and chest, like she’d been waiting to hear those words. Her mouth was sweet torture on my skin.

“That’s it, Angel,” I panted. “Suck on me.”

She licked my nipple, then sucked on it, and arousal shuddered through me.

Then she slid down and took my cock in her hand. It flexed at her touch. She pushed her other hand into her hair, holding the silky ribbons back from her face, so I could watch her. “So thick,” she moaned, then lapped her tongue up the side of my shaft.

I groaned as she licked and explored, just trying to stay calm. To enjoy every fucking second of this before I inevitably lost it. My balls were throbbing. If the first few times she made me come were any indication, Angeline Delacroix was about to blow my mind and body all over again—so fucking hard.

*Just calm down*, I willed myself as my heart thudded in my chest, while I watched her licking and kissing. My cock was so hard, it looked obscene wrapped in her slim fingers, and watching her soft lips wrap around the swollen crown to suckle a little taste was too much. “Fuck,” I breathed.

“So good,” she gushed. “You taste so fucking good.” Then she went to town making out with my cockhead, her tongue teasing my slit.

My ass clenched as spasms ripped through me. *Jesus Christ.*

“Angel… slow down,” I begged her.

She did. She pumped my cock slowly in her hand and gave the head a luscious kiss.

I couldn’t stand it anymore.

“Now take the whole thing in your mouth and come sit on my face.”

I just hoped she was in the mood to change her game plan and start following my orders.

She looked at me, her cheeks flushed. Then she rearranged herself, straddling my face on her knees. “Give me that pussy,” I murmured, as she wriggled into place, serving up her pussy to my mouth. I kissed her soft flesh, making her moan.

At the same time, she tipped my cockhead into her mouth, and as I slid my tongue over her pussy, she slowly swallowed my cock. She pushed down, taking me deep, and I groaned, digging my tongue inside her cunt. We screwed like that for a while as the world went blurry around us, her mouth slowly devouring my cock again and again, my tongue lavishing her pussy.

Then I danced my tongue over her sweet little clit, teasing. When she suddenly wriggled, her hips jerking, and gasped, I knew her orgasm was imminent. I lifted my bound hands to slide them over her ass and grip her, holding her in place. I took a breath, letting her dangle for just a moment, her body quivering.

*Yes.*

She moaned desperately.

"That's it, baby," I whispered, trying to hold back myself as she kept sucking me off. I licked her pussy indulgently. "I'm gonna make this pussy come so hard." Then I sucked her clit into my mouth, deep. She started to cry out, and I pushed my cock deeper into her mouth.

Then I pushed two fingers inside her soaked pussy. I alternately licked and sucked her clit, fucking her with my fingers as her core spasmed around them and she moaned in bliss. Her entire body was shuddering in climax on top of me.

I rasped against her flesh, "Suck my cock like a good girl while you come."

She moaned, sucking on me gratefully as she shuddered. The girl was a fucking angel, for sure.

Somehow, I'd managed to skip the dying part and went straight to heaven.

My fingers slid out of her to draw slippery circles over her clit as I flexed my hips, slowly fucking her mouth.

As her orgasm subsided, she picked up the pace, the suction, working my cock with her mouth and hands, and that deep spasm hit—as she drifted her fingers over my balls, pushing me into sensory overload. I couldn't hold back.

She knew it.

She drove her mouth down on my dick, sucking me harder.

I tried to relax my hips and just let her take it. "Fuck… yeah… Milk me, Angel." As she sucked, my cock and balls convulsed in her grasp and she moaned with anticipation. I poured my come into her heat with a deep groan, my head spinning violently as I unloaded. She sucked with deep, greedy pulls, and I came and came as she swallowed, wanting everything I gave.

I groaned helplessly as the deep quakes reverberated through my body. My hands slid up over her ass cheeks again, gripping her tight, and I heard myself rasping her name, *Angeline, Angeline…*

She kept sucking, kept milking me, root to tip, in a slow, heated rhythm—like she was savoring every drop of my orgasm—until I finally stopped pulsing into her mouth.

I caught my breath enough to lap my tongue over her pussy in appreciation. She wriggled in pleasure, slipping her mouth off my dick and giving the head a soft kiss. She was still stroking my shaft gently. The cock ring was keeping me hard. I didn't want her to stop.

Jesus Christ, she was an incredible fuck.

Maybe I really should've fucked her years ago.

No. If I did that, maybe it wouldn't have been this way. There was something about the intensity of her desire for me, right now, that lit me on fire. And the intensity of my desire to please her… that's what it was, right? I wanted her. Not just in my bed, fucking me. I wanted to make her feel good. I wanted to please her.

I wanted to make her stay.

I couldn't believe I'd actually entertained the thought of keeping my hands off her after that night—when I'd put her to bed and she'd gushed all over me about her crush.

Why? Because other people thought I should?

She collapsed on top of me, moaning and stretching a little. She kissed my groin. "Holy fuck, I love blowing you."

"I love being blown," I said weakly.

She laughed. Then she groaned, wriggling. Her pussy was still in my face. "Johnny…"

I lapped my tongue alongside her pussy, softly. "You need something?" I already knew the girl was practically insatiable.

I loved it.

She rubbed her face against my skin. I could sense her hesitation, even as her hunger burned her up. I could feel her heat pulsing through her. *Arousal.* She wasn't done yet.

"You need another come?" I asked her, placing my hands on her ass again and drifting my thumb over her pussy. I tugged her hips toward me and started kissing her clit as she sighed with relief. "It's okay, baby," I murmured between kisses. "My angel needs to come, she gets to come."

"Please…"

I teased her opening with the tip of my tongue. "This pussy still hungry, Angel?" She moaned against my skin. "Let me kiss it better…"

She giggled, then sighed softly. "You're an angel yourself, you know that? My wicked angel." She wriggled her hips a little as my kisses turned to teasing licks. "You know, I've pictured you like that. With sinuous black wings, your naked, tattooed body standing over me as you fuck me on a slab of rock."

I paused, trying to picture that. "Yeah?"

"Uh-huh."

"That make you come?"

"So hard."

"You have an incredible imagination," I told her appreciatively.

"I've had a lot of time," she said vaguely. "To imagine all the things."

"Things?"

"Oh, God." She moaned as I drifted my tongue over her pussy, shuddering with pleasure. "You know, all the fantasies. I've been single a lot, historically…"

Well, that was a damn shame. This was a woman who should be enjoyed. And satisfied.

"You don't have to fantasize anymore," I murmured against her skin. Then I sank my tongue inside her sweet cunt. Licking her, inside-out.

"Oh, fuck."

My cock flexed. The cock ring was still keeping me semi-hard, and her hunger was keeping me aroused. I felt the heat of her breath on my cockhead. I felt her tongue drift across it, tasting, like she couldn't help it.

It made my breath catch.

"You like that cock, Angel?"

"Mmm," she moaned, flickering her tongue over my slit.

"Take it in your mouth."

She sucked my cockhead into her mouth, no hesitation, and I groaned, momentarily distracted from pleasuring her pussy.

"More, baby. Suck it in deep. Stuff yourself."

She did as she was told.

"Keep it there. I want to feel your mouth wrapped around me when you come."

She moaned again, suckling in languid but hungry pulls, her tongue caressing me.

I drifted my thumbs over her pussy, spreading her open. "Baby…" I teased her clit with my tongue. "You're going to come, hard, with that cock stuffed in your mouth. Aren't you."

She gave up a muffled cry when my lips sealed around her clit. I sucked in rhythm with her soft pulls, and I didn't speed up or increase the pressure unless she did. When she slowed down or paused, panting, I matched her pace. I matched every move of her mouth with mine, putting her in control.

When she suddenly sucked harder and faster, I did the same. I felt her quivering on the brink of ecstasy as she moaned around her mouthful. Her hips bucked, the orgasm thrashing through her. Her pussy spasming while I kept sucking, latched on tight to her clit.

Then I stuffed my swollen cock into the back of her throat.

I couldn't come again. I just wanted to feel that connection. To know she was filled with me, stuffed deep, while she climaxed.

She could've pulled back, but she didn't. She sobbed and shivered, letting me fuck her mouth while her climax tore through her.

When she collapsed, panting, I licked her dripping pussy in long, slow strokes, making her shudder. Then I kissed her soft flesh, again and again.

"So beautiful, baby," I murmured as she slid me out of her mouth.

"Johnny," she whispered. "Can you come again?"

"No. I'm fucking spent. But come here."

She turned, crawling up over me as I stretched my bound hands above my head again, resting them on the pillows. She knelt over me, straddling my hips, her face above mine. She reached up and planted her hands on my biceps, pinning my arms. She held me down like that, looking into my eyes.

She had a kind of power over me when we were together. Maybe she knew it.

I had a kind of power over her, too.

It was a heady thing, this thing between us. As erotic as that exchange was, it was about so much more.

I'd never had a connection so erotic with a woman.

Sexual, sure. But performing intimate acts with another person in order to achieve sexual release did not equal intimacy.

It did not equal connection.

She stared into my eyes and I stared into hers.

My heart thudded in my chest, pumping blood through my body. While the rest of me silently shuddered. Part of me couldn't believe she had my wrists bound and my dick in a cock ring, and me, pinned beneath her. I couldn't believe she made me come like that. I couldn't believe she said all those beautiful things, about me.

I couldn't believe she thought I was beautiful.

I'd had women say that before. But they didn't really know me. They weren't around me enough to start to know.

Angeline had been around me a lot over the years. She'd been around me almost constantly for the last several days. She wasn't a stranger, getting swept up in the way I looked and having no idea what lay beneath.

The more time we spent together, I knew she was starting to glimpse beyond the outer layers.

I didn't expect that to happen, but I knew it must be happening.

I could hardly believe this was real.

But it was real.

She was vibrant and luscious and real, the force of her desire for me holding me down, stealing my breath. I didn't even want to move.

I didn't know what to say to her. I'd never prepared myself for this moment. I'd been keeping her at a distance, even when we spent time together, like I always kept women at a distance.

That was what I told myself.

She wouldn't get near me. I wouldn't let her near me.

It was instinctual.

A base impulse, stronger than any other drive I'd ever had.

Stronger than the drive to succeed, and that was a powerful fucking drive.

Stronger than the need for love or connection.

Stronger than anything I'd ever felt in my life.

Until… this.

"I want to kiss you," she whispered. Like she wasn't sure if she was allowed to, post-sex.

"Good."

She softened, maybe with relief.

"But could you take the cock ring off first? I may never get my circulation back."

She giggled. "Shit. Sorry." She climbed off me to reach for it, and when I groaned a little, she ended up using her tongue to lick the surrounding area, soaking my skin before rolling it off. "I don't know why I did that." She tossed the ring on the bedside table.

"Because you wanted to."

She met my eyes, softening again. I could tell what that meant to her.

She felt respected, again.

I understood that. I was feeling something similar, maybe. Like she was seeing me in a way no one ever had before.

"I'm scared," she said softly, looking deep into my eyes. I wondered what it was that she saw there.

"I know, Angel. Me, too."

I wasn't lying, exactly. I just didn't know what I felt. It was still buried so deep, I didn't know how to access it. And whatever was rising to the surface when we were together, right now… I couldn't understand it. It wasn't bad, but it was making me uneasy.

Maybe I was scared. Terrified.

But whatever was happening, I wanted more of it. When she stripped me naked and bound my wrists, I knew I would've done any-fucking-thing she wanted me to.

Anything.

"Do you want me to take off the belt?"

"When you want to," I told her. "Now come lay your beautiful body on me. And kiss me like I'm the last man you'll ever kiss."

Angeline's eyes went wide.

I wasn't sure where those words came from. Somewhere deep inside, so deep that I didn't recognize the source. I was disconnected from it, still. And whatever spurred it, it wasn't calculated. It was an impulse. An urgent desire for her to be as wrapped up in me as I was in her.

Because the last several days? I'd thought of little else but her.

She spread herself on top of me, fitting her naked body to mine like I told her to, and she kissed me.

# Chapter Twenty-Eight

**Angeline**

I woke up in the night to the bed moving.

"Johnny?" I gasped out in half-sleep. The bed was *shaking*.

Johnny's bed. I'd finally stayed the night with him like he'd asked me to. After having dinner with Shayla, I'd snuck back over here.

He gasped next to me. The sound was sawed off, like he was choking.

I reached out for him in the dark, my heart thudding with instinctual alarm. When my hand touched his back, he startled. He was already sitting up.

He sucked in a violent breath, a terrible, strangled sound. Then he exhaled in a burst and started panting. "*Fuck.*"

I sat up. I couldn't see him well in the dark. "Johnny? Are you okay?" I ran my hand up the back of his neck, gently. He was damp with sweat.

I could feel him moving, maybe rubbing his face as he breathed raggedly.

"You had a bad dream, I think. Are you awake?"

"Yeah." He sounded anguished.

I shifted closer.

"It's okay," I told him softly. "It's just the stress…"

"What…?" He sounded disoriented. Or maybe like he'd finally really woken up. I wanted to see him, but it was so dark in his room at night.

I knew he had to be stressed about things with Breakneck. Yash had laid out the whole situation for me at our meeting the other day. Johnny had seemed so calm and cool about the whole thing, and the last few days had been a delirious blur of mindblowing sex as we spent every possible moment together… but I should've known. I should've known he couldn't be taking it all that well. To me, it sounded like he was on the verge of a potentially huge legal battle.

And for all I knew, maybe he was feeling guilty about sneaking around behind Shayla's back, too. I knew I was, but we hadn't really talked about it. Shayla was preoccupied with the Players video shoot this week, but that didn't make it okay.

"Do you want me to turn on a light?" I asked him.

"No." He pulled away. I felt the bed move as he relaxed back into it all at once. He blew out a breath.

"You weren't breathing well," I said softly. "It was like you were suffocating. You were holding your breath."

"I'm okay."

I waited, but he didn't say anything else, so I lay down again. It didn't sound okay. His breathing had sounded… pained. Jagged.

Violent.

I could feel that he didn't want to talk about it, though. Maybe he was still half-asleep. I felt him pulling away, even when he didn't move again. His breathing was returning to normal. He didn't move toward me for comfort, though.

It made me want to pull away.

Both of us were still guarded around each other, in some ways. And wide open in others—mostly sexual. I knew that. But at the same time, there was something about this thing between us that was wildly different from anything I'd ever known.

It was special.

I could hardly believe we'd just recently become lovers. We just *fit* together. As soon as we started having sex… it was like we just melded into our togetherness.

I liked Johnny way more than I'd ever hated him, that was for sure.

It wasn't just the sex. You couldn't have sex that raw, that intense, that focused on the other person's responses and pleasure—as we both were—and have it mean absolutely nothing beyond the physical. I couldn't possibly bring myself to believe that.

The way he looked into my eyes… a guy didn't do that with a woman he was fucking if he didn't mean it. Unless he was a psychopath or something, and I knew Johnny was not that.

And if I started second-guessing things, pulling away now, in fear… I knew I'd fall right back into old patterns. Thinking I wasn't good enough, I wasn't special enough for someone like him.

Making the wrong decisions. For the wrong reasons.

For once, I wanted to make the right decisions in my relationship with a man. Or at the very fucking least, the wrong decisions for the right reasons.

I could try to rewind things between us, keep our relationship strictly professional. I could completely stop seeing him and give him up as a client. But I didn't want to do either of those things.

I wanted to reach forward.

The right decision, right now, was to lean into the feelings I had for him. Feelings that were starting to worm their way so deep in me, it made me feel breathless listening to him struggle to breathe.

Maybe I could be his publicist and be his lover.

Maybe we'd fall madly in love.

Maybe we'd fall apart.

Right now, it didn't matter. We had a chance. I had a chance at something magical with this man, and for once in my life, I was taking it.

So, I reached for him.

I found his hip under the blanket. He was lying on his back. I slid toward him, pressing my body against his side.

Johnny made a soft sound in his throat, a sound of surrender, maybe, as my fingers traced the lines of his hip, his groin. By the time I'd reached his cock, it was firm, and his lips found mine.

As we kissed I slipped off my panties. I moved slowly on top of him, straddling him, still kissing. I pressed my pussy against the hard shaft of his cock as it flexed, hungry for me.

Whatever that dream was that had ruined his sleep, waking him in a stressed panic… I wanted to make him forget it. I wanted to cleanse his mind and body of it and flood him with pleasure and peace instead.

I could feel myself growing wet as my pussy slid up and down his shaft. I lifted my hips a little higher, letting the head of his cock press against my opening. I kept kissing him, my tongue lapping against his in a decadent rhythm, as I pushed down. The crown of his cock split me open, the incredible sensation of taking him inside me tingling through my body and making me feel lightheaded with desire.

I pushed down, taking him slowly deeper. I slid back up, then down again, pushing harder, until I'd taken him all the way. I did it again and again, finding a hot, slow rhythm as we kissed.

Johnny groaned as his cock plunged into my depths. His hands roamed over my body as I urged his pleasure onward in a steady rhythm, kissing and fucking, until his breathing grew heavy and his fingers dug into my hips.

His hips rode up, restlessly. He was so stiff inside me… I rode him a little faster. I loved being in control of him, taking control of his pleasure.

I broke our kiss so I could sit up, and I reached to turn on the bedside lamp. Soft, golden light flooded over us. My eyes met his, blinking in the soft light. He looked sleepy and so fucking sexy, his blond hair all mussed.

I sat back, settling my weight on him as I took him even deeper, his cockhead pressing against my limits, my pussy squeezing him to the base of his shaft.

Johnny sucked in a breath, then groaned as I kept riding him, his eyes roaming over my body now. His hands slid up to my naked breasts, jutting from under the hem of my cami. He cupped them and pinched my nipples, sending a sweet shiver through me.

When I felt his body tense, his hips locking, I knew he was close. Fighting the orgasm or urging it onward. Either way, I knew he'd come soon, as soon as he knew I wanted him to, and warmth flooded through my body like a sweet aphrodisiac.

"Yes," I whispered. "Come inside me, baby."

He swore as I changed the motion of my hips, from up and down to back and forth, grinding slowly against him. He watched my breasts moving in front of his face. He growled a little, his hips bucking slightly as he started to come.

I milked him as he climaxed, rocking my hips slowly back and forth. I felt his thick cock spasm, his hot come spurting deep, even as his body relaxed, as he gave himself over to the pleasure. I pressed my hands to his chest, holding him down, and he gazed up at me as he filled me in long, throbbing spurts, his mouth dropping open in silent awe, his heart beating in his tattooed throat.

"Mine." The word fell out of my mouth as our eyes locked in shared ecstasy. "This is mine, Johnny."

"Angie," he breathed. His cock spasmed violently inside me when he said my name.

My slow gyrations became slipperier as our slick juices coated us, as he filled me to overflowing. "Your cock and come are all for me." I savored each spasm, drunk on knowing that I was giving him this release. That this state of extreme pleasure we achieved together was just for us. Him and me.

I knew, without having to ask, that the pure, raw ecstasy we experienced together was different than anything he'd ever had before. Just like it was for me.

It was in his eyes. In the helpless sounds he made. In the way he held onto me, his fingers digging into me so possessively.

I increased the force of my movements just a little and he moaned. His cock spasmed inside me again. His swollen balls slid wetly against my ass, slick with both our juices. I could feel how thick his shaft was, stretching me open as I rode back and forth. "Baby," he gasped, his fingers plucking gently on my nipples, and arousal coursed through me. When he throbbed inside me again, I climaxed.

I went still.

"Angeline," he breathed, holding my gaze as my inner muscles shuddered around him, my pussy squeezed around his cock like a fist, jerking with uncontrollable convulsions of pleasure. "Don't look away, Angel," he said gruffly. "Don't close your eyes."

I panted softly as the pleasure rolled through me. I dug my fingers into his pecs for stability. I rocked my hips a little, savoring the feel of him inside me. My pussy spasmed around him for what felt like long minutes, in shuddering pulses that resonated through my core. I couldn't believe how long it went on.

If Johnny could've come again so soon, I knew he would've. The slack, absolutely awestruck look on his face told me so.

"Tell me," he said in a daze. "Tell me what you feel."

"Your thick cock," I said, sounding more dazed than he did. I sounded drunk. "Making me come."

He squeezed my nipples gently as my pussy pulsed again. "You're so beautiful, Angel."

I murmured something that wasn't really words, lost in the haze of pleasure as the orgasm mellowed out. I sagged a little against him.

He slid his hands up to my neck, my face. "Come here."

I sank down over him, meeting his lips with mine. We kissed slowly, wet and hot. And as we did, he bent his knees up to brace his feet on the bed and flexed his hips, driving his cock into me in slow, deep pumps. His hands slid down to my ass. Gripping my cheeks and squeezing, he held me open as he pumped into me wetly. I was dripping with his cream, we were both slick, and his thrusts felt indulgent. He was half-hard but hard enough, his thickness still stretching me as he sought to continue my pleasure.

It wasn't long before my swollen, sensitive pussy responded, and my core shuddered as his thrusts set off another deep, pulsing climax.

I cried out into his mouth and when our kiss broke, he soothed me, "Good girl. My sweet Angel. Come for me." His cock kept up the slow, torturous pumps as I climaxed helplessly around him. He held my eyes, devouring my pleasure. "Keep coming, Angel." When I whimpered, shuddering on top of him, he muttered, "You don't know how much you turn me on." Then he caught my mouth in another hot kiss.

We kissed and kissed as the orgasm rolled through me and faded, as he slowly pumped into me. He gradually stopped as I settled into the limp aftermath of all that pleasure. I lay heavily on him and he kissed my face, smoothing my hair back so he could look in my eyes.

We both lay still as he kissed my cheek, my lips, slowly, reverently. His cock was still inside me, softened, but thick and heavy as he continued to possess me.

"Tell me," he said. "Tell me how good it is."

"It's so good," I panted. "I've never felt anything like this."

"Tell me it's not like this with anyone else."

"It's not. It's never been like this with anyone else."

"Tell me how hard I make you come."

I laughed breathily as he tipped my chin up to lick my throat. "I've never come like this in my life."

"Tell me. Tell me how much you need me."

My heart squeezed with fear. I didn't want to say those things. I didn't want him to know.

But he was asking, almost like he already knew. Or at least, he desperately hoped.

"I need you," I whispered.

Johnny groaned in his throat, kissing my neck. His hips shifted a little, and he pushed into me, making sure he was still buried to the root. "More," he panted.

"Nothing satisfies me like you do," I told him softly, instinctively knowing what he needed to hear. Just truth, and lots of it. "I get so hot just looking at you. And you give me what I need."

"I'm the only one?" he said hungrily, kissing my face with his soft, luscious lips.

"Yes. The only one." He knew that by now. How could there be anyone else? I was with him almost all the time. "You're the only one I come for, Johnny."

He groaned, the pleasure rippling through him. "You make me come so hard, Angel," he reciprocated, kissing me with a fervor, sucking on my lips. "You're the only one I come for. The only one who gets me off."

"Your cock is mine?"

"Anytime you want. Any way you want."

"You're the only one I want."

"Keep my cock inside you. Keep kissing me. I can't get enough of you, Angeline."

I kissed his face as he kissed mine, and our words of promise and praise enveloped us in a warm, safe place as my hair fell around us and our breath heated our skin.

"I do need you, Johnny. You make me feel so good." I wriggled my hips a little, feeling his cock swell inside me.

"You need me?" he panted, wanting to hear it again. Needing to hear it again.

"I need this cock," I teased, wriggling again. He swelled, his length filling me. His cockhead stretching me at my limits again when he flexed his hips, pushing deep.

And all at once, he was rolling over, taking me with him. Then he was kneeling up over me, his cock still buried to the root as he clutched my hips and dragged me to the edge of the bed. He stepped down to the floor, standing next to the bed while he spread my legs wide around him. I bent my knees and let them fall back as he pushed my thighs up, forcing me roughly open. He grunted, a very male, primal sort of grunt as he started fucking me again with single-minded focus.

I instantly melted, my head spinning with arousal at the sensations. His cock, hard again, pumping into me. His fast, greedy rhythm.

He wanted me again. He needed me again.

He pumped into me like a god. Pounding his cock into my swollen pussy as he stood over me. Abs bunching, muscles tensing, chest sweating. All tattoos and golden skin over the beautiful, muscular planes and curves, the tight cords of muscle along his arms.

His eyes roamed over me, my body wrenched open for his pleasure, as he said gruffly, "Spread for me, Angel."

I groaned with lust, my fingers sliding down between my legs to draw myself gently open to take him. It wasn't so much making it easier for him to fuck me any deeper—he was fully in control of that. We both knew it. No, it was an act of willingness and surrender, of doing exactly what he said, spreading myself as wide open as I could to take as much of him as I could, without hesitation. And it made him absolutely shake with lust as he stared at the place where he possessed me.

"Good girl," he grunted softly. "Open up for me. My beautiful cock slut…"

I moaned, feeling like I was slowly dying of pleasure as he fed me his dick. Stroking with such incredible control, despite the rest of him shaking over me, flushed with sweat.

His eyes suddenly tangled with mine. The flash of vulnerability I saw there made me suck in a breath.

"You need me, Angel?"

"Yes. Without you… I'm empty."

He groaned, long and low, and I knew he was about to lose it. His whole body flexed, muscles shuddering as he shoved his dick into me in quick, deep pumps.

"God, yeah," I moaned. "Fill me with your come."

"Angel." His hips stuttered. His body quivered.

"Give it to me, Johnny…"

He moaned, burying himself deep, stretching me, filling me so good it almost hurt. I felt the helpless pulses as he exploded inside me with a desperate groan, his body locking up as that singular part of him convulsed. Root to tip, spasming inside my sheath. "*Fuck.*" He pressed into me, savoring the connection as the last of his climax shuddered through him. Then his legs seemed to give out. He collapsed on top of me.

He buried his face in my neck as he gasped for air. And finally, when he could breathe, he whispered, "You need to come again, Angel?"

I laughed shakily. "All night, baby. I could come for you all night."

Truth.

He groaned. "We're gonna kill each other."

I grinned and kissed his temple as he buried his face in my neck again. He kissed me there with a hot, ardent suck.

Then he smoothed my hair back from my sweaty face. He nuzzled my neck, brushing his stubbled jaw lightly against my skin. He rasped in my ear, "No one else. No one else gets to have you this way." He was still buried to the root in me, keeping me spread wide with his weight. "It would kill me."

I knew, somehow, that he meant that quite literally.

# Chapter Twenty-Nine

**Johnny**

There's a dark street.

I'm in the backseat.

The windshield wipers beat back the weather, a slow, monotonous thud. The rain runs down the glass. It always turns to blood under the streetlights. Always.

There's an old rock song playing on the car radio.

And a stranger in the front seat.

Maybe he doesn't know I'm here.

I hold my breath until it burns in my chest. I can see the terrible thing through the gap in the seats. It's lying on the front passenger seat where he dropped it when he started driving.

I know I can't go where he's going. You don't go with bad men.

You don't let them take you.

I reach for it, between the seats. The metal is hard and cold, heavy in my small hand.

I've never held a gun before.

# Chapter Thirty

**Johnny**

The nightmare woke me early in the morning.

Lately, it just kept pushing to the front of my mind. Trying to tell me that something was wrong, before I even knew what it was.

I couldn't feel all the things.

But my body knew.

So I got up, to get away from it. I left Angeline sleeping in my bed. I was in and out of the sauna, the cold plunge, the gym, before the sun was fully up. Then I called Yash to get the daily update—and I went into a tail-spin unlike anything that had hit me in a long time. It was like the momentum took me by the wings and sent me flying.

I couldn't even remember getting in my car and taking off, but I had Lamar to drive me, so at least I didn't have to pay attention.

I was already focused on something else, something outside of myself. Shane; I went straight to Shane's place and got him out of bed. We hit his MMA gym, the one he trained at, then went for lunch. Then we started drinking.

Mostly, I started drinking.

Shane wasn't usually one to let a man drink alone, but he had a fight tonight. So I basically followed him around for the rest of the day. We met some of Lamar's buddies for a while. Lamar made me eat dinner. Then we rounded back to Shane's fight; it was in some derelict warehouse down by the Port of Vancouver cargo terminals. Illegal fights tended to happen in seedy places like that.

I bet a shit ton of cash on the fight. On Shane.

He lost, which was rare.

I knew that meant he'd be having some woman licking his wounds for the rest of the night, so I cleared out.

We hit another bar, then Lamar finally convinced me to go home. He was the only one I'd told what happened; I didn't tell Shane. So Lamar was looking out for me, trying to make sure I didn't self-destruct.

Smart man. I was actually considering finding myself some blow.

What a stupid idea.

Fucking reckless. Not who I was anymore.

So instead I ended up sitting on the patio outside my bedroom, smoking up, playing "Long Train Runnin'" quietly, too slowly, on one of my acoustics. It was a form of fucked-up therapy, but it worked for me. At least I wasn't high on blow, fucking some random fangirl, like in the old days.

Angeline found me like that. Just playing the song over and fucking over. Trying to desensitize myself. Raze memories by anesthetizing myself.

The truth was, I didn't want to feel.

"Hey, you." She'd come quietly up the exterior stairs and rested a hip against the railing. She studied me, her head tipping slightly like I was no longer right side up.

Maybe I wasn't.

I straightened and looked at her. She was wearing another one of my T-shirts. I wasn't even sure why it bugged me.

"What is that song?" she asked me when I said nothing. "You play it so much…"

"It's nothing."

"I recognize it. I think. CCR?"

That fucking bugged me, too. Because the Doobie Brothers sounded nothing like Creedence Clearwater Revival. "It's just an old Doobie Brothers song." I put the guitar aside.

Her lips quirked. "*Doobie Brothers.* Is that really a band?" She wandered over and sat on my lap, draping an arm around my shoulders.

"You really don't know music, do you."

She sighed. "Much less than my sister. I'm not gonna pretend it's my life's passion or anything." She played with my hair. "I like music. I follow some bands. I'm not an authority on the subject, as you noticed." She frowned a little. "I'm not really an authority on anything."

"Maybe you will be, one day."

That just seemed to make her sad, or something. "Yeah. Maybe."

I couldn't really handle her sadness right now, or whatever put that look on her face. I nudged her off my lap, getting up.

"What's wrong?" she asked me.

I lit up a blunt. "What's wrong with you?" I countered, but my tone said I didn't really want to know.

She hugged herself uncomfortably, looking out into the night as I smoked. Then she met my eyes again. "I guess I was just thinking… my sister was an authority, so young. She was so talented on the bass as a teenager, already."

"She probably practiced a lot."

"Yeah. So I was thinking, why is it taking me so long to catch up?"

"Maybe you don't need to catch up. Just stop comparing yourself to your sister."

She didn't say anything. She watched me smoke for a long moment, until I couldn't stand it anymore. I crushed out the blunt and headed into my bedroom.

She followed me, even though I didn't invite her in. The clock on my bedside table said it was two-something in the morning.

Was she waiting up for me all night?

Something churned in my stomach, fueling my unease.

"Something's bothering you," she said gently. "What is it?"

"Well, Breakneck is done. So there's that." I picked up the vodka I'd been drinking earlier and continued where I'd left off.

"What do you mean? What happened?"

"I talked to Yash. Apparently, this is the only way to avoid a lawsuit. Breakneck is no more."

"What does that mean, exactly?" She shook her head when I offered the vodka to her.

"It means that the band I gave the last eight years of my life to is done."

"But… what does that mean for you and Noah?"

"It means, since Breakneck is no longer a thing, no one can use the name or move forward with it. Including us. This is a slight problem because it also kills the record deal and forces me to basically start over."

Angeline breathed a soft, wounded sigh, for me, and I looked away. "Are you sure about the record deal?"

"I'm sure. Trey was crystal clear. The deal was with Breakneck. And since there is no Breakneck… no deal. Also, I can't use the songs we already wrote together. None of us can. So everything I've been writing the last six months or so… gone."

"Shit…"

Angeline followed me as I went to flop into a chair in front of the fireplace wall. She crouched down in front of me, her blue-gray eyes flooded with emotion.

I looked away.

"Johnny. I'm sorry. But this isn't the end."

"Of course it's the end. Did you not hear me?"

"I heard you. But just because your band—"

"Would you stop? Just stop." I really tried not to look at her, but it was impossible, with her soft eyes sucking me in like that.

She took a breath. "Johnny, did it ever occur to you that maybe you're just not meant to play with Breakneck anymore? And maybe the whole reason the band struggled so much and the whole dynamic just didn't work, in the end, was because it wasn't the right dynamic for *you*."

"What does that mean?"

"It means, maybe you're just not a lead guitarist in a band, period. Maybe Johnny O is a solo artist."

I stared at her.

How was it that this girl always said the exactly right thing? Even if it was nowhere near anything I was ready to hear.

She was annoyingly, kinda frighteningly like Rory that way.

"Hear me out," she said gently. "My sister recorded a solo album because she had things she wanted to do, musically, that didn't quite fit with Dirty. And so did Jesse Mayes. There have been many exceptionally successful rock stars who've had a period of their career where they've been a solo artist leading a band. Tom Petty and the Heartbreakers, Paul McCartney and Wings… Elton John, Jimi Hendrix, I don't know, I'm sure you can think of way more examples than I can. They could've called themselves something else, a band name instead of their own name, but they didn't. Because they were clearly the star of the show—"

"Yeah. And you know what all those artists had in common? They sang lead vocals. If you sell yourself as Tom Petty or Jimi Hendrix or Elton John, someone else isn't singing your songs."

Angeline stared at me. Maybe she knew I was right.

Maybe she knew I was just defeating myself before I even considered what she was saying.

"Well, then maybe you can sing lead vocals. I've heard your voice on Breakneck's songs—"

"Everything doesn't have a happy ending, Angeline. And maybe it doesn't have to. Just let it go."

She moved to sit on the corner of the coffee table in front of me. "Well, you're not letting it go, are you? You can't just pack up and quit."

"I'm not packing up and quitting."

"Good. I should finish the press release for you now. I can talk to Yash—"

"Yeah. Why don't you go call Yash and write your press release." I wasn't even sure why I was so… pissed off. At her. But everything she said was grating at me right now.

She said she'd been holding off on actually putting out a press release for me so far because there wasn't anything newsworthy to put in it. Well, this was news. But fuck if I cared who put it out there or how. Didn't change facts. And the fact was, my career was dead in the water right now.

"I mean, I just thought—"

"I don't care about the fucking press."

"But we should really get a statement out there, before JC—"

"Fuck JC. I don't give a shit what he says about me."

"But if we get ahead of it—"

"There's nothing to get ahead of. You can't outrun the truth." I looked into the shimmering fake flames of the fireplace, my heart beating too hard as the truth of that statement resonated in my bones.

I knew what I was doing. Pushing her away. *Running.*

Yash was right about me running away when things got hard. I was itching to run right now.

But I couldn't stop myself.

Why the hell did I even come home tonight?

"Is this really about the band?" she asked me. "The record deal? Or is it about what happened last night?"

I didn't even look at her. "What, you think fucking you is so transcendent that I couldn't actually want you to get out of my face right now?"

I felt her silence like a stab.

*Fuck, you hurt her.*

"I wasn't talking about the sex," she said in a small voice. "I meant the nightmare."

I stared into the fake fire, letting the light burn into my eyes. "What nightmare."

She leaned into my line of sight and met my eyes. "The one that woke us both up in the middle of the night."

"I didn't have a nightmare."

"Maybe you don't remember it now," she said gently, "but you did."

"I don't have time for this, Angeline, okay? My entire career just stopped in its tracks, so I have slightly more important things to deal with right now."

"Okay. Good. You should deal with it. Maybe we can—"

"I didn't ask for your opinion."

She sucked in a breath. Her eyes said *Why are you being mean?*

*Haven't we come so far?*

I looked away. "Can you just go? I need to take care of some things."

"Right now?"

"Yes. Right now."

"Okay." She hesitated, though. "I know you're not in the right headspace right now to be thinking about the press release. But I can get working on it, and then when you're ready—"

"I don't care about the fucking press release, Angeline. I don't. Fucking. Care. Do you hear me? I don't give a fuck. The only thing I fucking cared about just fucking up and left."

She blinked at me. "So… you don't care about me. Is that it?"

I didn't say anything as she stared at me, waiting for me to say something.

When I didn't, she got up and left the room.

# Chapter Thirty-One

**Angeline**

Johnny had disappeared.

I hadn't seen him in almost seventy-two hours. Not since he'd told me that he lost his record deal and he didn't care about any press release I might put out about it—and inferred that he didn't care about much of anything other than his career. Including me.

If he'd been around the next day or the next, or come home at night, I didn't see him. I slept in my room at Shayla's and stayed away from his house. He wanted me out of his face, so I got out.

But three days into the silent treatment, I was getting worried with a side of mad and a sprinkling of depressed.

I met Courteney at a coffee shop where she was working on her laptop. She was writing again, working on pitches for her next book with her agent. I was so proud of her, and when I saw her sitting there, glasses on, typing away, and I thought about how far she'd come from the sixteen-year-old girl I'd met at an industry party at Brody Mason's house, in a closet no less, crying because she'd felt rejected by her crush—her future husband, Xander—I couldn't believe I had my head so far up my own ass right now.

She lit up when she saw me and I gave her a huge hug. "You!" she exclaimed. "I miss you."

"Me too." I slumped into a seat at her table. "I hate myself for what I'm about to do to your day."

"Oh, shit. What's wrong?"

"I'm gonna cry. The tears are coming. I can feel it." By the time I got the words out, I was already crying. In a café. *Again.* At least this time I had the foresight to bring a damn hat. I tugged my ball cap down a bit, trying to hide my embarrassing face which displayed my every emotion to the wide world. "I'm so sorry, Court. I'm so excited about your new book. How is it going?"

She shut her laptop. "Angie, we can talk about that later. Whatever's bringing you to tears is more important."

That made me want to cry harder. I tried to suck it back. You know, like a mentally sound grownup who was in public, for fuck's sake.

"What is it, babe?" Courteney reached over the table to give my hand a squeeze. "You know you can tell me anything. I give terrible advice about sex toys but I'm a wonderful listener."

"I know you are." I tried to smile at her. "Johnny's upset with me. Or something." I breathed out through the sharp pain in my ribs. It had felt, for three whole days, like I couldn't take in a full breath. "We had a bit of an argument the other night. I don't know. He just wanted me out of his face because he was upset about losing his record deal."

Courteney's hazel eyes went wide. "He lost his record deal?"

"Yeah. I need to do a press release before the rumor mill gets going. But he doesn't even want to talk about it. Now, do I do the release without him, with his manager, or will he hate us for taking over?"

"Uh… I don't think it's taking over. You're doing your jobs. Part of which is basically protecting his career, right? Or at least helping to ensure that he continues to have one."

"True. It's what he hired me for." I sniffled. I'd been doing my best to keep business and pleasure—and pain—separate these last three days. I'd rewritten the press release several times, but I didn't send it to him. I was afraid he'd tell me to go away again. "I've been doubling down on it, trying to do my job so well that he'll love me for it. How sad is that?"

Courteney gazed at me with sympathy. “You want him to love you? Is that it?”

“Yes,” I whispered. I pulled my hat down lower so even she could barely see me. “I’m falling for him,” I confessed. “I fucked up, Court. I fucked him. I fucked him like crazy and I’m totally falling for him.”

I heard her soft gasp. Or maybe it was a sigh.

Maybe she wasn’t shocked at all.

I mean, she knew me. And how head-over-heels I fell for men. I’d fallen for men like Johnny from afar all my life. Was it really any wonder I’d gotten so carried away with him, up close?

“I’m so stupid.” I sniffled. “The moment I actually believed he really liked me… I was all in. It’s so beautiful and sad. I’m lame.”

“You’re not stupid or lame,” she said firmly. “You’re you. And your ability to fall in love *is* beautiful.”

“Yeah. But what if he’s not falling? Am I just in for a lifetime of hurt, with my stupid, squishy heart? Does it always have to hurt so damn much? Why can’t it just be… love?”

“I don’t know, babe,” Courteney said sympathetically. “Sometimes… the love is worth it, though. That’s all I can tell you. You know, after you get through all the other crap.”

I tried to laugh. There was a lot of crap to get through.

I could feel it.

Johnny had a ton of crap going on, and I didn’t even know what it was.

And I couldn’t even ask Shayla if she knew.

It was killing me trying to act normal around the house in front of her so she wouldn’t know anything was up. I had no idea if she knew where her brother was the last three days, or what he was doing, and I couldn’t exactly ask her without tipping her off that there was drama between us. She’d know, if I so much as mentioned his name in a certain tone. I couldn’t hide my feelings from her. So, I’d just been avoiding her as much as I could.

Besides, she’d been shooting the Players video this week, and I didn’t want to distract her from that with all this drama. She had more important things to focus on. And thank God for that.

But I was going to have to tell her, somehow. I just hoped that when I did, I'd have something better to tell her than… this.

"Can you please not say anything to Shayla? This is exactly what she didn't want to see happen. She'd be so pissed if she knew he'd hurt me, and that's the last thing he needs right now."

"You're protecting him." Courteney seemed kinda surprised.

"Of course I am."

"You really care about him," she concluded.

"I do." I sighed. "I'm tired of this shit, Court. I've cried so many tears over guys who didn't even know how I felt about them, because I never told them. Am I doing that again?"

"You did that because you put those guys on pedestals and worshipped them," she said. I knew she understood. She'd done the same thing. With Xander, in the early days. "Take it from me. You've got to let this one down off the pedestal if it's going to work. Even if that means you've got to take a step back and let him fall."

"I know. You're right." I still had him on that pedestal, didn't I? Somewhere deep inside, I still wondered if I was good enough for him—and if he was right to kick me to the curb.

But that was bullshit. I deserved better than that.

"But Angie, after you do that?" Courteney looked me dead in the eyes. "No matter what happens, promise me you'll burn that fucking pedestal to ashes. I don't care how hot or talented or special he is. No man should ever be above *you*."

---

It was Merritt, of all people, who called me—from the bar at Champagne—to tell me where I could find Johnny.

When I arrived at my sister's nightclub in a cab, I walked in to find the place fairly quiet. It was early, which meant it was closed. The bouncer at the door recognized me and let me in. Music was on and staff were buzzing around, setting up, some having a drink before their shifts started.

There were no customers inside yet. Except for one VIP at the bar with a couple of girls.

I stopped when I saw him. Johnny, sitting on a bar stool and leaning heavily on the bar. I could tell, just by his posture, that he was wasted.

Merritt, from behind the bar, met my eyes across the room. She came around the bar and over to me as I just stood there. "Hey. Am I to take it… that's yours right there?" She indicated Johnny with sympathy in her voice.

I sucked back a breath. "Yeah. I'd like to think so."

"I figured. I saw you with him at Talia's housewarming party. So when he came in tonight looking like… that… I texted Elle. She told me to call you."

"Thank you for doing that."

She glanced at Johnny and the two girls. They were on him like headphones, one at each ear, whispering. "He showed up about an hour ago and went from coherent to *not* pretty fast. I already gave him a drink, but I told him I can't serve him anymore."

"Great," I breathed, acute pain lashing through my chest as I watched one of the girls. She was leaning on Johnny, her head tipped close to his. Her fingers played with his hair as she talked to him. The other girl had her hand on his arm as she sipped her drink. "What about… them?"

"You mean busty and bustier? According to one of the waitresses, they were sniffing blow in the bathroom a few minutes ago. I would've kicked them out already, but I figured you might want him to stay put until you got here."

"Yeah," I forced out. "Thank you."

"They were drinking at Misty's before this. That's all I got out of them."

Misty's. That was the strip bar where Johnny and his friends used to hang out. *Used to…* because maybe I'd hoped these days he had better things to do? More enjoyable things? With me?

*Guess not.*

"You need my help, or one of the bouncers, let me know." Merritt squeezed my arm, then went back behind the bar.

I took a deep breath, trying to calm my raging heartbeat as I walked over to Johnny. I stood next to him, just behind the girl who was all in his face. They weren't kissing or anything, but she was murmuring to him about something, and that almost made it worse. Meanwhile, his head dangled like he was barely conscious.

"Johnny," I said, loudly enough that both girls turned to look at me.

He turned much slower.

When he saw me, recognized me, his glassy eyes widened. But not like, *Oh shit, I'm caught.* More like, *Oh, it's you; I adore you.* "Angel," he croaked, and my heart split right down the middle.

I didn't imagine it. I knew I didn't.

He cared about me. A lot.

I almost couldn't believe he'd called me that special name right now, though. In front of these women. It felt wrong.

"The two girls touching you right now need to go away," I told him. "Or our relationship is over. Do you understand?"

He stumbled off his bar stool to reach for me. I caught him because he looked so unstable, and while he clung to me he said, "Don't go."

I held onto him as he held onto me. I could see it in his eyes; as wasted as he was, he wanted me. He'd promised me I was the only one.

I wanted to believe him.

*Trust.*

"Go away," I told them, and when they didn't move, just kind of laughed as they looked at each other, Merritt came over.

"Time to go, ladies," she said, somehow neutrally yet forcefully. "Don't make it awkward." She swept what was left of their drinks off the bar. I could feel the male bartender at the other end of the bar watching us.

The girls huffed and started gathering their purses, slowly.

I ignored them. "His bodyguard is outside," I told Merritt. "His name is Lamar. Can you get him to come help us?" Johnny was kind of leaning on me and I propped him up against the bar. No way I could get him outside myself.

He kept saying my name and trying to drag me closer to him.

It would've been really nice if, when we went home, he explained everything and it all neatly made sense. This was all just a misunderstanding, and we made up and made love.

But it didn't happen like that.

Instead, Lamar drove us home and he had to help me get Johnny upstairs and onto the bed. After Lamar left, I undressed him as best I could. He was barely awake. I tucked him in and then lay beside him, on top of the covers, watching over him for a while to make sure he was okay.

Who knew what those girls had fed him? Not coke, probably, or he wouldn't be such a drunken slug right now.

I texted my sister to let her know I'd brought him home and to thank her for telling Merritt to call me, and also to thank her for not getting involved.

When I finally slid under the covers with him, Johnny stirred. He draped his heavy arm over me and muttered, "You're such an angel."

I sighed. At least he knew who he was in bed with.

I knew he was suffering. I wasn't dense.

I had eyes and a big, squishy heart.

But I couldn't let him shit all over it, or break it, no matter how broken he was.

I knew I had to talk to him about this shit tomorrow when he sobered up.

Better yet, I probably should've woken him up right now and given it to him.

But a funny thing happened, sometimes, when you were back in the bed of someone you knew you were falling in love with, someone you feared you might've already started to lose… and you felt how much they still needed you when they curled their body around you in sleep.

You gave in.

Sometimes… you just fucking gave in.

"You're an angel, too, Johnny O'Reilly," I told him, stroking the soft hair at his temple as he slept. "You just don't realize it."

# Chapter Thirty-Two

**Johnny**

"Have you thought more about the door? The one in the fortress?"

I was pacing around Rory's courtyard again, surrounded by his plant/pet obsession. This time, there were a couple of frogs chirping somewhere and he was tending to an array of orchids. Like, dozens of them.

"Yeah, I've thought about it," I grumbled. I was uneven today. Wildly uneven. I'd come straight to see him, first thing in the morning. Before Angeline woke up.

Because the thought of having to look her in the eyes after what I did last night…

I didn't fuck anyone. I didn't cheat on her, technically.

But I also wasn't with her, wasn't communicating with her, wasn't treating her or myself well. I'd probably been putting her through hell, if she cared about me at all.

And I fucking knew she cared.

Pretending otherwise, or that she deserved to be treated otherwise, was bullshit. Even I knew that much about relationships.

Lucky for me, when I arrived, Rory was up. He'd probably been up all night.

That made two of us.

I'd spent most of the night awake in bed, just watching Angeline sleep with a sinking feeling bottoming out in my stomach.

"Did you find it?" Rory asked me.

"What?" I looked across the jungle of plants at him, so irritated with myself I could barely string together my thoughts. I'd been agitated all night, uneven, unsettled, all that shit. And now I was wickedly hungover to boot.

"The door," Rory repeated patiently. "Did you find a door, in the fortress?"

I kept pacing. "What happened to the peace lilies?"

"Hmm?" He glanced up from his work. "Oh. I gave them all away. They're poisonous to cats."

Well, that was typical. He probably tended them with no intention of keeping them, gave them all away in prime shape to his friends and neighbors, the fucking mailman; anyone he thought might need some filtered air in their life.

"The door," he pressed, looking at me expectantly. "Have you found it?"

"Yeah," I muttered. "I found it."

Rory actually looked surprised by that. And keenly interested.

I looked away.

"How do you feel about that?"

"I don't know." I sat down in a chair. "Confused, maybe. It's disorienting, in a way. It wasn't there before."

"Can you picture it, now? In the wall of the fortress?"

"Yes."

I could practically hear the gears in his head turning that over. He seemed way more optimistic about this discovery than I was. "Then I wonder… if there's more than just the door? Other things that you haven't noticed before?"

"Like what?"

"Like where does the door go?"

"It goes outside."

Rory eyed me. He took off his gardening gloves and came to sit in a chair across from me, on the other side of the low table where Vivian had laid out tea for us. "Have you tried opening the door?"

"Yes."

"And what do you see?"

I rubbed my jaw. "It's… This is getting stupid."

"What is?"

"This metaphor."

He fixed me with his patient gaze. "It's much more than a metaphor, Johnny."

Yeah. I knew that.

The boy, the wall, the fortress, these had been key components of my therapy at one time. The only way I'd really ever been able to talk about any of it, as a kid; through the lens of the boy in the fortress.

It was still the only way I could talk about it, most days.

But I wasn't sure yet that I liked that fucking door. It made me uncomfortable.

It made me feel out of control. Like the fortress was no longer my own.

And yeah, it made me feel stupid. Because how did I never see it before?

"What do you see outside the door, when you open it?" Rory prompted. One of his cats, a kitten, jumped into his lap and I watched him stroke it.

It was so easy for him, caring for other creatures. Empathizing. Nurturing.

Feeling.

Maybe that was why I'd sometimes resented him so damn much.

"It's really fucking stupid."

"Then let's be stupid for a minute. Indulge me."

I sighed quietly.

He picked up the kitten and shoved it into my lap. "Hold the kitten, Johnny. It's good for the nerves."

I took it. It was so delicate and soft. And probably the cutest thing I'd ever held in my hands, gray stripes with white around its big golden eyes and a tiny tail. It was purring. "Where'd this one come from? Are they multiplying?"

"He's new. His name is George."

"That's a dumbass name for a kitten, just so you know."

"I named him after my late father-in-law."

"Oh."

"Purring heals, smart ass. It can heal you, too."

"Yeah? Can I get a prescription for that?" I rubbed the kitten with my thumbs while it melted into my lap.

"What do you see outside the door?" Rory pressed, ignoring my smart ass question.

I groaned inwardly. I could hardly believe these stupid words were about to come out of my mouth. "There's a moat."

"A moat? Outside the wall?"

"Yup."

He took a moment, like he was picturing this, or maybe calculating what this next layer of the fortress might mean. "How wide is it? Could you walk across it?"

"No."

"Is there a bridge?"

"No."

"Can you see what's on the other side?"

"I can't see anything. I just see a moat."

"Then, could there be a drawbridge?"

"Why would there be a drawbridge?"

"Because maybe you're not meant to stay in the fortress alone forever."

I didn't say anything.

He settled back in his chair. "And because maybe I had it wrong all those years ago. Maybe the next step in the boy's evolution wasn't to grow up, but to get curious. Maybe the curiosity precedes the growing up, and one naturally flows from the other."

"What do you mean?"

"You need to want something in order to get somewhere," he told me, like he'd told me many times. "You know this. Just like with your career, you have to be hungry. You have to be willing to do what other people aren't willing to do. Most people stop where the discomfort is. Pushing through the discomfort is where you'll find the greatest success. It's the same with where you are now in therapy. You've been through almost all available treatment for PTSD. You've broken old behavioral patterns. You're exceptionally focused, in general. It's a great strength of yours. What that means is that you have tools to go very far in anything you apply yourself to. It also means you can get stuck, when what you apply yourself to is not helpful, or worse, destructive. But imagine directing that superpower you've got, that intense focus, at something that truly matters. Imagine what you could accomplish."

"Uh-huh. Imagine." Right now, I couldn't imagine having any superpower. I was so hungover, I could barely follow what he was saying.

"I'll take your sarcasm as grudging interest until you convince me otherwise." He poured himself a tea but didn't drink, then stirred the tea with a spoon, around and around, going through an old ritual, from back when he used to allow himself to eat sugar. The man was a lot like me, in that way. Had a hard time sitting still. He always said he did his best thinking while doing something with his hands.

And as I watched him, I knew he was right; I was interested. I was always interested in what he had to say, even when I hated what he had to say.

When the kitten made a tiny mewling sound, I realized I'd tensed up. I was squeezing it a little and tried to relax my hands. He was still purring.

"You've described the boy to me, in the past," Rory said, finally, setting down his spoon. I noticed he still didn't drink the tea. "He's changed over time, but not much. Can you describe him to me now?"

I sighed again, and reiterated it for what felt like the thousandth time; naming the emotions he'd helped me attach to the boy. "He's lonely. He's scared. He's confused."

"Is he curious?" He asked the question with obvious curiosity of his own. This was one of the things that I liked the most about Rory. This genuine curiosity of his. It was one of the things that made me as comfortable as I was with him, that alleviated the discomfort of talking to a mental health professional at all. He was different than the other doctors and therapists I'd talked to over the years.

"What, curious like you?" I poked.

"I'm very curious about you. As I was about all my patients. Some more than others." He smiled a bit. "But let's talk about the boy. Is he curious? Most children are."

"About what?"

"What if he heard something on the other side of the wall? Not frightening. Just something in the distance. Something that piqued his curiosity."

"I don't know."

"Has there ever been something like that?"

I didn't answer that for a long moment. But the man was patient. He waited. And fucking waited.

"There was," I said finally. "Once. It was a long time ago. What does it matter?"

Rory leaned forward, interested. "What happened to it?"

"It went away."

"Why did it go away?"

"Because I made it go away."

"Do you know what it was?"

"It was… a girl." I cleared my throat. "A woman."

"Did this woman get inside the fortress?"

"No. No, I didn't let her in."

"Did you want her to come inside?"

"No. Maybe. I was too scared."

"You asked her to go away?"

"No. I hurt her. I made her go away."

He considered that. "Did she love you?"

"I think so."

"How did you hurt her?"

"I didn't let her into the fortress."

Rory held my gaze for a moment, then looked away, into the thickets of plants that surrounded us, like he was picturing something else. The fortress, maybe.

I wondered if, after all these years, it was as vivid for him as it was for me.

"What do you think is outside the fortress, Johnny? Beyond that moat?"

"I don't know how to answer that."

He sat back in his chair and studied me. "Can you picture it? The wall of the fortress, from the inside, right now?"

"Yes."

"Do you hear things, beyond the wall? Sense things?"

I shook my head, battling the uneven feeling. "My friends are there. Sometimes. Sometimes I hear their voices. Sometimes they speak to me from outside."

"Do they try to come in?"

"No."

"Why not?"

"Because they don't know the fortress is there."

"Why?"

"Because… I think it's invisible to them. Because I hide it from them."

"But they see you."

"They see… what they think is me."

"Did she see you? The woman who came and tried to get in?"

"She saw a version of me. But she didn't try to get in."

"You said a moment ago that she left because she couldn't get inside."

"The fortress was invisible to her, too. She just knew something was in the way."

He looked… intrigued or something. I wasn't sure why. As usual, he was probably way the hell ahead of me. More so, since I was so fucking hungover. "This is excellent, Johnny. It might not seem like it to you, but these are important details. You've never mentioned this woman before."

"You never asked."

Rory smiled slightly, maybe amused. "Ah. Yes. I try to ask the right questions. After so many years, I'm still learning what they are." Curiosity honed his features again. "Is she a real person?"

I rubbed my jaw uncomfortably. "Yes."

"Talking about it makes you uncomfortable?"

"Yes."

"I haven't asked you who she is."

"She was my wife. Briefly."

He nodded. "Yes. You did mention her. Years ago."

"I don't want to talk about that today."

"Why?"

"It's irrelevant."

Clearly, he disagreed. "What else is outside the fortress, Johnny?"

I leaned forward on my knees, sending the kitten scurrying from my lap, as the tears burned in my eyes again. So fucking fast. This place, Rory, was one of the only places it felt safe for the tears to come. Most everywhere else… I felt mostly numb. Emotionally numb. The wall was high and I was safely inside.

But the pain rose up now, so fucking fast.

"My mom. She used to be there. Before she died."

"Not anymore?"

I looked up at him. "She's dead." He knew that.

"So, she's silent now? You don't hear her anymore?"

"No. She's gone."

"I know you miss her from your life. Do you also miss her outside the wall?"

"No."

"Why not?"

"Because… she never tried to come in."

"She knew the fortress was there?"

"She knew I built it. That… my dad built it," I amended, remembering our last conversation, what he said about my dad being the first builder of the wall. "She watched it get built, from the outside. She never did anything to stop it. To stop us."

"She abandoned you."

I rubbed my face.

"She abandoned you in your life. And she abandoned you inside the fortress, too, didn't she."

I didn't answer that.

"Do you see that, Johnny?"

"Yeah. I see that."

Rory was silent for a moment. I wasn't sure if he was thinking, or just giving me a moment to digest.

"We've talked about your dad and about your mom, who could see the fortress. And about your ex-wife, who could not. And your friends, who cannot. Can anyone else see the fortress?"

I took a breath. "I think… I think she can."

"Who?"

"Angeline. My new… friend. My publicist. My…" I didn't know what to call her. "At least, she can feel it. And sooner or later she'll see it. If…"

"If, what?"

"If I kept seeing her."

"You say that like your relationship is in the past."

"I'm not sure what it is. I… I pushed her away." My head hung low. I didn't even want to look Rory in the eye on this. "I know I hurt her. I must have."

"Have you seen her since? Spoken to her?"

"Yeah. She came after me. I pushed her away, and she came back." I pressed my fingers into my eyes. "I don't know how to not do that."

"Was this all before or after you received the news that you'd lost your record deal?"

"After."

Rory was silent as I just breathed. When I lifted my head again, he was watching me with the same calm understanding and openness as always. There was no wall with Rory. There never had been. Not from his side. His specialty was dealing with children and teenagers suffering from PTSD stemming from a singular traumatic event.

He understood the fortress better than I ever did, and I'd lived in it for a large part of my life.

He'd told me, many times, though, that I couldn't live in it forever. Not if I wanted to stop suffering. The fortress was a key to my survival, once upon a time. But it wasn't the end.

It wasn't my grave.

"You don't need to die in the fortress, Johnny," he said gently. Which he'd also told me many times. He held my gaze as he let that sink in. *You could've done that already, if you wanted to.* That was what I felt like he was saying to me with his silence. But I couldn't be sure.

Then he asked me, "What if there is a drawbridge, and the boy lets it down?"

"Why?" I sniffed back the tears that were starting to come again. "Why would he do that?"

"So she might take a step inside."

I looked down at the floor again.

"You told me, long ago," he said, "that it was a relief to tell me about the wall. About the fortress. And about why you ended up inside. Do you think it might be a relief to tell her?"

I didn't answer that. I wasn't ready, maybe, to answer that.

It was so much easier to keep the wall high around me. It was all I knew.

But Rory wasn't done yet. "What if she does, eventually, see the fortress?"

Questions; the man always had more questions than answers. *Because the answers depend upon asking the right questions*, he would always say.

"What if she sees across that vast moat?"

I looked up into Rory's eyes, and I could see the compassion and wisdom at work there.

"I don't know."

"What if she sees the door in the wall, and finds it closed?" he asked me. "Have you ever thought about that, Johnny? Have you thought about what happens to her then?"

# Chapter Thirty-Three

**Angeline**

When I woke up to find myself alone in Johnny's bed, and no sign of him or Lamar on the property, no note, no text… after the shape I found him in last night… I got myself an Uber and headed to my parents' place.

My safe place.

*You're safe, Angeline.*

Yeah. *Bullshit, Johnny.*

I listened to Harry Styles on repeat in my earbuds all the way to Mom and Dad's, because no one could make me cry—or stop crying—like Harry telling me to stop crying when he sang "Sign of the Times" to me. I mean, it felt like he was singing to me. And by the time my Uber dropped me in my parents' driveway, I'd managed to run through the full cycle: ugly crying until the well ran dry, silent, wracking dry sobs, and finally, just focusing on breathing as I started to feel better about the whole thing. I had my crying song, I had my parents, I had my friends. I even had a sympathetic lady Uber driver.

I'd get through this, no matter what happened with Johnny.

I only hoped it wasn't obvious I'd been balling my eyes out as I tried to touch up my makeup before heading into the house.

Yeah, it was obvious.

Mom was making brunch and Dad was reading the paper in the breakfast nook when I walked in. Their usual position on a Saturday morning. They didn't ask me what I was doing here when I let myself in. I just gave Mom a hug from behind while she was plating omelettes, got a mug from the cupboard, poured myself a coffee and sat down at the table with Dad.

"Why didn't you tell us you were coming?" Mom said as she went to pull more eggs from the fridge. "I would've made some for you."

"Don't. Please. I'm not hungry. All I need is coffee."

"Angeline," she gasped when she really saw my eyes. "Are you alright?"

"Of course I am," I said lightly. "I'm here."

She eyed me with concern but sat down to eat when I insisted, again, that I didn't want any food.

Then they passed concerned looks between them as they asked me questions about the work I was doing for Johnny—what they probably assumed was a safe, neutral topic—and I answered while neatly avoiding the fact that I was also screwing him, falling in love with him, crying my eyes out over him, and that I had no idea if he was about to imminently shatter my heart into pieces.

As soon as Dad was done eating, he got up to make me breakfast even though I told him not to. I wasn't even sure what I was doing here except that it felt comforting having my parents dote on me, even when it annoyed me a little. They loved me so much, I could never be mad at them for trying too hard. They just wanted me to be safe, healthy and happy.

The doorbell rang while I was picking at my food and Mom went to get it. I'd been indulging my dad, encouraging him to ramble about the state of the housing market and rising interest rates, his favorite topics, when Mom returned. With Johnny.

The eggs on my fork missed my mouth and tumbled into my lap as his aquamarine eyes met mine.

"Good morning," he said, looking so fine in his white slub cotton T-shirt, tight jeans and tattoos. His hair was neat, but he could've used a shave and he looked tired.

I stood up, eggs tumbling off my lap to the floor. "Hi." I brushed off my dress. I wore a yellow cotton baby-doll because it was supposed to be warm today but all I really wanted to do was stay in bed, and this felt like pajamas. I was half sure I was going to go crash in my old bedroom and feel sorry for myself after I forced myself to eat.

But Johnny's gaze drifted over me like I was the best thing he'd ever seen, and the sick feeling I realized I'd been clutching deep in the pit of my stomach—ever since I woke up in his bed this morning to find him gone—melted away.

"Do you mind if we talk?" he said gently. I wasn't totally sure if he was talking to me or to my parents.

"Why don't you go out on the patio?" Mom suggested. When I looked at her but didn't budge, still a little stunned that Johnny had just magically appeared, she prompted me, "I'll bring out some lemonade."

"Okay." I glanced at Johnny. "I should just clean up this mess…"

Mom shooed me away before I could bend to scoop the eggs off the floor. "I'll take care of it. You go on outside and enjoy the sunshine."

"Thank you." I gave her cheek a quick kiss, which surprised her, then crossed the room to grab Johnny's hand and lead him straight outside. If my parents thought there was anything suspicious about me holding my client's hand—they did, for sure—they didn't say anything about it as we headed out the sliding door to the patio. I shut it firmly behind us. "They're nice, but nosey," I explained.

Johnny pulled out one of the chairs at the outdoor dining table for me, then one for himself next to it, angling them to face one another. "So… what are you doing here?" he said, as we sat down.

"Well…" I glanced at the house, but I couldn't see my parents through the windows into the kitchen. The mid-morning sun glaring off them was too bright. *Fuck it.* I was going with the truth. I met his eyes. "The thing is… the other day, when you disappeared and I decided to keep working, for you, and then I found you drowning your sorrows at a bar last night with those girls all over you… it terrified me."

I could see his remorse, written all over his face.

But when he opened his mouth to speak, I touched a finger to his lips, silencing him. "Listen. If you're headed down that road, the one where you disappear to get wasted whenever life gets shitty and then let random girls climb all over you as some sort of fucked-up avoidance therapy, that's your prerogative. I've seen that road, while hanging out in my sister's word. I'm really not as naïve as I am nice. I know some men choose that road at some point in their lives. But I am not coming along for that ride. I deserve so much better than that. Not only from my client, but from my boyfriend."

Johnny swallowed, taking that in. His dark eyebrows twisted. "You're right."

"Layered on top of that truth," I went on, "is the fact that I care about you. Deeply. If that comes as a surprise to you, then maybe you're the naïve one. I know I haven't said it out loud before, but that's just because I'm scared. My history with men is… messy. My entire experience as a girl growing into a woman has been in my sister's shadow. I've admired men like you from afar all my life but hooked up with other ones instead, denying myself what I really want, all because I never felt special enough to deserve a man like you. A man who's in the spotlight all the time because he's so talented, special, gorgeous—"

"Angeline…"

"I'm not done yet. I put you on a pedestal to create distance between us. Then I pulled you down off that pedestal and hated you after you kissed me that night, years ago, because I thought I couldn't really have you. That you didn't really like me. Then when we started working together, spending time together, I realized I'd put you back up on that pedestal at some point. I don't even know how that happened. I really thought I hated you. I'd convinced myself that I did. But then I realized… maybe I could have you. Maybe you did really like me—"

"I did. I do."

I took another breath, really letting those words sink in. I knew he meant them.

"I let myself feel for you, Johnny," I told him. "I do feel for you. And when I feel… I feel *everything*. And that's what scares me. So, I guess that's why I came here." I sighed, relieved to let it out, though a little sorry that I'd cut and run just like he did, more or less. "When I woke up this morning and you were gone, again, I just couldn't stomach following you down that road. I want a whole person, even if he's broken. I can handle that. I can't handle only getting pieces of you when it suits you."

He leaned forward onto his knees and studied my face. "I hear you. And that's fair. You deserve a whole person. But you're not in anyone's shadow, Angeline. You shine so bright, you make me see stars."

My insides instantly turned to hot liquid, like a candle engulfed in flame, and I fell forward, taking his face in my hands and kissing him hard. "Why do you say things like that?" I gushed. "You're gonna kill me, Johnny O'Reilly."

"It's the truth."

I kissed him again. He kissed me back, but he didn't seem happy. I clung to the kiss, scared to death that he was here to break up with me. Was that why he said those lovely things? To let me down easy?

I released him, taking a breath and settling back in my seat. "How did you know I was here?"

"I didn't. I was just kind of in the neighborhood. I was heading home to talk to you, but… I, uh, stopped in to see your parents."

Okay, now I was confused. "Oh."

"They said 'Come by anytime' after dinner that night. And I realized they actually meant it."

"They did."

"Yeah. So…" He cleared his throat. He seemed nervous, which I wasn't sure how to take. I'd never seen Johnny nervous before. Far from it. Cool, calm, controlled, yes. And maybe pissed off a time or two. But never nervous. "Your dad mentioned he likes Elton John, and I got these tickets for his farewell tour. He's playing Vancouver in October. I, uh, got the tickets for your parents."

"Really?" A stupid smile spread across my face. "My dad is going to love you."

Johnny didn't look happy about that either, though. "Yeah. I'm not sure I should give them to him."

"Why not?"

He took a deep, measured breath, avoiding my eyes. "I have this kind of… mentor. He was my therapist for years. He still kind of is, even though he's retired. His name is Rory. That's who I was with this morning.

I was at his place. We're kind of friends, actually, so… I kind of care about him a lot."

I took that in. "Well, that's good. Having someone to talk to…?"

"Yeah. It is. He's good for that. He always was. Talking to him is kind of like having this hippie uncle who's super wise and insightful, knows way more about you than you ever wanted him to, and is ridiculously patient and compassionate even when you're being stubborn and pissy with him. I honestly think he's the main reason I'm not dead."

"Johnny…" I leaned toward him and slid my hand onto his knee. That *dead* thing rattled me, but I tried not to show it. I wasn't sure what to say, so I went with, "Thank you for telling me that."

He rubbed his jaw and met my eyes. "There's more."

"Okay."

"There's much, much more, Angeline."

A hint of dread trickled down my spine at his tone and the nervous vibes he was giving off. He seemed tense, the air around him crackling with unease. He wasn't his usual cool-yet-tightly-wound. More like jittery, even though he wasn't moving.

I squeezed his knee reassuringly. "Okay. I'm listening."

Just then, the patio door slid open. "Lemonade!" Mom announced, and Johnny got up to take the wooden tray she was carrying. "Oh, thank you, Johnny," she said, and her gaze slid over to me.

I gave her a sharp look and rolled my eyes toward the house.

She took the hint. "Enjoy!"

"Thanks, Mom."

She disappeared back into the house, shutting the door firmly behind her as Johnny set the tray, complete with a glass pitcher of lemonade, two glasses and tea biscuits, onto the table.

"Sorry," I said as he settled back into his chair. "My parents are a little overly enthusiastic about ensuring my comfort. She's probably fighting herself back from coming out here again with pillows and a menu. Or my dad is."

"They think you're awesome," he said simply. "Can't blame them for that."

I smiled a little as he poured me a lemonade. I noticed he didn't pour one for himself.

"And your mom's super sweet," he added. "Loving and caring and kind. I see where you get it from."

I groaned a little. "Yeah. I'm probably way more like her than I want to know. She thinks you're super fucking hot, by the way. Never, ever tell anyone I said this, but my dad kinda looked like you when he was young."

Johnny looked mildly amused. "Did he?"

"Minus the tattoos. He was more blondish before he went so gray. And his hair was thick like yours before it thinned out. He was built like you. When I was like thirteen, he'd have his shirt off mowing the lawn in summer and my friends would be all, 'Your dad is so cuuute.' Thank God he finally started losing his hair and put on the middle-age belly. Or I'd be in a world of trouble with Shayla."

"Hate to say it, but you're probably right."

"She still tells me he's cute, just to irritate me."

Johnny settled his elbows on his knees again, his expression growing serious, and I could feel the conversation was about to shift. That prickle of dread crept down my spine again.

"I was telling you about my mentor."

"You were." I glanced at the house again. "Are you sure you want to talk about this here, though? I can't guarantee she won't come gliding out here any second with finger sandwiches and tea."

"It's okay," he said softly. "This is the best place. If what I have to say is upsetting to you, I wouldn't want you to be anywhere other than a place where you feel so loved."

Tears burned suddenly in my eyes and I bit my lip to keep them at bay.

"I'm listening," I reassured him.

"This is really hard to explain. I've been trying to practice how to tell you, and I can never seem to get it right." He took a deep breath. "The thing is, Rory has been trying to help me see beyond myself. Just like you have. Like, how I interact with the world. And the impact that has on others, not just on myself. I have this problem where I get stuck in my own head so much that I fail to see what's going on around me." He paused, and

I could tell he was really struggling for the right words. "You know how sometimes when someone's sick, for example, with alcoholism, they don't treat people the way they should, but it's not really them, it's the sickness?"

He waited for me to respond to that, but I wasn't sure what he was getting at. "Are you telling me you're an alcoholic?"

"No. I'm not an alcoholic. It's just an example that I thought might make sense to you. The issues I'm dealing with…" He blew out a breath. "I don't always see how they cause me to behave. Or how I treat others. But it's harder to explain to someone than being a drunk. When someone says, 'I'm sorry I hurt you, I was drinking,' it might not excuse the behavior but at least you get what they're saying. It was the alcohol at work. The disease. When I'm hurtful, I can't say 'I was hurt, so I became an alcoholic, and then I hurt you.'" He shook his head. "I'm simplifying this, I know, but I'm trying to simplify something that's really complex." His deep, aquamarine eyes met mine, and it really touched me, that he was trying so hard to get me to understand what he was trying to say.

Even if I still wasn't really getting it.

"For me," he went on, "it's more like, 'I was hurt, so I adapted a whole bunch of survival behaviors that ended up being destructive, and then I hurt you.'"

I sucked in a breath. I didn't like hearing that. That he'd been hurt. Though I was relieved to know that he realized he'd hurt me. Still… "You didn't hurt me that bad, Johnny. I just got scared. When I realized that more hurt was to come if I let us go down that road I described."

"Yeah. I know. I've been really trying not to head down that road." He shifted uncomfortably. "It's a road I've spent a lot of time on, historically."

"You mean, drinking and women?"

"Among other things. I've hurt a lot of people. Including myself. Actually… a while ago, Rory encouraged me to make a list. Of all the people who I think I've hurt, or should've treated better. It's a long, long fucking list," he confessed.

"It's okay. We've all hurt people, even without meaning to."

"It's not okay. There are people I hurt really badly. Like my mom. And my ex-wife. You know… Amber." He glanced up at the house. "And there are people I just plain should've treated better. Like your parents. I came into their house playing nice to impress you, and all the while I just wanted to fuck you. It was disrespectful to you and to them. And you know how I know that? Because I got concert tickets for your dad. Rory has been telling me to stop doing things like that. Stop trying to buy people and use people for my own gain. Because when I do that, I'm not really forming a relationship with them. I'm treating them like a means to an end. And he's right. The worst part is I never let anyone actually get to know me. They don't see who I am. It's artificial."

"I see who you are," I told him softly.

He held my eyes. "You see *some* of who I am. A hell of a lot more than anyone else, probably. And it's happening way too fucking fast." He shook his head a little, like I'd annoyed him but not really. "I've never wanted to be so transparent with anyone before. It's not my natural way of interacting with people. Especially women."

"Then that's meaningful, isn't it? Maybe there's something special between us, and we should both lean into it."

"Yeah." A haunted look flooded his eyes. "I wish I could. It's so fucking tempting…" He shook his head again. "But it wouldn't be fair to you to do that, to lean in and let you lean in too, let you feel like you had something solid to lean on. And then let it crumble around you when you realize the truth."

There it was again, that creeping dread. "What truth?"

His eyes dropped. "That I never told you the most important thing about me that there is to know. The thing that shaped me more than anything else in my life."

I could see, *feel*, how hard this was for him, whatever it was he was referring to.

I leaned toward him a little more. "The most important thing about you, to me," I said in a whisper, "is that I'm falling in love with you, Johnny O'Reilly."

He met my eyes, and his shone wetly.

"And that means," I went on, "that nothing you could say would change that on a dime."

"You might not love me," he said in almost a whisper, "when you learn."

I reached to take his hands. "Then teach me. And trust me that I can love you through anything, because that seed has already been planted and it has room to grow. Well… anything except that road littered with empty bottles and other women, and empty promises. Because I won't put myself through that, even for you. And even if I still love you."

We held each other's eyes for a long moment.

Then he forced out, "I suffer from symptoms of PTSD. I have for a long time. From a single traumatic event in my childhood."

I squeezed his hands tighter, my heart thumping in an increasing rhythm. I knew that my heart was going to break from whatever he told me. I could feel it, in the way he spoke.

"Tell me," I whispered.

"It was a carjacking." He said it plainly, like he'd removed himself from it. Like he was describing something he'd seen on TV. "My mom was driving me home. To my dad's. They were divorced. Dad had custody of me, but I'd just spent a few days visiting my mom. It was nighttime. It was already dark out and it was raining. The car was stopped at a red light. And a man opened the car door. My mom's door. He got in the car."

He stopped talking abruptly. He'd looked down again, avoiding my eyes as emotion started to color his voice, taking him from describing something he'd seen on a screen to something he'd witnessed firsthand. Something he'd lived through. Just barely.

Something that was still so very real for him, vivid and alive. Something buried that was clawing to get out, just under his skin.

I just held his hands. I could feel his anxious heartbeat thudding in his fingers, but I didn't release the tight hold. I didn't move. Birds chirped distantly in my parents' yard and a breeze whispered through the trees of this safe place, my childhood home, where nothing terrible had ever happened to me.

I barely breathed because I didn't want to disturb him as I held on for his next words.

When he didn't go on, I offered tentatively, "Johnny, that's… awful. I can't imagine going through something like that." All the while, my thoughts were spinning madly.

What happened next?

Did he get out of the car? Did he get kidnapped? Hurt? My stomach squeezed into a sick knot, the dread coalescing.

"The memory is muddy." He paused, like he was choosing his words, rather than actually trying to remember. "It's hard to go back there, even with Rory's guidance. But I know for sure the man had a gun. He had a gun and I picked it up." His eyes met mine, filled with pain and a terrible, searing guilt that took my breath away. "I shot him."

Those words, just a whisper on his cracked voice, seemed to ring through the air and whisper through the trees. I could feel the anguish in those words, the anguish that hadn't fully healed.

"I knew if I told you," he said quietly, "you might hate me. But I also knew I couldn't not tell you." He looked at me with a kind of helplessness in his eyes. And in that moment, he looked so young. "I've never wanted to tell anyone so badly."

I heard the truth whispered beneath those words. *I've never wanted to trust someone so badly.*

"Hate you?" I said softly, my voice wobbling. "He… he had a gun. He could've shot *you*. He could've done terrible things to you."

He looked away. "I know all that. But I still shot a man. I killed him."

I sat in stunned, pained silence, with no idea what to say. I was scared that anything I said wouldn't help. I couldn't stand the thought of hurting him with my words right now. So I just sat in silence, holding his hands tight so he'd know I was right here.

"I killed him," he said again, like he was making sure I heard. Or maybe to make sure I understood.

"Johnny, how old were you when this happened?"

"Eight years old."

I couldn't stop it; I started crying. The tears ran soundlessly down my face. "Does Shayla know about this?"

He looked at me again. There was a faraway look in his eyes, like he'd gone somewhere else in his head. But he refocused on me now, and for just a moment, I glimpsed so clearly the scared little boy that he tried so hard to hide. "No. Please don't tell her."

"I won't," I said automatically. I had no idea why he didn't want her to know, but right now, that didn't matter. "But how is that possible? Your dad must know…?"

"Yeah. My dad knows. He's the only one."

"How?"

He took a deep, shaky breath, staring at me, like he was trying to digest the fact that he'd gotten this far and I was still here. "Afterwards… I had a long recovery in the hospital. I don't remember most of that part. I was too young to be charged with any crime. My name wasn't in the papers or anything. So no one knew. But as soon as I got out of the hospital, my dad decided to pack up and move us across the country. His girlfriend and their new baby—Shayla—and me. I'd grown up in this small town in Ontario and my dad relocated us to West Vancouver, and he married Shayla's mom. So, suddenly I had this whole new life, in a new city, in a new home, with a new family. My mom stayed in Ontario. She wasn't very… mentally stable at that point."

"Shit. Johnny. I had no idea about any of this."

"Yeah. It's pretty fucked." He rubbed his hand over his face. He looked pale and exhausted. "I barely even saw my mom after that. Not until I was older. I didn't understand why I couldn't go back or talk to anyone from that part of my life. Dad just wanted us to start over somewhere far away, so no one would ever know. He even changed our last name. He started going to church, he got deeply into that, and he focused on work, building up his wine import business and his standing in our new community. He was trying to protect me from what happened by running away and pretending it didn't happen, I guess. And the result of that was that he was always too busy with other things to talk to me about it. He sent me to therapists so he wouldn't have to. And it was kind of an unwritten rule in our house that you just didn't talk about it. That it was inappropriate to tell my stepmom or my sister. That's what the doctors were for, so I had someone to talk to. So… I guess I have abandonment issues," he concluded.

Another oversimplification, I was sure, but it made so much of his behavior make sense.

He was probably more scared than I was of this thing between us not working out.

"I'm not blaming my dad," he added. "He was doing what he thought was best for me. But it kind of made it worse, in the end."

"Because it became a secret," I said gently.

"Yeah."

"And you've carried that secret for a long time. And you thought… it would change how I feel about you if I knew?"

His eyes held mine, looking both scared and guarded. There were tears in them now. "Doesn't it?"

I considered that carefully. "Johnny…" I said gently. "The fact that you trust me enough to tell me the hardest thing you ever went through… that only makes me love you more."

Johnny blinked at me, looking stunned and relieved and so fucking tired, I just wanted to wrap him up and take him home with me and keep him safe forever.

Then he looked down at our joined hands and said quietly, "I'm so glad I met you, Angeline."

I was pretty sure he was crying and trying to hide it, so I hugged him and pretended not to notice. "Same here."

I climbed into his lap and his arms went around me, holding me tight. Then he whispered in my ear, "No matter what happens… you are the best thing that's ever happened in my life."

"Good. Then don't ever let anything change that."

# Chapter Thirty-Four

## Johnny

Lamar and I pulled up along the row of nondescript gray buildings that looked more like garages than artists' studios. Access was from the back lane. He'd drop me off and go find somewhere to park until he was needed, but not before he gave me a gruff, "You want me with you?"

He was eying the biker leaning on the wall, next to the door with the number on it that Dylan Cope had given me.

"No. It's fine. I'll call you if I need a ride to the hospital."

Lamar turned his dark eyes on me with an unamused look.

I got out and he took his time pulling away, probably eying the biker up and down. His name was Connor, he was a member of the West Coast Kings, and the man was nothing if not a public service for bikers everywhere with his white toothed smile and jolly giant vibes. Tall, blond and handsome, with a casual man-bun, the dude could crush a skull with a bicep curl.

He shone his many-megawatt smile at Lamar and gave him a little wave. Then he plucked the toothpick out of his teeth and flicked it aside, his eyes narrowing slightly as they landed on me. He pushed off the wall and sauntered toward me. "Johnny O'Reilly. What a pleasure meeting you again on such a fine summer day."

If our first-ever meeting didn't result in a bar brawl—over my ex-wife, Amber—that ended with Dylan Cope punching my lights out, I might actually believe him. Since Connor was Dylan's bodyguard though, and I'd just called Dylan to ask him where I might find his lovely wife for a quick chat, I knew exactly why the man was here.

Shoulda probably been a little more suspicious when Dylan gave me the address to his wife's photo studio without the slightest concern.

"Connor, right?" I extended my hand. "Dylan told me I'd find Amber here."

He shook it, squeezing so hard my bones ground together. *Jesus.*

"You might. What do you want to find her for?" He asked with a jovial smile that told me he'd snap my spine if he didn't like my answer. The man had a certain delivery, that was for sure. The fact that I was tight with Lex and he and Lex were club brothers didn't seem to have much currency with him. Not for me.

"I'd say that's between a man and his ex-wife."

"The way I heard it," he said, the pleasantry only slipping a notch, "you were married for, what, two weeks, followed by an annulment? 'Ex-wife' suggests a relationship that you barely had."

"That may be so. But she's an adult. Maybe you can ask her if she'd like to let me in or not."

He held eye contact with me for way the fuck longer than two heterosexual men should ever hold eye contact. Then his smile widened. "Let's do that." He turned, knocked on the regular door next to the large rolling door, then opened it and leaned in. I heard him say Amber's name. Then he disappeared inside.

I took a deep breath as I waited outside. I felt nervous, and I didn't often get nervous. Mostly because I usually avoided situations that might make me nervous, like my life depended on it. Feeling anxious or uncomfortable about anything used to be such a powerful, panic-inducing trigger when I was a kid, after the shooting, that I'd somehow learned to avoid feeling pretty much anything.

But talking to Angeline about the shooting had torn a bandage off. It was one of many, but I'd started to feel things in the last few weeks with her that I wasn't sure I was even capable of feeling anymore. I thought so many emotions were just dead to me. Gone.

Stubborn as I was, I didn't even believe Rory when he told me that wasn't the case.

But now I knew. I'd felt so much with Angeline in such a short time, I knew he was right all along. The feelings were just buried, deep inside the fortress, with everything else in me that had been wounded.

I tried to control my breathing and remind myself why I was doing this.

Because it was essential.

I used to only do things that were essential to my survival. Then things that were essential to success in my career.

Now I was focusing on things that were essential in order for me to grow.

Rory was right, about so many things. That boy I was when I was so deeply traumatized would never leave the fortress or even see whatever lay beyond if he didn't grow into a man.

And being a man meant owning all your shit. Even the worst shit.

I cleared my throat when Amber appeared in the doorway. She squinted out into the daylight.

"Hey," I said gently. I didn't want her to be afraid of me. I wasn't here to hurt her. But for all I knew, the sight of my face was a painful trigger for her. "Sorry to drop in unannounced."

She looked guarded, for sure, but no surprise, I couldn't read what she was feeling. "It's okay. I guess. Dylan said you wanted to stop by."

Of course he'd called her, too. I knew he would. The fact that she'd answered the door was a good sign though, maybe.

"I just wanted to have a quick talk. It won't take long."

"I'll be here the whole time," I heard Connor say from where he was looming behind her.

"Okay," Amber told me. "You can come in." She stepped back to let me in and Connor shut the door behind me. I followed her into the studio. It wasn't huge, but it was large enough you could drive a vehicle through the big door. There was a makeup station and storage cabinets along the back. In the middle of the room, a giant roll of white backdrop paper was suspended, unrolled to the floor and across to where she had her lights and camera set up.

Looked like she'd just finished shooting. There was a guy tearing down her equipment.

"Do you want coffee or something?" she said neutrally, turning to me.

"No, thanks." I took a good look at her. My ex-wife, because that's what she was. Connor's opinion aside, thinking of her as anything else would be disrespectful to her. It would dismiss the vows she'd made to me, and even though I'd broken them and ended the brief marriage, she'd meant those vows.

We both did, for a short time.

She wore ripped jeans and a flowery peasant blouse, casual, pretty. Her caramel hair in waves to her shoulders. A dusting of freckles across her small nose. Pale green eyes.

She looked much like that girl I'd married. But she didn't look *at me* anything like she did then.

Now, I was just that guy she gave her heart to, once, who then turned around and smashed it into the dirt, like it was something that had no value at all. I mean, from her side of it, that must've been how it seemed.

"We won't really have time for coffee," I told her. "I came here to apologize to you."

If she was surprised by that, she didn't show it. She stared at me, like she was weighing whether or not I was serious.

I was.

Then her eyes drifted over to Connor. "Con, could you please wait outside?"

"I'm comfy right here."

I glanced at him. He stood a few feet away, arms crossed over his broad chest.

"I'd like you to wait outside," she said, not any more forcefully, but I could see that the man was wrapped around her finger. Or at the very least, incredibly loyal to Dylan.

"Alright. I'll be outside." He gave me another warning smile with casual murder in his eyes and walked out the door.

Amber turned to her assistant. "Could you give us a minute? Maybe go grab me a tea from the café?"

"Sure, Amber." He set her camera down on a table, glanced at me and headed out.

"Well, I've cleared the room for you," she said, eying me warily. "Say whatever you need to say."

"You didn't have to do that. But thank you." I looked around a bit. "You have a studio now."

"That surprises you?"

"You said you hated studio work. You liked working out in the world, photographing people in their natural environment."

"You were listening," she said, almost suspiciously.

I met her eyes. "Of course I was."

She looked away, crossing her arms over her chest. "It's a co-op. Shared space with other photographers. I'm only here when I need to be. When I have a specific need or desire to photograph something with totally controlled lighting conditions. Or a celebrity client who requires privacy." She glanced at me. "I had a shoot with John Colton Bissette today. He's doing an interview for a high-profile magazine. I have some connections there, so they put us together."

She didn't say which magazine, maybe to soften the blow, but I'd already heard. Dylan had mentioned the photo shoot over the phone. Normally, that might've bothered me; JC doing an in depth tell-all with a major industry magazine so soon after our breakup. I might've been pissed that whatever he said might reflect badly on me. I'd probably be rushing to try to get in front of it, get an interview out first. Make sure my story was told in my own words, not his.

But right now, the only story that mattered was the truth. Specifically, the truth between me and the people I cared about.

Including ones I should've cared more about in the past.

I tried to consider what this photo shoot meant for her, instead of focusing on any lingering animosity toward JC, when I said, "That's cool. I look forward to seeing the photos."

Amber looked at me like *Who are you?* "I thought you all just broke up."

"We did."

Understanding seemed to dawn on her face. Maybe she was thinking about *our* breakup, how I'd walked away from it so unscathed. I was sure it probably looked that way to her.

"Band breakups are not fun," I explained. "But it was necessary. We weren't a forever type of band. We were figuring it out."

"And what did you figure out?" she asked, not with interest but more like she was going through the motions of this conversation. Probably wondering what the hell I really wanted.

Was I here to ask her to photograph me? To use her connections with Dirty to help my career somehow?

All I wanted was to apologize, like I said.

"I figured out that I was in the wrong band. With the wrong people. Noah Vaughan aside. And it was time to let go. Build something new."

"That happens," she said evenly. *Where the hell are you going with this?* her guarded expression seemed to say. If I was here to make excuses about why I'd broken up with *her*, clearly, she didn't want to hear it.

I couldn't blame her.

But I didn't have any excuses.

I'd realized, through a pretty deep conversation with Noah last night, on the heels of similar conversations with Shane and Lex—conversations where I'd told them all basically the same story I told Angeline about the carjacking and the shooting from my childhood and my PTSD—that I'd fucked up. Badly.

I couldn't make any amends with my mom; it was too late for that. She'd died, and there was nothing I could do about the way I'd hurt her by refusing to see her those last few years. But there was one more person who I needed to speak with, someone who'd suffered serious collateral damage from that traumatic event in my life through no fault of her own.

Amber had loved me, and I'd hurt her. Badly.

I had no idea if she'd forgive me. But I needed to try to make amends. I couldn't just run from the damage I'd suffered and the damage I'd caused forever.

"I also realized recently that I never did tell you I was sorry."

She frowned, entirely skeptical. "You just realized that?"

"Yes."

"It's been nine years, Johnny."

"Yeah. I know. I'm a slow-ass learner."

She studied me, like she was expecting to catch me smiling, making a joke. I wasn't joking.

"I cheated on you." I didn't say it to hurt her. I was trying to take ownership of the shit I'd done. "Many times." I realized this probably wasn't news to her. She knew about at least some of those times.

"We were only together for a very short time," she pointed out.

"Yes."

"Seven months," she said. "Really seems short now. But, seven months of my life, Johnny. And married for only sixteen days…"

"Yes."

"And you were with multiple other women."

"Yeah."

"Why did you marry me?" she asked me, kinda like she'd wanted to ask me for years, and yet the answer really didn't matter, because it didn't. Not anymore.

"Because I wanted to."

She actually rolled her eyes slightly.

Maybe it didn't matter. But I knew she deserved more than that.

"I was drawn to you," I told her, "because you had this thing about you. This soft, down-to-earth thing that made me feel safe, and at the same time, you had a guardedness about you, like you didn't want to give your heart away too easily. I think I partly liked the challenge of winning you over."

"So I was a game to you."

"No. You were something lovely that I didn't know if I deserved. And I liked how hard for me you fell. It felt good."

"Yeah," she said dryly, "it felt good from my side of it too. For a minute."

"Maybe I sensed," I added, going for the full truth, "that there was a part of you that would never let me in. That we could just hide from each other together. And for a minute, I actually thought we might be safe like that, forever."

She actually seemed mildly curious now. "So what happened?"

I shrugged. "I got scared. I realized I was wrong about you. You loved me enough, so fast, that you would've wanted more of me. More I couldn't give. So…"

"So, you pushed me away," she concluded, "horrifyingly."

"I'm sorry about that."

"Are you?"

"Yes. I really am."

"You wanted me to find out. You knew I'd walk in on you. At the resort. In that hot tub in the middle of the night, with those women."

"It was cruel. I know that. I didn't mean it to be cruel. It was thoughtless and selfish." I tried to find words to explain, but there weren't really any that would do her any good. So I just went with the truth. "I got wasted that night on purpose. I didn't plan the rest, but I didn't think about you when I did it. After the drinking binge and all the coke, the rest was just me checking out on you. Before you could check out on me."

"Wow." She shook her head. "I must've been naïve as hell. I was married to you and I didn't even know you were doing coke."

"I didn't want you to know."

She seemed to consider that for a moment. "When you sat me down and gave me the big breakup talk, you said we 'rushed into things.' I'll never forget that, you know? That was the part that really hurt the most. I knew we rushed. I wanted to rush. It was finding out that you regretted rushing into it *with me* that really crushed me."

"I'm sorry you were crushed. You didn't deserve that, Amber."

Maybe she actually believed me this time. I wasn't sure. She didn't seem angry.

She sighed a little. "I used to think I'd never heal from the damage you did. I felt like you left this crack in the foundation of my trust that might never heal."

"Did it heal?"

"Of course it did. If it didn't, I wouldn't have gotten married again. Dylan makes all the things I feared I'd never have seem possible. Not just possible… imminent. He loves me in a way that I never have to worry it will just evaporate tomorrow."

"I'm glad you found that."

Amber was silent for a long moment. She still had her guard up with me. I didn't expect that to ever change. I didn't expect her to let me anywhere near her heart, ever again, even as a casual friend. But I could tell that being genuinely glad for her and what she had with Dylan got close.

"You know, I probably wouldn't believe a word you had to say," she told me bluntly. "Even now. After all this time. But Ash told me what you did."

Well… *shit*.

I did not know what she meant by that. Ashley Player was the lead singer of the Players and Dylan's best friend. What the hell did he tell her about me?

"He told me about how he tried to kiss you that night, at that ski resort in Alaska."

Oh. That.

That was years ago, after my marriage to Amber. I'd kind of forgotten about it, actually.

"Uh…"

"He told me how drunk he was," she went on, "and how messed up he felt over his breakup with Summer. He said he made a move on you, when the two of you were alone in a hotel room. You could've reacted to that any number of ways. There was no one else there to witness it. But he told me how you treated him. He was hurting that night, and you were so nice to him. To Ash, and to me, that spoke volumes about who you really are."

I didn't know what to say.

I'd never told anyone about what happened that night, out of respect for Ashley. I knew he was bisexual. Most people did. But whatever he was going through that night seemed pretty messy, and it wasn't mine to tell.

"This, right now," Amber added, "also shows who you really are."

"Thank you."

"So why are you such a dick in public?" she inquired.

I laughed shortly. I wasn't sure I had an answer for her, even now.

"Fear?" she guessed. "Weakness?"

"I don't know. All I can say is I've been hiding a lot of things, holding onto them, for a long time. It's not a pleasant existence."

I wasn't about to tell her about the trauma from my childhood. That, I'd only started to tell people I trusted, people I knew—or hoped—would support me through pretty much anything. And I wasn't looking for her sympathy. I wasn't even looking for her forgiveness. That was up to her.

I just needed to apologize. Sincerely.

If I didn't… I didn't know how I could honestly look Angeline in the eye and expect her to believe in me. I couldn't ask that of her. Look how I'd treated the woman I married. If I couldn't take ownership of the pain I'd caused her, how could I even believe myself that I wouldn't cause Angeline pain?

This was for her, as much as it was for Amber, and as much as it was for me.

"I don't know what you mean by that," Amber said carefully. "Hiding things? But I really don't need to know. I do appreciate you coming here, though. You didn't have to, and I'm sure it was hard. I also appreciate that you did it without asking me for anything in return." There was a warning note in her tone. *Please don't ruin this by asking.*

I lifted my hands, showing her my empty palms. "No ulterior motives. Just trying to grow as a human. I don't expect anything from you."

"Good." She studied me with her pale green eyes, giving me this strange feeling like I shouldn't move. So I didn't. She frowned. "You've changed, Johnny."

"I hope so."

Then she pushed her lips out in a thoughtful pout, like she was contemplating a subject before photographing it. I'd forgotten that look, but I'd definitely seen it on her face plenty of times, all those years ago.

"Do you have a few minutes?" she asked me. Then she picked up her camera.

I was momentarily stunned. She wanted to photograph me?

"Right now?"

"Yes." Her keen photographer's eyes slid over my face. "Right now." Then she smiled at me, genuinely, for the first time since I'd broken her heart. "Why, you have something better to do than be photographed by your ex-wife?"

# Chapter Thirty-Five

**Angeline**

"I don't know where he is."

I hated saying those words, sounding like one of those pathetic girls who didn't want to admit that her man was a train wreck. But maybe I was one of those girls.

Was Johnny ghosting me? Yet again?

Courteney gave me a supportive look across the table. "I'm sure he's just stuck in traffic. It's thick out there."

We were sitting in a restaurant lounge waiting on our men. She was meeting Xander any minute. The two of them were going to see some band play at a club. I didn't even pay attention to the details, I was so distracted. I'd been texting with her while I waited for my date, and when we realized we were two blocks apart, she'd ditched the bar she was supposed to meet Xander at to come meet up with me.

I was supposed to be meeting Johnny here for dinner, like half an hour ago.

I checked my phone for what I promised myself would be the last time. "Yeah? Is traffic so thick it's jamming up his cell signal? Because he hasn't even texted."

"I'm sure he'll be here," she said, sounding unsure. She could hardly vouch for Johnny, even if she wanted to make me feel better. She didn't know him that well, and what she did know… well, we all knew his reputation. "How's it going otherwise? When we spoke a few nights ago you still seemed unsure where the two of you were at."

"Oh, it's going. He's been in and out. I don't even know."

Sadly, I'd called her crying about it a few times this week.

I couldn't exactly go crying to Shayla about her brother when I hadn't even told her yet that we were seeing each other; I wanted to at least tell her when I could frame it as a positive. However, there really hadn't been a moment for that, in between him disappearing, then finding him wasted at a bar with other women all over him, then him disappearing again, resurfacing to tell me the terrible secret from his past… and disappearing again.

So, unfortunately for Courteney and Larissa, they'd had to carry the weight of the emotional dump I'd usually distribute more evenly between the three of them.

I didn't tell Courteney or anyone else about Johnny's big confession, about the traumatic event from his childhood, and I never would unless Johnny said it was okay. But I'd been struggling—to process what he told me and to deal with his uneven behavior.

I sipped my drink, trying to pretend that his behavior didn't bother me as much as it did. I wasn't sure why. Courteney and I were way too close for that. She'd see right through it.

Maybe I was just tired of everyone hating him.

"Also, I made the mistake of mentioning to my sister that he and I were going through a rough patch," I admitted. "That was fun."

Courteney made a *Dear God, you didn't* sort of face, because she knew what that meant. She had a protective older brother. I had a protective older sister. But mine was way more nosey.

"Did she get all helicopter parent on you this time?" she asked with sympathy, knowing full well how my sister had circled, prepared to attend to my scrapes and bruises as soon as she gleaned that things between Flynn and I were less than copacetic. Damn, that went on for a long time.

I actually felt sorry for Elle. That must've been worrisome for her.

But hey, I didn't ask her to worry about me.

"Worse," I sighed. "She told Summer." My sister's bestie had called me last night, to say all the shit my sister was trying not to say so I wouldn't shut her out. Summer never did mince words.

"And how did that go?"

"Oh, it went as you can imagine it went. Getting a lecture from the alpha female of the pack is not fun. 'Angie, the bad guy is the one you screw when you're in your early twenties,'" I recited, channeling Summer's sassy yet emphatic confidence. "'You bang him out of your system, then wise up, grow up and move on. It's natural, sweetie.'"

"That does sound like Summer," Courteney commiserated. Since both her husband and her big brother were Summer's bandmates, I was assuming she'd experienced the alpha female lecture herself a time or two by now.

"'But you don't *stay* with him,'" I continued the lecture, verbatim. "'And you definitely don't try to make him your husband or your baby daddy.'"

"Oh God." A horrified look swept across Courteney's face. "Are you pregnant?"

"No. But I don't actually think Johnny would be a horrifying dad or anything so please get that look off your face."

"Sorry." Her expression melted back into sympathy. "And… what about Shayla? Have you told her?"

"*Fuck.*" I slumped on the table. "No, I haven't told her. She's been flying so high on the whole video shoot experience. She had the time of her life last week, and this week she's got the stars in her eyes. She already told me if she ever gets famous enough to need a publicist, she's hiring me. How could I ruin that?"

Courteney sighed with understanding. "She is flying. So high. I went by the set while they were filming to check it out. She did an amazing job, from what I could see."

"Really? You went to watch the shoot?"

"Of course. Xander would've flipped if I didn't. He's so stoked about the new album. You could've come with me, though. I left you a message… but you seemed… preoccupied."

Holy shit. "I totally missed that message. Oh my God. I'm the worst friend."

"You are not." Courteney reached to squeeze my arm across the table. "Tell me about it?"

"Well, I wasn't allowed to take any pictures and I'm not supposed to talk about the song yet, but it's this dark, heavy ballad, that apparently Ash wrote with Cary and Summer, for Matt, and they were shooting on this dirt road outside of town. Shayla wore this wispy black thing and danced on top of these wrecked cars… it was so hot. They put a bit more red in her hair and backlit her and she's like… fire. Just wait 'til you see it."

"Wow," I marveled, envisioning that. I'd seen Shayla's new hair. And considering how hot the Players and their music was… Shayla was gonna get a lot of attention and probably more dancing gigs out of that video. "Our girl is growing up."

Courteney laughed. Of course, she was the youngest of all the Lil Brats. But we could all argue that Shayla was the youngest in spirit. Shayla O'Reilly was a *free* spirit. I knew she adored me and wanted me to be happy. And as feisty as the girl was, she'd never been mad at me, ever. As friends, we'd never really fought. She'd always had my back.

Every time I thought about launching this Johnny grenade into our relationship, it made me want to weep.

Of course, when I thought he might be worth it, I thought I could deal with it.

Now… I wasn't totally sure.

I thought we'd had a giant breakthrough when he told me about the shooting and his PTSD… but I'd barely seen him this week. He'd barely touched me. He'd been preoccupied and distant. Unreachable, most of the time.

With his and Yash's approval, I'd finally put out a press release about Johnny's split with two of his band members and the end of Breakneck. I was officially representing him as his publicist. It felt like I was actually starting to earn the generous pay he'd offered me, yet it was anticlimactic. Because I still didn't feel any more certain about our future together.

Like I told him, I could love a broken man. But how long could I put myself through this in and out, up and down crap? And never knowing what was going on, or where he was, or if he'd leave me hanging in some restaurant, waiting for him?

Flynn… Flynn had been so solid, so reliable. Maybe I just wasn't prepared to be with a man who wasn't.

But what did that mean for us?

"Angeline…" Courteney squeezed my arm again. "We all just want you to be happy. You were the best friend in the whole world to me, all that time when I was hurting over Xander before we finally got together. I just want to do that for you."

"I know. You do. You took me sex toy shopping, and answered all my emotional late night calls this week. What more could a girl ask for?"

She smirked. "Actually, I think you took me sex toy shopping."

As she spoke, her husband strolled up behind her, and he slid his strong drummer's hands up her shoulders. Her eyes widened when he said, "Who's buying sex toys?"

I sighed. "Me. Always me."

Xander smirked and gave Courteney a soft kiss on the lips that made my stomach clench. The way he loved her was… the stuff of my deepest fantasies.

Xander had a lot in common with Johnny, actually. Worked his body at the gym to the point of sculpted masculine perfection, lots of visible tattoos, always impeccably groomed. Stylish. Well-dressed. Kind of cocky. But where Johnny had golden skin and really suited the blond color he enhanced his naturally dark hair with, and usually went clean shaven or with a five o'clock shadow, Xander had dark hair and usually wore a neatly trimmed beard. The two of them were so hot, I suddenly wondered what it would be like to go out on a double date, Courteney and Xan with me and Johnny.

Fun yet annoying, probably. Like going anywhere in public with my sister; having to sit there while she fielded requests for autographs and selfies…

As gorgeous as Xander Rush was, though, he'd never really made the butterflies go off in my stomach. Probably because I only went for men who were messed up and/or hardly knew I was alive. Xander had always looked me in the eye and treated me like a human worthy of his respect, probably because of who my sister was.

"You ready, babe?" he asked Courteney, in that smoldering tone that said without words how happy he was to see her.

"Yeah." She gave me an apologetic look as she downed the remainder of her drink. "I'm sorry we can't hang out. We have to be there, like, now. Xan knows the band."

"You coming?" Xander asked me.

"No. Thank you for asking. But I'm waiting for someone."

"She has a dinner date," Courteney supplied, sliding out of her seat.

"Johnny O?" he said knowingly. It wasn't like Xander to be nosey. He usually disappeared whenever the girl talk got going. Out of respect for Court and her friends, or because it made him uncomfortable, I wasn't sure. But he held my eye, steady, like he wanted me to know that he knew about me and Johnny.

"Yes. Johnny O."

"There's a lot of talk going around about the two of you."

Courteney elbowed her husband lightly. "Xan."

"What? She should know. It's just buzz. Questions, mostly."

"I know." I tried not to roll my eyes. "Like 'What's he doing with her?' 'Is he gonna break her?' 'Should we warn her?' Trust me, I've been warned, ad nauseam."

Xander's dark eyebrows lifted a little. "Actually, it's more like 'What's she doing with him?' And 'Should we be concerned or butt the fuck out?'"

"The butt fuck thing."

"Right." The corner of his mouth ticked up, amused. "Later, Angeline. Have a nice night." He gave me a fist bump which I returned half-heartedly.

"Good thing you're married. You are incredibly unsmooth with women."

"Hey." Courteney curled herself around his waist. "You hurt the little geek boy inside him when you say that," she teased.

Xander rolled his eyes and put his arm around her, steering her away. Apparently, he was a geek in high school; I had a hard time picturing it.

"We love you!" she tossed over his shoulder.

"Love you guys," I tossed back, giving Xander's bodyguard, Lucas, a little wave.

As I watched the three of them make their way through the lounge, I spotted Johnny and Lamar and my insides coiled tight. Xander gave Johnny a fist bump as they passed. Johnny then looked right at me and when our eyes met, my heart thumped. My whole body warmed. Nerves, adrenaline and anticipation. Pretty much the way I felt every time I saw him lately, but now it was tinged with something else. Pain, for him. And a restless anxiousness, a fear that maybe he was going to pull away from me, completely.

That I'd find him wrecked at some bar again dripping with women, or worse.

That maybe this time I wouldn't find him until afterwards, when the full damage was already done.

Could I forgive him?

Would I even want to?

These questions spun through my mind as he walked over to me, looking apologetic.

"Angeline, I'm sorry. I just fucking realized how late I am."

I got to my feet and he kissed me. "Our table should be ready. They've been waiting for us." Our waitress circled by, noticing the blond god who'd just strolled in with the giant bodyguard right behind him.

She seated us in a corner of the restaurant at a fairly private table, where I hoped we'd be safe from autograph seekers, while Lamar hung out at the bar.

"So, where were you?" I asked him as soon as we'd gotten settled and put in our drink order. My third, and I told myself it should really be my last. I didn't want to get all boozy and emotional if things went sour tonight. I really wasn't sure where we were at, or where *he* was at, since the last week he'd been so busy… meeting up with his friends, spending time with Rory, and hardly home or around me at all.

He'd even been coming home late and slipping into his bed—where I'd wait for him every night—to sleep with me without instigating sex. It felt strange, since we were so early in our relationship and we'd been so hot and heavy up until the day he'd told me about his painful past.

He met my eyes, and I could feel his hesitation about whatever he was about to tell me. "I was with Amber. I hope that doesn't bother you."

"Why would it bother me?" It was an automatic response, defensive. But… I really wasn't sure if it should bother me or not. Amber was pretty, she'd won over the likes of Dylan Cope, and she was once married to Johnny. I couldn't say I had no reason whatsoever to be bothered, considering I'd seen him with two women wrapped around him several nights ago.

"I just needed to talk to her. To apologize about how I treated her in the past. That's all."

"Oh. Well, how did she take that?"

"Really well."

I considered that. "How did you treat her in the past?"

Before he could answer that, a couple of waitresses, not ours, came up to the table. "Excuse us! Hi! Johnny… I'm Cleo, this is Elaina. Could we please get a picture?" The taller waitress was talking to Johnny, in a rush, like she wanted to do this quickly, before she got in trouble for it. She already had her phone in-hand.

I knew what this was. It happened all the time with Elle, even with staff who should be expected to behave better. *Fans.* Fans who'd knock down their own grandmother to get a selfie with a celebrity they admired. They'd probably steal the cutlery after we left, because Johnny licked it.

My sister had a hell of a lot of these fans.

Johnny glanced at me. I just rolled my eyes and waved him on. I could see Lamar getting off his barstool and heading over already.

"I'll take a photo for you," I told her, putting out my hand for her phone.

"Oh. Thanks." She handed me the phone, like she'd just noticed me sitting here.

The girls leaned in on either side of Johnny and smiled prettily. He gave the camera a practiced look, an expression that looked nothing like the Johnny I knew. This was Johnny O, rock star. Gorgeous and composed, sly and utterly unknowable. A fiction. A fantasy.

I took a few pics, then shoved the phone back at the waitress. "Thank you!" she said, her eyes glued to her phone while the other girl shook Johnny's hand.

"I love your music. 'Up in Smoke' is my favorite. You should sing more."

"Thank you. I'd love to," Johnny said graciously. I studied his face as the girls hovered. That practiced mask he'd slipped on, so quickly. His body language even shifted, his angles sharpening. Heated and closed all at once. *Look but don't touch.*

Lamar stepped in when the girls didn't promptly clear out, thrusting his massive arm between them and Johnny. "He's on a date," Lamar said blandly, an impassive wall of take-no-shit. "This isn't the time." He swept the girls out of our sight, post haste. One of them met my eyes briefly, looking confused, probably about the "date" part.

Yup, to some people I was utterly invisible. Making peace with that fact was rather freeing. I was getting there. I could accept that I was of zero value to some.

So long as I was of extreme value to my man.

His eyes met mine, the mask slipping. "Sorry about that."

"Not your fault. I've been with Elle in public a time or two. I know some people have no clue."

"Where were we?" he said.

Then our waitress came by to drop off our drinks. We gave her our dinner orders and Johnny told her, "We'll take it to go, as soon as possible," then handed her a credit card.

When she'd gone, he told me, "I need to get out of here."

I understood. He didn't want to have an emotional conversation in a restaurant. If I'd known it was going to be one, I wouldn't have agreed to meet him here.

Maybe he didn't know it was going to be one, either.

"You were about to tell me," I reminded him, "how you treated Amber when you were married to her. But we don't have to talk about that here."

"I treated her not well," he said bluntly, but he seemed to have trouble holding my gaze. "I hurt her pretty badly. I cheated on her. I was a different person then than I am now. At least, I behaved differently."

"Not that differently," I said, holding his gaze.

This time, he held my gaze right back. "I didn't cheat on you, Angie."

"There were other women touching you, and you weren't stopping them. They were leaning on you, touching your hair… there has to be a line, Johnny."

We hadn't talked about that part, not really. But I definitely couldn't stop seeing it in my mind and wondering, *What if? What if I didn't show up when I did?*

"I know that," he said.

"What if some guy, or guys, were pressing their bodies up against me and putting their fingers in my hair, whispering in my ears? How would you feel about walking in on that?"

"That's not happening," he said darkly.

"Then why did it happen with you and those girls?"

"Because that's an old pattern of mine. It's default behavior. But I went home with you."

"Because I showed up."

"You have to know how important you are to me."

"Then treat me that way."

His eyes softened as he gazed at me with a kind of hope. "I do. I told you…" He faded off.

"About the shooting."

"Yes." He looked down at his drink.

"That was hard for you. I know."

"Not just hard." He looked into my eyes. "I'd never told anyone before. No one but Rory."

"I'm really glad you told me."

He blew out a rough breath. "I'm really sorry about that night, at Champagne. I'm sorry for anything I've ever done that's hurt you. The sad part is I probably don't even know all the things I've done that've hurt you."

I sipped my drink and thought about how best to respond to that. I wasn't going to hold anything back, tip toe around so I didn't hurt him or somehow trigger his PTSD, re-traumatize him. I couldn't live like that in a relationship. I didn't want to hurt him, but we had to be open and honest.

So I went with the one thing that hurt the most.

"You hurt me that night you kissed me, three years ago. Do you remember that?"

"Yeah. I do."

"I was already with Flynn. I had a boyfriend. I'd just stepped outside to call Courteney. She was on her way to the party. It was too loud to call from inside. I wasn't expecting to run into you. I wasn't expecting that to happen."

"I wasn't either," he said sincerely. "My mom died that night."

"What?"

He rubbed a hand over his face. "I'd gotten the call while I was at that party. From my dad. And I handled that by getting wasted. And kissing you, apparently."

"I'm sorry," I breathed. "I didn't know."

I knew his mom had died, a few years ago. Shayla had mentioned it in passing at some point, but it must've been after the fact. If I knew it happened that night, I might've connected those dots. But Shayla hadn't said much about it. She never knew Johnny's mom, personally.

"It doesn't excuse that I hurt you," he said.

"I know. But I'm sorry anyway. Were you ever close to her? I mean, after what happened…?"

"Yes. And no. I didn't see her much in the years before she died. It was sudden. An overdose of pills. Not really sure if it was on purpose or not. But she really struggled with depression. After… the carjacking."

"Oh."

"She was totally different in my memories from childhood. She was kind of wild. Loud, in a good way. Always talking, always laughing, always up to something. She'd take me to festivals and concerts and she'd always have music playing. We'd have dance parties all the time, just the two of us. My dad would watch us dance. It seemed to make him happy." He got a faraway look for a moment, like he was reliving some memory. "They seemed really happy together. Before the divorce."

"Maybe they were," I offered. "For a while."

"I stopped visiting her when she got really sick. I mean, mentally ill. I didn't know how to handle it. I hurt her a lot, I think." He refocused on me. "I don't know why I'm such a dick to people, Angie. It's a chronic problem."

"You're not a dick."

He laughed, humorlessly. "I left you waiting for me tonight and I didn't even realize I was late."

"Why?"

"Amber wanted to photograph me." He shook his head, like he couldn't make sense of it. "She took photos of me. Of my face. Why would she want to do that? After what I did to her? I was so blown away by that, I didn't even know how to process it. I had all these strange feelings about it on the way here. Guilt, mostly, I think. I don't know. I don't even know how to name the emotions. I just kind of zoned out while Lamar was driving. I forgot where we were going."

Wow. I could relate to that feeling; I'd lost my sense of place and direction many times after some emotional argument with Flynn. But I'd never not known what I was feeling. I felt too much, at times, for sure. I'd felt confusion about my feelings. I'd never been totally unable to name what I was feeling, though.

"Maybe Amber's forgiven you," I said gently. "And she can see something beautiful in you, something worth preserving, without wanting anything from you."

Johnny looked uncomfortable with that idea. I wasn't sure why.

"Not every woman you meet wants something from you, Johnny," I told him. "Including your mom. She probably just wanted *you*."

His eyes shone a little and he tried to hide it by looking down when he sipped his drink.

As we waited for our takeout, the conversation turned to other things. The Players' video, which Shayla had danced in, would be released soon, along with the Players' new album. Dirty's new album would release next month, and according to my sister, it was their best work in years. But I joked that she always said that, about whatever her band was working on.

Johnny seemed to take it in stride, but with him, it was so hard to tell what he was really feeling about these things.

He mentioned to me that Amber had done a photo shoot with JC, to accompany some magazine interview. But he didn't seem upset about it, just… neutral. I wasn't sure if that was evidence of growth or not.

Maybe he was just shutting down on that subject.

When our dinner came, Lamar walked us out to Johnny's car. Then

Johnny drove me home while Lamar took a cab so we could be alone. In the car, Johnny told me about how Noah had signed some endorsement deal with one of the big drum companies, despite him and Johnny being "regrouping" their band; it meant he'd have service at concerts on both sides of the Atlantic when they got touring again, which was a step up in his career. In turn, I told him about how Courteney had started work on her next book, a retrospective on the Vancouver music scene, and maybe she'd want to interview him for it sometime.

Lots of good things were going on around us. Maybe we were hoping that some of it would rub off on us.

When we got home, Lamar vanished into his suite. He seemed to have a knack for knowing exactly when to disappear. I unpacked our food at the long dining table between Johnny's kitchen and living room. He made us both a vodka and juice and we sat down to eat, and to continue our talk.

"What does Rory say about it?" I probed gently.

"About what?"

"About the dick thing. You know, your habit of hurting people."

He blew out a breath. "He says I've been living inside a fortress."

"What does that mean?"

"He says I've built a wall around myself, to keep myself safe. He said I did it when I was a kid, after what happened. The shooting." He swallowed. "He said that it's the place where the boy I was went to hide from what happened. It's the place we have to go sometimes, to find out what I'm feeling. Because I don't know how to tell him how I'm feeling in any other way." He stopped.

"Go on. Please. What do you mean by that?"

"I mean that emotionally, I'm numb. I've been that way for a long, long time. I don't know how to go inside myself and put whatever I'm experiencing into words. The boy in the fortress, that's how we talk about it. It makes the feelings more accessible to me. The boy might be in pain, but I'm just… numb." He shook his head a little. "I sound crazy."

"No. You don't. But… I've seen you have emotions. Like anger, for sure."

"Yeah. I've gotten angry lately a time or two."

"So then you're not really numb."

"Maybe just not as numb as I used to be. But anger, frustration… I think those are the only feelings that have ever run rampant in me as an adult."

"What about good feelings?"

"Like what?"

"Happiness. Joy."

"I don't know if I know what happiness is."

"I know you feel pleasure when we're together."

"Pleasure." He seemed to think about that. "Yeah. But it takes a lot. Like drinking or music, I have to do those to the extreme to get a rush off of it. It's not one drink, it's gotta be twelve. It can't be a top 100 song, it's gotta be number one."

"And when that doesn't happen?" I was pretty sure, from my research on his career, that Breakneck had never had a number one hit on any chart.

"That's where the frustration and anger sets in," he admitted. "And with women… hooking up with some fan or some woman I meet at a party doesn't really do it. It's not the same rush as the girlfriend of my bandmate taking me back to her hotel room."

I tried to digest that. My meal was getting less appetizing by the minute.

"I know that's wrong," he said.

"So… what about sex? Isn't that pleasurable?"

"Sex is… discardable. It's barely worth it. Having to potentially deal with another person's needs, their emotions, for any length of time… Sex often comes with those things, at least for the woman, if not for me."

I sucked back a breath, quietly, trying not to take what he was saying personally and freak out. He was opening up. I knew this was hard for him. I knew this was rare for him. I also heard what he just said, about how hard it was to put his feelings into words. So I tried, really hard, not to be hurt by his words.

Then he reached across the table and took my hand. "Unless it's like it is with us."

"Us?"

"Yeah. With you… the pleasure is so intense… I crave it. Because I've never felt anything like it. It's not just physical pleasure. The emotions are overwhelming, even if I don't fully understand what they are. That's probably why I fell for you so fast."

"You… fell for me?"

"Yeah. I fell for you. Hard." He squeezed my hand and I couldn't hold back my smile. "Even that first time we kissed… I probably could've fallen for you way back then, Angie. But even so, I really should've apologized to you for that. I would've, maybe, but I didn't want to upset Shayla. Or upset you. So I just went on pretending it didn't happen. I thought maybe you'd assume I was just being a drunken asshole that night and let it go. But it wasn't like that for me."

"What was it like?"

"It… overwhelmed me. Whenever something bad happens, I have these two coping mechanisms. I run. Or I reach out for the nearest distraction, if there is one available. And the distraction has to be all-consuming enough to work. Occasionally that means getting stupidly drunk. Or stupidly high. Or smashing up a hotel room. Or… sex. When I got the news about my mom that night…" He sighed shortly. "I grabbed on to you. But when I kissed you, I don't know… something happened. It got to me. It bothered me, when you pulled away. I thought it was because I was so raw about what happened to my mom. But it was more than that. It was disturbing how much I wanted you."

"Yeah. Well… that was how it felt for me, too."

"I'm sorry," he said, sincerely, with all the regret he'd obviously felt about it since that night.

"I'm not."

We stared at each other as that sank in, for both of us.

"You had a boyfriend. I should never have fucked with you like that."

"Honestly…" I swallowed, admitting the truth to him that I'd never admitted before, even to myself. "If you'd pressed it that night… I would've broken up with Flynn a lot sooner."

Johnny got up and came around the table to sit right next to me. His hands slid into my hair, holding me close. "I'm sorry, Angeline. I never, never meant to hurt you."

"I know. But if you'd really wanted me… I would've been yours."

We breathed together for a long moment, our eyes tangled together. "Angie." He breathed out a heavy sigh. "I really wanted you."

I sighed, too. "*Fuck.*"

He kissed me, lightly.

"We're stupid," I whispered.

He smiled. Then he looked deep in my eyes. "I would've hurt you," he said soberly. "If we'd hooked up back then. Without meaning to. I would've hurt you… much worse."

"So, maybe… things happened how they were meant to happen."

"Yeah," he said, though I could feel his lingering regret. That *what if…?* feeling. I felt it, too.

What if we'd gotten together sooner?

"Flynn was good to me," I told him gently. "So, there's that. I don't regret my relationship with him. At all. I just regret hurting him."

"Yeah. I get that." Johnny sat back and took a sip of his almost forgotten drink. Neither of us seemed all that interested in the food. "I'm not good at relationships, Angie. The ones I keep in my life… they're sort of calculated. They serve a purpose. There are very few people besides my dad, my stepmom and my sister, who I really trust and call a friend. Noah, Lex, Shane, Dane. Lamar, too. Yash. I feel safe with them, maybe because they know a version of me that I let them know. But even they think I'm a jerk. That asshole the world knows as Johnny O is basically the only way I know how to function in the world."

"There's so much more to you than that, though," I told him. "I hear what you're saying. But just because you have a hard time expressing your feelings doesn't mean you're not capable of them. Your fear of abandonment is a driving force in your life, I get it. But what happened to you when you were eight years old is a part of who you are, forever. It didn't make you a bad person. Maybe it just made it harder for you to connect with the good person you are. And to connect with other people."

"Yeah. Definitely."

"You're so protective of that part of you that got hurt. But working so hard to protect that boy… it comes at a cost, Johnny. I know it does. I've seen your nightmares."

He gave me that haunted look, the one I'd glimpsed in his eyes a few times now. "So… what if I open up, tell people everything there is to know about me, and they don't like who I really am? Or what I've done?"

"Then fuck them."

"What if they're horrified?"

"You were just a boy, Johnny. It was self-defense."

"What if they think I'm evil? To some people, it's murder, any way you look at it."

"They're wrong."

"What if I embarrass my parents?"

"You were a *child*."

"What if my friends don't want me around their kids? What if my sister looks at me differently?"

I knew this was his worst fear, finally expressed. I could hear it in his voice. It was a debilitating fear; one that had stopped him from getting close to people.

*What if they think I'm a monster?*

Because deep inside, that was what he thought he was, because of what he did.

It broke my heart to know that was how he really felt about himself. That the horrendous experience he'd been through as a child had warped and destroyed his self-worth like that, his self-image.

"Shayla really doesn't know?" I asked him gently. He couldn't possibly think Shayla would think he was a monster. And yet… I was pretty sure that was his fear.

"No one knows. No one but my dad and Rory, and now you, and Noah, Shane and Lex. I never told anyone because I knew my dad didn't want me to. He changed our whole life, gave us a new home, so no one would ever know. But sometimes…"

"You wish he didn't. So everyone would already know and then you wouldn't have to tell them. Or fear telling them."

"Yes."

"We all have things that are hard to say, Johnny," I told him. "And hard to live. I may not have a lot of experience with this kind of thing. But I know that my sister's husband, Seth, survived being abandoned as a kid, being orphaned. And he managed to overcome addiction to some nasty drugs. I know that my best friend Courteney's brother, Cary, survived the death of a dear friend. And he managed to overcome debilitating grief and anxiety. Both of those guys are extremely successful in their careers now, and they have families. They have love. And none of that happened overnight. So I know you can continue to survive this and thrive. Some things are harder to survive than others, sure. But we all keep secrets because we're scared to tell people and have them turn away from us."

"Even you, Angel?" he said gently.

"Of course." I took a deep breath and confessed to him, "I didn't tell you the whole truth about my breakup with Flynn. He didn't exactly say he didn't want to have kids. He said he didn't want to have kids *with me*."

"I'm sorry," Johnny said. "That's a shitty thing to hear from someone who's supposed to love you."

I took a deep breath and gathered my will to be grown up about it. It had been a hard thing to do, in the end. "I don't blame him, though. He spent three years with a woman who always had her eye on something else. I was trying so hard to figure out who I was, where I fit in, I was always looking to see what I was missing out on. And that included men. I couldn't stop dreaming of another man, and he felt it."

"Another man?" He considered that. "Who?"

"You really want to know?"

"Yeah. I do."

"No one specific." I sighed. "And… a lot of specific someones. Just… someone who wasn't him." Then I took a breath and added, "Someone like you."

Johnny didn't look happy to hear it. More like he couldn't believe I would say such a thing.

"I'm not a good man, Angeline."

"When you say things like that to me, I know you're trying to run away again."

"I'm not. I'm right here."

"But I can feel you pulling away. Trying to hide from me. If you really want to make amends and build trust, you need to open up to people. Including me. People need to know who you are if you want them in your life. *I* need to know who you really are. Not this overconfident jerk you try to be," I added, trying to drive home my point with a touch of humor.

"Yeah," he agreed. "I'm realizing that."

But I could tell he was still afraid.

That night, when we went up to bed, we made love, slow and passionate, for the first time since he shared his dark secret with me. And I could feel that he was holding back. Not just physically. I could feel his inner turmoil, his struggle, his pain. I could feel him… *feeling*.

And I wondered, what would that be like—burying your feelings so deep, for so long, that you could barely identify what they were… and then experiencing them starting to surge up to the surface, outside of your control, pulsing through your body and soul?

I knew how to feel.

What would it be like to not feel at all, then to learn how to feel again?

I wanted to make him feel *better*; to make every feeling he had when we were together a good one. No, not just good. Incredible.

But that wasn't really in my power. I couldn't control someone else's feelings.

I wanted him to feel better now that he'd shared his traumatic experience with me.

But I really wasn't sure that he did.

# Chapter Thirty-Six

**Johnny**

I woke from the nightmare, struggling to breathe.

The light of near dawn was creeping over me, and I realized I hadn't closed the blinds all the way last night. The air felt filmy, murky, like it did on an overcast day.

I caught my breath.

I found Angeline lying next to me, the sheet wrapped around her waist. And I remembered the intense sex we'd had, late into the night. Her tits peeked out below her cropped top, which had ridden up, and my dick started to harden.

I eased toward her and carefully slid the shirt up a little more, fully exposing the soft swells of her breasts and her perfect pink nipples. They were soft in sleep, but when I wrapped my lips around one and sucked gently, the pink bud hardened and Angeline started to stir.

She slithered on the mattress a bit, arching her back and stretching, and I sucked a little harder. Wet, slow, luxurious sucks that quickly had her panting.

I moved down and slipped her panties off as her eyes drifted open, blinking at me. "Don't move," I told her.

She smiled a little.

I slid my hands under her thighs and gripped, tugging her toward me, straightening out her hips. When I let go, her thighs relaxed open a bit, presenting her clit to me perfectly.

I breathed hotly on her clit, making her squirm. "Don't move an inch. Even when you come."

She sighed. "Okay, Johnny."

"If you move, then I can't make you come. Then you'll have to go about your day knowing you could've started the day coming on my face, and instead, you were naughty and got nothing."

She giggled softly. "That's okay. Then I'll just wait until you go to your meeting, and then I'll put on one of your shirts and lay in your bed playing with my pussy and I'll make myself come. Maybe if you're lucky, I'll take a picture of it and send it to you."

Damn. Girl was impossible to top.

Even when I was topping her.

I stirred, my hard dick digging into the bed.

"Then I'm afraid I'm gonna have to come home and tie you down, naked, with your legs spread, and jerk off on you." Her eyes glazed over as, hopefully, she pictured that scene. My dick throbbed against the bed. I wasn't sure who I was torturing more. "And I won't make you come, no matter how much you beg me."

"Bullshit. You love it when I beg."

"I do. That's how you'll know how upset with you I am."

"So upset… you'll come all over me."

"Yup."

"What a terrible punishment. Please, don't," she said sarcastically.

"Shush now and keep still." I drifted the tip of my tongue over her clit, then wriggled it around. She inhaled sharply, and I could feel her straining not to move. "Good girl. Do you want your morning orgasm or not?"

"Yes, please."

"That's more like it."

I licked my lips and wrapped them around her clit, then sucked in a slow, luxurious rhythm, making sure to keep my mouth wet, until my spit was running down between her legs, mingling with her juices. She was crying out softly, and I just kept going, patiently, content to suck on her sweet little clit all morning. She was trembling faintly, trying so hard to do as she was told and keep still.

I rewarded her, finally, by sliding a finger inside her dripping wet cunt as I sucked, and her hips suddenly bucked, hard. She spasmed around my finger, crying out, and I pulled back, releasing her clit and taking my finger back. "Bad girl," I admonished, watching her pussy convulse.

"Johnny! Don't stop! Oh! God!" She whimpered with relief as my mouth met her clit again, sucking harder. Then she screamed and her hips went wild, bucking against me. Very bad. We'd have to work on that. Later.

Right now, I didn't give a fuck if she was following my orders or not. Her body convulsed helplessly as I gently suckled and the pangs of orgasm rolled through her. I watched her soft tits bounce, her soft mouth drop open, her head rolling from side to side as I gave her pleasure.

This… I could get totally lost in this. I was stupidly addicted to it.

Getting Angeline off. Getting off with Angeline.

If she walked into a business meeting and said she needed to suck my cock, right then and there, I'd probably take it out. Except that the thought of another man seeing her like this…

In my mind, a heady montage of Angeline played out as I suckled her clit and she sobbed my name. Her sweet mouth stuffed full of my cock. My hard, swollen shaft, pulsing with veins, sliding in and out of her wet pussy, her legs spread high and wide, as she whimpered for more. Her tongue flickering over my nipples, licking down my abs, the hungry, needy look in her eyes just before I fed the head of my cock into her mouth or into her cunt. The way she moaned or gasped my name…

"Johnny…" She came again and I realized I'd been sucking harder, getting carried away. Her body pulsed and writhed, and I kept at it until she settled back down. "Oh, baby…" She moaned languidly, and I lifted up to crawl over her.

I kissed her breasts, then her sweet mouth, slow and hot, and she wrapped her arms around me.

I nudged her open with my cock and thrust into her, slow. Sank myself deep, until I'd bottomed out, my cockhead shoved against her limits. I'd barely seated myself when I was coming. I groaned as my climax shuddered violently through my body, pumping hot come into her in long, aching convulsions. My heart pounded as I emptied into her.

Her sex drunk eyes met mine.

I lay still, holding her there, holding her eyes with mine. My cock stretching her, my hips tight against her as I sought some unreachable depth, some impossible closeness.

I kissed her face, over and over again.

When I pulled back just to look at her, she gazed up at me with soft eyes.

Those eyes seemed to say *I love you.*

It was like a punch in the gut.

I folded, burying my face in her neck and closing my eyes.

---

Maybe I was backsliding. Already.

I couldn't tell.

It was like one step forward, three steps back, every day. Today, I woke up with Angeline and things were good, and then as the day progressed they just got worse.

I was going to talk to my sister today, because Rory had encouraged me to. Because Angeline had encouraged me to. I was going to tell her the truth. About the car in the rain and my mom and the man with the gun, but I ended up in a bar instead.

At least I had Lamar with me, to be my good conscience.

After a couple of drinks, he drove me home and deposited me in my studio. He left me there with my guitars. I picked one up and started playing.

And that was where Angeline found me, sometime later. The same way she so often found me: playing "Long Train Runnin'," over and fucking over.

"When did you get home?"

I looked up to find her leaning against the door frame. At least she didn't startle the hell out of me this time. I was used to her being around now.

"I don't know. What time is it?"

"It's six. Are you hungry for dinner?"

"No." I probably was. I felt mildly sick from the vodka and tequila I'd drank at the bar. But I just kept playing the song.

She watched my fingers on the guitar for a moment. "I know you're sad," she said sadly, when our eyes met again. "I always know you're sad when you play that song."

"I'm not sad."

"Johnny, something is upsetting you. And whatever it is, I know you're not talking to me about it."

"You want me to talk?"

"Yes."

"Okay." I thought about how to put it. It was fucking strange as hell, trying to put things into words that I'd never talked to a woman about before. "I don't feel sad. I feel numb. I always feel numb when I play this song."

"What song is it, Johnny?" She stepped into the room, hugging herself as she drifted toward me.

"It's called 'Long Train Runnin'.' Would you believe there was a time I couldn't stand this song?"

"Really?"

"I couldn't stand to hear it. It used to trigger something terrible in me. Something… helpless." I felt that helplessness, like a ghost, lingering in the cobwebs of my subconscious. Like something foreign to me. An intruder. "Then I learned to play it on guitar. I played it until my fingers bled, literally, just trying to purge it out of my system. So maybe I'd stop hearing it in my dreams."

Angeline's soft eyes filled with tears as she listened.

"I played it until I could get numb when I heard it, instead of my stomach dropping out and my anxiety spiking through the roof. This song… it used to make me shake so hard. Out of nowhere, boom, I'm in some restaurant and this song comes on, and I fucking freak out. Shake, sweat, go throw up in the bathroom. But now… nothing."

Angeline was watching me carefully. "I don't know what that's like," she said gently, because being her, she was trying to understand. To empathize. Something she did easily and well. But on this… I wasn't surprised that she was out of her depth. Regular people didn't usually throw up just hearing some random song. "But I guess it must be a relief to be able to play it now?"

"Relief…" I turned that word over in my head. "Maybe. I never thought of it that way. It's more like… a curse. A vice. Something I'll never be rid of but I have to learn to live with. And something I can't live without. So. I played it over and over until I was desensitized, detached from it completely."

"So, now it's just a song? And you can enjoy it?"

"I don't enjoy it. It is just a song. It's a good song. But for me it's like a painkiller or something. It nullifies whatever I'm feeling. Playing it over and over, focusing so hard on purging its power, saved me from having to face feelings. I'd just focus on the song and play until whatever I was starting to feel was gone. But that's terrible, right?"

"I don't think it's terrible," Angeline said carefully. "It sounds like a coping mechanism."

"It's a crutch." I put the guitar aside. I was still playing the song, without even thinking about it… the chorus, over and over, and when I realized it, I saw how it made Angeline uneasy.

She watched me, but stood in front of me with her arms wrapped around herself.

"It was the song that was playing when that man got in the car," I told her.

I didn't say, *when I shot him*. She knew the rest.

Her eyes looked pink and I knew she was trying not to cry. I knew that was hard for her, fighting back her feelings. I knew she was doing it for me.

"You could've told me that," she said softly. "It might've helped me understand, if you'd just told me that."

"How am I gonna tell you that?" I said lightly. "I'm gonna ruin the song for you, too?"

Maybe that was terrible of me to try to make light of the subject, but Angeline just shook her head. "Let me share in it."

"In what?"

"In whatever you're going through. That's what a relationship is."

"I'm not loading all my crap on you at once, Angeline. You'd drown."

"I'm not kidding."

"Neither am I."

"It's not loading all your crap on me, Johnny. It's allowing me to know you. And while we're being honest, I'm not taking on all your crap, believe me. I don't expect you to take on all of mine. But can't we, like, hold hands and skip down that road together or something?"

I laughed a little, because leave it to Angeline to paint that picture. "Did you actually just make me smile?"

"Yes."

"Come here."

She came, and I pulled her onto my lap. Her arms wrapped around me. "Why won't you trust me to let me get closer to you?" she asked me, and I heard the pain in her words. "All I want is to be close to you."

"You want to know the truth?" I took a deep breath and just fucking told her, because if I didn't, I'd just be hurting her, and somehow that took the choice away. I couldn't not tell her. "The truth is that she left me."

"Who left you?"

"My mom. She left me in the car."

"What do you mean?"

I blew out a breath, rubbing my hand over my face. It was still so painful, the memory of that moment… what I remembered of it… that it was hard as hell not to cry. Even when I didn't particularly feel anything about it, on the surface… the tears would come. Because inside, it was still a deep, raw wound.

But I forced the words out, dry-eyed. "She got out of the car… and he got in the car. The guy with the gun. She left me there."

Angeline appeared speechless.

"I mean, what was she supposed to do, right?" I said dryly. "He put a gun in her face. What the fuck was she supposed to do?"

"Johnny… I didn't know. I didn't really think about… how it all happened…"

"What the fuck was she supposed to do," I repeated, the ghost of that old helplessness drifting in the cobwebs at the back of my mind. "But still… she left me."

Angeline searched my eyes. "That's it, isn't it?" she said breathlessly, her arms tightening around me. "That's the part that hurt you the most."

I looked away. "All of it hurt me."

She was right, though. That part had fucked me up so badly, I could never make sense of it.

Being hurt by a stranger… being hurt by myself over something I did in self-defense, as a child, when I didn't even comprehend the consequences… those were hard hurts to survive. But being left by my own mother, in that car, to a stranger with a gun…

I'd forgiven her. Of course, I'd forgiven her. As an adult, I could see it from a point of view that was impossible as a teen.

He had a gun.

What the fuck was she supposed to do?

In that moment… it probably happened so fucking fast anyway. She was probably in shock. For all I knew, he forcibly pulled her out of the car and tossed her aside. I really didn't remember. I didn't see it all happen that clearly.

From what Rory and I pieced together, he figured I'd either been asleep in the backseat and woke up after the man got in, or I'd blocked the details out. The first theory would explain why I didn't scream or call out to my mom or make any sound. Though maybe I was in shock.

So many fucking questions… questions maybe I thought someday I'd get answers for, from my mom… when I was brave enough to actually ask her. When I thought I could ask her, have a conversation with her about it, without melting down in rage at her or hurting her by making her remember. I didn't want to do that, so I never had that conversation with her.

And now I never would.

"Do you want to talk about it?" Angeline asked me when I remained silent.

"I don't know how to talk about it." I laughed bitterly. "Every time I think I'm finally 'healed,' I end up having a resurgence of symptoms because I'm triggered or stressed, and it's not always the same trigger or the same symptoms. So I don't even know, at first, that it's happening all over again. It fucks with my head. It's maddening. It just never ends. And after all these fucking years, all the hours in therapy… all the hours spent talking about it… I still don't know how to."

Angeline held my eyes. Hers were soft with sympathy. "All you have to do is tell the truth."

Yeah. She made that seem so beautifully simple.

I thought about all the things I could say. But there were literally thousands of words, between all those hours of therapy. Which were the ones that would explain to her what it all meant to me, without dragging her, or myself, through every painful detail?

What were the words that would help her to understand *me*?

"So, here's another truth," I said carefully. "After it happened, I couldn't talk for a while. That was why they kept me in the hospital so long. And then when I did talk, I stuttered. So then I avoided talking. For years. And talking about what happened… that's the scariest conversation to have. Because what if the stutter comes back? What if I spiral into depression about it or start snorting lines again?"

Angeline's arms tightened around me, like she wanted to comfort me. Nothing I said ever seemed to repel her. I couldn't imagine how that was possible, but it was.

She was like Rory that way, maybe. Both of them cared enough about me to stick around and talk it through, even when it got ugly.

I looked into her beautiful, sympathetic eyes, as hard as it was. "It was Rory who gleaned my interest in music and recommended singing lessons. Maybe that's why I've always loved him so much. He fucking saved me. But more than that… he saw me, *me*, better than anyone else ever did. Better than I ever did."

"Wow. I love Rory."

"You will when you meet him, I'm sure."

"So… it was Rory who basically nudged you into becoming a musician?"

"It was more than a nudge. When I took to the singing lessons so well, he bought me a guitar. What psychiatrist does that?"

"I don't know," she said. "I've never actually been in therapy or anything. My life has been mercifully trauma-free."

I squeezed her gently. "I'm glad. But believe me… it's not common to have a doctor take that kind of interest, or that kind of risk. He did a lot of things that were probably frowned upon by his peers. But that was why I connected with him, maybe. He was a rule breaker."

"Like you," she mused.

"Maybe." I shook my head, remembering how my dad told me, when I was seventeen, that it was Rory who bought the guitar for my thirteenth birthday and gave it to my dad to give to me. Rory didn't want credit, and he didn't want it to seem inappropriate. But he'd seen what even my dad hadn't picked up on right away: that music was bringing me back to life.

"Singing was the thing," I told her, "more than speech therapy, even, that helped me get over the stutter. It still comes back every once in a while when I'm really stressed out. I just kind of choke and can't get the words out. And I shut right up to try to hide it. That's why I hate singing in front of people. I'm afraid it'll happen when everyone's watching. So I do everything I can to avoid that. Record my vocals alone in the studio. I'll sing backup onstage, but only because the pressure isn't on me to carry the vocals."

"That's wild," Angeline said, her eyes going wide. "We need to get you singing, then."

"Of course you would say that," I teased her. "You love my voice."

"I'm serious. You have to face your fears, baby. It's like the song you play over and over. You have to desensitize yourself. You need to fully immerse yourself in the thing you're afraid of in order to diminish its power over you. I think it's called exposure therapy or something."

"Uh-huh. I'm sorry, I didn't know you had a degree in psychology."

"Actually, I might have. If I didn't flunk out."

"Seriously?"

She shrugged. "A few semesters in, I decided it was too much work. What can I say. I was young and lazy."

I laughed a little. "You would've made a terrible therapist, Angeline. I'm sorry, but you're way too soft. You'd cry at every appointment. You'd bum your patients out."

She sighed, not even a little offended. "That's true."

"So, let's get back to this exposure therapy bullshit. What are *you* most afraid of, by the way?"

"Uh… I don't know. Nothing?"

"Nice try, brat. What are you afraid of?"

"Well… I mean, ax murderers are scary."

"Okay. So how about we toss you in a dark cave with a bunch of murderous men wielding axes and see how fast you get over your fear."

"That's hardly what they do in exposure therapy, just so you know. And I am not enjoying that you're shitting all over my point right now. Murderers with axes are dangerous. Choking while singing in front of a crowd is embarrassing but it will not kill you."

Shit. Should've known that would backfire on me. Girl was way too clever.

"I'm not enjoying," I told her, "that you just turned around and fucked me up the ass with my own argument."

"It's what I do," she purred, running her finger over my lip. I bit it and she gasped. Then I licked it and she made a soft, hungry noise. Her eyes sparked, then warmed over… then went molten with desire.

And my guts went molten just looking at her.

"If I gave you a ring right now," I asked her, "would you stay with me forever?"

She sucked in a soft breath. Neither of us seemed to know I was going to say that.

But I said it.

"Johnny." She kissed my face, over and over.

"I'm not kidding, Angeline."

She looked into my eyes. "A ring is just a symbol, baby. It would have to be a promise. I'd need to know you were here to stay. If I knew that…" She shivered as I pulled her closer. "Yes, I'd stay."

I caught her lips and kissed her, warm and soft. I breathed in her scent, asking myself what the fuck I was gonna do to show her I was here for her. And how I was gonna man up the courage to give her everything she deserved.

*Trust.*

I had to trust her, just like I wanted her, so badly, to trust me.

I pressed my forehead to hers and closed my eyes.

"Would you have gotten out of that car?" I asked her.

"*Oh*… you can't ask me that. Johnny… You can't ask yourself that. It's not fair."

"I wouldn't have." I opened my eyes and looked into hers. "If that was my kid in the backseat. If that was *our* kid…" I tightened my arms around her. "I swear to God, Angeline, he would've had to shoot me before I'd get out of that car."

She took my face in her hands. "And what would that have done, if your mom had that conviction in that moment?" she said softly. "Think that through. You're eight years old, you're in that car, now your mother's dead, and you're still in danger."

"I know." I shuddered. "Believe me, I've thought it through."

She sighed, her arms sliding around my shoulders. "I think the answer to this question is that there is no answer. And that's the part that must torture you. Because it's so unfair. There's nothing that could be done differently because you can't turn back time. And even if you could… there might not have been a better outcome. You've heard the saying, hurt people hurt people? Well, bad people do bad things that ruin other people's lives. It's up to us not to allow it." She kissed me softly. "Please, don't let him ruin yours."

"Do you think he knew I was there, in the backseat?" I asked her through the lump in my throat, like I'd asked myself, and asked Rory, so many times.

"Do you?" she asked me right back.

"I don't know. Why would he put down the gun, if he knew I was there?"

"He probably didn't, then. He probably didn't even know you existed,

Johnny. Why would you give him the power to control your life for the rest of your life?" She hugged me tight.

"How is it that I can talk to you about this stuff?" I marveled, stroking her hair.

"Because I'm awesome."

"Tell me something I don't know," I murmured.

Her soft eyes met mine again. "I think you need to tell more people the things you've told me. Take down the wall of that fortress you built."

"I really don't know how to, Angel."

"Same way you built it," she said. "Brick by brick."

# Chapter Thirty-Seven

**Johnny**

That night, after hours of working in my studio, playing around with song ideas, I came up to bed late and found Angeline in my bathtub.

She looked like she'd been crying and it wrenched my guts, a hot, painful squeeze around my vital organs. There was a half-empty wine bottle next to the tub and a glass in her hand.

I sat down on the edge of the tub and took the wine from her, setting it aside. We'd had dinner together when I took a break from work, but I thought she'd gone home to Shayla's after that. She'd said they were having a girls' night.

"Hey, sweetheart," I said gently. "How long have you been up here?"

She looked at me, unfocused, through the tears in her eyes. "How long does it take to turn into a raisin?" She held up her fingers to show me her little fingertips, pink and wrinkly like raisins.

I took her hand and kissed them. "What's wrong?"

"I told Shayla about us." She sniffled. "She flipped out."

I cupped her face in my hand and looked into those watery blue-gray eyes, wondering what she was feeling. Pain? Sadness? Despair?

All of the above.

I could see that. I could feel that, when I really let myself. It was terrible, like having a giant scab peeled off my ribs, from the inside out. It hurt like hell. It was so uncomfortable, I knew now why I'd avoided feeling these things. Feeling for a woman. Falling in love.

But I felt it all now.

Her pain, acute, in my body.

I got up and got undressed, then slipped into the tub at the other end and drew her toward me. "Turn around, Angel." She turned and sank back against me, resting her head on my shoulder. I kissed her temple, then her neck, as her head lolled to the side, relaxed. I ran my hands up her arms and kneaded her shoulders. "You feel that?"

"Uh-huh," she said drunkenly, more relaxed from my touch than the wine, I was sure.

"That's me holding you. We're staying together. You and me. No matter what anyone else says or does about it."

She melted into me.

"Shayla will be okay," I assured her. "She loves you. And she loves me."

"I know. She'll accept this, once she gets past being mad at me."

My hands faltered mid-massage. "Why would she be mad at you?"

"Because she warned me not to do this. Not to fall in love with you."

My heart thudded, a dark, brutal rhythm. Fear. I felt an excruciating fear when she said those words. I also felt a hunger like nothing I'd ever known. A desperation to hear her say it again. Need scorched through me, and it wasn't just sexual. It was visceral. Painful.

I pressed my face into the crook of her neck. "Why?" I whispered.

"She thinks you'll hurt me."

"I am hurting you. You're fighting with Shayla because of me."

"We're not fighting. She just got upset. She feels a bit betrayed that I didn't tell her the moment you kissed me. I told her tonight, about what happened, three years ago…" She sighed, growing heavier against me. "I think it helped her to understand, quickly, that this wasn't some whim. That it's deep with us and it's not going anywhere. But… it also hurt her that I didn't tell her back then."

"She really didn't know?"

"No. She trusted me. I mean, she's not dense. She knows I've been spending a lot of time with you. But she believed me when I told her, early on, that there was nothing going on between us. And then she stopped asking. Because… she trusted me." She sighed again. "I'm the worst friend."

"You're not. But… should we have told her sooner?" I wondered. Because how the hell would I know. I didn't know the first thing about being that honest, even with my closest friends. But I was trying to learn.

"No," she breathed. "It's better that she find out now. Now that I'm with you."

"Right," I said, letting a little sarcasm slip in. "I mean, clearly I am making you incredibly happy."

"Johnny… you make me feel better than happy. You make me feel so much more *me* than I am without you. You tap into all the best parts of me and draw them out, and you fucking cherish them."

I didn't know what to say to that. "Well… I love all the parts of you." It was the closest I'd come to telling her I loved her, but the words didn't slide smoothly out. They got choked up in my throat.

"I know you do," she said.

We lay silent for a moment, my heart beating against her.

"I think you need to tell her everything," she said softly. "Otherwise, there are things about you that Shayla will never understand. Things that have probably always caused a rift between you two. People you love can tell when you're not telling them everything there is to know. When you tell her… things will come into focus for her. She'll understand you more. And she'll be glad that you told her."

"I really don't know if I can, Angeline."

"Because you're still afraid it will change things?"

"Yes."

"So, if you can't say it… then why don't you put it in a song?"

"Sure. I'll just write a jingle."

"Johnny O'Reilly. Don't get smart," she said smartly. "You said music and singing helped you to find your voice, right? So can't that still be true for you?"

"Sweetheart," I told her, my voice rough as I kissed her neck, "I think that's always been true for me. There are things I've put into songs that I'd never say to someone in real life."

"Then maybe the best thing you can do for yourself and the people who love you is to put what you went through into a song somehow."

I sighed. And I confessed to her then, something else I'd never told anyone. "I already did."

"You wrote a song about the carjacking and… everything?"

"Actually, I wrote a lot of songs about it. Just none that were any good."

"Are you sure?"

"I'm sure."

"Why aren't they any good?"

"I don't know. Maybe because they're unfinished."

"Did you ever plan to finish them?"

"No."

"Then they're not really songs, are they?" Angeline looked up at me over her shoulder. "I mean, what is a song if no one ever hears it?"

"You're sexy when you're wise."

"Thank you."

I blew out a breath. "I just don't know if I can write those songs, finish them. Play them for people. It feels too big. And too small. And too… everything, all at once."

"That's why you have to play them for people."

Maybe. Maybe not.

"I mean, if you prefer," she said, "you could just write 'Up in Smoke, Part Two.'"

"It *was* Breakneck's biggest song," I mused. "It basically paid for these houses…"

"Uh-huh."

"Can I tell you a secret?"

"Baby, tell me all your secrets."

"I hate that song," I whispered in her ear.

"I know."

"What? How did you know?"

"I can just tell. If you were proud of it, you'd lean into it more. You never talk about how much it sucks to lose Breakneck, meaning the guys and the songs. You seemed to regret losing the path you guys were on. The momentum. The plan. But not the actual music. And for a music lover, that speaks volumes."

"You're being wise again. It's turning me on."

"Good. If I were to give you one piece of advice—"

"One?" I teased.

"One for today, okay? You need to write the songs that are actually meaningful for you. They'll have the best chance of being your biggest successes *and* they're the ones you'll love the most. And if you're playing them hundreds of times at concerts over the course of your career… you better love them, baby. Or you're gonna end up very bitter and unhappy."

"And you know this because…?"

"I have a sister who's in a band."

"Right."

"Also… I can imagine it makes you feel naked and exposed," she said gently, "the idea of singing about those personal, painful things. But you can get the emotion into it without spelling out every detail of the experience you went through. Songs don't have to be literal."

"Thanks. I never thought of that."

She laughed. "Sassy!" She elbowed me gently. "Look… I heard that the Players' first lead single off their new album, the one they shot the video for with Shayla dancing in it, was written by Ash. For Matt. Ash wrote a love song for the man he loves, and in the video there's a woman dancing. How would anyone know what the song is really about unless someone tells them? They won't. Because it's not even that important, for the listener. When you listen, it's about *feeling*."

I listened and I thought about that, but I didn't say anything.

"Dirty's most famous song is 'Dirty Like Me,' right?" she went on. "And no one even knows what it's about. Not really. Why does the songwriter feel dirty? I don't know. You don't know. But we all know what it is to feel dirty, even if we've never had that experience. The beauty of it is that your version of feeling dirty and mine are different. It resonates on so many levels, and yet it's deeply personal."

"So… just write a song as good as Dirty's biggest hit. Sure. No problem."

"Just write the truth, Mr. Sarcastic. And don't worry about sugar-coating it for anyone." She wrapped her arms over mine, around her waist. "Things that are the most personal resonate with the most people. It's a human experience. And even if we haven't had that experience… Johnny, I've never had that specific experience that you had. But I can feel what you're feeling when you talk about it. You make me feel."

"But you feel things so easily," I half-teased.

"Don't let that be your excuse not to write your songs."

"Honestly… even if I write the songs, I don't know if I could play them. I just don't know if I can bare my soul like that to the world, Angie."

"Then start with Noah. Play your songs for Noah. And when you survive that, which I know you will, play them for Shane. Then play them for Lex. Then play them for Dane. And by that time, if you realize that it feels good to play them for other people, play them for Yash. And for Trey. Just take it one set of ears at a time. And I'm telling you, you'll be glad you did."

"What if you're wrong?"

"Then you can go back to hiding in your fortress and shutting people out." She glanced up at me. "I'm serious. You've been there before, right? For a long damn time. What have you got to lose?"

I sighed. "I'll think about that."

"Good. And when you think about that… think about how willing you'd be to die on that sword. To stand by what you write, so that you'll only write songs you believe in so strongly, it won't even matter if no one likes them but you. That's where it starts. That's what Elle always tells me. And when you write songs you believe in that much… other people will love them, too. I know it."

"I get what you're saying. I do. But writing those kinds of songs… It's harder than it sounds."

"It sounds incredibly fucking hard." Angeline turned herself over, pulling up her knees to straddle me, and wrapped her arms around my neck. "That doesn't mean you shouldn't do it, baby."

I raised an eyebrow at her. "You're really trying to be stern with me while your beautiful tits are in my face?" My hands smoothed up her body to cup them gently. Then I leaned in and fed a perfect nipple into my mouth. I gave it a soft, sucking kiss.

She squirmed a little in my lap. "Don't try to change the subject with sweet sex talk," she breathed. "Nothing is going to be easy if you want to heal." She lifted my face in her hands and kissed me softly, and I bit her lip, but she didn't let me turn it into anything more.

Instead, she stroked my hair back from my temples with her thumbs while gazing into my eyes.

"Write your songs, Johnny. And go to therapy. Tell your friends and family what you're going through. *Everything* is screaming at you that you can't build your future anymore unless you take care of the damage caused by your past." She pressed her hand gently to my chest. "Think of it as a bullet," she said softly, "that's still lodged in your heart, encapsulated in layers of scar tissue. It takes painstaking surgery to unearth it and repair the damage."

I took hold of her hand and held it against my pounding heart. How did she always say the right thing? I couldn't even say anything back worth a damn. But my eyes were starting to burn.

"Your injury is psychological," she told me, with so much compassion, I felt it like warm rain, soothing me. "It's invisible to the world. But I see it. Rory sees it. It's an emotional wound, so deep, you need help healing it."

I swallowed. "I know."

"Please tell me you're going to do everything I just asked you to do." She pleaded with me with her pretty gray-blue eyes.

My arms slipped around her. I opened my mouth to answer, but she quickly pressed her finger to my lips, stopping me. "But don't say yes if you don't mean it."

The look in her eyes was so sad and so filled with hope at the same time, it broke my heart to think I'd ever made her doubt me.

"Actually," she said with gentle conviction, "don't say yes at all. Don't say anything. Your actions have always told me far more about where your heart is at. So show me. Show me who you really are, Johnny O'Reilly. Because you're much more than my best friend's brother. You're much more than a rock star. And you're much more than that boy who was left to fend for himself in that terrible moment in that car. You're all of those things, and so much more."

She kissed me, and the sweet strength in this girl… it coursed through me like a cleansing fire. I didn't even have words for how much she made me want to be a better man. It was a bone deep, soul deep urge, to want to break myself apart and fit myself back together, better and stronger than before, so I could be worthy of the woman she was.

"Don't be afraid that people will think less of you when they know the whole truth," she whispered to me.

My heart thudded, because she'd just tweaked a raw, exposed nerve. The fear of abandonment was still acute. Maybe it always would be. "But what if they do?"

"Just be you, Johnny. Write your songs. I'm telling you," she promised me, with conviction. "It won't change a thing."

But she was wrong about that.

It changed everything.

# Chapter Thirty-Eight

**Johnny**

*Sixteen weeks later…*

It was storming out. Rain, wind and darkness… it was eerie, sliding through the downtown streets, so black, the rain sheeting over the car. A huge section of downtown was completely blacked out as we drove into it. A power outage. The police weren't even out yet to direct traffic; it must've just happened.

I wasn't driving. I couldn't drive right before a show, and not in the sheeting rain and dark.

"Just spoke to Elle," Angeline said next to me, hanging up her phone; she'd been on a call while I was texting with Noah. "Champagne is fine. Most of downtown still has power."

"Good." I gave her a slight smile. I didn't want her to know how tense I was. The dark fist in my gut was tight tonight, growing tighter as the storm lashed down around us.

We were heading to Champagne nightclub for a special show. Me and my backup band were going to play my songs for an intimate crowd of industry VIPs and my family and friends. My new songs.

Including *the* songs.

It was a chance to play them for more than just a few friends in my small home studio. So far, only Angeline, Yash, Shane and my band had heard the songs. And tonight, key people in the industry, including reps from several record companies, would be in the room. Along with many of my peers. No media. No fans. Just special guests invited by Yash, Angeline and me.

Yash said the music was so good, we weren't taking it to Trey. We were going to make him come to us. And if he wouldn't, someone else would.

Maybe he was right.

Maybe he was wrong, and this was the last show I'd ever play. But hey, I made a promise to Angeline that I'd die on this sword. I believed in these songs. So did she.

Right now, that was enough for me.

And the fact that Yash and my band believed in them, too, reassured me that we weren't totally crazy.

My phone buzzed with a text and I glanced at it. Yash had been texting me all evening. *What's your ETA?*

I texted him back. *About five minutes.*

I knew he was concerned that I'd choke. Bail. Run. That I'd somehow fail to pull through tonight. I'd never bailed on a show. But there was a first time for everything. And I'd definitely never played a set featuring such deeply personal music.

Or one where I was singing lead vocals.

We rolled up to a red light, finally reaching a set of working street lights. Sort of. They were flashing red. The red light colored the rain on the windshield in between each slash of the wipers, making it look like blood. Rain water, blood. Then clean again. Rain water, blood.

I swallowed and looked away. I was in the backseat of Lamar's car, holding Angeline's hand. There was a time I thought I'd never ride in a backseat again, but Angeline Delacroix, and her love for me, made almost anything seem possible.

"Everything okay?" she asked me lightly. I knew she was worried, too. About me, more than the show. But also about the show. Because she knew how important it was to me.

"All good."

"I'm trying to zip it. You know, not talk," she said. "So you can think and go over the songs in your head and whatever you need to do. Sometimes Elle tells me to shut up before shows because I get babbling backstage and Zane likes quiet before he goes onstage… He does this thing where he stands just offstage checking out the crowd, and no one's supposed to talk to him so he can just be in his head, but if I'm too close, sometimes I forget and get in the way of that. So, I've learned to—"

I was smiling at her and she smiled back.

"Oh. I was just doing it, wasn't I?"

"Yup. But I'm not Zane."

"Then… you want me to babble?"

"I want you to do whatever makes you happy."

Her smile faded. "I love you, Johnny."

I squeezed her hand. "I know."

"Nothing that happens tonight can change that." She meant if I choked. If I bailed or failed or completely fucked up onstage, or whatever.

"I know that too," I told her.

She looked out into the street. "We've got power again," she noted, maybe misreading the reason for my tension. "It's much brighter here."

"Yeah. Hopefully the power outage doesn't affect anything. And everyone can make it."

"As long as Trey is there. I want him to hear what he missed out on. We'll make him rue the day he tossed out your record deal."

"Maybe," I said neutrally. "But that was Breakneck's record deal, not mine."

"True." She smiled at me. "Larissa said she's coming with him, and they were on their way a little while ago."

"Then everything is as it should be."

"Trust me," she said, looking into my eyes. "You're going to make him regret that he ever considered not making an album with Johnny O."

I hoped she was right. But honestly, for me, this night wasn't even about that.

It was just about the songs.

And it was about *her*.

I'd asked her to trust me. To trust this thing between us.

So, I'd worked my ass off for the last few months, pouring my heart and soul into these songs, my guts and my every emotion, every feeling I could scrape up from that deep, dark place in me where I'd locked them down so tight. I wanted to give her something to trust. Something to count on. Something to believe in.

I wanted to be the kind of man who was available to her in every way, whenever she needed me. Because God knew I needed her, and she'd been there for me, in every way.

She'd told me that she wanted all of me, even if I was broken. Well, I was fucking broken. But I was working on it. And meanwhile, I was here to offer her every broken shard of me that I could find, in the truest way I knew how.

With music.

When we pulled up behind Champagne, security had blocked off part of the alley and Lamar rolled us up to the door. A bouncer let us in and a member of Ronan Sterling's security team walked us to the green room; Yash had contracted some of Ronan's guys for tonight's show. I was the first musician to arrive. My band wasn't here yet.

"Do you think you could go find my dad," I asked Angeline, "and bring him back here? Shayla was coming with him. They should be here by now."

"Of course." She gave me a sweet kiss, then headed out.

Alone, I paced the length of the room. Champagne's green room was nicer than any other I'd been in at clubs around town, but none of the other clubs in town were owned by rock stars. It was quiet, sound controlled, with charcoal gray walls and contemporary furniture, one of Katie Mayes' colorful, abstract paintings dominating one wall; an anonymous, faceless guitarist playing his instrument. The couches and chairs were upholstered in emerald-green and sapphire-blue. There was a massive mirror and a makeup table to suit a queen, and a large TV on one wall.

I didn't touch any of it, just paced as I waited for my dad.

I just hoped he got here before the band did. I wanted a moment with him, alone. I didn't plan this moment. I didn't think a lot about how it would go down, just knew that it would. That it would have to, at some point, before he heard my new songs.

Maybe I'd just avoided it for as long as I possibly could, and now time had run out.

Finally, there was a soft knock on the door and Angeline reappeared, with my dad.

"Hey, Dad," I greeted him as he came to clasp my hand and pulled me in for a quick, tight hug.

"Johnny. You look great."

My dad always told me I looked great. I never let him see me looking otherwise.

"I'll give you two a moment?" Angeline offered, lingering by the door in her pretty, pale-pink dress and suede booties.

"Thank you," I told her.

"You'll sit with us?" my dad asked her, and she smiled. I knew she'd met my dad over the years, and my stepmom, Miranda—Shayla's parents—and I wasn't at all surprised that he liked her. But it did make me happy to see it.

"I will. Thanks! I'll go keep Shayla and Miranda company." Angeline beamed at my dad, then blew me a kiss and slipped out, shutting the door.

"Angeline," my dad said thoughtfully, meeting my eyes. His eyes were blue, brighter than mine. His face was etched with knowledge, and the lines that came from the kind of torment known only to a parent who'd watched their child suffer terrible pain. I couldn't even remember him not having those lines on his face, but he must've been young, once. "I always thought she's quite something, that girl," he mused.

"She is."

He took that in, like he wasn't quite expecting that response. He knew I'd been seeing her. I'd mentioned it. But that was all. He'd probably expected me to be over it by now. Moved on. "Are you planning on keeping her around?" he asked me.

"Yes. Definitely. If she'll stay."

"She will. So long as you love her." He studied my response to that.

"Yeah. I figured that one out."

"Good." His eyes twinkled the way they did when he was amused. "Then you're learning."

"I hope so."

"And how is Shayla taking it?"

See, just when I thought my dad was maybe getting out of touch. He always somehow showed me that he was still tuned in. Still watching. That he understood his kids much more than he let on. Donal O'Reilly was all business, most of the time. Practical, tactical, driven. Very successful in business. And very cut and dry when it came to emotions.

Maybe he'd learned, like I did, to bury them, for the most part.

Whatever the reason, he generally seemed to like to pretend that Shayla and I were doing just fine, even on our worst of days. And the idea that the two of us might ever fight? He didn't even want to hear about it. *Don't waste your energy on fighting your family,* he'd say. *You should have each other's backs, no matter what.*

"Well. She's taking it." I scratched my jaw. "I believe she said something to the effect of, 'Worship her or you'll wish you were never born.'"

"Not bad advice." My dad smirked. "Though you'll want to make sure the worship flows both ways. Keep things in balance."

"Yeah. I'm pretty sure we've got that down."

He nodded appreciatively. "So, you're all ready?" He looked me over in my ripped jeans and T-shirt. My dad had always appreciated my style, even though he dressed way more conservatively than I did. He was a suit guy. Tonight, he wore dress slacks and a collared shirt, expensive, clean lines, but in dark colors; his version of rock 'n' roll. He looked somewhat like me, similar build, just older, his hair a pale shade of blond that was starting to turn white. He liked to joke that I got my good looks from him, but we were all in on that joke; any good looks I'd been lucky enough to get came from my mother.

My mom was a drop-dead gorgeous Italian woman with dark hair and darker eyes who'd swept him away with her wild, passionate heart—his words—and then broke his heart when she had a string of affairs that ended in their divorce. He never spoke ill of her in front of me, but he'd told me why they split up, when I was a teenager and I asked him for the truth.

I knew I got more than my looks from her, for good and bad.

My dad was steady as a rock. My mom was… self-indulgent, to put it nicely.

Maybe I was just lucky that he loved me so much—and through so much dark shit—despite how like her I was.

I gestured at a couch. "Have a seat, Dad."

He sat down on the edge of the couch and looked up at me. "This feels serious," he said lightly.

"It is. Potentially. I just feel like I should warn you. That you might not like some of the songs I've been writing. But I'm writing them anyway. And one day, I may put them on an album."

"Why wouldn't I like them?"

"You just might not like the lyrics when you hear them."

"What kind of lyrics? Because once you've heard that 'Wet Ass Pussy' song," he said dryly, "you've heard it all. And thanks to your sister, I'm afraid I have." Maybe he was trying to keep things light. Steer this away from things he didn't want to hear. He was good at that.

But we weren't playing that game tonight.

"I wrote a song to my mom."

His smile faded. "Oh." He recovered quickly. "Well, that's probably a good thing, then. I hope it's a nice tribute."

"Yeah. Maybe. And no, it's not." I wasn't sure how to put it. The song I wrote about her was nice, and it wasn't. Just like my feelings for her. "It's a lot of things."

My dad seemed to be digesting that, thoughtfully.

Years ago, I knew he would've been more upset about this. Today, though, he appeared to be taking it pretty well.

We hadn't talked about my mom in a long time. Not since shortly after she died. But maybe time had finally healed some of those wounds.

"Well, I trust you know what you're doing, Johnny," he said.

"Yeah." I rubbed my forehead. "I also wrote a song to the man in the car."

I didn't say his name. We both knew his name.

But to me, he'd always be the man in the car. The man whose life I took, without meaning to. The man who took so much from me. In that horrendous moment, he wasn't a whole person. Not to me. He was fragments. He was hard, cold metal. He was blood on the glass. He was a terrible mistake.

He was a horrifying set of actions, taken for reasons I'd never understand, that ended in his own death.

I'd forgiven the person who took those actions, for my own sake.

But the actions themselves would probably haunt me for the rest of my life.

"This song," I went on, when my dad didn't seem able to say anything, "has been in me for a long time. Deep in me. In this place I've gone to hide over the years. Rory calls it a fortress."

My dad nodded slowly, taking that in. "Fortress," he repeated. I knew he was giving weight to the idea, because he thought highly of Rory, and of the work he'd done with me, how much he'd helped me, even when he didn't always understand Rory's unorthodox methods.

"The fortress is… this wall I built in my mind." I didn't bother telling my dad what Rory had said about him helping me build it. I didn't want him to feel like I was putting any blame on him. "It was a place that kept me safe, when I was young. But I'm on the outside of it now. And the songs are coming with me."

"Johnny… You know, whatever you need to do to… to feel better about what happened… then that's what you need to do. Especially if it's not hurting anyone."

"Well, this is what I need to do. I couldn't stay trapped in that place forever. The songs couldn't stay trapped in there forever. It was making me crazy."

"You were never crazy. We don't use that word."

"I was going crazy, Dad. I was torturing myself by shutting down. I couldn't feel anything. Unless I drank too much, or fucked too much, or when I was up onstage… That hit of dopamine. Acceptance. Approval. From the fans. From the critics. From *you*. And from women… I've been so fucked up with women for so long. And that's not my mom's fault. Or yours or Miranda's. It's not the fault of any women I've dated. It's my fault. I know that. But I can't keep torturing myself. I can't keep silent anymore. So, I had to write these songs. They're not literal stories. No one's going to know exactly what happened when they hear them. But I know you'll know, so I wanted to prepare you. These songs are very visceral. Emotional. I'm… I'm going to sing them, too."

I could see what that did to my dad. His eyes glistened with tears. He sounded choked up when he said, "You're going to sing them?"

"Yeah."

"Onstage?"

"Yes. That's the goal."

"But, do you think you can do that—?"

"Don't ask me that. Of course I can."

I could see my dad digesting that. A sort of wonder softened the wounded lines of his face as he stared at me. He blinked back the unshed tears. "Of course you can."

"I want you to be proud of me, no matter what I sing."

"I am."

"Even if it's about pussy."

Dad choked out a laugh. He got up and came over, his arms out, and gave me a hug. "I am proud of you, Johnny. Your mother would be, too."

I closed my eyes and hugged my dad for a long minute.

"I just hope I don't kill my career with this show," I muttered. "And if I do, please let me crash in your guest room when the bank takes my houses."

He chuckled. "You won't." He held me out at arms' length and looked me in the eye. "Something tells me… that this is going to be the best show of your career so far, son."

And the very next second… the power went out.

---

What the fuck.

*No.*

The room had gone black, but the emergency exit light came up. I stared at my dad in the dull glow. "*Shit.*"

"Oh, son," he said.

"Hang on. I'll figure this out." I got on my phone, calling Yash. When he didn't pick up, I called Lamar. I heard his phone ringing as the door opened and Shane sauntered into the room, Lamar helping light his way with the flashlight app on his phone. I hung up.

"Do you want the bad news first?" Shane asked me, no preamble. "Or the other bad news."

"Give me all of it."

"Well, the power doesn't seem to be coming back anytime soon, but the party is rocking. Yash says the turnout is fantastic. I saw, like, every member of Dirty and the Players out there. And Brody Mason, Trey Jones, Cary Clarke… everyone you want to see tonight. And I'm pretty sure if you bail on this you'll never forgive yourself. So there's that."

"Fuck."

The door opened again, and Lex and Dane walked in.

"Hey. You tell him?" Lex asked Shane.

"Tell me what?"

"The power went out," Lex quipped, always the fucking joker. "And no, you're not bailing on this show."

"*Fuck,*" I repeated and sat down. I put my head in my hands.

Lex sat down next to me, slapped me on the back. "Remember in high school? We'd go into the guys' empty showers and you'd play your guitar because you liked the acoustics, the sound of the music bouncing off the tile walls? No electricity?"

"Yeah, fuck electricity," Shane said. "Who needs it?"

My hands dropped and I looked up at my friends, and my dad, all staring down at me. "Uh, let's see. I do. And my band does. The drums will destroy everything else. No one will hear anything, least of all my voice or the songs."

"Not to mention that the bar probably can't pour."

We all looked at Dane.

He shrugged. "Their whole computer system is down, right? So they've got no way to input orders and take payment."

The door opened again and my band piled in. "Johnny," Noah said. "What are we doing?"

"I don't know." I got to my feet to greet my bandmates, hugging Noah, Raf and Coop.

"You can still play the show," Noah said. "The songs work without us."

"There's no need to call off the show," Coop agreed. "Raf can still join you on some songs. Guitars and vocals, that's all you need."

Raf nodded. "Whatever you need, brother."

"That's how this all started," Noah said. "You had us into your home studio and played us the songs, acoustic."

"That was how you wrote them," Raf added. "Just do your thing.

"We'll get a chance to rock at our next show," Coop put in.

Of course, that was true. If there was a next show. We didn't exactly have anything else booked, though. This was a special night. A one-off. For Yash, it was a chance to showcase the songs and the band and *me* to record labels. For me, it was a chance to play the songs, if only once, and see how it went.

I needed to know if I could play these songs. If I could sing them in front of people. I needed to play them, once, for my friends and my family and my peers.

After that… I wasn't sure yet. How would I know until I knew how it felt out there tonight?

I took a deep breath.

Then Yash walked in, with Elle—and Flynn, sort of. He hovered near the open door. "Hey, Johnny," Yash said. "What are you thinking?"

"I'm thinking…" *Shit.* I took a breath, looking at Yash and trying to tune out Flynn. He was kinda the last person I wanted to see right now, but I knew he'd probably be here, with Elle.

"You need to do this," Yash told me, sincerely, because he knew what this show and the songs meant to me. But his eyes said, *This is your call, brother.*

Because he really was a great manager. He'd never force me to do this for his own reasons. Not if this wasn't right for me.

"I can play the show," I forced out. "We'll just need to make a few changes to the setup, so hopefully everyone can hear me."

"That's what we were thinking," Elle agreed. "If you're game, we can make it work."

"Great. Then let's do it."

"You can do this," Noah told me, patting me on the back. "We're all here for you, Johnny. The songs are special. Just focus on the songs."

"Thank you."

The guys all gave me another hug, and I watched Flynn leave with Elle and Yash. My dad headed back out into the club to get seated. I tried not to think about anyone being in that room out there but Angeline and my family.

Everyone else got to work.

And the way my team and the bar staff rallied to make this happen for me was awe-inspiring. I watched from backstage with Lamar and Noah.

The staff lit candles and passed them around. The emergency lights were on around the edges of the room, illuminating the exits. But everything else was an undulating flicker of candle flames.

"If the fire inspector comes by…" I said to Elle when she came by to check on me again.

"Then we'll deal with it," she said. "We've got a lot of strong negotiators in this room. Between Ronan and Jude and Summer, we'll appease them somehow. Even if we have to clear the place out. We'll make sure you can play for the execs, no matter what happens. Even if I have to take you all back to my house."

"Thanks, Elle." I gave her a hug. She'd been incredibly supportive of this whole thing, from allowing Yash to book the show here tonight, to checking in on me a few times over the last several weeks, even while she was on the road with Dirty. Asking me how writing was going.

I knew that meant Angeline had pled our case to her, and done a great job. Somehow, Angie had convinced her sister that I was someone to believe in. Or at least that I was someone to give a chance to. And she was giving me that chance. Not just with her bar, but with her family. She was treating me like I was her sister's boyfriend, and that was that.

It was almost like she liked me or something.

"This feels wrong," she said thoughtfully, looking out across the small stage, where the staff was setting up candles, trying to provide the best lighting they could.

"I know. I'll be so quiet, and so far away."

"Maybe if we just have everyone move forward, onto the dance floor. We could move all the chairs."

"Actually…" I eyed the dance floor in front of the stage. It was huge. "What if I play in the middle of the dance floor? And we ask everyone to just gather around me. People in the front seated on chairs, then standing at the back? In the tightest circle we can."

"Like a human amphitheater," she mused. "I like it."

"It's probably the best chance we have of everyone actually hearing me."

"We'll make sure the execs and your family are seated in the front 'row.' That way they'll be comfortable and they'll hear you for sure."

"Perfect."

"I'll get the crew on it."

"Hey, Elle?" I stopped her as she started away. "Also, can you have someone announce that the drinks are on me and Yash? Just have the staff keep track of it somehow, and we'll clear up the tab at the end of the night?"

Elle smiled. "You've got it. I'll talk to the manager."

I watched her get the crew going, moving a bar stool to the middle of the dance floor for me and surrounding it with candles. A stool was set up for Raf, too, along with the stands for our guitars. Then they started moving the audience of about a hundred people, table by table, relocating them to the dance floor, in a circle around the stools.

Elle really didn't have to be this involved. She co-owned the place, but she could've had the manager and everyone else do the work. But there she was, helping move chairs and working with the crew to make sure the small audience was arranged for the best possible chance of hearing every note off my guitar and every word I sang.

Just like a loving, supportive sister-in-law. It really fucking got to me.

My stomach felt tight, but the tense fist was slowly melting into a warm excitement. Happy nerves and adrenaline.

Meanwhile, the bar staff kept the drinks flowing on that open tab. After the last guests were arranged around the stools and candles that constituted the "stage," Yash walked into the middle of the circle and stood by my stool. He thanked everyone for coming. Then he told them there would be no video or audio recording allowed, and to please make sure their phones were on silent. He never liked being in the spotlight and got his part over quickly.

Then Elle stepped into the circle. "Thank you for coming tonight to hear our friend, Johnny O'Reilly, play some new songs. Johnny?" She looked over at me, and the small crowd applauded and whistled for me as I walked out, making my way through the bodies with Lamar's guidance. I took my seat and strapped on my guitar. When I looked out at all the expectant faces, the fist clenched in my gut, but I took a breath and ignored it, just letting the warm nerves wash through me.

I saw Angeline. And my family. And my band. My friends. My peers. The faces of so many people who were important to me, whether I'd really done a good job of letting them know that over the years or not.

I just hoped I was half as important to them.

I hoped they'd like the new songs as much as Angeline and Yash and my band did.

And, I hoped no one would walk out when they heard the words in the songs. At least, no one who mattered. Dad. Shayla.

Angeline.

It was the worst pain I'd ever experienced, being left. When my mom left me alone in that car, then left my life, then left the world… I could see now how it all fit together. How it was all connected. I also realized that it was only because of Angeline that I'd somehow found the courage to start exposing my scars to other people. And to accept that I'd always have scars, but the music—and Angeline—could help me live with them.

Thanks to her, I'd written some incredibly painful songs. Cathartic songs. Freeing songs. And love songs, too. Beautiful songs.

"I've got about a half hour of music for you tonight," I told my waiting audience. "A sampling of new songs. If the power comes back up, my band can join me. If not, well, wish me luck."

There was applause and some sympathetic laughter.

I started to play, beginning with a song I'd written for my beautiful muse, Angeline. "The Way You Do."

Because of the nature of it, even with the storm making a distant rumble, it was quiet in here. Everyone had to be silent in order for the music of my single guitar, and my voice, to carry. It felt like playing around a campfire or at a party in the old days, just me on a log or on a couch, or in the showers at school, playing to friends.

Only back then, I wouldn't have been singing. I'd sit head down, hiding in the sounds of my guitar.

Today, I looked out into the crowd of faces around me and all those flickering flames. And as I played that love song for Angeline, the first love song I'd ever written for a woman, it felt like the start of a whole new era or something.

Then I tore right into it and played the hard songs, one after another.

"Words Can't Say," the song about losing my ability to speak and the stutter that kept me silent for so long.

"Blood on Glass," the song to the man in the car.

And "Without You," the song for my mom.

When I survived those, I just kept playing. Raf accompanied me on "Without You," and then again on the next song, a lighter song. I called it "Pastel Dreams." Angeline loved this song. It was sugary and optimistic, like her.

The crowd seemed to like it, too. I'd pretty much shut out their responses during the harder songs, but I could feel the undeniable energy in the room. That connection, when everyone was tuned into every word, every note. I knew the songs were going over. There was a flow in the room that only came when there was harmony between the performer, the songs and the crowd. They were stone silent at all the right times, and murmured or whistled at others.

When "Pastel Dreams" wrapped up, I thanked Raf and introduced him and my band, even though they didn't get to play. They got a nice round of applause.

Then I took a deep breath, cleared my throat, and spoke to my audience.

"My girlfriend, Angeline…" I looked over at her, and she smiled as people looked at her. "She has this song she calls her 'crying song.' This girl, who's lived mercifully trauma-free all her life, in her own words, listens to this song when she's feeling down. A song about, of all things, running from bullets. It makes her cry and it lifts her up. Well, I've been running from bullets for a long time."

I went silent, looking down at the floor for a moment as I gathered my thoughts and tried to find the right words. I didn't rehearse this. I just knew, in the moment, that I'd know what to say.

"My own 'crying song' is about the importance of love in your life," I went on, "and a train as a metaphor for… well, I'm sure the guys who wrote it heard it much differently than I ever did. It was the song that was playing during the worst moment of my life. When my whole world changed. And it always reminds me how songs are so personal and so universal at the same time. How we all hear something different even when we hear the same words. But we can all share in a feeling, right?"

I looked up, and I saw Noah. I saw Shane. I saw my friends in kind of a blur, as I tried not to focus on a single one of them and let it derail me.

"That's why it's been so hard for me to sing. I had a painful stutter as a kid that I managed to overcome largely by learning to sing. And I used that as my excuse not to sing lead, and not to sing much at all in live shows. I'd even record my backup vocals for Breakneck's albums alone, so no one would be there when I sang. Because when I sang… I often broke down in tears, over and over again, for no reason. Or at least I told myself it was for no reason. But the reason was that singing and music allowed me to feel what I couldn't bear to feel any other way. I couldn't stop the flood of feelings with music. The truth is, singing in front of a crowd was terrifying. It still is. The difference is, today I'm doing it anyway."

That got a burst of supportive applause. I waited until everyone was quiet again to keep speaking.

"Angeline encouraged me to play my crying song as part of my set tonight. Many of you know it. It's a song called 'Long Train Runnin'' by the Doobie Brothers. I told her there was no place for a cover song in a showcase like this unless there was a damn good reason. Unless I could make utter magic with it, there was no point. I don't know if I can make magic. As the listener, that's kind of up to you. But tonight, I'm gonna try."

There was more applause and some whistles. Then gradually, my small audience fell silent again.

I waited for a few breaths into that silence, to start strumming.

Everyone expected me to play 'Long Train Runnin'' now. I knew that. But as soon as I started to play, they discovered they were wrong. I could feel them leaning in around me as they struggled to make the switch in their heads. What song was I playing?

It was "Sign of the Times," and I played it for Angeline, totally stripped down, acoustic, just me and my guitar in the candlelight. My voice was huskier, deeper than Harry Styles' and I made it my own, but I could tell by the feeling in the room, the deep silence of the crowd, that it felt as magical for them as it did for me. It was like the calm before a storm. Like they were all holding their breaths.

Like a sharp intake of breath before a burst of tears.

By the end of it, I could see Angeline full-on crying. I knew she'd tried not to. I didn't play her crying song to make her cry, but I loved her tears. By now, I knew she cried for so many reasons, and not one of them was wrong. The fact that she was crying just meant she was feeling.

I wished I could've felt as freely as she did.

But she was still the only one in my life I fully trusted with my feelings. Even now… the songs expressed what I couldn't really say.

And because she was my muse, and my heart, I closed the show with a song I wrote for her. One she hadn't heard yet. One she didn't even know I wrote.

It was my gift to her.

My way of saying thank you, for everything she'd done for me.

It was a song about love. About an angel on earth. And in that song I told her the things I still found hard to say.

Without me even saying the words, she'd know, when she heard this song, how much I loved her. And that this song was for her.

As I sang, I saw her sitting at the table with my dad, with Shayla and my stepmom. I saw Angeline trying so hard not to cry.

---

When I got to my feet at the end of the show, the crowd stood, too. I had a standing ovation, as it was.

Lamar was already at my side. "Clearing out?" he asked me.

"I'll just give it a minute." Lamar knew I didn't want to stick around tonight. That I wouldn't have much left to say after my set. That I'd be tapped out.

I knew some people would want to talk to me, though. I knew Yash would want to see me talk to them.

Trey was the first person who approached to shake my hand. "Brother," he said. "Let me be the first to tell you how exceptional that was."

"Thank you."

"And without a band, and electricity… you really stepped up."

"I just hope it sounded decent."

"Johnny," he said, with a charming, dimpled smile, "you're better than decent. We need to talk about a new deal. You need to record *that* and get out on tour."

"We'd be happy to negotiate, Trey." Yash angled in. "I'm sure Johnny will have a few offers to consider."

Trey smirked. "I'm sure he will. But my offer will be the best."

"I appreciate it," I told Trey, sincerely. "But I'm not really looking for a record deal tonight. I just wanted to play these songs. See how it all feels."

Yash stared at me like I'd been abducted by aliens and deposited back on earth, possessed by some foreign life form. *Feels?* he mouthed at me. Granted, he'd probably never heard that word out of my mouth before.

But he wisely kept quiet.

"Well, the offer stands," Trey said, surprised maybe, but too cool to let my response shake him.

"I hope so. I have more music to write. Maybe we can talk about a record, when I'm ready."

"Alright, brother," he said. "Respect. My door's open."

"Have a drink on me," I told him. "I've gotta head out."

I gave Yash a squeeze on the shoulder. "Make sure you clear up that bar tab," I told him.

"You're leaving?"

"Yup. I did what I came here to do." I gave him a smile and turned to find people waiting to talk to me. They congratulated me on the show.

Telling me how much they liked the songs. Asking if I was cutting an album. All that.

I still didn't have answers for those questions, though.

"My publicist will let you all know," I told them. Then I let Lamar and Ronan's guys clear a path for me to backstage. I knew it was highly unusual for the star of the show not to stick around to schmooze after a showcase like this. But there was only one person I wanted to see right now. I leaned into Lamar as we ducked backstage. "Where's Angeline?"

"She's waiting for you."

When we walked out the back exit, I found her waiting by his car, with Flynn. The rain had stopped. And Flynn had walked her outside, apparently.

She looked at me uncertainly, her eyes drifting over to Flynn for a moment. He stood back, eying me. Cool, stoic. Just part of the scenery. I knew he had to be thinking—feeling—something, though.

"Angel." I reached for Angeline and felt Flynn drifting away. I wrapped my arm around her waist, pulling her against me.

She beamed at me. "Well, hello, rock star."

"Hello, muse. Don't tell me you were out here the whole time?"

She slapped my chest. "You didn't see me!? I'm your number one fan! I was crying my eyes out in there!"

"I know. I saw." I glanced back, but Flynn was gone. "You okay?"

"Yeah. He just walked me out. Asked me how I was doing."

"And how are you doing?"

"Much better than I let on, I'm sure." She smiled at me tentatively. "I mean, you sang some beautiful love songs about me in there. And I cried my face off. He was probably confused about what that all meant."

I cupped her face in my hand. "Then I guess he doesn't really know you."

Emotion flickered over her sweet face. "No. He really doesn't. But that's not entirely his fault."

I tightened my arm around her, holding her close. "As long as there's nothing left for him to know."

"There isn't," she vowed, her blue-gray eyes wide. "Whatever there is to know about me, Johnny O," she said softly, maybe aware that Lamar was so close by, "is for you to discover."

"I love you, Angeline." I brushed my lips against hers, feeling what those words did to her. How her body came alive in my arms, hyper tuned to my touch. I knew I didn't have to say the words. Hearing how I felt about her, in a song, more than cut it. She loved being my muse. But she deserved every word, and every feeling I had to give.

"I love you, too." She shuddered a little, an echo of all those tears. "I'm sorry I got the feels so hard at your show," she whispered. "I hope I didn't embarrass you."

"I love how much you feel."

"Yeah?"

"Yeah. So how about I take you home… and I make you feel all kinds of things, all night long?"

She licked her lip thoughtfully, seductively. "How soon can we get there?"

"As soon as I finish kissing you."

I kissed her, long and slow. While I kissed her, I pulled her into the back of Lamar's car. And true to my word, I kept kissing her, all the way home.

# Chapter Thirty-Nine

**Angeline**

*One year later…*

I walked into Little Black Hole recording studio with a bounce in my step. Merritt, who was on the phone at her desk in the reception area, smiled and waved me through, and I headed deeper into the studio—through a door and down the long hall toward the large Studio A. When I pushed through the studio door, I found Johnny, Noah and Cary Clarke lounging on the couches, talking.

"Hello, rock star," I greeted my man. I slid into his lap when he reached for me, giving the other guys a little wave.

Johnny nuzzled my neck and kissed my ear as Noah and Cary kept talking. "Hello, muse," Johnny rasped, and a thrill of heat rushed through me. I would never not get wet at the sound of his voice rasping in my ear.

I was doomed once we got out on tour.

Every night, every show… I'd be a horny, sopping wet mess waiting for him backstage, quivering and begging for it by the time he took me… in his dressing room, in the tour bus, in our hotel suite, wherever.

I wriggled in his lap as his fingers drifted slowly down my spine. His deep, aquamarine eyes met mine, and a thrill pulsed through my lady parts.

He knew he was driving me wild, and I couldn't exactly do anything about it with Noah and Cary sitting right there.

I hadn't seen Johnny since yesterday morning. He'd worked late last night, while I'd worked during the day. I'd been asleep when he came to bed, and he'd been gone when I woke up this morning. He didn't usually work so around-the-clock, but right now his band, officially known as Johnny O and the Trust, was just putting the finishing touches on their debut album in-studio.

"You want to hear your song?" he whispered in my ear.

I gasped. "Yes!"

He gave a signal to the sound engineer, visible through the window into the control room, and the song started to play.

Cary got up, patted Johnny on the shoulder, and headed out, giving me a little salute. *Thank you!* I mouthed at him, waving goodbye. "Well, look at him," I purred in Johnny's ear, "heading home to his wife and child at a reasonable hour."

"Very responsible. You gonna punish me for working late last night?"

"Yes."

He bit my ear and I glanced at Noah, but he wasn't looking at us. He seemed lost in listening to the song, gently drumming on his knee with a pair of drumsticks.

I sank back against Johnny as he reclined into the couch. Together, we listened to "Angel," one of the songs he'd written for me. But it was no longer a simple, acoustic, one-guitar song, like it was when I'd heard it for the first time, the night of his showcase at Champagne, a year ago. A whole band, an orchestral string section, a deep, resonant bass drum… I heard all kinds of sounds rising into it as the song built. Everyone who'd collaborated on the album in the studio had taken Johnny's songs and made them into so much more.

The Players and Dirty were both home on an extended tour break in the middle of their tour, and Cary had been producing the album. Johnny had taken his time to do things right; the way he wanted them done. He'd signed with Brick House Records a while ago as a solo artist; this time, the contract was in his name, so other musicians could come and go on the project and it wouldn't change a thing. But that said, he'd had a solid band backing him up for over a year now, and it looked like they'd be sticking together. Andy Cooper on bass, Rafael Serrano on guitar, and of course, Noah Vaughan on drums.

The whole band was loving the songs, and playing them together… They all couldn't stop talking about the upcoming tour.

And this song… my favorite song of the whole album… it was stunning. Maybe there were better songs on the album, in some ways; songs that would be singles before this one. But some of those songs were still so hard for me to listen to, knowing the truth behind them. The love songs were the easiest for me to get swept up in.

I had a stone in my throat by the time it finished.

"You like?" Johnny nuzzled into me, his arms encircling me. Like he instinctively knew that I had all the feels coursing through me right now, and the only thing that would make them feel even better was him, touching me.

"You've finished it?" I asked him, with a glance at Noah.

"It's as finished as finished gets with Johnny and Cary in the room," Noah said.

"We'd probably tweak it forever," Johnny admitted. "If we could."

Noah poked Johnny's knee with a drumstick as he got to his feet. "Perfectionism. It's a terrible disease."

"It's an affliction," I agreed solemnly, playing with the soft hair at the nape of Johnny's neck.

"It's finished," Johnny admitted, grudgingly.

"I love it," I told them both, sincerely. "And not just because it's about me. The whole album is amazing."

"Cary said he's bringing the Players in to listen on Monday," Noah said. "Think you can get your sister in here?"

"I'll see what I can do," I said coyly. My sister would be here in a heartbeat if I told her Johnny's album was finished, and she was invited to listen. For one, music was her jam. And two, she'd love to give him her two cents on it. She wanted his band and his album and his career to be a huge success. Because it mattered to me. "Nervous?" I grinned at Johnny.

He smiled back. "Not at all." He kissed me, then nudged me off his lap so we could get up. "See you back here Monday, bright and early?" he said to Noah.

Noah was stretching languidly. "Savage. I'll be here sometime in the afternoon."

"Alright, brother." They hugged, then Noah headed out the back door.

The engineer seemed to be busy with something on the other side of the window, and I slipped my arms around Johnny's neck. "Your music gets me hot." I bit his lip, and his strong arms went around me. He squeezed my ass.

Then I pulled away. "I am punishing you, though."

He gave me a devious look, interested. "How?"

"Hmm. By not fucking you right here, right now?" I tugged him toward the door. "And taking you to a party instead?"

"Cruel."

We pushed out through the back exit, into a stairwell that led down to the parking area along the back alley. Johnny slung his arm around my shoulders and I cuddled into his side as we headed down. I was so fucking proud of him, I could burst.

Some scars told stories. His wrote songs.

And what incredible songs they were.

That was the name of the album… *Scars.*

He kissed me on the top of my head, like he could feel my pride in him. "How was your day?" he asked me, like he always did.

I fucking loved that, because seriously: he was a rock star. His days, no matter how mundane, were way more interesting than the average person's. I knew that because my sister was a rock star, too. And now, living with Johnny in his house—our house—I'd learned that even a "nothing" sort of day was comprised of things like working out in his state of the art gym with his personal trainer, swimming in his heated pool, eating at the hottest new restaurant in town with friends, playing guitar, writing songs, front row tickets and backstage access to whatever he wanted to see, etcetera. Of course, I got to enjoy those perks too, with him, but the fact that he still wanted to know every detail about my day… it warmed my heart.

Because I knew he cared. He cared about all the little things that made my life mine, especially when he wasn't around. Because he didn't want to miss a thing.

"It was epic," I gushed. "I had the big meeting with Danica and her team. The photo shoot is a go."

As he knew, I'd taken on a new client a few months ago. Danica Vola, wife of the Players' lead singer Ashley Player—and their bassist, Matt Brohmer. Technically, Danica wasn't legally married to both men, but Danica, Ash and Matt had been in a committed three-way relationship for a few years now.

Danica made custom jewelry for VIP clients, and while she handmade each piece and had no interest in expanding her business to a whole line of products, her work—and her relationship—got a lot of media attention. And now she and her work were being profiled in some popular fashion magazines—thanks to her publicist, *me*.

"Danica will be in the editorial images, as planned," I went on, "but Ash and Matt are now going to be in them with her. The idea is we have the guys on either side of her, both of them with their shirts off, and wearing her jewelry. It's going to be so fucking hot."

"You think the world's ready for that?" Johnny said thoughtfully, as he opened the door for me and we stepped out into the evening light of the back alley, but I knew he was kinda teasing.

"Hey, the world is changing. My client can be photographed with both of her men and speak freely about her relationship with them. The magazines we've pitched to are loving it. Honestly, they're probably *all* gonna run a feature on her. You throw a couple of hot rock stars into the bargain and go figure…" I teased him right back, "people are all salivating to snap up the story."

"I'm sure," he said mildly. We'd stopped walking and he'd encircled me with his arms.

"I love my job," I gushed. "I have no idea why I didn't realize earlier in life that I'd be a fabulous publicist. I love talking up my clients to the world and cheering them on."

"You are good at tooting horns," he said darkly, and I felt the heat in his body pressed against mine.

"If that was a blowjob reference," I said smartly, "I thank you."

He kissed me in answer, deeply and thoroughly. But just as I was really getting into it, my hands roaming down to his tight ass, he stopped.

"You know," he mused, "one day, you'll be the queenmaker in this town." He smirked at me and I grinned, smacking his chest lightly, because he was teasing me. I'd told him long ago about the whole conversation I'd had with Danielle Duke when she dismissed me. And the result? He'd never let me forget it. Until I'd dethroned Danielle in that regard, he wouldn't let it rest. To say he detested the woman because of how she'd treated me would be an understatement.

But he was also super proud of me. Because I was making it there, bit by bit. I was nowhere near Danielle Duke's level in my career. But I'd get there.

"One day," I agreed, smiling up at him. "I'll get there. One queen at a time."

"I know you will."

I took a deep breath, absorbing his words. His belief in me was so… empowering. It was intoxicating, like a super drug. A triple shot of caffeine. Pure gasoline beneath my wings.

But his belief in me had also helped me to see that I probably had what it took to make it all along; I just didn't recognize it. I was no longer living in my sister's shadow. It was a long shadow, but I was the one who chose to keep myself tucked safely under it.

Maybe I just had to find the right person to help bring out the best in me. Someone to believe in me. Someone to believe in. I needed that collaboration; someone to cheer on.

I wasn't like Johnny. I wasn't a solo artist.

"But you know," I told him, "along the way, working with a king isn't bad."

"Ah, you say the sweetest things," he teased me, but I knew how it floored him when I praised him. His eyes flared with desire. Because he knew I really meant it. My love was an aphrodisiac for him, a healing balm and a powerful turn-on. Just like his love was a power source for me, an electric charge. It lit me up and sustained me, and it helped me to grow.

He kissed me again, deep and slow, until my toes curled. My fingers curled into his waist, just like that night he'd first kissed me. When he drew back and smiled at me, a wry and raw kind of smile, I knew he was probably remembering that, too. How I'd clung to him that night, for just a few moments.

"Thank you for kissing me," I whispered.

He chuckled softly. "You really don't have to thank me. It's my pleasure."

"I meant… back then. That very first time."

He kissed me again. Then he slid an arm around my shoulders, steering me away from the studio. And that's when I saw the freaking limo.

It was a black stretch limo, parked along the alley. Lamar was leaning casually against it, on the far side, obviously trying not to eavesdrop. His head was tilted down, like he was reading.

"Johnny! What's with the limo?" We were heading over to North Vancouver tonight, to a party at Brody Mason's house. It was Zane Traynor's birthday, and since Dirty and the Players were home from the road, there was a big birthday party. But I'd expected Lamar to pick us up in his SUV.

Johnny shrugged. "Why not ride in style?" We walked over to the limo and Lamar mobilized to open the door for us.

"You first," I told my boyfriend sweetly.

He gave me a suspicious look, then slid into the limo.

"Do you take song requests?" I asked Lamar quietly.

"From you, Angie," he said, "anytime."

"Great!" I leaned in to whisper my request in his ear, then slid into the limo with Johnny. As Lamar shut the door and went to sit up front with the driver, Johnny reached to pull me against him and tuck me into his side. We got rolling… and the music came on.

Johnny looked down at me when Drake "Best I Ever Had" surrounded us in stereo. "You made Lamar put this on?"

"Have you seen Lamar?" I fluttered my eyelashes innocently. "He's a tank. I didn't make him do anything."

"Uh-huh. Because you couldn't possibly have any influence over a tank-sized man." His eyes drifted down to my chest.

"It was a request. And it's for you." I grinned when he rolled his eyes but smiled. "It's just one song. After this, he can put on whatever he wants."

"Sure. You were telling me about your day…" He changed the subject as his hand slid up my bare thigh, beneath my skirt, and squeezed. "Did you see the new tour dates?"

"Oh, yes! I saw. I'm so happy." Johnny and his band were going on tour soon, and they were playing a few shows with Dirty and the Players. Brody Mason himself had invited them to join the bands for some dates next summer. "I can't wait to go on tour with you. It's going to be so much fun."

"I've never toured with a woman before," he said thoughtfully. "I hope you're prepared to fulfill my every sexual desire."

My eyebrow rose.

"What?" He feigned innocence. "That's what women are for on tour, right?"

"Yes," I said smartly, "and rock stars are there to fulfill a woman's every sexual fantasy… so… it goes both ways, buddy."

"You're telling me… I better be ready to fuck you anytime you demand it?"

"Yup."

"And make you come, over and over again…?"

"Yup."

"Sounds terrible."

I sighed deliriously just thinking about it. "It's gonna be incredible. You pursuing your dreams, me pursing mine… The best part about my job is that I can do it from anywhere."

"So, you're not gonna follow Danica around, telling her to be nice?" His hand slid higher up my thigh.

"She doesn't need me to. She's extremely nice… And by the way, I'm not sure how well you learned that lesson. This is very rude of you." My voice grew breathy as his fingers flirted with my clit through my panties. "We're having a conversation, sir."

His aquamarine eyes hit mine. "Are we?" His finger hooked into my panties, wrenching them aside, and then he was teasing me for real, his fingers drawing delicious figure eights over my clit and the soft flesh between my legs… and my thighs were spreading of their own free will.

"You better fuck me, you go starting a conversation like this…" I told him.

"Unfortunately for you," he said solemnly, "I can't get it up while Drake's playing."

I ran my hand over his thick erection. "Liar." He groaned as I massaged his firm length through his jeans, then eased back in the seat, spreading his legs as I tore open his zipper.

Then I tossed his teasing hand aside and got down on my knees on the floor between his thighs. I spread his jeans open, peeling his boxer briefs down to get at that beautiful cock of his.

"Babe," he breathed as I sank my mouth down over him, taking him deep, "… I was just… teasing you…"

I slid my mouth off his dick, licking the hard, silken, veiny length of him, luxuriously. "Well, it worked. Now I'm horny and we're gonna fuck."

I worked him with my mouth for a delirious minute while he groaned in pleasure. Then I slipped off my panties and climbed into his lap. I straddled him and pushed his head back so I could look right into his eyes while I sank down on him.

"We were supposed to wait until we got there…" he protested half-heartedly.

"Fuck you at Brody's house? Hmm. Why not just fuck right here…?"

I sealed my mouth over his, swallowing his growl as I started riding him, slowly. Then more urgently. His hands clutched at my hips as I rode him, obviously trying to slow me down and failing.

"Baby," I gushed as I broke the kiss. "I love the fuck out of you. And your dick is my crack."

He laughed, the sound strangled as I sped my thrusts. "Angel…"

"I can't wait…" I panted.

Then he grabbed me around the waist. He lifted up off the seat, taking me with him, keeping his cock seated deep inside me. I squealed, wrapping my arms around his neck and holding on as he laid me back on the seat behind me… and started driving into me.

My knees fell open and my arms slid away as he leaned up over me, grabbing onto the back of the seat for leverage. Then he fucking gave it to me.

"Take off your shirt," I gushed.

He paused just long enough to rip it off over his head, giving me a glorious view of his toned torso as he gripped the seat back again and resumed slamming into me, again and again. I reached up and held onto his strong forearms.

"This what you wanted, Angel?" he panted.

"Yeah. Call me your cock slut." He hadn't done that in a while.

His eyes heated with molten lust, burning into mine. "Yeah? My little slut can't even wait until we get to the party, can you."

"No. No I can't wait. Give it to me."

"You were supposed to wait, sweetheart," he breathed, his eyes raking over me as he fucked me. "But… I can't say no to you…"

"Good. Give me what I want."

His eyes locked onto mine again. "What do you want, Angel?"

"You. That thick cock, so deep…" My voice broke into a gasp as his fat cockhead thrust in and out, his hips sweeping up with each thrust so he stroked me at an angle so excruciatingly sweet, my core shuddered… and then I was coming, screaming, on his cock. Slightly self-conscious that Lamar and the driver might hear, but not really giving a fuck. I was too far gone, tumbling into sheer bliss as my body shuddered and shook for him.

"So pretty…" Johnny drifted a hand down my throat and over my chest, squeezing my breast through my thin dress. Then back up my throat as I whimpered, my core shivering around him.

"Johnny, come," I breathed, fucking loving this view as he started to lose his rhythm above me. His face flushed, his throat constricting as the muscles all along his neck and chest tensed.

He hooked his thumb into my mouth and I sucked, then bit down. With his other hand, he wrenched down my dress and bra, exposing my breast so he could grab it. He pushed his thumb deeper into my mouth and shoved his cock into me, deep. He clutched my breast and my mouth, greedy, possessive.

His eyes, wet and dark, raked over me.

Then I felt him explode, releasing hot jets of come, lashing my insides as he growled. He emptied himself inside me in long, shuddering spasms.

"God I love you," I gushed, when his thumb slid from my mouth.

He collapsed over me and kissed me, his hands sliding into my hair. Deep, mind-melting kisses, his tongue lashing mine as his hips rocked into me, slowly, over and over, his body quaking with aftershocks. "You…" he gasped into my mouth. "I love you, Angeline. You have no idea."

"Not as much as I love you," I teased, panting.

His aquamarine eyes hit mine. "Angel," he warned, "shut that dirty mouth. Or I'm stuffing it with cock."

"Promise?"

He groaned. Then he tried to shut me up by kissing me, deep, and I laughed as I kissed him back.

# Chapter Forty

## Angeline

The limo had parked, and we managed to get all our clothes back on properly. Mostly. Johnny had ripped a strap on my dress, so I tucked it into my bra to keep it from falling down. Then he opened the door for us. Lamar had wisely left it shut, waiting for us outside.

I knew with one glance that we were not parked outside Brody Mason's house.

Brody and his wife and kids lived in an upscale but homey residential neighborhood in North Vancouver, his house surrounded by large trees. Right now, we were parked on the curved, neatly landscaped and stone-paved driveway loop in front of what looked like a hotel. *The Westshore* said the gold letters over the grand glass entrance. It didn't feel like a hotel, though; there was no concierge or bellhop stand, and it was too quiet.

"Uh, where the fuck are we?"

Johnny helped me out of the limo and I looked up at the building that soared high into the dark sky above us. It was a tower. I blinked at the beautiful lanterns on posts along the curved drive, leaning into his warmth; it was cool out and I gathered the wrap I'd brought around me.

Johnny draped his arm around me and we followed Lamar toward the entrance, where a large man in a suit, with an obvious earpiece, opened the door and spoke with Lamar.

I elbowed my boyfriend's ribs. He still hadn't answered me.

"Oh, is this not Brody's place?" he said casually, as if he didn't fucking know. He'd been to Brody's plenty of times.

I actually caught the scent of ocean air as we followed Lamar in through the door, which the doorman was now holding open for us. I craned my neck to see what I thought was a slice of water through the windows on one side. "Are we on the waterfront?" *Which waterfront?*

"We're in West Vancouver, sweetheart."

I tried to calculate how long we'd been driving. "Wait… We're in West Bay? How did I not notice that we turned the wrong way after the bridge?" Honestly, I couldn't even remember driving over the Lions Gate bridge. I was probably orgasming.

"I guess that's what happens when you fuck a guy instead of paying attention to where he's taking you."

"And I'd do it again…" I glanced around the lobby. There was a massive chandelier over a grand piano that no one was currently playing. We were the only guests here. "So, what is this place?"

"Condos," he said. "For the uber-wealthy. Dane's friend owns this tower."

"Oh, like one of his billionaire friends?"

"Yes."

Lamar came back and handed Johnny an envelope and a key card. "Keys and welcome package. Take the last elevator."

"Thanks. We'll see you in a bit."

"Uh… bye!" I waved goodbye at Lamar, who obviously wasn't coming in with us, as Johnny took my hand, leading me toward the elevator bank.

As we stepped into the last elevator in the row, Johnny swiped his key card over the sensor. There was only one button to push. It said *PH* in scripted gold letters.

"Oooh the penthouse," I marveled as the door shut and we started to rise. "Did you know West Bay has the most billionaires per capita in all of the Greater Vancouver area? I mean, Vancouver only has like a dozen billionaires. But still."

"Yes," he said dryly, "and most of them are too old, hideous and married for you to date, so don't even think about it."

"Wow, I *was* really thinking about it, but old, hideous *and* married? I guess that's three strikes," I teased him.

He gave me a warning look. It was a look he usually reserved for when I'd been a brat and he was about to fuck the ever-loving hell out of me as a consequence.

I grinned and licked my lip gratuitously, egging him on. "I just think it's cool. Imagine being so rich you can buy whole buildings and do whatever you want."

"Money doesn't buy everything, Angeline." Johnny gazed at me with affection, and this certain wondrous look I sometimes glimpsed in his eyes… like he just saw me in a certain light and couldn't believe I was his.

"I love you," I said simply. "Money didn't buy that."

"No, it didn't."

The elevator door slid open and we stepped out into a grand foyer. A man in a suit was waiting for us inside the expansive penthouse suite; the elevator had opened right into it. "Mr. O'Reilly," he greeted Johnny. "Everything is as you requested. If you need anything at all, just pick up the gold phone." He indicated an old-school gold phone sitting on an elegant console table in the foyer.

"Thank you."

The man nodded, gave me a polite smile, then departed by way of the elevator.

When he was gone, I pretended to pick up the gold phone and hold it to my ear. "Hello? Three shirtless waiters, two hookers with hearts of gold, and one pound of blow, please?" I hung up my invisible phone receiver and Johnny's eyebrow crept up.

"Sounds like a party."

"Isn't that what we're here for?" I asked innocently. "A rock star party?"

He tugged me against his body and my arms slid around his shoulders.

"When is everyone else getting here, by the way?" I inquired, wondering if we had time for more sex stuff.

"They're not. Disappointed?"

"Not at all." I couldn't contain my grin. "So what are *we* doing here?"

"Showering?" He brushed my hair off my cheek. "Wash off the limo sex? Then go to the party."

"We're still going to Zane's birthday party?"

He smiled, a wicked grin. "Disappointed now?"

"Nope. Brody throws a great party."

He did. This night would be kind of like old times, in the best way; epic industry parties had been going on at Brody's house for years. We'd both been to many of them. But now, Johnny and I were no longer on the outskirts of that crowd. I was looking forward to feeling more like I was in a room full of my peers at one of these parties, and no longer just Elle's little sister.

I knew Johnny was looking forward to it, too; feeling more like an equal amongst that crowd, now that his music and his career felt more authentic to him.

"We're like a fifteen minute drive from Brody's place," he explained. "So yes, we're going. But afterwards… we'll come back here and be naked freaks all night. I mean, if that sounds good to you."

"That sounds… decent." I gave him a teasing grin.

He took my hand and drew me deeper into the penthouse. Lights were on throughout the contemporary suite, the floor to ceiling windows all along two sides darkened out by some kind of smoked glass situation. Everything was luxurious, exquisitely tasteful and obviously cost a fortune.

"Johnny, it's beautiful. Don't tell me you bought it…?"

"You wish." He smirked. "It's slightly out of the budget, babe. We already have two houses in Vancouver."

"Darn," I sighed, in mock disappointment.

He led me into the massive main bedroom, where a custom bed, obviously larger than king sized, stood on a raised platform in the middle. The entire thing was dusted with white and red rose petals. White and red roses were gathered in several massive vases around the room. There was Champagne on a table by the bed.

And draped across the bed, there was gorgeous lingerie and a beautiful dress. I went over to the dress and touched the fabric. It was a slinky, soft dress in a pastel turquoise, with matching heels. And blush-pink lingerie, a matching panty and bra set.

"What's this for?"

"It's for you," Johnny said simply.

"You're amazing," I gushed. I told him so at least once a day.

Then he took me by the hand again and led me into the massive bathroom. He undressed me, then undressed himself while I tied my hair up in a knot. Then we showered together in luxurious silence as he ran his hands all over me.

After he'd lovingly washed me and I'd done the same to him, he insisted on us drying off to get dressed instead of diving onto the bed to sixty-nine, which was my suggestion. He looked at me from under hooded eyes as he drew me out to the bedroom, then watched me watch him slide into fresh underwear and a pair of dark jeans; there were clothes laid out on the bed for him, too.

He picked up the lacy panties that he'd bought for me and ogled my pussy. "Let's get you dressed for the party."

I grinned as he crouched down and held the panties for me so I could step into them. I slid my hand down between my legs, right in front of his face, and caressed my clit. "You sure you want me dressed…?"

He leaned in and gently nipped my finger with his teeth. "Naughty." He gave me another warning look, his eyes darkened with arousal.

I sighed, and stepped into the panties. "I can really do this myself," I told him, as he slid them slowly up my legs and I wiggled into them. When the soft, expensive lace brushed my clit, a warm shiver ran through me.

"I love dressing you. It's almost as enjoyable as undressing you." His fingers skimmed my breasts as he "helped" me slide on my bra.

I giggled and gently slapped his hands away so I could do it up. "Hey, if I can't touch, neither can you."

"Fair."

"I really thought you'd put up more of a fight."

He smiled wickedly. I had no idea what he was really up to here, but whatever it was… I was loving it. I watched him pick up a strawberry from the silver tray by the Champagne. He held it for me so I could take a juicy bite, then ate the rest himself.

"Wow," I mused. "Billionaires eat really good strawberries."

"Who knew."

I watched him pull on his shirt, a fresh new button-up, a deep blue that brought out his eyes and hugged his torso perfectly. And of course, he left a few buttons undone. I watched him roll up the sleeves, revealing his forearm tattoos, his rings and bracelets.

"This is so romantic," I told him as I slipped into the sexy turquoise heels he'd picked out for me. "You have to tell me why you brought me here."

Johnny's eyes drifted over me appreciatively. I was standing in front of him in heels, panties, bra and nothing else. "It's a special night."

I laughed a little. "Zane's Traynor's birthday?"

He just smiled.

He was always doing stuff like this for me, no matter if it was a big occasion or not. No matter how busy he was, he always made time to whisk me away to a spa or a beautiful dinner, take me up into the mountains, or fly me out to wine country in the interior, or down to Seattle for a quick overnight to go to a concert or a hockey game. Or if there wasn't time for that, he'd surprise me with a catered picnic in our backyard. For my birthday this year, he had a chef come to our place and cook my favorite meal.

It was like he always wanted to make sure I knew that he was thinking about me, no matter what else was going on or how focused he was on his career.

That I was always in his thoughts.

And he always made time for me, to celebrate us.

"This is amazing, Johnny. But we have a beautiful house. We can drink Champagne there, and have sex all night…"

"Yeah, but here we get room service. Now that the album is done, I thought we could celebrate. By turning off our phones and telling no one where we are."

"Really?" I bounced, excited.

"Really. I mean, if you're into it… I was thinking of keeping you here for a few days and doing nothing but feed you and fuck you. With maybe a few massages thrown in."

"Holy God."

"I wanted to take you away somewhere, honestly, but there wasn't time for it in the schedule right now. So I figured this would be a perfect escape, for now. Oh. And… we get this." He went to pick up the envelope Lamar had given him and pulled out a fancy booklet. He flipped through it, heading over to a smart panel on the wall. With a few taps of his fingers, the smoked glass windows cleared. And the view beyond… it was utterly breathtaking.

I actually gasped.

We were facing Vancouver, across the water. Just far enough away, and just high enough up, that we got a jaw-dropping view of the city against the dark sky and the dark world beyond, with all the evening lights glittering. They sparkled like jewels, like treasure strewn across a dark reef. But maybe the underwater vibes I was getting were just because my eyes were glistening.

I looked at Johnny. "Johnny, it's…"

"Beautiful," he said simply. "Like you."

Another tap of the panel, and the floor to ceiling windows slid open. Johnny came over to me, ditched the booklet and picked up the dress, and held it so I could step into it, too. "Get dressed, Angel," he said, his voice choking up with emotion. Whatever this was, we were both getting emotional. And if he was getting emotional… I was fucking done for.

I held onto his shoulders for stability and stepped carefully into the dress. He slid it up over my curves and zipped up the back for me. Then he took me by the hand and led me out onto the private wraparound patio.

The city glittered across the water, so beautiful against the inky dark sky and the dark waters surrounding it. "This view is incredible," I marveled. "It's so pretty. I've never seen Vancouver from quite this angle. How high up are we?" I leaned over the railing and peeked down.

"In order to really see something, sometimes, you have to take a step back from it," Johnny said behind me. I could hear the regret in his words.

I turned to look at him, and I could see the admiration in his eyes as he looked at me, standing against that breathtaking view.

"So you can truly appreciate it," he added.

I knew, from that painful but appreciative tone, that he was talking about the little step back he'd taken last year, from us, for those few short days… right before he told me everything: all his secrets. His darkness. His pain.

Before he decided to trust me with all of it.

When maybe, for just a split second, we'd both thought about walking away.

"I'm so glad you took that step back," I told him. "Because it made it all that much sweeter when we both stepped back in. And stayed."

"I never trusted anyone like I trust you," he said simply.

"I know that."

"You reminded me of what's important, when I was so focused on other things. I was obsessing about my career falling apart. And you brought it home for me. You reminded me how putting down roots in Vancouver, building family and community with my sister, was *the* most important thing. Probably the smartest move I'd ever made. You told me to lean into that. You were right."

"Good. I'm glad you stayed. If you took off to L.A. or something, to pull together a band and record an album… who knows when we would've crossed paths again. I mean, maybe I would've hooked up with Dean Slater, and the rest would be history. I'd be having his juicy-lipped babies by now—"

"Jesus. Stop." Johnny pulled me up against his body. "What the fuck are you talking about?"

I shrugged. "Dean Slater has juicy lips."

"I meant…" He slid a hand up my throat and grasped my jaw. "What the hell are you smoking thinking I'd let you hook up with Dickhead Dean Slater?"

"Baby, I like rock stars. It was time I ended up with one."

"*Me*. It was time you ended up with me."

"Who knows?" I said vaguely.

"Are you torturing me on purpose?" he growled.

"Yes. So you jealousy-fuck me later. I love it when you get possessive." My heart was beating faster already. I could feel it thumping in my throat under the grasp of his hand.

He growled again and kissed me… deep, possessive strokes of his tongue, basically fucking my face. "Do not," he breathed, after pausing to lightly bite my lower lip, "ever talk to me about ending up with another man."

"*Mmmmm.* Jealousy."

"You're mine."

"Say it again."

"*Mine.*"

"I mean, you really need to wife me up if you're gonna talk like that." I was goading him, only because it was fun, and because every time he got possessive—when we weren't in bed—I liked to tease him about putting a ring on it. Mostly because I knew he would, one day. And I loved fantasizing about how it would happen.

He pressed his forehead to mine and took a deep breath, like he was either sucking in my scent and relishing it, or trying to restrain himself from putting me over his knee and spanking me raw.

Maybe if I pushed just a little harder…

"Dean's got a nice ass, too. I really think he'd—"

"Angeline Delacroix," he growled, "will you marry me?"

"What?!" I yanked back to look in his eyes. "I thought we were kidding. Did you just pop the question?"

He didn't even need to answer that. He just got down on one knee, magicked a ring out of somewhere, and presented it to me. "If you'll stop rambling about another man's body parts… please allow me to ask you to be my wife."

"Oh my God! You did not let me just ruin this glorious moment by acting like a sassy brat!"

"I did, actually."

"Why!?"

"Because." His lips curved in a fond smile. "You were being you."

I sank onto my knees on the patio in front of him, which was absolutely painful in these heels. "I love you, you ridiculous man! Of course I'll marry you!" I was full-on crying, already.

He slid the ring onto my finger.

I threw myself on him, hugging the shit out of him. "You're so beautiful! I love you!"

"That's my line." He kissed my face, many times, as I cried, then smoothed the tears from my cheeks with his thumbs. He held my face and kissed me over and over, just letting my emotions run free.

"Good God, you get me," I wept.

"I love you, Angeline," he said softly.

"My knees and ankles hurt so bad right now."

He got up, pulling me to my feet. I sagged against him, melting down with emotions.

"You're the best," I sobbed. "I can't believe you did all this for me…"

"Are you kidding?" He gazed into my eyes, searching. "I've taken too much and not given enough back. It's what I always do, but I have to stop, or I know one day I'll lose you. And I won't lose you."

"You won't lose me."

"I've been working too hard."

"You've been working hard on something you love," I corrected him.

Johnny shook his head at me, like he still couldn't understand how I stood by him so unfailingly.

"You know, when I was playing that showcase, a year ago…" he said, "and I could see you there, listening so intently, crying along to my songs… it struck me so hard, that if I didn't ask you to marry me, I'd regret it for the rest of my life."

Oh my God. He was killing me dead. "So what took you so long?" I sobbed.

"I had to be sure you'd say yes."

"Really?"

"Yes. Really. I needed to prove to you that I'm not running anymore. I already had a failed marriage. I needed you to trust me that I'm here to stay." He took a breath. "Amber said, when I went to apologize to her, that the thing that hurt her the most was that she felt like I regretted rushing into things with her. And I did regret it, with her. I never wanted *you* to feel that way. I never wanted you to worry that we rushed into things. I never wanted you to have any regrets about us, because I know I don't. I just know it would've haunted me, though, if I didn't do this right. If I didn't ask you to marry me, and know that if you said yes, you meant it with every piece of your heart. And that I'd make good on my vows to you."

"I say yes."

He looked deep into my eyes. "Don't say yes unless you mean it."

"*Yes,*" I promised him, with every piece of my heart. I gave him a wet, tearful kiss.

Then I looked down at the ring he'd put on my finger, which I'd barely been able to get a glimpse of, what with all the emotions and the tears. I wiped my eyes. "Jesus, Johnny. This is… gorgeous."

"It's got the diamond from my mom's engagement ring."

I looked up at him in awe.

"See this?" He nodded toward the ring. I looked down, and he touched his finger to one of the off-center stones. "This was Mom's. I had a bigger one set in the middle for you, and some others around it. I wanted you to have something really special. And just so you know…" He looked into my eyes again. "Amber never wore this ring. It didn't even exist when I married her."

"Well… thank you. I'm glad to hear that."

"It's yours," he assured me. "After Mom died… I went to clean up her things and I found her engagement ring in a little box with my name on it. I guess she wanted to give it to me. But she never got the chance to, because… well, I didn't go back to see her the last few years. I'll never be able to stop regretting that, I don't think, but I want you to wear it. I know she'd love you. Everything about you. She'd love you for me."

Oh, Christ, I was a freaking mess.

"Johnny! You don't do this to a girl when she's supposed to show up at a party," I sobbed, "without warning her! I didn't bring fresh mascara and wipes…"

"Then we'll stop to pick some up on the way to the party," he said easily. "Whatever you need."

"I need you."

"Stop it. You're making me hard."

I grinned through my ecstatic tears. My hands were creeping down to his crotch to verify this… when they suddenly stopped. "Oh, *shit.* Devi owes Taylor a day at the spa. I have to let them know…"

"Huh?"

I dabbed my tears away with my fingers. "That night, at Lex and Talia's housewarming party… the girls made a bet. That you'd end up with me. Or, wouldn't."

Johnny's eyebrow hooked. "So you're saying Devi bet against us?"

"I mean, her and basically everyone else."

"So… Taylor's the only one of your friends who believed in us from the start?"

"Well, more like she was the drunkest one involved in that conversation."

"Nice."

I laughed. "Don't worry. You know you've won them over… gradually."

"Yeah," he said grudgingly. "I guess they can all come to the wedding."

I almost passed out at the glorious vision of Johnny in a rocked-out white tux or something. "Wedding! *Wow*. You really are making all my dreams come true, you know."

"I hope so."

"Actually… I had this dream of you proposing to me while you're inside me."

"Is that so?"

"Uh-huh…"

"Well, sorry to disappoint." His eyes darkened with lust as I reached down to discover that he *was* hard. I slid down the zipper on his jeans…

"You never disappoint," I told him, slipping my hand inside his underwear and down his hot, silken shaft. His cock flexed hungrily. He was hard as rock, just standing here talking about marrying me.

Our eyes held and he cupped my face in his hands. "Angel," he sighed as I stroked him. The fact that we were doing this on the balcony was such a turn-on. I mean, it was dark. But that didn't mean no one could see us. "I want to eat your sweet pussy," he murmured. "All fucking night."

"Mmm. I want you inside me all fucking night."

His eyes flared.

His hands slid down my body to my hips, and he spun me so my back was to him. He slid up my new dress and my heartbeat sped up.

Then he bent me forward a little. I leaned on the patio railing as he tugged my panties down. My eyes rolled closed as his fingers grazed my sensitive thighs. He kissed my neck, nuzzling into me, the stubble on his jaw scraping me and sending shivers across my skin. "Open your eyes, Angel."

I opened them.

"You see that?" I gazed out at the view before me as his hands slid up my body and tugged down the bodice of my dress, then my bra, so my boobs spilled out. "That beautiful city?"

I swallowed. "Yes."

"What do you see?"

"Home."

"I see the world, laid out at your feet." He grasped my nipples, tight, making me gasp. "You're my angel, and I'll give you everything."

"You already give me everything."

"Baby, we're just getting started…"

He bit my neck as he squeezed my nipples. My eyes rolled closed again.

God. This man. The way he touched me…

He released my breasts, one hand suddenly grasping the back of my neck. He squeezed possessively and bent me a little further over the railing, making my heart race. His other hand slid around the front of my body, his fingers dipping under my dress. He pinched my clit, rough and possessive.

"Purr for me, kitten," he rasped in my ear.

I shivered, crying out as he tugged on my clit. His hot body pressed to mine, his cock against my ass. I mewled and moaned as he worked my clit, setting fire to my body.

"Johnny?" I gasped helplessly.

"Yes?"

"You're my angel."

"No, babe. I'm nothing without you."

"You're everything."

"Don't argue with me when I'm about to fuck you."

I laughed breathlessly, floored by the rough promise in his voice.

"My fucking wife…" he murmured against my neck, and I melted. "You want my cock, wife?" I felt his warm cockhead nudge between my legs, slide through my wet lips, and I shuddered in anticipation.

"I'm not… your wife yet," I breathed.

"Oh, but you are. Now open for me," he rasped, "my sweet wife."

*Yes.* I gripped the railing, my new ring and the city before me glittering like promises of our future together. I blinked to see clearly through the tears in my eyes.

He squeezed my neck and pushed into me, slow and hot, possessing me inch by inch, until he'd filled me completely.

"Are you… getting off right now…" I teased him breathlessly, "on calling me your wife?"

"Yes, baby. Yes, I am." He tugged my body tight against his as he started to fuck me in deep, possessive strokes, achingly slow.

"Then I guess… we'd better get married soon. So I can make you this happy all the time…"

Johnny groaned as he buried himself deep inside me, his arms tightening around me. "If that's what you want, Angel, then that's what you'll get."

---

THE END

Thank you for reading!

Don't miss *Irresistible Rogue*, the next book in the Vancity Villains series!

Need more of Johnny and Angeline's happily ever after?

Get the free bonus epilogue:
https://jainediamond.com/bonus-content/

Enjoy *Wicked Angel*?
Have you read about Elle and Seth yet,
and Xander and Courteney, and all the others?
Vancity Villains is a spinoff from my Dirty/Players series.

# Books by Jaine Diamond

**For the most up-to-date list of Jaine Diamond's published books and reading order please go to** https://jainediamond.com/books/

**Dirty Series**

*Dirty Like Me*

*Dirty Like Us*

*Dirty Like Brody*

*A Dirty Wedding Night*

*Dirty Like Seth*

*Dirty Like Dylan*

*Dirty Like Jude*

*Dirty Like Zane*

**Players Series**

*Hot Mess*

*Filthy Beautiful*

*Sweet Temptation*

*Lovely Madness*

*Flames and Flowers*

**Vancity Villains Series**

*Handsome Devil*

*Rebel Heir*

*Wicked Angel*

*Irresistible Rogue*

**DEEP Duet**

*DEEP (DEEP #1)*

*DEEPER (DEEP #2)*

**Never miss a book**—join Jaine's **Diamond Club Newsletter** at jainediamond.com to get new release info, insider updates, giveaways and free bonus content.

# Note to Readers / Acknowledgments

Angeline first appeared and Johnny was first mentioned back in *Dirty Like Seth*. (You may remember Angie adorably grilling Seth over family dinner.) I adored Angeline from the first moment I met her. I have no idea what I imagined for Johnny's journey at that time, LOL. But along the way, we've gotten to know the two of them bit by bit. It wasn't until recently though that I/they realized that they were going to fall in love with one another. I just knew Johnny had a story to tell. And that Angeline would be *the one* he'd let into his heart.

As for Flynn… For those of you who love that man, I love him too. I promise you that. And I wouldn't break a good man's heart without making sure he gets an HEA of his own one day.

To my lovely PA, Alyssa Giselbach, thank you for everything you do for me and my readers, running my readers' groups. To my publicist, Autumn Gantz, thank you for taking so much off my plate so I could really immerse myself in this book.

To my fabulous narrators and the team at Brick Shop Audio, thank you for producing such gorgeous audiobooks for my readers'/listeners' ears.

To the enthusiastic members of my readers' groups, Jaine Diamond's VIPs and Jaine Diamond's Spoiler Room, thank you for being such a fun and supportive community. Your knowledge of my books and your hunger for them humbles and astounds me.

To my author friends, my friends and family, thank you for supporting me and always cheering me on.

To Mr. Diamond, thank you for always being there to support me through all the highs and lows of writing a book. As you know, it's an emotional journey for me, always, and you're always there to (calmly) have my back. You're as solid as Flynn, and Johnny wouldn't be who he is without you.

To my lovely, passionate, enthusiastic readers: THANK YOU for reading this book! I'm so honored that you chose to read this love story; my intent as a romance author is to spread love. As an independent author, I could not do what I do without you. If you've enjoyed Johnny and Angeline's story, please consider leaving a review and telling your friends about this book; your support means the world to me.

With love and gratitude,
Jaine

# Playlist

Time for another extensive playlist! I love this one so much… it was so much fun listening to songs for Johnny and Angeline's story, ranging from sexy to quirky to dark… and of course, we can't forget those crying songs!

As always, some of the songs on this playlist are mentioned in this book; others are songs that captured the feel of a certain scene or that I listened to while writing the book.

*You'll find the links to the full playlists*
*on Spotify and Apple Music here:*
https://jainediamond.com/wicked-angel/

---

*Blush* — Allan Rayman
*Don't You Wait* — CLOVES
*Stormy* — Dragonette
*Cold Blooded* — Our Last Night
*Bad Habit* — Black Pistol Fire
*Circles* — Post Malone

*Megalomaniac* — Incubus
*Nothing Good (feat. G-Eazy and Juicy J)* — Goody Grace
*Better Now* — Post Malone
*T-Shirt* — Dragonette
*forget me too* — Machine Gun Kelly & Halsey
*Ice Cold* — Highly Suspect
*Side To Side (feat. Nicki Minaj)* — Ariana Grande
*California Numb* — CLOVES
*Bad Habits* — Ed Sheeran
*Just Like You* — Emotional Oranges
*All That* — Emotional Oranges & Channel Tres
*The Motto* — Tiësto & Ava Max
*Could You Love Me?* — Black Saint
*Long Train Runnin' (Acoustic)* — Meg Birch
*So Much For Everyone* — Dan Mangan
*I Like You (A Happier Song) [feat. Doja Cat]* — Post Malone
*One Track Mind (feat. A$AP Rocky)* — Thirty Seconds to Mars
*If U Like That* — Marissa
*Wow.* — Post Malone
*Dangerous Night* — Thirty Seconds to Mars
*Feel It In My Bones (feat. Tegan & Sara)* — Tiësto
*Angel in Your Eyes (feat. Sia, Diplo & Labrinth)* — LSD
*For Free (feat. Drake)* — DJ Khaled
*Sweet Surrender* — Extreme Music
*Midnight Demon Club* — Highly Suspect
*Up and Down* — CLOVES
*Caught On Fire* — Highly Suspect
*Sign of the Times* — Harry Styles
*Used to Be* — Goody Grace
*Dug My Heart* — BØRNS
*Softcore* — The Neighbourhood
*Long Train Runnin'* — The Doobie Brothers
*Wild Eyed Son* — Highly Suspect
*Doubt* — twenty one pilots

*Remedy* — Thirty Seconds to Mars
*Best I Ever Had* — Drake
*Heaven Can Wait (feat. Sia, Diplo & Labrinth)* — LSD
*Baby Let Your Soulshine* — Michael Franti & Spearhead (BONUS EPILOGUE SONG)

## About the Author

Jaine Diamond is a Top 50 Amazon bestselling author of contemporary romance. She writes badass, swoon-worthy heroes endowed with massive hearts, strong heroines armed with sweetness and sass, and explosive, page-turning chemistry.

She lives on the beautiful west coast of Canada with her real-life romantic hero and daughter, where she reads, writes and makes extensive playlists for her books while binge drinking tea.

**www.jainediamond.com**

Join the readers' group Jaine Diamond's VIPs on Facebook
to chat with Jaine and other readers:
https://www.facebook.com/groups/jainediamondsVIPs/

# Preview of Irresistible Rogue

Don't miss the next book in the Vancity Villains series,
***Irresistible Rogue***—Shane and Jolie's story!

*Irresistible Rogue is an angsty and suspenseful enemies-with-benefits romance, featuring a mysterious alpha antihero, an inexperienced heroine on the verge of a steamy awakening, and a one night stand that ignites an all-consuming mutual obsession.*

---

## PROLOGUE

**Jolie**

"Ugh. Where am I?" I clawed the wet hair from my eyes and peered out between the dripping curls. I'd stumbled out of the rain into the refuge of what appeared to be an upscale restaurant lounge. Dark floors, thick slabs of wood and stone everywhere, massive plants and subdued lighting.

The storm blew the door shut behind me and the Instagram model at the hostess stand actually gasped at the sight of me.

"Uh, welcome to Black Bear Grille," she said dubiously. She had a pretty Australian accent. A lot of the staff here in Whistler were Aussies; they came for the Canadian mountains during ski season. I was born just over an hour away in West Vancouver but I could've been an alien the way this Aussie was eying me. "Perhaps you're looking for Filthy Joe's?" she provided helpfully.

"And Filthy Joe's would be…?"

"The burger truck parked in the lot at the end of the block," she said, straight-faced.

I dabbed under my eyes. Did I look *that* bad? I'd just come from a beauty salon. "My mascara is running down my face, isn't it."

"Oh, it's much worse than that, hon."

Okay, I was gonna go ahead and believe her. About a minute ago, I was shuffling along the sidewalk in my spa slippers and the sky had ripped open, a torrential rain crashing down on me out of nowhere, because that was how my day was going. A dead car battery on the highway, an hour in a tow truck with an obnoxious tow truck driver, a soul sucking evening of forced "salon pampering," *my mother*, and now this.

The door opened, wind and rain gusting in as someone stepped in behind me. The hostess stood up straighter, lifting her boobs in the direction of whoever it was.

"Good evening, sir," she said breathily. "Welcome to Black Bear Grille."

"I'll just take a seat at the bar," I told her when her eyes remained glued to "sir" behind me. "To wait out the storm. Should I seat myself?"

She almost gasped again as her eyes darted back to me. "Not like that."

"You have a powder room, I assume? I'll clean up."

Her eyes raked down my Prince *When Doves Cry* T-shirt and wide-leg sweatpants. "We have a dress code."

"But it's pouring rain out there, and—"

"Darling," a man rumbled behind me. "Aren't you going to say hello?" His voice was as sultry and playful as it was rough.

I turned to find this guy looking at me. I made a squelched squeaking sound in my throat as I did a whiplash double take. *Holy fucking hell.*

Was he talking to *me*?

I was never prepared to cross paths with an attractive man, especially without any warning. And this fucker was tall, dark *and* handsome. He wore a sleek but simple black blazer, black T-shirt and jeans, effortlessly beauti-fucking-ful. Everything about him screamed: *expensive.* And also: *will fuck you in every sense of the word.*

That last part was due to his luscious full lips, stunning pale-greenish eyes and thick whorls of dark "please grab on and let's go for a ride" hair.

And the bruises. He had three of them on his face. Forehead, jaw, and a dark one that followed the curve of his left cheekbone.

He also had what looked like either a doozy of a hickey cluster or strangulation marks on his neck.

He held my eyes for way too long to be an accident.

Yup. He was talking to me.

I laughed nervously and turned hot pink. "Um. Hello?"

As his eyes slid down my body, the hot pink crept down from my face and sizzled across my senses like wildfire. He looked at my mushy, wet, dirty slippers and the bits of Kleenex that were stuffed between my toes to keep them spread apart while the turquoise nail polish dried.

That was what set Mom off at the salon: the nail polish color I chose. After that, it all spiraled downhill.

I turned back to the gaping hostess who was apparently dumbfounded that I might be seen in public with *that* man while looking like *this*. Which made two of us. I gathered my scattered brain cells to speak when his low, sultry voice said, "We'll take your best table."

The hostess appeared as speechless as I was, but she recovered quicker. "Of course. Right this way." She turned and headed into the lounge.

Wow. Somehow this hot Nascar driver or whatever he was had so much currency with her that it totally negated my lack thereof. I wondered, as I shuffled along behind her in my slippers, if it was his looks or his money that had her so agreeable.

*Both.*

"How is this?" she said sweetly, presenting us with a table in the middle of the lounge and gazing at the man behind me like I wasn't there.

"We'll take that one," said Mr. Gorgeous and Bossy.

"Of course." She rushed to escort us over to the one he'd pointed out in a dark corner. She pulled out our chairs while avoiding looking at me, left us with a menu and elegantly disappeared.

I glanced at him. He seemed to be waiting for me to sit down before he took his seat. How far was he planning to take this hero thing?

"Uh, thank you. But I'd never expect a hot race car driver like yourself to sit with me. Especially looking like… this."

"Why not?" He smirked faintly. "I mean, you do have a little something, right here…" He made a little circle in the air in front of his gorgeous face with his finger.

Okay, I was way too flustered to deal with his level of hotness right now. I wouldn't know how to exchange witty banter with this guy if someone handed me a script. If he asked me to sit on his face instead of the chair, I'd seriously consider it. And something about him said that he might, just to see what I'd do.

*Dangerous.*

I broke eye contact, because I was way out-matched here. "Thank you. But obviously I need to clean up. Have a nice night. Um, thanks."

*Stop thanking him. You sound desperate.*

Then I shuffled off in my soggy slippers in search of the ladies' room, floored that the last five minutes of my life had actually happened.

*Thanks, Mom. Thanks a lot.*

I pushed through the door into the beautiful washroom, shuffled to a mirror and exhaled. I'd never been so mad at my mother in my life. We'd made such a stupid scene, arguing in the salon in front of all the staff. I'd stormed out like *I* was the difficult one, and now look at me.

The lashing rain and my hair whipping around me had somehow scribbled mascara and lipstick all over my face. I looked like I'd been graffitied. I was a grown woman, and I'd let the makeup artist Mom hired slather on way more makeup than I'd ever wear. As I set about peeling off the false eyelashes and washing off as much of it as I could, I tried to ignore the other women who came and went, hoping they'd just ignore me too. I didn't really want to talk to anyone right now.

Shit, I couldn't believe I'd talked to that smoldering hottie looking like this. He had like, dewy, sexy rain drops in his hair and on his sharp blazer. And I looked like I'd been swallowed by a hurricane and spit back out.

The hair stylist hadn't even finished curling my hair, so the left side was twisted up in clips that were now falling out. *Jesus.* I looked like a nutcase. Who walked into a nice bar looking like this?

*This weirdo.*

It was official. My mother had driven me insane.

*Congratulations, Margot. You finally did it.*

I plucked the clips out, stuffing them into my purse and tussling my hair so maybe the whole thing would look intentionally messy-cute? Nope. Just looked crazy. I hadn't cut my blondish hair in a while, so Mom had paid for the cut that she'd insisted on today. It was too short, cut above my shoulders, shorter in the back and longer in the front. It wasn't me.

I tried to tuck it behind my ears and smooth it down a bit. Sort of helped.

But I still didn't look like I belonged in this upscale bar. More like in my hotel room eating Cheetos out of the bag. *Dare to dream.* Probably what I should've just done tonight.

I sighed and tackled the slipper issue, plucking the soggy wads of tissue from between my toes and trashing them. Then I took off each slipper and dried it with the hand dryer. They were nice and warm when I slipped my feet back into them and I actually felt one percent better.

Then I remembered where I was. And where I was supposed to be.

I pulled out my phone and sent a text to my cousin, Danica. *Where are you guys?? I need backup! Margot is already going bridezilla and they haven't even set a wedding date yet!* I really couldn't handle my mom's mile-high expectations and her snooty fancy engagement party tonight without my wingladies.

And a few stiff drinks.

According to my phone, Mom had already tried calling me twice since I left the salon.

Well, I'd be coming to her party when I was ready, looking however I wanted to look. Maybe I'd make her sweat just a bit.

Served her right for being so goddamn overbearing.

When I headed back out into the bar, I could see through the front windows that the storm was still raging. I saw Mr. Gorgeous at his table in the corner. He was alone, he had a drink in front of him, and he was looking at his phone. He'd taken off his blazer and he did not look worse with less clothes on. His arms in that snug black T-shirt appeared to have been sculpted by horny demons.

I tore my eyes away before he could catch me staring. I'd already embarrassed myself enough.

Most of the seats in the lounge and a few along the bar were taken. The vibe was west coast chill, the music cool and subdued, and the dress code was more lax than the hostess's attitude had suggested.

I went up to the bar, where I sat myself on a stool and waited for the bartender to notice me. He was busy at the other end, lining up drinks at the servers' station for the sleek cocktail waitresses to pick up.

It hit me that I'd never actually sat at a bar all alone before.

I usually had my girls with me in a bar, and I'd really only been going to bars—legally—for a couple of months. While I waited, I decided to snap a few discreet photos of the beautiful wood bar for my aunt Madeleine, an interior designer and my employer. Then a text popped up from Danica. *Epic storm on the highway! We had to pull over. Will keep you posted. Love you!*

Then a text from her twin sister, Daniella, popped up. *Do not let Margot's bitch factor run rampant. And do not let her cut your hair.*

Yeah; too late.

Shit, I really needed my girls here. Maybe I'd just wait here until they came. Or at least until I ran out of beer money and maybe the rain let up and I could make it back to my hotel without getting washed away.

I texted them back. *Okay, be safe.*

I looked up as the bartender approached; he set a drink on a coaster in front of me. "From the gentleman in the corner." I watched him walk away without taking my order, then my eyes dropped to the drink in front of me.

It stood in a tall, curvy glass that was somehow reminiscent of a woman's figure. The liquid, on ice, was a perfect ombre of deep pink at the bottom fading up to blush, and it had an edible flower perched on top. It looked like a piece of art and probably cost thirty bucks. And while I would've loved to drink it, *what the fuck.*

I looked like shit. Why was this guy hitting on me?

I looked into the corner where he sat. He looked over at that exact second and I looked away.

Damn. I wanted this drink. Did I send it back and order up whatever cheap beer I could afford? Or just drink it and play his game?

Was this guy actually looking for a hookup?

*With me?*

I wasn't exactly here for a hookup. Plus, I had a party to go to.

I was wearing decent panties, though.

Really could've shaved the bikini line this morning…

"Hello again."

I startled as he leaned in casually next to me. He'd brought his drink over with him. And his blazer. My mouth drifted open as he joined me at the bar without asking, but two seats down, draping his blazer on the empty stool between us. Confident, but not too pushy.

I stashed my phone away. My brain was already rapidly calculating the odds that I'd let this stranger in my pants tonight. No, because he was a stranger. Yes, because he was insanely hot and I hadn't had sex since… January?

I wondered if he'd change his mind about wanting in my pants after I started saying weird, nervous shit and he realized that I had no game, and I wasn't the cutely flustered coed he thought he'd romantically crossed paths with on a stormy night but a total disaster who hadn't been laid in like six months.

"Hi." I stared at the pink drink in front of me. Fuck, it looked delicious.

When I made no move to touch it, he said, "Taste it."

*Whoa.*

His words gripped me unexpectedly, in a deeply intimate place. Not just the sound of his voice—low, sexy, almost taunting—but the way he said the words. It was a command, and it made my guts twist in an amazing, euphoric way.

Not good.

I looked at him again.

How old was he? The luscious lips made him look young. But the dark stubble combined with his eyes made him look much older. He really could've been anything from some college athlete in his early twenties who just upscaled very nicely, to a businessman in his early thirties.

He didn't seem that much older than me, but he also did.

"Why?" I pushed back. I didn't want this guy to know how flustered he was making me.

"Because I want you to."

I looked away. I could not keep contact with those wolfish eyes. They were so light against his tan skin. And so… hungry. Yet he leaned casually on the bar, so relaxed.

I slid the drink closer to myself, leaned in and took a sip through the straw. He watched me do it and my cheeks burned.

I swallowed. It was delicious. I tried to focus on that instead of on the strange sensation of knowing that I'd just done what he told me to do *because he wanted me to* and we were both hyperaware of it. It was unsettling and electric.

*What the fuck is happening right now?*

I needed to call a friend. Use a lifeline. Something.

But I didn't move.

"You're not a football player," I said tentatively. I searched for the right words, glancing at him. "You don't look… bulky enough for that. But you definitely play soccer or hockey or baseball. Or lacrosse. I don't know."

"You're trying to guess my profession, is that it?"

"You're an athlete for sure. Or a very athletic claims adjuster."

He chuckled softly, and it felt like flower petals dusting my skin. "You think I'm in insurance?" Damn, his voice was sexy. He was so… manly.

"You just seem like someone who's very comfortable handling financial matters. Are you here for a business conference?"

"You seem to enjoy guessing. So, guess."

I glanced at his clothes again, trying not to ogle his physique. "Maybe not business. A bachelor party? But the party was last night. The bruises are from your vigorous orgy with a cheer squad who was passing through. You met them in the lobby of your hotel."

I thought that might earn me a chuckle again, amuse him, make him seem less intimidating. It didn't.

He leaned a little more onto the bar, shifting a fraction closer to me. "You don't pay attention to detail, little dove. These bruises are over a week old." He ran his finger down his bruised cheekbone, touching himself as his eyes held mine in a way that made my mouth run dry. "So they couldn't be from last night's orgy."

"No? How about the hickies?" My eyes darted to the bruising on his neck. "Those are hickies and not strangulation marks, right?"

"You tell me."

"Hickies." *I think.* "See, I pay attention to detail." I tried to sound nonchalant and took another sip of my delicious drink, which I hadn't actually thanked him for. Maybe I wouldn't. "Do you?"

"Only when the details are interesting." His eyes were still on me, and I tried to read between the lines of that.

I liked flirting. Loved it, actually. I was just usually terrible at it. But this guy was definitely flirting with me. My heart was drumming and my cheeks were burning and I loved having his attention on me. It was intoxicating.

"So… I'm a detail?"

"You're the most interesting thing in this room."

*Wow.* I had not been hit on this hard in… ever? At least not outside of a crowded nightclub near two a.m. when dudes were drunk and desperate not to go home alone. I knew I wasn't ugly, but I'd never had a man who looked like this one laser locked on me like this.

"The hostess finds *you* very interesting," I informed him.

"Too bad for her, the feeling isn't mutual."

Why, though? She was an eleven out of ten.

"Are you drunk?" I inquired.

"Not even a little bit."

"Then maybe someone told you the really good prostitutes hang out at this bar, dressed in sweats? If so, you were sadly misinformed." I frowned. "I think."

"You're suggesting I pay for the company of women?" He took a slow sip of his drink. "Maybe it's the other way around. Maybe women pay for my company."

"So you're the prostitute?"

"You wouldn't pay for my company?" He was teasing me now, for sure. His eyes glimmered, and somehow he looked even hotter when he was giving me a hard time.

If he actually smiled at me, I'd probably pee my pants.

"I probably couldn't pay for this cocktail," I confessed, entranced by that glimmer in his eyes. "So I'm afraid you're slightly out of my budget."

He took another sip of his drink, set it on the bar, and said, "How about I give you a freebie?"

I laughed too loudly, nervously, as he seemed to be waiting for a response to that. "I'm sorry, did you confuse me with someone?"

"You seem to be the one who's confused. About how interesting you are."

I took a long, fortifying suck from my straw, pondering this mind fuck. "I think *you* need to pay more attention to detail. Your observational powers seem way off."

"So, then, tell me what's not interesting about you."

"Nope. No way." He wanted the goods on me? I felt much more comfortable awkwardly flirting and cracking jokes than actually divulging any personal bits.

"Just tell me one thing about you," he pressed. "You can even choose what it is." For a total stranger, he was very bossy.

I kinda loved it. Which was not great.

"I'm not telling you anything," I pressed back. "You get three questions that I will answer honestly, and beyond that you're on your own."

"Three?"

"Yup."

"Honestly, huh?"

"Swear to God. Use them wisely."

He seemed to think about that. "How old are you?"

"Nineteen. That's seriously what you wanted to know?"

"I didn't see the bartender check your ID. I just wanted to make sure you're not too young for the dirty thoughts in my head right now."

Okay, that didn't sound like he was teasing.

*This is not a drill. He's definitely trying to pick you up.*

I quietly cleared my throat, aiming for non-flustered. "How… responsible of you."

"Do you like delayed gratification?"

*Jesus.* I took a long, deep pull of my cocktail, the warm fuzzies making this conversation go down easier. "Um. Yeah. I guess."

He stared me down with those intense eyes of his. "Not a valid answer. You like or you don't like."

"Oh-kay." I tried to keep my expression neutral as my insides melted down. "I like. I mean, what's not to like? Gratification is gratification. Why not draw it out?"

"Do you like following orders?"

His fingertip was drawing a slow circle around the mouth of his rocks glass. The guy hadn't touched me, but his finger running down his bruised cheek and now stroking his glass set my panties on fire. When my eyes lifted to his again, he was still watching me, and he wasn't smiling.

"Do you like," he asked me again, "following orders?"

*I don't even know his name.*

"Um." *What does a girl say to that?* "Sometimes."

"No." His pale wolf eyes held mine. "You like or you don't like."

We stared at each other.

There was noise all around us. Music playing, ice and glass clinking, many voices layered over one another. But all I could really hear was his voice, a low, sultry command.

"Say it."

"Yes." I swallowed. "That's three questions. Now it's my turn. How old are you?"

"I never said you'd get a turn." His eyes glimmered again as he lifted his glass, taking a luxurious sip of the golden liquid.

"Well, that's a dick move."

He set his drink down and cracked a sudden smile. "You have a dirty mouth for such a little girl."

"Excuse me?"

Did he just call me a little girl? My brain was absolutely fried from that smile.

The smile faded, replaced by that hungry look in his eyes. "I said. You have a dirty mouth. For a little girl."

*Yeah. That's what I thought he said.*

And now he was looking at my mouth like he wanted to shove the entirety of his hard dick into it.

I had no idea what was happening right now. Because this, whatever this was, had never happened to me before. Not even close. I'd had a one nighter or two. A few casual hookups. But this was something else.

Who knew where it was going, but right now I really had nothing to lose, so damn right, I was getting a turn.

"Swear you'll be honest. How old are you?"

His eyes drifted back up to mine. "Okay. I swear. I'm twenty-six."

"Are you married?"

"Do you want me to be?"

"You can't answer the question with a question. And of course I don't want you to be."

He shrugged. "Maybe you're into that."

"I'm not!"

"Well, I'm not married."

"Of course you'd say that. Because I just told you I don't want you to be."

"All the same, I'm not married. I swore I'd be honest."

He did. But still.

I took a hearty suck of my cocktail. I was getting near the bottom and feeling a little buzz. I was also feeling bolder and took a moment to search for signs of a wedding band. He wasn't wearing one and there didn't appear to be any dent like he'd just taken one off. He wore only a signet ring on his pinky with some kind of engraved crest or monogram on it that I unfortunately couldn't read.

I met his beautiful, wolfish eyes again. "I really don't trust you."

"You probably shouldn't." He took another sip of his drink, and this time he sucked a chip of ice into his mouth and crunched it between his teeth, giving me a dazzling smile. "You just met me in a bar."

"Same here. Third question under the oath of honesty. Why did you pretend we were together so the snooty hostess would let me in?"

"Because I wanted the story on that outfit. Women don't usually wear spa slippers around town."

"Well, you could ask me. But you used up your three questions, so I guess you wanted to know those other things more." I smiled tentatively. I couldn't really pull off the level of sass that would probably be required to handle a man like him. He'd realize that soon and get bored, right?

He didn't even blink, his eyes locked on mine when he said, "Yeah, well, once I came over here and saw you without all the makeup, I got distracted."

I laughed a little. Was he for real?

"So. Tell me what you're doing in here in those slippers," he said.

Sneaky. He'd rephrased it so it wasn't a question.

It was more of a command.

I gave in with a small sigh. "I'm just avoiding the storm. And by storm, I mean my mother, actually."

"Then you should probably stay and have another drink with me. I imagine she'd love that."

Oh, she'd love it all right. Sex talk with a stranger at a bar? If Mom could see me right now, she'd be appalled.

I looked him over, eying those strong arms propped on the bar, but trying not to be obvious about it. He had some bruises on his hands and I wasn't even sure why that seemed… sexy. "So… what are you, really? If not an athlete or an unaffordable male prostitute?"

"I'm sorry, little dove. You used up all your questions."

Ugh. Seriously? He was using my game against me?

"Okay, fine. I'll figure it out. Drug dealer? Or maybe spy by day, secret porn star by night?"

"We prefer to film during the day. All that natural lighting does wonders for the skin. I do my spy stuff at night."

I shook my head. This was getting perversely fun. Even if he was just messing with me. "There's something clandestine about you. And mercurial. And definitely antiestablishment. No way you work for any government. Actually, I take back the porn star thing, too. You might've gotten your start on screen but now you definitely produce the porn."

"It is nice to step up in your career."

"Tell me which guess was the closest to the truth."

"I'm gonna say drug dealer. Although I'm not a drug dealer."

"So how close is close?"

"Well, technically I am a criminal."

"I don't even know if I believe you." He was toying with me, for sure.

"So, what am I then?" He leaned in a little closer. We were gradually eliminating the space between us, inch by inch. "Have you figured it out?"

"No."

His gaze dropped to my mouth. "Then tell me your fantasy."

Oh. My.

*This is hot.*

I glanced around. No one was even paying attention to us. Did no one notice that the hottest moment of my life was transpiring here?

Where were my girls to witness this crazy shit?

I tried to keep some semblance of cool as I looked at him. I wasn't even sure why this was going so well. Chemistry? Or maybe he slipped in the rain and hit his head and could no longer tell how out of my league he was?

"Okay. You're definitely an athlete, then."

Athletes had amazing physiques like him, right?

And there was just something about him… athletic and polished, mysterious and commanding… the kind of man who could crush an opponent with his confidence alone. The kind of man I'd never talk to unless he talked to me first.

He'd basically hunted me out across the bar and demanded I talk to him. I still wasn't sure why.

"And what am I?" I asked him.

"I already told you, little dove."

"Why do you call me that?"

"It suits you." His eyes drifted down to my chest. "And you literally have doves on your shirt."

"Oh." I glanced down. I did have doves on my shirt. His shirt, however, was blank. "And what should I call you?"

"Whatever you like. Big Daddy has a nice ring to it."

Hmm. I didn't like the little spark of disappointment I felt when he didn't offer me his name. But I tried to hide it. "Okay. If you're gonna make me guess…"

He sipped his drink and said, "I'm not making you do anything."

Well, that was cocky as hell. He wasn't making me do anything, true. But he knew I'd probably lick his abs in the men's room right now if he asked me to, right?

"Then I'm guessing your name is Maximus," I said. "You look like a Maximus. Destroyer of enemies, conqueror of worlds, lover of all women… am I on the right track?"

"Almost."

"Well, nice to meet you, almost Max." I sucked back the last of my cocktail and slid off my bar stool, maybe just to see if he'd call my bluff. "I'm almost leaving."

I stopped short when he extended his hand. "Hunter."

I shook his hand and he tugged me towards him. I ended up between his spread thighs. I took my hand back, but I didn't back away. Christ, he smelled good.

And he was forward as hell.

I didn't hate it.

"And your name is?" he prompted.

"Julie," I breathed. I could've told him the truth. Julie was kind of a running joke in my life; so many people just couldn't seem to wrap their heads around Jolie, plus autocorrect was the enemy of a name like mine.

But for some reason, I didn't tell him the truth.

His eyes roamed my face as my heart thudded in my chest. We were so close now. Even though we weren't touching, it felt super intimate.

"So, Julie… do you want me to buy you another drink?" His eyes met mine again. "Or do you want me to take you to my hotel room? Or do you want me to fuck off?"

I struggled to find my voice. "The second thing," I whispered.

We stared at each other.

"Or would you rather go to your room?" he offered.

Maybe he was considering the awkward who-gets-up-afterward-to-leave thing. But in my experience, it was better to get up and leave than to be left.

"Don't worry," I told him, "I won't stay the night. I won't ask for your phone number or anything. I know how a one night stand works." I held his gaze, waiting to see if he said anything crazy like, *This is not a one night stand. I must see you again.*

But he didn't say that.

He got to his feet, reminding me how tall and broad-shouldered and *fucking perfect* he was as he slid his blazer back on. "Come with me."

And I did, just like that, gripping the hand he'd offered me.

"Is your name really Hunter?" I practically panted as I followed him through the lounge. I knew this was against the rules. If he wanted to slip me a fake name, that was his prerogative.

I'd slipped him a fake name, too.

He didn't answer me.

Maybe I should've known right then that this was way too good to be true.

That Hunter *was* just a fantasy. A fiction.

A lie.

But hey, I'd lied to him too.

And I did stay the night.

Because somehow, having a hot stranger drive me to orgasm over and over that night, for hours on end, became more important to me than my mom's engagement party or any other thing on earth.

When I woke up in the morning, he was gone, and I found a note that he'd left for me on his pillow. It had a phone number written on it. And four little words that effectively ruined the best night of my life.

*My name is Shane.*

I knew right then that I'd been his fantasy as much as he was mine.

Unfortunately, his fantasy was sick as fuck.

Made in the USA
Thornton, CO
06/09/24 17:10:18

17932a1a-074e-41ad-9d05-268ab0c77dc4R01